The Delivery

THE DELIVERY

Mark Chisnell

C

CENTURY · LONDON

Published by Century Books in 1996

1 3 5 7 9 10 8 6 4 2

Copyright © Mark Chisnell 1996

Mark Chisnell has asserted his right under the Copyright, Designs and
Patents Act, 1988 to be identified as the author of this work.

First published in the United Kingdom by
Century Books Limited
20 Vauxhall Bridge Road, London, SW1V 2SA

Random House Australia (Pty) Limited
20 Alfred Street, Milsons Point, Sydney,
New South Wales 2061, Australia

Random House New Zealand Limited
18 Poland Road, Glenfield
Auckland 10, New Zealand

Random House South Africa (Pty) Limited
PO Box 337, Bergvlei, South Africa

Random House UK Limited Reg. No. 954009

A CIP catalogue record for this book is available from the British Library

Papers used by Random House UK Limited are natural, recyclable
products made from wood grown in sustainable forests. The
manufacturing processes conform to the environmental regulations of the
country of origin.

ISBN 0 7126 7554 X

Typeset by Palimpsest Book Production Limited,
Polmont, Stirlingshire
Printed and bound in Great Britain by
Mackays of Chatham plc, Chatham, Kent

ACKNOWLEDGEMENTS

Many of my friends have provided essential advice, criticism and encouragement – not to mention the space to work. There are too many to thank them all here, but I'm going to try anyway; Charlotte, Frances and Frances, Nick, Sian, Robin, Tim, Donna, Jonica, Jo Jo, Benita, Anna, Fiona, Lou, Bibs, Charles, Bev, Moira, Marina, George, Gordon, Eileen, Midge, Graeme, Rick, Craig, Sarah and Rhidian. And of course my apologies and thanks go to anyone I have forgotten.

Both William Poundstone's excellent book, 'Prisoner's Dilemma', and Douglas Hofstadter's writing on the same topic in 'Metamagical Themas' were influential. I owe an enormous debt to my agent, Susie Aikin-Sneath at David Higham Associates. Without her unflagging support the published book would have remained just a dream. I must also thank my editor at Century, Oliver Johnson, for his efforts to turn my erratic plotting and characterisation into something cohesive. The failings that remain are all mine.

Mark Chisnell

This book is for my family, Michael, Margaret and Su.
Thanks for your patience, and understanding.

FOREWORD

THE Prisoner's Dĭlĕmma – n. A philosophical conundrum enacted through a game with two participants which gives an insight into the behaviour of the individual in society

The Prisoner's Dilemma was 'discovered' by Merrill Flood and Melvin Dresher, two scientists at the American RAND Corporation think-tank, back in 1950. It got its name from the story told by one of their colleagues, Albert W. Tucker, to illustrate the 'game'.

Two prisoners are held in solitary confinement, both accused of collusion in the same crime. They are each given the chance to turn State's evidence to assist in the conviction of the other. If they both choose to remain silent, they will each be convicted for one year. If they both choose to turn in the other, they will be convicted for three years each. However, should one of them remain silent and the other turn State's evidence, the squealer will go free and the other will do five years.

In Prisoner's Dilemma terminology squealing to the authorities (hoping to leave your fellow prisoner to his fate while you escape scot-free) is known as defecting. To remain silent (hoping for the shortest combined prison term for the two of you) is known as cooperating. We can use these terms to write the Prisoner's Dilemma down in short-hand.

Two cooperators: both receive one year in jail.

Two defectors: both receive three years in jail.

One defector and one cooperator: the defector goes free and the cooperator gets five years.

The problem for each player is whether or not they can trust their fellow prisoner to remain silent. If they can, both of them get off lightly. But of course if one player, with both their interests at heart, decides to cooperate and remains silent whilst the other defects and squeals, then the cooperator ends up in jail for five years whilst the defector gets away completely. That would seem

ix

a pretty bad deal if you were the cooperator. So, the thinking goes, wouldn't it be better to squeal – just in case? But if both prisoners are thinking the same thing they both end up in jail for three years instead of one. If only they could have kept quiet.

Such is the train of thought which takes us to the most frequent result of a Prisoner's Dilemma in modern western society – mutual defection. But the Prisoner's Dilemma is not just a mind game, it appears everywhere, every day of our lives. It is the central metaphor for our interpersonal behaviour. Take the case of an unmanned barrier on a railway system that has no ticket inspectors. Hop over the barrier and you get a personal gain – you save the fare. But if enough people do it, eventually the rail company has to put the fares up – and everyone who pays will suffer for the free ride the barrier hoppers are getting. In Prisoner's Dilemma terms the freeloader is defecting, putting his personal welfare ahead of the group interest. Whilst the ticket buyer is cooperating, hoping that everyone else will do the same and prices will stay down.

The Prisoner's Dilemma can be found residing just as clearly in insurance cheats, tax dodges and traffic queue jumpers – all relatively innocuous examples. But what if the Prisoner's Dilemma were taken to the other extreme? What if the choices involved were life and death? And what if the lives belonged to people you knew and someone you loved? This book is about just such a dilemma.

PROLOGUE

İT WAS FRIDAY, and Fridays were always bad. This particular Friday was worse because of the rain. I love the place. Always have, and probably always will. Good old England. But I hate the rain, boy, do I hate the rain. And more than anything I hate driving in the rain. That day was typical, it was June and barely drizzling hard enough to get the wipers out of intermittent and into first gear, but there was a cloud of spray on the road so bad I could barely see the end of the bonnet on the BMW. And I was late. I was always late, I guess it was just a part of the lifestyle.

I saw the lorry a little late too, coming out from the slip road on my left. These guys, they think they own the road. And this one was typical, indicator on and just shove it out. I was doing nearly twice his speed and he only had to wait a few seconds and I'd be past him. But oh no, he wanted me to move over. I didn't, though, I flashed the lights on to full beam, thumbed the horn and floored it. I'd just burst through the curtain of solid spray kicked up by the front wheels as they moved to avoid me. He over-reacted a little, I must have surprised him. I felt it more than saw it. The cab rocking and the sqwoosh noise as the tyres let go on the wet road.

It was when I saw the trailer fill my rear view mirror that I knew it was going to be bad. Then there were the horns, the almost human wail of anguish as the inevitable slowly, hopelessly, became fact. The gate closed, the trailer just shut down the motorway behind me. I heard one crash, a high-pitched screech that lowered into a grinding, ripping tenor howl before exhausting itself in a dull wumph. But by then I was gone, mist and drizzle and spray swallowed up the scene behind me. There was nothing, no one in the rear-view mirror. I watched a raindrop slide down the back window. I was the last one that made it through. I drove on, there was nothing else to do. You have to carry on, don't you?

I

Seven months later: Ko Samui, an 'emerald island jewel set in the sapphire sea of the Gulf of Thailand' – or so the brochures would have you believe. But I knew it was costume jewellery, superficial glamour that barely hid a cheating heart. A heart I should avoid, but there I was, back on the dusty strip of bars and clubs where Ko Samui slinkily slipped out of its formal white sand and blue water into something more comfortable.

Chaweng Beach. The main drag. Midnight. 'Purple Haze' pounded the air from a couple of bars down, the lights flared and the darkness turned into day-glo orange, then red, then green. The bar-girls shrieked at the conveyor belt of passing humanity. The women tourists looked away as their men leered. I picked up the glass of Mekong and Coke and unsteadily raised it to my lips, ice was only a ghostly memory in the warm sugary fluid. I'd lost count of the evening's tally a while back. I gazed over the rim at the girl beside me. The beauty of Thai women is only matched by the country's reputation for selling it cheap: jet black hair, sultry eyes, the slim figure tucked neatly into the short, silk and very red dress. The brazen come-on was offset by a startling, almost luminous naïvety in her face. But it was the come-on quality I was interested in. The eyes said she was available – they all are, at a price.

The jet-black curtain of hair shrouded her face as she bent to light a cigarette, a match flared in the gloom, dangerously close to it. This was the moment I'd been waiting for, I lifted my hand to brush it to safety.

'No touch girl,' said the voice.

I looked round, a little surprised, my hand frozen a couple of inches from her. It was the barman. He'd been watching our slow conversation for the last hour, why the problem now? My nostrils wrinkled involuntarily at the pungent cloud of smoke in my face. I turned back to the girl. She exhaled towards me, the red lips kissing the air then spreading into a smirk. A twinge of alarm forced its way through the alcohol. The barman took off his apron and stepped forward from behind the bar. The T-shirt underneath was not much cleaner than the apron had been, and it was stretched tight round a substantial frame. He looked like he had muscles in his shit.

'No touch,' he repeated.

'Who says?' I replied, almost before I'd thought about it.

'I do,' he answered, simply. The face was expressionless, the eyes impassive. I could have walked away from it – if I'd been smart. But my mouth was quicker.

'And just who the hell are you?' I said.

The eyes flickered, off to his right. I followed his gaze, another Thai had appeared behind the bar, the expensively tailored, white button-down shirt at odds with the thick, tattooed forearms. It had to be the manager. But it was the iron bar he put on the wooden counter between us that got my attention.

'The boss don't like you touching girlfriend,' said the barman. Ah. The manager's girlfriend. 'You been hittin' on her all night, and he just about had enough.'

It was that moment in all conflicts, potential and resolved, when your deepest instincts either get you out of the mess or cast you hopelessly adrift in it. This time, the booze had the final word.

'Well, he shouldn't let her sit up here, dressed like a tart, along with the rest of the merchandise,' I slurred out.

I heard the whistle and saw five other Thais separate out from the isolated groups of drinkers. Lots of gold jewellery clashed with the understated Brooks Brothers shirts. Chairs screeched on the wooden floor as the rest of the clientele turned to watch the show. The five approached casually from my left. They didn't seem to think I was going to give them much trouble. I guess I didn't think so either. I could feel the swoosh of alcohol around my brain, thoughts were slow and movements slower. I couldn't deal with this. I saw the tyre lever hefted off the counter by the boss. He moved slowly to his right, trying to pin me between him and the barman. I backed off the stool, getting some distance, closing the angle between the groups. My eyes flicking between them. The girl had disappeared.

Primitive survival instincts clicked into gear. Blood was pumping, my head clearing. The Thais came in a rush, like the adrenaline that suddenly coursed through my body. I dived in under the swinging tyre lever and my kick caught the manager off-balance. He doubled up at the stomach. The tyre lever spun free. I lunged after it. I got half way to it before a chair slammed into the back of my knees. I went down hard, thinking that was it, they'd kill me now. I squirmed round, struggling to keep moving, lashing out at nothing and everything. Backing off, trying to stop them closing the circle. Aware only of the coming blow, the anticipated flash of pain. But it didn't happen to me.

They say in those books that glory in this kind of detail, that to win bar fights you have to be prepared to go straight to total violence. No pussy footing around with any of this wrestling stuff you see in the movies. Just hit the sucker as hard as you can in the softest spot you can reach with the hardest object you can lay your hands on. The head butt to the unprotected, fleshy nose, the knee to the groin and the finger in the eyeball are all good, solid, bar fight moves. But this guy, he must have written the manual.

He appeared behind the ring of encircling Thais. I hadn't noticed him before and he certainly didn't look like some kind of all-action hero; lightly built, five eleven tops and dressed in chinos and an open-collared shirt. The ginger hair was close-cropped, military style. No rippling muscles or martial arts stance. But he was fit, and the face was as lean and hard as the body, creased and freckled by too much sun. His expression had an almost surreal calm, no grimace as his left hand chopped down into the neck of one of my attackers. The man dropped heavily; heaving, retching, struggling to suck air through a traumatised wind pipe. His nearest companion turned, but too slow, something metallic flashed as the newcomer's right hand drove in a straight arm punch. The Thai spun away clutching at a bloodied face.

Then everything was still. Smart move I thought, if I was them I wouldn't be in any hurry to shift either. The newcomer quickly took the opportunity and stepped in between me and the Thais. 'You OK?' he asked over his shoulder. American.

'Sure, thanks . . .' I eased myself gently to my feet, brushing away the dust, taking some much needed deep breaths.

He didn't take his eyes off the five still standing as he slid the heavy steel watch back from his knuckles on to his wrist. In the silence I heard the catch on the strap close. 'We're leaving now,' he said to them. No one moved. 'We'll just move off nice and easy,' he went on in a lower voice. 'You go first, watch the back, I'll keep an eye on these boys.' I shuffled to the door, the stranger backing up, until he joined me on the street. We set off together, walking rapidly. He glanced over his shoulder once or twice, but no one was following. After about a hundred metres there was still no sign of pursuit from the bar. I started to slow and then stopped. I must have been a good couple of inches taller and several stone heavier than this guy, but I held my place against the flow of people around us with a difficulty he didn't appear to be having.

'Can I buy you a drink?' I said. 'You saved my hide back there.'

'No problem, those guys are pricks.' He finished with a grimace that might have been a smile, revealing some un-American yellow teeth. 'But I'll take the drink anyway. I know a place just down by the beach. The owner's an acquaintance – no one'll bother us there.'

I followed him down the hill towards the ocean, visible only by the line of white surf on the beach. We turned west along the sand and ducked through a T-shirt stand. I clattered against a bench of trinkets. Christ, how much had I had to drink already? The sobering effect of the adrenaline rush was beginning to slip away. We emerged in a back alley of wooden shacks, crackling fires and silent stares, walking another fifty metres to a bar well-hidden from the tourist strip. The kind of local bar where the clientele have to be friends of the owner or they don't get in. There were some bamboo chairs and tables scattered around a hard earth floor. Otherwise the place was empty. I sank gratefully into a chair and sucked at a split knuckle.

A waiter stepped out of the gloom like a ghost. The American spoke rapidly in Thai and the man returned with a bottle.

'What are we drinking?' I asked.

'Local stuff, but it's OK,' he said. The glasses clattered on to the table top and the amber liquid rolled into them. The waiter had started to move away when the stranger's hand flashed out, grabbing him by the wrist. 'We'll keep it,' he said.

The barman looked at him and then down at the hand imprisoning his arm. He quickly let the bottle go. In the silence I dropped a fistful of notes on the table. The waiter snatched them up, revealing the ugly red welt left on his wrist.

I picked up the glass gratefully, it slipped down easily. So did the second and the third. It wasn't until they had stopped that I realised how badly my hands had been shaking. 'Thanks for your help,' I said.

4

'It was nothing,' he replied.

I shrugged, swallowed the drink. The glow was spreading outwards. I gazed hazily at the roof. A spider crawled erratically down a bamboo pole, the single bare bulb throwing its shadow into gargantuan relief. I hauled in a deep breath, and slumped forward on to the support of my elbows.

'Better?'

I nodded, and held out my hand, there was only the slightest tremor 'See? No problem,' I said.

He nodded solemnly, but didn't shift his gaze from the rest of the room. 'It's scary that stuff, if you aren't used to it.'

'You look like you are.' I made the statement flat, no rising inflection, no question asked. His cold grey eyes swivelled slowly towards me. The memory of the sudden violence of only minutes before came back sharply. Two guys hospitalised with startling speed and precision. And complete indifference. You wouldn't mistake this guy for someone who gave a fuck. I sat, frozen in that frigid gaze for a full half minute. Until he picked up the bottle and the chuckle of alcohol into my glass broke the uneven silence. I heard my heart beating in time to the tick, tick of the ceiling fan. I wanted to leave, but that gaze had immobilised with its spell.

'So what brings you to Ko Samui?' His eyes swept across the room again as he spoke. Then settled on the open door. The door. How to get through it? I began to frame some excuses for leaving in my head, but first, his question.

'I just needed to get away for a while.' It sounded lame as soon as I'd said it.

'You in trouble?'

And suddenly we weren't small talking any more. How to get through that door?

'Not exactly,' I said, stalling, gazing down at the patterns of dirt at my feet. But 'no' was the right answer. I might have escaped all that followed if I'd just said 'no' right then. Made up some bullshit story about a holiday and got the hell out of there.

Instead, I glanced up and once more I was fixed in the glare of those penetrating grey eyes. I could feel them sucking it out of me. I'd not talked to anyone else, not since the accident. So why now? And to this stranger, who was already on the way to freaking me out? I still wonder about that. But the answer was right there in those eyes.

'It's a long story,' I said, throwing back the contents of the glass.

He smiled again, yellow teeth and gaunt face skull-like in the gloom. 'We got plenty of time,' he said, reaching forward and refilling the glass again.

I slumped back in the chair. The spider had gone. The bulb was swinging lightly under a puff of wind. My mind started to follow it, dizzily beginning to spin. I leaned forward again quickly, gazing ahead until the giddiness had gone. A puddle of beer was slowly working its way down a crack in the table. 'I guess it started about six months ago. There was a motorway accident, although I wasn't involved in the crash itself . . .' I stopped, thinking about the trailer filling my rear-view mirror, the horns, the rising alarm. And then that gentle wumph. That must have been the explosion that started the fire. 'It wasn't my fault . . . I mean, the other guy definitely screwed up. And no one even knows I was there . . . you certainly couldn't prove it was my fault. I cut the guy up and he lost control, over-reacted to the situation . . .' I stopped and took a deep breath, looked up again, but the grey eyes were cold, 'Eighteen people died. Several of them burned to death, trapped inside a minibus. I read about it in the papers the day after.'

The beer had made it to the edge of the table and was slowly dripping on to my leg. I watched another drop fall. The brown stain crept slowly across the faded denim. Somewhere I found it in me to care enough about it to move. I shifted and looked up.

'So?' he said

'So . . .?' I choked. 'So eighteen people died and . . .' the words tumbled out, then evaporated. I tried again. 'I don't . . . I mean . . . fuck it.' I shook my head. I hadn't got the words. I stared at him, but there was nothing in those grey eyes, no blame, no sympathy. Perhaps, and only perhaps, a little curiosity.

I snorted back a deep breath through my nose and wiped the back of my hand across my mouth. Why was I doing this? But having started, it seemed I couldn't stop. 'For weeks afterwards I caught myself doing the same sort of thing, cutting people up, not letting them into queues, driving like a real arsehole. It was like . . . am I always like this? Or did I want to get caught, get it out in the open. Almost like it was guilt. Shit, I mean, I knew it wasn't my fault but . . .' I lifted the glass and stared at the glowing amber light. I poured it back. 'I started drinking, a lot. Started to lose it at work. I was a currency dealer in a big London bank. And I was good, made a lot of money. But it started to slip and then there was a deal . . .'

I shuddered slightly as that day came back at me. The row with Jo that night, rolling in to the office at nearly ten the next morning looking like shit. Then the 'this is going to hurt me more than it hurts you' speech from the boss. I could still smell the power and money that hung in the air in that office, oozing out of the wood, the leather, the wool. It could have been mine. My secretary had brought me a coffee afterwards, no one else came near. The word had gone round. I was history. Bad news. A loser. Last seen leaving.

I slugged back the whole of the drink. I was numb now and the liquid no longer had its fiery effect, but I didn't have much more to say. I went on in a hollow, distant voice, slurring the words. 'I lost the job, then the girlfriend.' I smiled weakly. 'The money went, she went. Fuck her, I don't miss her. I packed a bag and took a plane out here. Bangkok blew my brains out, someone told me about the islands, I got on a bus and've been drifting around down here ever since.'

I looked at him. There was no expression, no response. I stared back into the glass and watched a final trickle of alcohol slip back down to the bottom. But looking down was a big mistake. My head started to spin, there was the hot rush of nausea. I bit back hard, struggled to my feet, stumbling backwards. I think I made it to the veranda before I threw up.

2

I MUST'VE SLEPT a while. But consciousness came like a painfully piercing light. The sun finally emerging through heavy, grey clouds in the aftermath of a wicked storm. I twitched my eyes open a crack and stared upwards. Gradually a little light started to filter through the matted roof. It must be morning. My head was pounding. Slowly I levered myself upwards. At this point my stomach registered a severe protest. I flinched quietly and rolled over on to my side, pushing my legs out and slowly easing off the edge of the bed. I was starting to sweat and my legs were shaking.

I staggered the few steps over towards the bathroom. Such as it was. Basically a bowl, toilet and a shower head in a screened-off corner. I groped around in the half light until I found the bottle of water. I slugged it back. Slowly I became conscious of my mouth. I felt round my teeth with my tongue, gently dislodging pieces of food. Probably vomit. Foul. I found a toothbrush and gingerly prodded around in my mouth with the help of lots more water. When I finally sat back on the edge of the bed I was feeling quite a bit better. I let myself drop back, landing heavily as my stomach muscles weren't quite up to the task.

The second time I saw the roof, daylight was streaming in. And it was hot. I was hot. I was soaked in sweat. I glanced at my watch, two p.m. I tried the sitting upright business again and this time it hardly hurt at all. I stretched gently and eased myself off the bed. The sordid clothes from the night before were swopped for a clean pair of shorts and I staggered out into the too-bright daylight. I had to close my eyes completely whilst my irises, which not unreasonably had assumed they'd got the day off, were summoned back from wherever they had gone and put to work.

The scene, when finally it revealed itself, was the same one that had greeted me each morning for the past couple of weeks. A few rather shabby bamboo beach huts scattered around a central covered area that passed as restaurant and bar. A couple of figures were dotted around the shaded tables and beyond them others were stretched out on the beach to fry in the afternoon sun. Dumb cancer-heads. But it was a stunning beach, the kind they make chocolate bar ads on, with white, white sand sliding gently under the ridiculously azure water. I took a deep breath, then turned back inside to find a beach mat, book and the water bottle.

'Martin!'

I turned, still moving smoothly so as not to disturb the delicately balanced equilibrium of my health, to see a small figure running down the beach towards me. It was Prachit, at least I think that was her name, the young daughter of the manager. She worked in the restaurant and bar and we'd struck up quite a friendship in the past couple of weeks. Strictly platonic, I hasten to add. She bounced up, panting anxiously, and said, 'You OK, Martin?'

'I think so,' I replied in a hoarse croak. She looked dubious so I carried on before she could find the words to express it. 'How did I get back here last night?'

'We find you in road with other man and bring you back on motorbike.'

'That's very kind of you, I was in a bad way. What did the other man look like?'

'Like you, Farang, but not so fat,' she paused and made a height motion with her hand, 'not so . . .'

'Tall?'

'Yes, not so tall, funny red hair.'

'Did he say anything?'

'Ask where you from, I tell him here.' The pretty features were breaking into a frown, so I smiled to reassure her.

'That's great, thank you. You know what I'd like? One of those special fruit shakes you do for me, could I have one please?'

She beamed, revealing a row of shining white teeth. 'No worries,' she said.

I did wonder whether the varied English influences in the little resort were having a positive impact on her grasp of the language. I smiled again and turned back to go inside the hut.

'Martin,' and I looked over my shoulder, 'you very funny last night,' she said, giggling, and ran off. The other question, it then occurred to me, was whether I was having a good influence on her. I retrieved my beach mat and book and settled under the shade of a palm tree to wait for Prachit to return with my drink. I flicked through the book to find the crease that marked my place. But my eyes refused to hold the focus and the page blurred out. I closed them ready to settle for more sleep and immediately a new image exploded on my conciousness.

Kate.

Of course, Kate. The drink had done the trick for a while, and I'd forgotten everything. I'd spotted her in the market yesterday afternoon. At first I hadn't been completely sure that it was her. There was nothing to connect her to this place, no reason why she should turn up here. She belonged three years and thousands of miles away. Maybe my mind was playing tricks. But even with all that time and distance the half glance I had caught of her was enough. The way she tilted her head, moved her body, there had been no doubt. The final, concrete flash of recognition had brought an almost physical pain, as past events crowded in, shrieking for attention. All so immediate it was overwhelming.

I stood, giddily, watching. It was then that I noticed the man beside her. She had turned to him and laughed, one hand flicking an insect off his shoulder. He had frowned at her, at the contact, and as he glanced up he caught my eye as I stared at them. I had dived away, pushed deep into the crowd. There had been no shout, no cry of recognition. I didn't know him either, but I could guess who he was.

I forced my eyes to focus in the present and down at the book. Struggling to shut out the image. But the words were no competition for the slight, blonde figure and the memories it brought. The one, single thing that I'd ever truly loved. And she had turned up here.

I could remember every detail about the night we had met. It'd been the autumn of 1986 and I had been dragged up to Oxford to go to a party by an acquaintance from the bank. I hadn't been too keen on the idea, but I'd been persuaded. Kate had been there, a vision of disillusioned, radical chic in torn jeans and oversized woollen jumper. But she could have worn a coal sack and looked good as far as I was concerned. We had argued intensely for hours, mostly about Thatcher's vision of the Britain we were going to live in, and then had crazy, passionate sex till the sun came up.

I'd been hooked from then on. She was a first-year politics student and made Marx look like Genghis Khan. The daughter of a wealthy businessman she had the financial stability to be able to afford such radical principles. Or so I used to like to tell her –

the true working class were busting their butts for a middle-class income, if not the social mores, and couldn't afford the luxury of principles. I had the advantage of my own background and could infuriate her in seconds – by asking how the hell she could know what the working class was about when the only one she'd ever met was me.

And that's how it had been. Discussions that became arguments that became rows. Conducted with a passion and intelligence that surprised us both. I suppose that's part of what the attraction was, we brought out the best and the worst in each other. There were times when we were so in tune, I'd been thinking maybe we could go and see that new movie tonight and she'd already have bought the tickets and booked a table as a surprise. Then there'd be those slow, sexy, Sunday mornings in bed, a walk in the park all bundled up against the cold, and coming home to a big roast dinner just as it started to get dark. We'd light the fire and settle down with the papers. And then she'd see some article, and get all outraged about the latest privatisation sell-off, and of course I'd know the guys dealing with the issue or have the prospectus and that would fire us off. We wouldn't talk for a week. Or two. Three was the record, I think.

Considering how good the reconciliation was it still struck me as amazing that we managed three weeks. Stubborn? Pig-headed would be closer. And those principles of hers? Contrasted with the oh, so comfortable background, they always used to wind me up. But, of course, in the end such people can only prove themselves by taking the final step and disavowing their inheritance. And the very passion that had so attracted me to her took her away. As the eighties got cranked up to its full clichéd frenzy even Gordon Gecko might have had a few principled shudders if he'd seen what I was up to. We had argued more, but with real venom. Finally she had dropped out of Oxford a few weeks before her finals, throwing away what her tutors regarded as a near-certain first class honours degree, told her father where he could shove her allowance and climbed on a plane to Australia. Which ticket, of course, he'd paid for.

It'd been perfect until then, hot-shot City boy with the BMW, gold card and fabulous looking girl on his arm. And not just fabulous looking either; smart, passionate, caring . . . But I could go on listing adjectives indefinitely and still not pin down what it was about her. She just had it, and I had never recovered. She left me to travel, and ended up with another guy. I shuddered a little, a cold shiver in the sweaty humidity at the thought of that final phone call. Scott, that was his name. A professional racing sailor. And that was him yesterday. I was sure of it. He would have been with her as long as I had, longer, just over three years. And they were still together.

I had skirted around and moved in closer to them from the other direction, but still keeping my distance. They were easy to follow, moving slowly through the throng of stalls and people. I tagged along, gazing blankly at a hundred sarongs and a thousand postcards. I bumped gently into ten thousand people and uttered a million 'sorrys'. But my thoughts and my eyes never strayed from her. I couldn't figure it out. Why was she here, crashing back into my life when I was least able to deal with it? No job, not much money and precious little purpose. It wasn't exactly the kind of situation that gave you confidence, was it? I must have followed them for hours, unable to decide what to do, unable to approach her, but equally unable to tear myself away. I should have got out, there and then. I could feel the old feelings growing even as I watched her. She was dangerous for me. I didn't know if I was strong enough to deal with her now. But I couldn't stop watching her, alone, and with him. Thinking, thinking it should be me.

They'd ended up on the courtesy bus to the Emperor's Hotel. I had drifted into the nearest bar and a substantial amount of Mekong and Coke.

A puff of wind stirred the pages of the book. I let them blow across, closing my eyes and trying to forget.

'Martin.'

The voice came through sharply, and I started awake.

'Damn.' The pain shooting through my neck made it clear I had not fallen asleep in an orderly fashion. It was stiff and sore where it had been propped up against the tree trunk. I rubbed it gingerly as I looked around for the source of the voice. The book still lay on my lap, the untouched glass was all but hidden in a buzz of insect life and beyond it the sun was plummetting towards the horizon in a red ball. Highlighted against it was a dark but recognisable figure. The last person I wanted to see: my saviour from the night before. I started to pick myself up from the sand, trying to think of something to say.

'I brought you this,' he said, proferring a drink.

I looked at it a little hesitantly, then back at him. 'Thanks,' I said, taking it slowly.

'I'm Janac,' he replied, stretching out a hand.

'Martin,' I said. He nodded. Of course, he already knew. I shook his hand. He looked one of those types who goes for the immediate psychological advantage by breaking your fingers, but I was pleased to find the grasp almost gentle. Of course I thought, he already has the advantage, he saved my butt from a beating.

'Thanks, for last night,' I said.

He shrugged. 'You already did that.'

I rubbed my forehead. 'Did I?' I nodded, as though remembering. 'So you found me,' I added, non-committally.

'Uhuh, pretty little thing that took you home last night told me where you were.'

I nodded.

'You don't mind.' It wasn't a question, I didn't have a choice. But the tone said he could care less anyway.

'No, no, of course not.' I went through the motions. After all, I'd be in some hospital right now if it wasn't for him. I took a sip of the drink and tried to relax a little. 'You want to take a seat?' I asked, indicating the bar.

'Sure. That'd be nice.' I led the way over and we sat down, one either side of a small glass-topped wooden table. I gently put my drink down and massaged my temples.

'So how are you today?' he asked.

I glanced at him. 'Better than I was earlier,' I said.

'Yeah, you didn't seem too good last night. I was quite happy when that young girl turned up, I had no idea what to do with you.'

'She works here, she's a good kid.'

Janac grunted and shifted in his chair. I watched the cool, grey eyes sweep the bar and then the beach. I could remember those eyes well enough. And the purposeful stillness. He was here for a reason. I waited, silently, to find out what it was. Finally he said, 'My car's parked out the back. You up for some dinner?'

Again it didn't seem so much a question as an order. I twirled my finger through the ice in the glass. Watching the cubes tumble over each other. I didn't want to do this. But he'd saved me from a beating and I owed him one. I couldn't say no. I took another sip of my drink.

'I really feel pretty damn rough . . .' I started. I let the silence roll for a couple of seconds, then I leaned forward, and picked up one of the loose coins someone had left as change on the table. 'Tell you what, heads I go with you, tails I stay here, take three aspirin and crash out. Agreed?'

It was the first time I'd seen him smile properly. It almost reached his eyes. I'd hit the right note. He nodded 'OK.' I flipped the coin and missed the catch. It bounced and spun on the glass table top. It seemed to take an eternity to settle. 'Heads,' said Janac, starting out of his chair. 'Let's go.'

3

'M ARTIN?'
'Uhuh?' I murmured, without moving.
'Martin!' The tone was much sharper. I looked round at Janac
quickly. He held out something, a rolled up bill. My heart jumped,
I looked down at the table between us. Two neat lines of white
powder on a shiny mirror. I'd been so absorbed in watching the
two girls shooting up a couple of tables away I hadn't even
noticed. I glanced around, no one seemed to be watching, never
mind caring.
'There's no problem in here.' The tone was insistent, the hand
extended a half inch further with the bill.
I scratched at the corner of my eye. Looked at Janac, the bill,
the coke. I needed something, I felt like death. I took the bill.

The meal arrived, the smell was stunning. I had no idea I was
this hungry. But then I hadn't eaten all day, and I must have
thrown up most of yesterday's. I grabbed a fork. It was good,
very good, brilliant. So was I. I glanced around the club. Lit by
flickering candles that created motion where there was none, and
disguised it where there was. Only a few people dotted around
in the shadows, despite the queue outside. The two girls with
the needles had joined us. Janac had snapped his fingers and it
had been so. It seemed everything had been like that. We had
cruised in here past three sets of doormen and a fifty-yard queue
as though Janac owned the place. He probably did. And I was
feeling pretty damn cool in the reflection of that presence now.
Empowered rather than uneasy. The coke had breezed away the
tiredness, the night was young, and we were in for a seriously
good time.
I felt a light touch on my leg, it crept slowly upwards. I glanced
at the two girls. One was now beside Janac and I had the undivided
attention of the other. A pink tongue crept out and slid across the

15

blood-red lips. I smiled and inclined my head. She moved round the table and slid astride my thigh. She weighed nothing. I put my arm round her tiny waist and felt the hot skin under the filmy, almost intangible dress.

'How's the food?' said Janac.

'Excellent,' I said, shifting slightly so I could still get at the meal. He was picking desultorily at his with a fork, the same hand holding a cigarette. The smoke drifted upwards to join the chemical cocktail in the atmosphere – an air sample would probably have been enough to get you busted for possession.

He nodded thoughtfully. 'Tell me how you lost your job.'

Some of my euphoria evaporated. I stared at the food for a second. 'I need another drink.' I pushed forward my empty glass. I'd been converting chemicals faster than ICI and didn't want to slow down.

His fingers snapped again, then he turned back to me interrogatively.

I rubbed my nose with a blunt forefinger. 'Middle of summer last year, just before the car crash. The European Union had signed the Maastricht treaty. The coming of a single currency required the exchange rates to be held for two years prior to the event. Failing to do so meant dropping out and being consigned to second string in a two-tier Europe – highly embarrassing for the government of the country concerned. This meant a lot of political credibility was invested in holding the rate parities, which in turn made the risks of currency devaluation very low. So, everyone was buying in the normally weaker, high-risk currencies, which had some very attractive interest rates compared to the Deutschmark. A high yield and low risk. All good news.'

I shrugged, adjusting the table mat as the waiter arrived with my drink. 'But along came the Danish referendum with a "No" vote on the treaty. And all of a sudden the political certainties were no longer certain. Some big players started to bail, getting back into the Deutschmark. It was about then that the accident happened. I was OK for a while, but I got on this guilt trip and somehow the deal got all mixed up in it. I wanted to believe in the single currency, that it was right for business, you know.' I looked up to find the usual dispassionate gaze from Janac. 'No, you wouldn't know. But fixed rates make it easy for people to do business. I thought we should support that. We spent so much time screwing with

16

the market for our own profit that I wanted to see those rates held for once.'

I reached out for the drink and a thin arm slipped round my neck, her body was warm and relaxed against mine. 'But I was hopelessly wrong. The fundamental reality was that the pound went into the ERM too high, it had to realign downwards. All the research said so. It was inevitable and everyone could see it. Except me. But there was all this rhetoric from the press, painting the traders as profiteering bad guys. I didn't want to be a bad guy anymore. Too much guilt. So I stuck with pounds. On a day when the Quantum Fund made a billion dollars, I lost big.' I shook my head bitterly, skin still crawling at the memory, the buzz in the office, the humiliation of being a loser. 'While Norman Lamont was singing in the bath I was pissing in the wind.'

I took another redeeming slug of the drink before I went on. 'I really fucked up, for the first time I confused right and wrong with profit and loss. They reckon the Central Banks spent fifteen billion quid trying to support sterling that one day alone. Whose money do you think that was? The taxpayers'. But it just got washed away. On average the London currency market deals with three hundred billion dollars a day. The fifteen billion was nothing. The markets just pummelled them.' I shook my head ruefully. 'When you've seen that kind of power, you want to be a part of it. I'll go back, got six months to sort myself out. You should have seen it that final day, God the market was just running with cash.'

Janac was eyeing me carefully. 'The currency markets aren't the only place you can make big money,' he said.

I watched him flick the ash off his cigarette. It was clear where this was going. It was in the air, literally. I should at least have tried to make a break then, but the coke was still pumping through my body.'

'You're a player, Martin,' he said, 'you could be a player here.'

I nodded, letting him reel me in, God help me. I forked in another mouthful of rice, but it was starting to get cold. I pushed the plate away. Janac had fallen silent, sipping at his drink. The girl fidgetted restlessly under his arm. She was obviously getting bored.

'So, if I told you we had a little action out here would you be interested?' he said, after a pause.

'What kind?'

He nodded down at the table, sticking his finger in the tiniest trace of white powder. I felt the girl tense under my arm, she was watching him hungrily. He saw the desire and slowly reached out and placed the finger on her lips. Her tongue slipped out and licked it lovingly. Janac shifted his gaze back to me and his eyebrows arched enquiringly.

I glanced away over his shoulder, trying to think of a response, wondering in a corner of my mind if he ever did that shit himself. The girl had followed my gaze, then quickly shifted, putting her arms around me, nuzzling her face in the nape of my neck. I ran my finger gently down her spine. Behind Janac a curtain had shifted to reveal a stage. I watched as a slight Thai girl crawled into the spotlight. She was shaking, crying. The distant professionalism of the sex shows was absent. Also missing was the cheap glamour, she was wearing a stylish silk dress.

An answer came to me, which had the dual benefits of being both a refusal and an early negotiating stance. 'I earned over two hundred thousand in bonus the year before last,' I said, 'and that was on top of my salary. And no personal risk. Whereas drugs are high risk, low return, unless you're close to the top.'

There was a long silence. I felt rather than saw Janac take a drag of his cigarette, as I watched the stage show develop. Five men surrounded the girl. Dressed all in black, bizarre, brightly-coloured masks hid their faces. A strobe light came on as they started to push her around, casting the scene in a harsh monochrome flicker. Now with jerky, brutal movements they tore at the dress. She twisted and turned, already half-naked, she fought to cover herself. Someone slapped her, another kicked her legs out from behind. She fell badly and strong arms grabbed her, pinning her down. It was a choreographed rape scene. I wanted to look away. But I was gripped by the anguish, the pain in the girl's face and in every torrid, freeze-frame movement.

'Jesus,' I breathed out. If pornography could be art, this was. 'What an actress,' I said, finally glancing away long enough to reach for my drink.

Janac glanced over his shoulder. 'It helps when it's real,' he replied, bluntly.

I heard him, but couldn't register the meaning. 'I'm sorry?' I whispered, glass half-way to my mouth.

'It's for real, they pull a kid off the street, run her up a dress, then throw her on the stage and rape her.' There was the cynical, yellow-toothed smile. 'It's a competitive market, there's only so much you can do with ping pong balls, razor blades and snakes.'

His hand came up with the cigarette. I watched the tip flare and die.

Back on stage she had almost stopped struggling, the remaining resistance seemed focused in her left hand, caught in a streak of light. It twitched, half unclenched, but she was desperately trying to hold on to something. Then with a sudden spasm her hand was flung open and a small, shiny object spun out and rolled across the stage. It seemed to have an energy of its own as it careered towards me, fleeing the nightmare behind. My eyes, and a single spotlight, followed it magnetically. What was so important to her? Slowly it looped into a spiral, tracing a series of ever smaller circles until it sank to rest only yards away. A button. A gold button.

I tried to wet dry lips, gaze hopelessly drawn back to the girl. Just her head was moving, almost imperceptibly, tiny flicks back and forth, shaking, no, no, no. I looked at her tear-stained, bloodied face, looked into her eyes. Stop them, she was pleading. I started to rise. There was a fevered grasp round my neck, as the girl on my lap began to slip off. And then Janac's hand was firmly planted on my wrist.

'No,' he said.

'But the girl . . .' I choked.

Janac shrugged. 'From one of the villages up north, an orphan. Nobody knows or cares about her. If she makes it through tonight and cooperates they'll put her to work on the streets, if she's good, she'll maybe even make it in here.' He nodded at our companions. 'These girls are the best.'

I slumped back. Washes of emotion crashed over me; nausea, revulsion, disgust, fear, anger – and shame. I looked back at Janac. He was still picking at his food. Watching me, with that half-smile, eyes glittering with a bitter amusement. 'What were you going to do?'

'Stop them.'

'You want to be next?' He was suddenly very still.

'God no.'

'I won't protect you in here.'

I stared at him through a long silence, the grey eyes never left my face. Finally I pulled some bills out of my pocket. 'How much would she cost, for the rest of the night?'

The gaze flickered down at the pile of notes on the table. 'That should do it.'

I pushed it all forward. 'Tell them.'

Janac shrugged, disbelief in the eyes and the motion. 'Where do you want her?'

'I don't want her, tell them to get her a hotel room, some good food, tell them to be fucking nice to her!' I was shouting the last words out.

Janac waved over a waiter, and spoke some words, in Thai. Handing over the wad of cash, he pointed to the stage, where the girl was lying alone in the spotlight. A crumpled, quivering heap of blood, shredded clothes and shattered humanity. The girl on my lap was listening, she shifted, staring at me. It was a confused expression. I stared back blankly. She started to move away, I let her go.

'I thought you were a player, Martin.'

I shook my head. 'I think I should leave.'

Janac nodded slowly, then turned and waved over another waiter, who started towards us. He turned back to me. 'See that guy over there?' he said.

I followed his gaze.

'Blond hair, denim shirt, a couple of tables down.'

I nodded.

'Australian narc, why don't you go tell him all about it?'

'What?'

'He's an Australian narcotics cop, go tell him, maybe he'll arrest somebody.'

'Christ! He could do something?'

'Like bust you for shooting those lines?'

I could feel myself redden hotly, anger and shame.

'Don't worry, he can't touch us, no jurisdiction, and the locals won't cooperate.'

The waiter was beside Janac, a few words in Thai and then, 'The bill please and a drink for my friend.' He pointed to the cop, speaking in English now for my benefit.

I watched the waiter go to the bar, lurid Hawaiian shirt clashing with the blackness, and then on to the cop. He put down the drink and indicated in our direction. The cop turned, surprised and concerned, staring straight at us. He hesitated, then rose, picked up the drink and headed over towards us. The waiter trailed anxiously in his wake, another joined him. Alarmed, I was half-way out of my seat when the Australian got to us. He was tall, over six foot, bleached blond hair and a deep tan. Rugged features and an arrogantly jutting jaw. Janac remained seated, one leg still nonchalantly crossed over the other. Arm still round the girl. But the grey eyes were watchful. I sat back down.

Without a word the Australian tipped the glass and the dark liquid splashed on to the floor. There was a light tinkling sound as the ice cubes followed. My heart had stopped. I didn't seem to need to breathe any more either. This guy was dead. Janac sucked his teeth and blew out a shred of tobacco. Eventually the eyebrows flicked up and that distorted smile returned to his lips. 'Get him another drink,' he said tersely, to the hovering waiter.

The waiter started to turn, but the Australian grabbed his jacket roughly. 'Don't bother, I don't want it.'

Janac looked unfazed, the smile still there. He reached into his jacket with a movement that was as casual as it was fast. It looked like he was going for his wallet. His hand emerged with a gun. An old-fashioned six shooter revolver, now levelled between the cop's eyes.

Time had stopped, all other sounds in the room had receded. The girls scurried away. All I could hear was the buzzing in my ears. The Australian's hand dropped off the waiter.

'If you don't want another, you'd better have the one on the floor,' said Janac. 'Lick it up.'

'Fuck you,' said the cop, but his words were undermined by the tremor in his voice.

The hammer clicked back, the cylinder sliding noiselessly round. Janac rose from his seat. The gun steadily advancing until it was between the Australian's lips. 'Lick it up,' he repeated.

In the silence I could hear the Australian's teeth click on the steel, he was visibly paling underneath the tan. He stood his ground for a couple more seconds, then slowly dropped to his knees. The gun backed off and followed him down. All four of us watched its progress.

'Lick it up.' The words were slow, heavy with menace. The cop bent, eyes finally lowered. Instantly Janac's boot slammed down on his neck, pressing his face hard into the floor. He snorted and struggled, bubbling the liquid. 'Suck, you arsehole.'

There was a gurgling, gasping, pain filled suck.

'Say thank you.'

There was more gasping before the cop ground out something that could have been 'thank you'.

In a flash of movement Janac dropped the hammer, reversed the weapon and slammed the butt down into the back of his head. The cop's face bounced off the floor, then he lay immobile.

A waiter dragged the body off as if it was a crate of empty bottles. No one in the club paid any attention. I looked back to Janac. The grey eyes were watching me again.

'As I mentioned, that arsehole has no jurisdiction here. This is a town for players – if you've got the balls,' he said, smiling. He laid the gun on the table between us with a heavy thud. 'So, how about it?'

'You want me to smuggle drugs, now? After this? Are you crazy?'

'Ten thousand dollars in it for you.'

'Bullshit easy money.' I started to rise.

'You're beginning to bore me now, Martin,' Janac said quietly, the smile was gone.

'I'm sorry,' I muttered, and I almost meant it.

'You've forgotten the bill too.'

At a movement from Janac the remaining waiter dropped it in front of me. I had no money left. I'd given it all to Janac for the girl. I swore under my breath, and sat back down. Two hundred and fifty-seven dollars. 'What about your half?'

'That is just your half.'

My mouth had gone dry on me. 'This is bullshit,' I muttered.

He shrugged. 'The prices are on the wall behind the bar.'

I looked around, I couldn't even see the bar. 'I can't pay this with cash.'

He nodded. 'The consequences of generosity and compassion.'

'So what do I do, they take credit cards?'

He laughed. 'I don't think so. But I tell you what. I'll spoof you for the bill.'

'I'm sorry?' I said, stalling, though I knew exactly what the game was.

'Spoof. It's real simple. Both players have three coins. Then out of sight of the other player, you put any number of them in one hand. Each player has a guess at how many coins there are in total. Whoever is right wins, the other guy picks up the tab.'

'I still don't have the money.'

'I'll lend it to you if you play, I'll cover the bill. If you lose you can get the cash and pay me back tomorrow.'

'And if I don't want to play?'

'Like I said, I won't protect you in here.'

I stared at him, I had no choice.

'What's the problem? You tell me you're a player, Martin. These are tiny stakes.'

I glanced at the trail of ice and cola, where the cop had been dragged away. Janac noticed, but didn't comment, the message was clear enough.

I slowly reached into my pocket. Despite the circumstances I was buzzing a little at the thought of the game. I was good at this. I'd played spoof for more restaurant meals than most people would ever eat.

'Whose first call?' I said.

'We'll toss for that,' replied Janac. He produced three coins which he laid on the table, flipped one, caught it and looked at me enquiringly.

'Tails,' I said.

He moved his hand away and we both peered forward. It was a tail. 'Your first call,' I said, fishing around for some coins. I put both hands behind my back and placed all three coins in my right hand, clenching it tightly, I placed it in front of me. Janac did the same.

He gazed at me impassively for a second or two before saying, 'Three.'

Three. The question was if he was trying to win with that call or just not lose. If I was first, I sometimes made a dummy call – for instance, I said three when I had zero myself. If you were trying to win with a call of three, you'd probably have one or two yourself. For some reason, people preferred to have one or two coins than zero or three. I had three though, which meant if he was playing for a win rather than a tied round, I should go for four or five. But I had a suspicion he was trying to spin me off in the wrong direction. I had a horrible feeling he had zero – in which case three was the right call, but he'd already made it.

'Four,' I said, opening my hand slowly. Janac raised those eyebrows again, his hand was indeed empty.

'See you, loser.' He started to get up. 'I'll settle here. My man will be round tomorrow about the money.'

'One more,' I replied, leaning forward. 'Double or quits.'

There was a long silence, while he gently eased himself back into the chair. He watched me carefully as he did it. The thin lips tight. 'A thousand bucks? Hardly worth it, let's make it ten thousand to the winner.'

'Ten thousand?'

'You lose, you can work it off.'

I swore fast and hard under my breath. Hooked in and played for a sucker. But there was no backing away now. Ten thousand would near enough clean me out. But it wasn't the money, it was the game itself. Spoof, stock markets, bond deals, currency speculation, property, it was all the same. I nodded my assent. I'd take this arsehole down.

'You surprise me, I didn't think you had it in you. You have the money?'

'I can get it,' I replied.

He nodded slowly. 'OK, let's play.' He presented a clenched fist in front of him.

I dropped a couple of coins into my hand under the table and matched his fist.

'Your call,' he said.

'Two,' I replied.

He smiled, I could almost see him going through the same routine I had, the wheels turning. 'Three.'

We both opened our hands and there lay four grubby coins, two each. I breathed a sigh of relief, my initiative now. And I already knew how I was going to play this one. I dropped all but one of the coins out and presented a tightly clenched hand.

Janac matched it, and he looked into my eyes for a long time. But he wouldn't find anything there. Too many deals, too many games.

Eventually he spoke. 'Three.'

Playing to win, or playing to draw? I was sure he'd play to draw again, he just seemed the type. I was going to say one, but then something made me think, that would be too obvious, to call three and have none again. 'Two,' I said.

He opened his hand with a slight grimace. There was nothing in it. Again.

I swore under my breath, I should've had him that time. Twice in a row when leading he had called three and had none. Ten thousand dollars had just slipped through my fingers. And I hadn't missed the import of that comment 'you lose you can

24

work it off'. If I wanted out of here I had to win. I licked dry lips. I could feel a little trace of sweat start around the hairline on my forehead. My heart was beating slowly, but hard, lots of blood pumping with each heavy thud. I was focused, there was nothing but the game. The higher the stakes the bigger the buzz. It was a good feeling, an old one, but a good feeling. I'd missed it.

I dropped all the coins out this time, and presented the fist. 'Two.'

Janac was much quicker, as though he'd decided in advance. He knew I'd give nothing away. 'Three,' he said and opened his hand, there was one in it. I added my zero and we both smiled grimly. I was worried. He had assumed that I would stick with my pattern, the last time I had led I'd called two and had two in my hand. And this was after he'd led with the same call and number of coins twice in a row. I carefully loaded two coins, and looked up. Janac was ready.

'Three,' he said, without a single flicker crossing his face. I breathed heavily. He was daring me to take him out. Three times in a row? Surely, no one would do that. But maybe that was the point.

Ten thousand dollars. Perhaps freedom too. All on the line. Bluff or double bluff? I had to go with the flow. 'Two,' I called and slowly opened my hand. The grey eyes glittered as he looked at the two grubby coins sitting in my sweaty palm. His hand remained clenched. I swallowed heavily. Slowly his fingers peeled open. Empty.

'Yes!' I hissed under my breath. Unbelieveable. Three times in a row. He'd dared me to take him out, and I'd done it. It was almost as though he had been prepared to lose, just to see what I did. Well, now he knew.

But he smiled, sort of, the thin lips curling back over the yellow teeth in an approximation. 'I didn't think you'd have the balls to make that last call.'

I shrugged. 'I want my money.'

'You'll get it. My men will find you tomorrow.'

I struggled to stand. 'They'd better,' I muttered, blood coursing with coke, alcohol and adrenaline.

Janac smirked. 'Or what?'

'Just get my money.' I turned and staggered towards the door.

'Hey,' he shouted. 'Keep this as a souvenir.' And, laughing, he flung something at me.

I caught it. It was the stage girl's button. But not gold. Plastic. A cheap plastic button.

4

I DROPPED THE second tablet on to my tongue and slugged back a mouthful from the bottle of water. Then took a couple more sips before screwing on the top and leaning forward on to the bar. 'Thanks Suchit,' I said hoarsely. 'Wish I'd known you had those before.'

He turned from where he was washing a glass. 'No problem, many people here have headache in morning,' he smiled.

I tried to laugh. 'Yeah, right. Can I have the usual breakfast? When you got a minute.'

'No problem.'

I turned and walked over to my corner table. God what a night. I'd been flying when I left that club. Buzzing, back in the game, ten thousand bucks up, I'd gone for the lot. I'd phoned Kate. I slumped into the chair and stared at the silent ocean. Thank God she hadn't been there. I took another swig out of the bottle. The pain killer was starting to help. I could remember leaving a message. Just the hotel name, I didn't know the phone number. Maybe she could find the number. Maybe she'd just turn up. Maybe she wouldn't get in touch at all. I closed my eyes and tried some deep, slow breaths.

And then there was Janac. I'd seen a lot last night. Too much. I should've got out when I had the chance. The buzz of winning had banished the memory for a while, but this morning it was hard to think of anything else. Maybe I should just get out now, get on a boat today. Get off the island. But what about Kate? I was going round in circles. And with the mother of all headaches I was in no state to do any thinking. There was a clunk. I opened my eyes and sat up as Suchit dropped the coffee cup on the table a little too heavily. 'Pancake come in two minutes,' he said.

I didn't see the figure approaching me through the tables until he stopped in front of me. The blond cop, whom I had last seen being dragged away unconcious, leaned heavily on the table between us – he looked like he needed to. I took in the bandaged arm and plastered face, half-way out of my seat, coffee spilling as I leapt up.

'We have to talk,' he said, emphatically.

'What do you want?' I asked quickly, darkly – either way, if it was a bust or information I was in trouble.

He twitched his head towards the door. 'Come on, let's walk.'

I checked around the bar with a quick glance, a couple of tourists were staring at us curiously. Better to take it outside. As I followed him I could see he was limping badly as well. He must have been really worked over, after he was dragged off the previous night.

I stepped in beside him as we reached the sand and he turned north. In the distance I could see the Big Buddha looming over the beach that bore his name. It was the middle of the day and blistering hot when you moved out from the shade of the restaurant.

He shuffled over the loose sand to the harder stuff at the water's edge. I glanced around uneasily, I didn't want to be seen with him.

'My name's Alex,' he said, tersely.

'Look,' I began, 'if this is about last night . . .'

He waved his hand dismissively. 'I'm here to warn you, Cormac – you're getting into deep trouble.'

I nearly laughed – looking at the state of him, he was the one in trouble.

'By now you'll know a little bit about our mutual friend Janac,' he continued.

'Maybe,' I interrupted, 'but why should I talk to you?'

'I'm an Australian cop, Sydney-based, with a special narcotics squad, put together to operate undercover and abroad.'

'Undercover?' I raised an eyebrow.

'Yeah, until last night. Or maybe Janac knew about me the minute I got off the plane. Either way, that's neither here nor there now. I'm on my way to the airport. His men gave me till tonight to clear off the island.'

'Great, so now you're compromising me,' I spat back at him.

He shook his head. 'No, I was careful. I'd give you a hundred to one he doesn't know I'm here. I watched for a tail, nothing.' He paused. 'I checked you out after the fight in the bar a

28

couple of nights ago. That was the first time you met him, wasn't it?'

I nodded, I could feel the sun beating harshly on the back of my neck. I flipped up my collar, no sense in getting burned.

'Far as I can tell, you're all right. That's why I came to look for you, partly to find out if you know anything and partly to warn you to be careful.'

'Seems like you're the one who should be careful. What were you doing last night?'

'When your target sends over a glass asking you to join him for a drink, you kind of know you've fucked up.'

'But why confront him?'

'Rush of blood I guess. I'm not proud of it.' He turned again and hobbled off up the beach.

I fell into step beside him. I let the silence run awhile before saying, 'So, tell me what I need to know.'

Alex stooped and picked up a stone, he didn't break stride. 'The man Janac is a hard core drug dealer, with an Interpol file as long as your arm. But nothing anyone can prove in a court that counts for more than diddlyshit. He has a lot of cooperation from the law round here. Big local employer and all that. We know he was in Vietnam with the Yanks and I have some of his military service file as well. A high IQ, but no formal education. He comes from one of those little country towns in the mid-west, and was starting to get a bad reputation as a trouble-maker with the local cops, when the draft whisked him off and paid him to do it for Uncle Sam.'

He spoke quickly and to the ground, pausing only for breath, flipping the flat stone through his fingers as he spoke. It clicked on a couple of heavy gold rings. 'The combat stuff reads like the story idea for *Platoon* – citations for valour beside reprimands for brutality. There's a couple of accusations of torturing prisoners captured on long range reconnaissance patrols and then the file closes.' He stopped, and the stone spun away over the calm water, as if to emphasise the point. I watched it skip, once, twice, three times before it caught an edge and plunged down.

Alex was still talking, 'The Americans say the rest is "classified". Although they admitted that he served in special operations over there. The Interpol rumours are that he was recruited into the CIA and was involved with their opium running operation to fund the covert activities in the border countries. When that was closed down, he bailed out and started up in business for himself, using the extensive contacts he'd made in that part of the world. He's spent twenty years developing it into one of the biggest operations in South East Asia. Unlike most of the Thai-based groups he handles the whole thing from growing to final distribution himself. That's how we came across him. He's directly responsible for about twenty per cent of the opiate-based drugs coming into Australia.'

I stopped and looked out to sea. This was heavier than I had imagined.

'So,' he said, 'I've told you what you're into. Take it anyway you want.'

I started to walk again. 'I only just met the guy. I got out of there straight after you last night.'

'That girl on the stage, she was really raped you know?' he said.

I nodded heavily, kicking at a rock.

'So, are you going to help me fix that bastard?'

'Look, I told you, I only just met him.'

'What about the drugs? He say anything to you?'

I stopped and looked him in the face. 'Why the hell should he? We were just having dinner. That's all.'

He met my stare evenly. 'No one "just" has dinner with Janac, Martin.' There was a long silence before he added, 'Think about it, Martin, it's not just me, thousands of people are having their lives fucked up by this shit.'

I sighed heavily, turned away and sat on the sand, staring out at the ocean. It was so calm. The mirror-like sheen stretching away. A few ripples came from one of the local fishing boats working a mile or so offshore. The hot silence now hung heavily. Alex was watching me as carefully as I was watching the view. At last he sat down beside me. We sat in silence for a long time. He glanced at his watch, but I ignored him.

Finally I said, speaking to the ocean, 'There is a girl on a stage being raped for public entertainment and no one does anything. Before I can draw breath there's a fucking huge revolver pointed in a guy's face. Then the guy, a cop, is beaten and dragged off to god knows what fate in front of my eyes. The next day he comes round, all fucked up, and tells me that the man I was with is some kind of heart of darkness psycho – which conclusion I had pretty much arrived at myself – and then asks me to inform on him.'

I shook my head. 'I don't know what's happening to me, but I want out, not further in.'

Alex stared at me for a long time, before saying, 'You ever seen a fourteen-year-old dying from an overdose?'

'Don't give me that civic responsibility crap. What you're asking me to do is way beyond the call of duty,' I responded sharply. 'Besides, like I said, I don't know anything.'

He nodded slowly. 'Maybe, but someone has to fight the dirty wars, don't they?'

I stared down at the sand, kicking it into a little pile.

'Anything you want to tell me, anything he's said, that could help us?'

I shook my head, still staring at the ground. There was another uncomfortable silence. Eventually I looked him in the eye.

'You sure?'

I nodded. 'I don't know anything,' I repeated.

'OK,' he said heavily. 'I've got to split. I've got a plane to catch.' He pulled out a pad and scribbled down a number. 'If you want out, I'd stay away from Janac. But you may not get a choice. If you get sucked in and you want to side with the good guys, here's my number.' He pushed himself awkwardly to his feet and held out the piece of paper. 'Ask for Alex. There'll be an answerphone if I'm not there.'

I nodded slowly, taking the note.

'My car's right here, you can walk back, huh?'

Again I nodded, and watched as he turned and slowly limped up the beach.

I sat for a good while longer, throwing stones at the ocean, before making my way back to the resort. I was very close to packing my bags and heading for the airport, but two things stopped me: Kate and ten thousand dollars. I knew I wanted to see her now, I couldn't leave without that. And if I was going to stick around, I wanted my money. Then I was out of here faster than you could say it. So I walked back into the restaurant, mind still racing with all that had happened, and discovered I hadn't got a choice anyway.

'Hey, Suchit,' I said as I strolled up to the bar. 'Any messages?'

'No messages, but,' he nodded towards a corner of the restaurant, 'man waiting for you.'

I looked round and saw a heavily-set local struggling out from behind a table, on which sat an untouched cola. He was maybe thirty or forty and dressed smartly if rather unconventionally in a sort of semi-military khaki outfit. He came straight up to me. 'Martin Cormac?'

I nodded.

'Please follow me.' He turned on his heel and headed out through the door.

'Hey?' I followed him slowly. 'What's the deal?'

'You come to lunch with Mr Janac.'

I swallowed, heart starting to thump. I looked at the impassive brown eyes and blank face. 'Why?' I asked.

'You want money,' he said, simply.

'No.' I shook my head. 'I want the money here. I don't want to go to lunch.'

'You want money you come to lunch. You come to lunch, you want money or not,' he said, face still expressionless. He turned and walked five paces to a car, where he opened the passenger door. I stared at him, trying to figure the options. Once again, there were none. It was an island, and Janac ran it. I got in.

We bumped out of the dusty drive and on to an equally dusty road. Turning south we drove parallel to the beach for a couple of miles before diving into the hinterland through an obscure turning. The car bounced and jolted as the rough got rougher and we slowed to a crawl as the driver fought his way round potholes and encroaching undergrowth. The gradient steepened and it was clear we were gaining height. After thirty minutes of this, concern had turned to palpable fear. Whatever was going to happen to me, no one else would ever know about it.

We finally burst through a gap in the branches and emerged on to a cultivated driveway. In front of us stood a beautiful one-storey, colonial-style house, built in timber and surrounded by a balustraded veranda. The freshly painted white glistened in the sun. The drive led up through a small area of landscaped garden and we came to a halt at what looked like the back door. The engine died and the tick, tick of it cooling joined the buzz of the forest and the hum of the ceiling fans spaced at intervals along the porch. A hammock gently swayed in the afternoon breeze. Janac was standing at the top of the steps, hands on hips, master of all he surveyed. 'Glad you could make it,' he called.

I got out of the car, walked up the steps and shook his hand.

'Beautiful place,' I said. Every sinew, every tendon, every muscle and every nerve was tense enough to snap.

'You haven't seen the view yet,' he replied, turning to lead the way inside. 'Drink?' he asked over his shoulder.

'A beer would be fine,' I answered. It wasn't smart, but I needed a drink. We stepped through the door into a hallway, which led into a living room. The room was large, in front of me the two outside walls slid back in a succession of panels to reveal a stunning view down the mountain, towards the ocean.

The driver had disappeared and Janac was talking quietly to a pretty Thai girl. I turned to survey the rest of the room. One wall was occupied almost exclusively with books, the ceiling-high shelves broken only by a doorway. The other, the one I had walked through, was sparsely decorated with a couple of paintings I didn't recognise. The white walls, varnished hardwood floors and gentle whoosh of the ceiling fans created a peaceful and tropical atmosphere.

I stepped over towards the bookshelves and ran my hand along the spines. It was all neatly catalogued and some of the titles looked highly academic. The only ones I recognised under warfare were Paul Kennedy's 'Rise and Fall of the Great Powers' and Michael Herr's 'Dispatches' – two more disparate volumes on the struggles of empire it would be hard to imagine. Then there was finance: 'Barbarians at the Gate', 'Liar's Poker' plus all those American 'how to make a million' books, along with a few academic volumes on economics. Further along I found philosophy. Hofstader, Putnam, Dennet and Skinner were new to me along with a lot more; Nietzche and Machiavelli I did know. Politics was there, Marx and Lenin, and a copy of *Mein Kampf*. I raised a hand to pull it off the shelf, and then thought better of it.

I felt someone behind me and turned, tensing. Janac proferred a beer. I took it and said, 'Impressive, very impressive.'

He nodded. 'I'm interested in the human mind, how it works, how it thinks, how it behaves in different circumstances. I think there is a great deal to be learned about such matters from books – all products of minds. Please have a seat.' He extended an arm and I led the way to a couple of chairs and a table by one of the doors. I sat back and gazed out at the view. It was cool, despite the heat outside, but it was the delightful cool that comes from the intelligence of good design rather than the power of air conditioning. Unwillingly I started to relax a little. I took a handful of the nuts that were on the table and looked over as Janac sat down.

He smiled, and took a sip of his beer. 'I'm sorry that last night got a little heated. I hope you don't think any the worse of me for it.'

I said nothing, surprised by the conciliatory tone.

'I took care of the girl for you, she's had medical attention, I'll get her a job in town somewhere when she's fixed up.'

I recovered enough to manage, 'What kind of job?'

'Hotel, cleaning job, something like that. You can't expect too much.'

'That's very good of you,' I said, unsure of this sudden display of magnanimity.

'Not at all. Your outburst made me think a little about what was happening. I have asked the club to stop that act.' He leant forward and took a single peanut, chewed it slowly, thoughtfully. Again I couldn't think of anything to say. I took a long swallow of the beer to fill the silence.

'So have you thought about my offer any further?' he asked, eventually.

'I think I've explained my reasons for not wanting to get involved,' I said slowly.

'It's possible that we might be able to set it up rather more generously for you, perhaps, a little risk, a little game to play. But bigger stakes.'

I forced a smile. 'Unfortunately, I'm quite happy to get out while I'm ahead.'

'Ahead? Yes, of course.' Janac eased a thick leather wallet from a back pocket and slipped out ten thousand-dollar bills on to the table. I looked at the money carefully, but didn't reach for it, yet.

'Lots more where that came from.'

'I'm sure,' I replied evenly.

'You see, you interest me, Martin. There is a conflict struggling away inside you, even as we speak. Transposing your guilt from the crash to the selfishness in your City lifestyle showed compassion. And there was your sympathy for the girl last night. Demonstrated at a moment that could have wrecked what might be a profitable relationship with me. And yet there is your greed – you want to go back to the City. You consider my offer, not on the basis of the immorality of smuggling drugs, but on a risk/benefit ratio. And of course . . .' he nodded at the ten thousand dollars on the table. Then leant forward and pushed it towards me. 'You know where the money has come from.'

I hesitated, I guess this was the moment I had been worried about. Would accepting the money dig me in deeper? The grey eyes were watching me carefully. I couldn't get any deeper. And I certainly wasn't going to let him moralise me out of taking it. I'd won it fair and square. I leant forward and picked it up. Stacked it and put it in my pocket.

I looked up. He was smiling. 'I have a better game for you too, Martin.'

I shook my head.

'But this is different. A non-zero-sum game.'

'I'm sorry, I . . .'

'You're not familiar with Games Theory?'

I knew a little, of course, but decided to stall, 'No,' I said.

'Zero-sum is winner takes all, what you win I lose. Like spoof. They are relatively simple, the objective is clear. More interesting are non-zero-sum games where winning and losing are blurred.'

'Such as?'

'Lunch is ready Mr Janac.' The sing-song voice of the Thai maid interrupted.

He turned to her, the faintest trace of annoyance crossing his face. 'Oh. Well, we'd better eat. It's not the kind of meal that will wait.' He faced me again and the tight smile was back. 'Please, follow me.'

I trailed through to the dining room, another vision of wood panelling and tropical elegance. We sat down at a long polished table as the girl poured a glass of white wine. I sipped delicately, it was chilled perfectly. Janac was silent whilst the girl bustled around serving the first course. Finally she was gone. I waited for Janac and then began investigating the rather curious vegetable that had been served with my prawns. The beer was beginning to work, the tension was ebbing away.

'So Martin,' he restarted, 'I was telling you about non-zero-sum games.'

'Yes,' I murmured non-comittally. I took another sip of wine and a mouthful of vegetable. It was sweet and crunchy. Not vegetable at all, some kind of fruit.

'The Prisoner's Dilemma is the best. It explores exactly that distinction you appear so confused by, between self-interested greed, and concern for one's fellow man. You haven't heard of the Prisoner's Dilemma?' he sipped at the wine, the grey eyes watching me still.

I shook my head.

He put the wine glass down, templing his fingers. 'The classic formulation, and the one that gives the problem its name, is with two prisoners in solitary, who are unable to confer. They are both accused of the same crime and, as in the finest traditions of American justice they are both offered a deal. They are each given the chance to turn State's evidence to assist in the conviction of the other. If they both choose to remain silent, they can each only be convicted for one year. If they both choose to turn in the other, they will be convicted for three years each. However, should one of them remain silent and the other turn State's evidence, the grass will go free and the other will do five years.'

He smiled and picked up his fork. 'The central problem is whether you feel you can risk remaining silent, in an attempt to cooperate with the other prisoner, so that you both get off with one year. Aware that he could then grass on you and walk away free while you go down for five years. The pressure is on you, and him too, not to take that chance and so you grass on each other. When you do, you get three years each, rather than the one year you both could have got, if you had kept your mouths shut. The game is a metaphor of man's behaviour in society – do you look after yourself, or are you prepared to take the risk and act selflessly so everyone can be better off.' He forked up a mouthful of rice and sat with it poised. 'I have a machine that I had specially built. We'll have a game of the Prisoner's Dilemma after lunch. Then you will understand. It'll be a good opportunity for you to test yourself.' He swallowed the forkful.

I prodded thoughtfully at a prawn. He seemed much less intense, less intimidating now. Fork poised over a battered prawn, glass of chilled white at his elbow – the picture of a man at ease pondering an intellectual problem. But the lean face had a taunting half-smile, and the eyes flickered inquisitively. I was still unsure of him, more so of his interest in this Prisoner's Dilemma. Just a game? Perhaps, but I'd already learned that nothing was 'just' a game with Janac.

5

STEAMING COFFEE SPLASHED into the china cup in front of me. I poured in some milk and watched as black and white blended into a murky brown. I had almost relaxed. I just had to get through the next game, without getting sucked into some high stakes play-off, and get the hell out of there.

Janac pushed his chair back from the table a couple of inches and crossed his legs. The thin, almost delicate fingers lit a cigarette from an engraved silver case with precise, careful movements. The lighter was a Zippo. He dragged deeply on the butt and exhaled a cloud of smoke. 'You see, Martin,' he started, 'your struggle between behaving out of self interest or for group interest – in this I see the whole history of the world. The struggle between personal sacrifice for the community and looking after number one. It was clear in the eighties which took over and you are a product of those times. Can you shake off those values for the new, more caring decade?' he chuckled.

I smiled, neutrally.

'This game, this Prisoner's Dilemma, is your problem. Come, I want to show you.'

He eased his sparse frame out of the chair and, stubbing out the remains of the cigarette, headed towards the door. I poured down the last of my coffee and followed. The meal and its surroundings had quelled most of my fears, but I wouldn't be happy until I was out of there.

The door led into a third room, much smaller than the others. Windowless, it was lit only by the luminous glow of two computer monitors on a table in the middle of the room. They faced away from each other, both connected to the same processing box, but each with a separate mouse. There was also a couple of wristbands with each monitor, connected on long flexes to a second box. The only other items in the room were two hard-backed chairs.

'Take a seat,' said Janac, sitting down opposite the chair indicated. I glanced at the screen, feeling the flicker of the refresh on my cheeks. Numbers danced across the monitor in ever-changing patterns. My blood stirred. But Janac was talking again. 'You'll see on the screen two boxes.' The numbers dissolved into a shower of coloured pixels and the screen reformed itself in two halves. The boxes appeared in the top half as he described. He went on, 'You can use the mouse, you are familiar with mouses?'

I nodded yes.

'You can use it to click on one or other of the boxes to make your decision. You can choose to cooperate or defect. The computer will work out the result depending on both our decisions according to the pay-off table. You should be able to see it on your screen now.' There were a couple more clicks and the bottom half came to life. Numbers marched on to the monitor again. I smiled, thoughts crowding in of a thousand games played through trails of shifting numbers; buy or sell, win or lose. Slowly they began to stop, the patterns fixed, the game defined.

Janac described what I was seeing, 'Player one is myself, you're player two. You will see from this table that if we both cooperate there is a level one punishment for each of us. For mutual defection we both get a level three punishment and for a defect/cooperate response, the defector gets no punishment, the cooperator a level five. This is exactly the problem the prisoners faced, they can cooperate with each other by remaining silent, or defect to the authorities. I can alter the pay-offs to my preference, but these are the same as the classic problem and will suit us well.'

I stared at the screen in silence for a while, thinking. It was a simple matrix of decision and consequence, cause and effect. I could see the link with the earlier problem, with one major difference. I said, 'What's the punishment?'

'A points score.'

That was harmless enough, but there was one thing that wasn't clear. 'So, is the idea to minimise our personal score, or our collective score against the machine?'

Janac smiled. 'I see you have a grasp of the situation already. As I said, in these games winning and losing are not so clearly defined. Do you want to beat me, or minimise our collective punishment? That of course, is the essence of the game. What do you consider to be winning?' Before I could answer he went on, 'Let's try a round. You can have a minute or two to think.'

So I thought about it. The hotshot broker with numbers to balance and a game to play. It was that old feeling again. The buzz of the trading room came back to me from the past; phones, slapping keyboards, hustling conversations, the shouts of triumph and defeat. Always moving inexorably onwards, no time to rest, barely time to think. I shook my head, but this was a static problem. It should be easy. Forget the memories and concentrate on the now. Play the game.

The first thing that became apparent was that as an individual, whatever he did, I was better off if I defected. Since if he cooperated then I got zero – compared to one if I had cooperated also. If he defected I got three as a defector – whereas if I cooperated I would get five. Defection was the option that best protected my own self-interest.

So far so good. But Janac obviously understood that, so we'd both end up defecting and getting three points. And here was the rub, because if we could, somehow, both cooperate, we'd get one point each, which was both an individual and a collectively better result. But could you afford to take the chance on cooperating and have the opposition defect on you? Who wanted to take the big loss while the other guy got off scot-free? The greatest mutual benefit, cooperating and taking the point each, was exactly the option that self-interest said you shouldn't follow.

The rationality of the market. Trading. Sell early, because if you're still holding that position when everyone else runs for cover you'll lose big time. But of course it is the actions of you and others like you, trying to get out early, that push the price into freefall. You may cover your own position, but you help create a chronically unstable market, dominated by short term profiteering. And an economy in which no one can get on with the real businesses that the market was originally created to support. Which, in the final analysis, is not good for any of us. What do you choose, the personal or the public good?

I shifted uncomfortably, gazing steadily back at the numbers lighting up my face. Torn between memories of the glamour and excitement of the games I had played, and the realisation of their consequences. The game did have a point, Janac was right, this was my problem. Was I a cooperator or a defector? I thought about the City, about the smash, about the life I'd led before and after. About the real evil I had glimpsed in the past couple of days. Slowly, and almost unwillingly, I clicked on cooperate. I could be a good guy.

'Done?' said Janac.

I looked up and nodded.

'OK, I'm making my choice now.'

'You can't see what I've done?' I said, ever suspicious.

'No, not until I make my choice, when the computer displays the results – like that.'

The screen flashed again:

Player One Defect	Player Two Cooperate
0	5

'Got you, sucker. I'm disappointed in you.'

I looked back at Janac. Only numbers, but I hated losing.

'Another round. Let's play it again.' Once more the screen dissolved and reformed, the boxes and the pay-off table were back.

'OK,' I said slowly, 'you make your choice first this time.'

'Trusting, aren't you?'

'Too much time in the City. Go on.' I heard the click. It was pretty clear what mine had to be. I slid the cursor over to defect and pressed the button. The results popped up immediately:

Player One Defect	Player Two Defect
3	3

Janac glanced up. 'Predictable, isn't it? Looking out for number one comes naturally to you, Martin,' he said, with a knowing smile.

'What the hell am I supposed to do?' I retorted. 'The way it's structured the only rational answer is to defect.'

'That's the point, that's why it's so powerful. It's like life. You're forced out of self interest into behaviour that is damaging to the common good. The machine got six points out of us then, rather than two, if we had both cooperated. Another round. But this time let's play it properly. Put the wrist and ankle bands on, please.'

I looked at the Velcro and copper straps lying on the table next to the mouse.

'The point score denotes a level of pain, the wrist and ankle bands administer it via an electric shock.'

'What! Hang on a minute! I'm not into this at all.' I started up. I should have known.

'Please,' Janac's voice was soothing. He remained seated, opening his hands in a conciliatory gesture. 'Please, not so much excitement. The shock is a mild one. It's so difficult to think of a worthwhile penalty – to make the game real – like life. You're a player, Martin. A troubled one, and this game allows you to test exactly that which is troubling you. Playing the game is not the downside, playing badly is, against what you believe. But for points? Really, where's the value when there is no risk? And money? What value has it? What is money? Nothing, it comes it goes, you've already walked away from what ninety per cent of the world's population would regard as a fortune. But pain, now there's something that we can all relate to equally.'

'How much pain are we talking about?'

'I will administer myself the level five punishment, so that you can see the effect for yourself.'

I slowly sat back down and watched as he fastened the wrist and ankle bands and then clicked away on the mouse. There was a final click, a hum and he looked up at me smiling. Then the humming stopped with a cracking phizz sound, and I saw his arm jolt. He gasped briefly and a shadow crossed his face. His eyes flickered and closed and he remained still and silent for a couple of seconds. I breathed out gently, this exercise had at least given me a little time to think. And I didn't think I wanted to get a level five.

I could run through the open doors and back down the track. But I'd been through that loop before. I had no doubt that he could make me play this if he wanted to. And he did want me to. That was why I was here. Wined and dined, sweetened up, lulled into feeling secure – and then this. Same deal. The high stakes play-off. But the stakes weren't that high, yet. I had to tag along, keep him happy, keep it low key, then get clear and run like hell. I wouldn't stop till I was out of Thailand. I glanced at my watch and looked back up.

'OK,' I said in a voice that was intended to betray a certain amount of resignation, but not too much – yes, I will play your childish game, I wanted to say, to please you. It's not the pain that bothers me, just the pointlessness of it. 'OK, I have a dinner engagement tonight that I should leave for soon, I would hate to be late. But I'll play a couple of rounds with you first – then I must head back.'

Janac nodded, unsmiling, but he looked satisfied. 'All right. Make your choice.'

I dragged the cursor across to defect, and clicked.

The machine whirred and ticked and up came the result. Two defects. A level three. Then the phizz sound, I flinched protectively and jerked my arm involuntarily as the charge shot through it. For a second the universe exploded in a sensation of pure pain. It faded slowly, translating into a buzz of colour and feeling. 'Fuck,' I whispered. I could barely make Janac out through watering eyes.

Janac sat with a fixed smile. 'Please, I thought you were made of a little sterner stuff than that.' The words were brave, but his face was flushed. Another blast coming so soon after the first hit must've taken something out of him.

'That was a level three?' I said.

'Sure. That was good though, Martin, I was worried you might have another go at being a nice guy. But you won't, will you? Let's play it again.' His voice was firmer now.

I took a deep breath. This was crazy. I had to defect. So did he, but I wasn't sure I could take another shock like that. But I couldn't believe he would ever cooperate. And even if he did, I was still better off defecting. It was insane, we'd both get another level three. Insane but . . . there was no other rational choice. I clicked defect. Reflexively tensing, muscles singing out. I barely heard the machine this time. I saw the two defects come up and tried to shut down my senses. There was a couple of seconds that seemed like hours and then . . .

This time I didn't even manage a yell, the pain shot through me and I just gasped, frozen in my seat. I closed my eyes and sucked in a deep, deep breath and waited, slowly, but so slowly the pain subsided. It was much worse. The pain had gone higher and had lasted longer. A whole world of hurt. I stayed slumped in my chair, eyes closed, trying to recover my breath, the aftershock echoing through my body.

'Wonderful.' It was Janac, his voice hoarse with pain, he was hurting too. 'Everybody does it. No matter how moral they think they are the bastards always try to look after themselves. You've just proved it. Civilisation, acting for the group interest, is forced

42

on us. But that's not the natural response, when it comes down to it, we would all prefer to act selfishly. The world would fall apart if we weren't forced to cooperate with society.' I looked up, there was triumph in his face, even through the pain. 'Power, Martin, enforcing control, that's all that counts. The job of governments is to punish defectors. But remember – you're above that, you're a player, a defector, don't let that go.' His face was flushed, delighted by his proof of man's selfish inhumanity. 'One more time,' he said, and I heard the mouse scrape and the button click.

I stared across at him. There was no question, he would never cooperate. He would sit there and take level three shots till he died, rather than believe there was any other way. And he thought we were all like him. That I was like him. I trembled as I realised what I had to do. I had to show him I was different. Maybe it would break me free. I dragged the cursor over to cooperate and, heart pounding, vision already blurred with pain and sweat, I clicked.

I remember the first flash. Then nothing. It all exploded, blazing out in a starburst of white hot light. I think I came to quickly, survival instinct helping conciousness struggle through. The jolt had flung me backwards off the chair. Giddy with pain and nausea, I recognised the ceiling, I had to be lying down. I tried to figure out where my limbs were. It was as though all the nerves and muscles had overloaded. There were no signals coming in, my brain couldn't figure out what was where, which muscles needed to pull and which to push to get myself upright. I knew I had to get up, to get away. But nothing would respond. I struggled and collapsed. I heard Janac's dry laugh, getting fainter. I felt it slipping away again . . .

The second time I came to with a start, the cold splash of water on my face. I shook my head, sitting up quickly. Startled, staring around, trying to work out where I was, what was happening. Then I saw Janac, standing over me, hands on hips, face calm, with its cynical half-smile, back in control.

The pain was still coming in waves, each one making me nauseous, but I could feel my legs and arms now, work my body. I struggled and rose, uncertainly, to my feet. I stood for a second or two, still dazed, still hurting, but aware. I swallowed heavily, and struggled to pull the copper bands off with thick, unwieldly fingers. Finally free of them I looked up.

Janac had moved away from me, towards the door. 'You

disappoint me, Martin, and intrigue me. But I guess that's another round to me. Good job I had the level set as low as possible. You looked like you were hurting there.'

I choked. I'd felt like I was dying. 'You can scale the pain level up?' I said in a crackly voice.

'Of course,' he replied, turning and moving towards the back of the house and the car.

'How high does it go?' I croaked, hobbling after him, sure now that I could get away, that this was the end of the game. Maybe it had worked.

'In the US they recommend an electric chair voltage of two thousand six hundred and forty volts alternating current. Two thousand should be enough but if you want to be sure, and being sure is humane in their books, then go for the extra six forty on top. You have to be careful about the current, if it gets above five amps it tends to cook the flesh off the body, very messy when you want to move it afterwards. My system will deliver that, at maximum on a level five. Of course at that point death is almost instantaneous, which isn't really the idea. But the electrode connections are probably inefficient enough to cause sufficient pain and burning.'

I could feel a lightness come over me, as though my mind was detaching from my body, Janac's voice was growing distant. He glanced over his shoulder as he moved into the sunlight bursting through the outside door. 'You know it only takes thirty-one cents of electricity to kill a man?'

My heart had stopped. All the muscles seemed incapable of movement, except my shaking hands. My throat had dried, I tried to swallow, to move forward towards the door and the sunlight, the waiting car. 'Kill a man,' I croaked.

Janac was on the veranda now, he turned to face me, that cynical, half-amused smile drifting across his face. 'Sure, that's when it gets interesting, when there is something of true value at stake – life itself. Physical pain is one thing, at high enough levels it's unpleasant of course, but the real agony is in the mind. That's why it's so important to understand the mind, to know what does and does not inflict pain. The fear of death inflicts such pain in most people, and interestingly enough the fear of the death of a loved one is nearly as strong.'

'Is that what you learned from your books?' I said, in the same strangled voice.

'Yes,' he replied, turning the grey eyes on me, 'of course, I don't often get people to play for those stakes.' He stopped by the car and turned, smiling, flashing those yellow teeth, in an open, disarming way. But I had caught the implication only too well. 'My man will take you home. Thanks for your company.' He paused. 'And think about my offer, Martin. We will make it worth your while.'

'No, no, I'm sorry. No way.' The words stumbled out involuntarily.

Something flashed across his face, but it was gone before I could recognise it, the smile was back. 'Well, here's to the next round of the game.' He extended his hand and I took it, briefly, my arm still tingling horribly.

I nodded agreement, forcing a smile, and thought: in your dreams, buddy, I'm out of your life.

6

I FELT AS though I had just escaped from Death Row as the car bumped back down the mountain. I sat in the back seat in silence. I had no desire to talk to the driver. I had to get off this island. Finally the car lurched back into the resort drive and drew to a dusty stop. I jumped out and headed for the bar. I ordered a double Mekong and Coke and sat down heavily in my chair, I was still shaking. Suchit brought the drink.

'Some friend of yours come here this afternoon, want to meet you later.'

'Friends, here? Who?'

He fumbled in a pocket and pulled out a flimsy piece of paper. I grabbed at it, 'Dear Martin,' I read, 'So surprised and pleased to get your message. Sorry I missed you, but love to meet with you, perhaps we could have dinner at our hotel tonight? Meet about six for a drink first? Call me if there is a problem, number's on the letterhead, room 318. Lots of love, Kate.'

A friendly message, more than I could have hoped for. I was conscious of the irrepressible and ridiculous grin I had developed. Janac was temporarily forgotten. I read the note again and looked at my watch, it was already quarter past five. I wanted to see her. Badly. But then, Janac . . .

'Suchit, are there any more planes or boats today?'

'To mainland?'

'To anywhere.'

He shook his head. 'No, tomorrow.'

I nodded, that settled it. If he came looking for me, it would be here. I'd be better off at Kate's hotel this evening. Get back late, leave early.

I downed the drink in one go and headed over to my room. I took a quick shower and threw on a cleanish pair of jeans and a T-shirt. I dug the keys to the bike I had hired out of my bag. I retrieved money and credit cards from their hiding spot under a rock in the corner and went back out. I climbed on the bike and kicked it into life. It started with unusual ease. I flicked it into gear, blipped the throttle, dropped the clutch and was gone.

It was five past when I pulled up outside the hotel. The shower had been a complete waste of time, I was covered in dust again. I found the courtesy phone and dialled up to room 318. Kate picked it up.

'Kate, it's Martin.'

'Martin, where are you?'

It was that voice again, three years on and it already had my heart pounding. 'I'm in the lobby.'

'We'll be right down,' she said confidently.

I paced around impatiently, checked myself in the mirror a couple of times, tried to brush the dust off, paced around some more. How was I going to feel when I saw her for real?

'Martin?'

I spun round and there she was. I stepped forward into her arms and held on tight for a long couple of seconds. But she was tense and all too quickly started to pull away. I let go unwillingly, stepping back and taking in the slim figure, dressed simply in jeans and a strapless top, no make-up and, of course, the characteristically bare feet. 'As beautiful as ever,' I said quietly.

She laughed, a little nervously now. 'You haven't changed at all!' She turned to the man accompanying her. 'Martin, this is Scott.'

I turned to face him. Three years on and she was still with him. He was two or three inches shorter than me, but stocky, with a shock of jet black hair and a beard so closely cropped it was almost stubble. Slowly I held out a hand, he took it brusquely, and shook with a firm grasp and pumping action.

He spoke to Kate, 'I just have to check for messages, why don't you go through to the bar. Mine's a beer,' and he turned and left.

I watched him go as I tried to think of something safe to say. Finally, I turned back to Kate. 'This is one hell of a coincidence, what are you doing here?'

She looked distracted, a hand brushed away imaginary hair from her eyes, but slowly she smiled, transforming her whole person, 'I was going to ask you the same thing, but let's get that drink first, hey? It's this way.' She led me into the bar. It was expensively decorated with hardwood furnishings that were a little too heavy for my taste. It had an in-your-face opulence that I wouldn't have thought Kate would go for. I followed her towards a table for four in the corner. I sat down opposite, leaving the seat beside her for Scott.

'So, how did you know we were here?' she started quickly.

'That's easy, I saw you in the market, but you hopped into the hotel's courtesy bus before I had a chance to get over to you. It was simple enough to find out about the hotel, then I just phoned up and left a message.' I looked up to see a waiter patiently waiting for an order.

'Scott will have a beer, mine's a Coke,' said Kate.

'Make that two beers and a Coke then please,' I said.

The waiter nodded and disappeared as quietly as he had arrived.

I looked at Kate in silence, she stared down, spinning a ring on her right hand with the thumb and index finger of her left. 'I missed the way you play with that ring when you're nervous,' I said.

She looked up, eyebrows raised, a half-smile. 'Yeah, well I'd smoke but I couldn't handle you and Scott giving me a hard time.'

I smiled. 'It's good to see you, Kate,' I said slowly. 'I wasn't sure if you'd call, I wasn't too, er,' I looked away, and then back, 'I wasn't too cool when we split up. I'm sorry, I wish I could have dealt with it better.'

'I don't think either of us did ourselves any favours,' she said sadly. 'I suppose we were younger.' She reached out and gently pulled my hand away from my face. 'You know, I've missed the way you scratch at that eyebrow when you're nervous.'

I smiled. 'Fifteen all.'

We both laughed. I realised she was still holding my hand. I caught the blue eyes. There was a sudden awkward silence. And the hand was gone.

I studied her carefully, the rampaging blonde hair tumbling over the bare, tanned shoulders. The face that broke your heart. God I'd been so in love with this girl. She hadn't changed much, a few lines around the eyes that I didn't remember. But those lines looked as comfortable being worried as they were laughing. And now they were definitely worried. 'So where have you been all this time?' she said.

I looked away.

'Everyone is frantic, Martin. Your parents phoned half of

England trying to track you down. They even managed to get hold of me to find out if I'd heard from you. No one knew where you'd gone.'

'That was the idea,' I butted in, a little tersely. 'I sent a card saying I was OK.'

'A month later. One postcard from Bangkok, saying you were going "walkabout". You were so together, Martin, what the hell happened?'

'Apart from you leaving me?' I said, and immediately regretted it.

The lips tightened and her eyes closed, as though in pain, 'That's not fair, Martin. I left the life, the place. And anyway it was three years ago, why take off now?' She glanced over to where Scott was picking his way back towards us through the tables.

'Sorry,' I said, and meant it.

'You, or I, must contact your family,' she said, slowly.

I gave her an askance look, but before I could respond Scott was there.

Kate looked up. 'Anything?'

He looked concerned. 'Yeah, from Ben, there's another message, problems, but I can't get hold of him to find out what.'

She smiled uncertainly. 'It'll be OK, Scott, we'll be back there soon.'

He scowled. 'I hate not knowing what's going on, I knew we shouldn't have come up here so close to the regatta.'

Kate bit her lip. 'We'll talk about it later,' she said, tightly.

No one said anything while Scott sat down.

'Drinks are coming,' I said to him, awkwardly.

He nodded, distant, troubled.

'So,' Kate said, with what was obviously a big effort at good humour, and a change of subject, 'what are you up to, Martin?'

'Well,' I started, 'I'm out of here first thing tomorrow morning.'

'Really? Are you going home? Why didn't you say . . .'

'No,' I shook my head, 'I don't know where I'm going, but I'm not staying here.'

'What's the problem?' she asked.

'Oh, there's this American I ran into in a bar,' I hesitated, but I could see no reason not to tell them, 'to start with he just seemed good company,' I shook my head ruefully, 'but he got me wrapped up in these games . . .'

'What kind of games?'

I shrugged. 'You know, spoof, Prisoner's Dilemma . . .' I tailed off. My propensity to turn everything into a game or a gamble had been a continual source of friction between us.

'Oh, Martin, you're not still at that? I thought maybe because you were out here, and had given that job up you might have stopped all that betting rubbish too.'

'Well, yeah.' I stared at the ceiling, watched a fan complete a couple of laps. Damn, I should have seen this coming. 'It was only one game you know, and before I knew it I was mixed up with this real bad guy, major league drug smuggler.'

'Martin!'

Even Scott turned round and looked interested.

'It's OK, I mean that's why I have to leave. I told him I was out of it. First thing tomorrow I'm on a plane or a boat.'

'Jesus! How on earth could you get involved with drug smuggling?'

'Kate, keep your voice down! I just got sucked in, he picked me out, there was nothing I could do.' That wasn't entirely true, but true enough for the moment. 'I'm out of it now. No problem.'

'You think it's that easy?' said Scott, out of nowhere.

I turned to look at him, and shrugged. 'I hope so, I'd have liked to have left tonight, but there's no way off the island.'

'Don't blame you,' said Scott. 'There's some pretty bad shit goes down around here, behind all those friendly smiles.'

I nodded. If only you knew how bad, I thought.

There was a clink in front of me as the waiter put down the two beers, the Coke followed. I distributed them and paid him.

'Well, I've told you all about me, what are you doing here?'

'Not all about you, Martin . . .' Kate started.

'As much as you're going to get,' I said firmly. 'At the moment.' I glanced at Scott, who had gone back to staring round the room.

Kate sighed, but there was an almost imperceptible nod. 'Well, we're just on holiday,' she said, 'we needed a break, we've had a hard time recently.' She smiled at Scott and laid a hand on his arm. I caught Scott's eye without meaning to and he stared me down.

'Oh?' I said. 'What kind of hard time?'

'Just boat shit,' said Scott. So far he hadn't been exactly friendly, but the question provoked an even more negative response. I guessed it was a sensitive subject.

Kate looked at him, concerned, there was a silence and she obviously felt that she had to fill it. 'The boat is down in Sydney, we've been getting it ready for a regatta down there. But it's been a lot of hassle. The sponsor won't part with any money and the racing skipper . . .' she stopped, and I glanced up just in time to catch Scott giving her a very old-fashioned look.

'The skipper?' I said, as innocently as possible.

Kate glanced back from Scott. 'Just boat politics,' she said.

There was another silence, this time I was happy to break it.

'So my family's call didn't have anything to do with the choice of holiday venue?' I said, backing a hunch, and trying to appear innocently mischievous. Ko Samui was, after all, the most obvious place in Thailand to look for someone gone 'walkabout'.

Kate smiled, a little guiltily. 'Maybe.'

'Yeah, you're the reason I'm here instead of doing my job,' said Scott to me, openly hostile now.

Kate turned on him quickly. 'That's bullshit and you know it, you promised me this holiday weeks before I heard about Martin.' And then back to me, 'We weren't looking for you. I just thought, well, that if you were around we might bump into you, and we did.'

I sat back, things were becoming clearer. I tried to pour a little oil. 'Look, I really appreciate that you're here, whatever the reason. I'm glad to see a friendly face, this guy has me a little freaked.'

Scott took a big swallow of his beer, and stared fixedly at the ceiling. Kate said, 'So where are you going next? You won't stay in Thailand and you won't go home?'

I shrugged. 'No, not home for sure.' I stopped my hand half-way to the giveaway eyebrow and redirected it to the beer. I wished she'd stay away from that subject. 'I'll go anywhere else, somewhere the sun shines and the living is easy.'

Kate glanced at Scott, a mixture of emotions crossing her face. She seemed to come to a decision. 'We're going back to Sydney tomorrow. Why don't you come to Australia? It's the perfect place, great weather, great people. You can relax, get in touch with your family. I can help you sort things out. Scott, Martin can come with us to Sydney can't he?'

To say that Scott didn't look too impressed with the idea would be an understatement. 'I guess,' he muttered, eventually.

And Kate leaned forward, smiling. 'So, Martin, what do you think?'

I looked at her again. It was a long way from Janac. It could be a good half-way house on the way back to normality. I looked at Kate and knew I was rationalising a decision that I'd made the second I saw her. I'd lost her three years ago, I wasn't going to let her slip away again. Scott or no Scott. 'I'd love to,' I replied.

'Excellent.' Kate looked genuinely pleased.

I felt euphoric. 'I'll go down to the airport in the morning and catch the first plane I can get on.'

'I think our flight is a little later,' said Kate. 'After lunch.'

'Well, I'll get to Bangkok and just keep going to Sydney.'

'Exactly. Come and find us at the boat. It's called *Gold*, and it's in the yacht club marina at Rushcutter's Bay.'

'I don't have a pen,' I said.

'No problem, we'll get one at the desk later.'

'Great.' There was a silence. 'Well, shall we eat?'

The meal was every bit as good as I expected. And Scott relaxed after a few more beers. Kate made a fuss of him and he kept a territorial arm round her for much of the time. But I wasn't fazed, everything comes to those who wait. And so it was a much happier man that left dinner, than the one that had left lunch. The resort was darkened and quiet when I arrived back a little after one in the morning and I slipped into my room unnoticed. I set the alarm for just before sunrise, so I could leave equally unobtrusively.

7

THE CRASH AS the door flew open had me sitting bolt upright in bed instantly. 'What the hell!'

'Shut up.' The words were English but the accent was Thai. A torch shone in my eyes and I put my arm up to protect them – too late, I was completely blinded. 'What the hell is going on! Who are you?' I asked in a voice as panicked as I felt. There was a whoosh of air before the blow landed heavily on my shoulder and I gasped with the pain of the impact.

'I said, shut up. We're police, searching your room for illegal substances on the basis of information we've been given.'

'That's bullshit,' I started to protest, but this time no one responded. I peered out from behind my arm and could vaguely make out several figures through blurred eyes. Torch beams swung through the air, flicking over the floor, my gear . . . There was another bang and some scraping, then voices. One of the torches swung round and lit up an arm, then a hand.

'What's this!'

I peered at the hand and the package. 'I don't know, I've never seen it before.' My protest sounded pathetic. I'd heard the stories about this type of thing, but never met anybody it had happened to. It didn't really happen.

'Bring him along.'

'No!'

Several arms grabbed and started to haul me off the bed. I was scrabbling for the sheet, bizarrely worried about my nakedness more than the arrest. Then it hit me. I couldn't let them take me. I started to yell, and that was all, a flash of pain and then nothing.

It was the throbbing in my head that I felt first. A deep booming pulse that echoed through my body. I shifted slightly and realised two things: my head hurt a great deal more when I moved, and

I wasn't lying down. I was sitting on a chair. I could remember going to bed, but nothing after that.

Then it came back, the hut, torches, men, the blow on the head. I heard some voices, they must have seen me move. I stayed still and tried to regulate my breathing evenly. A hand grabbed me under the chin and my head snapped back. Involuntarily I opened my eyes. A torch shone straight in them and again, involuntarily, I shut them. My head was allowed to fall forward and ripples of pain echoed out through my body. But not so bad this time. They couldn't have hit me that hard. There were more voices and the shuffle of steps on an earth floor, moving away.

It went silent and I kept my head down, opened my eyes again to try and find out more about where I was. I blinked a few times in the harsh flickering light of a fluorescent tube. I flexed my arms and discovered that they were tied behind my back. Out of the periphery of my vision I could just see a couple of pairs of booted feet and a dusty floor, blue-edged shadows on the dirt. That was it. Then there were more voices, and one I recognised. Now I understood.

'I'm terribly sorry you've been treated so badly.' The voice was heavy with sarcasm. I looked up to find Janac standing squarely in front of me, hands on hips, a concerned, but mocking, expression on his face. He spoke some words in Thai and hands reached behind my back and loosened the bonds. I struggled free and rubbed my chafed wrists, glancing round the room; grey concrete walls, crumbling plaster ceiling, no window and the single door. All coldly lit by the humming, sputtering tube above. A pile of clothes came flying towards me, I caught them. Not mine and not clean, but I wasn't in a position to be picky. I dressed quickly, while Janac watched silently.

'Sit. Please,' he ordered when I was finished, and I slumped back into the bamboo chair, staring at the floor. Everyone else had left the room.

There were a couple of seconds of silence before I said, 'I suppose this is your doing?'

There was another pause, I watched him walk over to close the door. He kicked it shut with a flurry of dust, then leaned back against it and tapped a heel into the floor.

'What do you want?' I said, dully.

'What do I want?' Janac repeated the question lightly, then smiled. 'What I've wanted all along, Martin.' He pushed himself off the door and moved towards me before continuing. 'As I said before, you interest me. From that moment when you wanted to play spoof for a thousand dollars – you wanted to up the stakes on me!' his tone was incredulous, 'I thought then that here was a player, a man after my own heart. Someone I could mix business and pleasure with. Since then you have been, although not altogether cooperative, at least entertaining company. I was disappointed at your decision not to participate further. So it is fortunate that the opportunity now appears to have arisen where I can apply pressure to encourage you to play on. As I know that you want to, Martin, deep down.' He laughed and the grey eyes flickered. 'Someone tipped the police off and they found a considerable quantity of drugs in your room. Considerable, the sort of amount you get executed for in fact.'

I was motionless. 'Why don't you just cut the crap and tell me what you want.'

Janac smiled, good humoured now he had complete control. 'Well, it is true that I carry a lot of influence with the police in these parts, model citizen and all that. I'm sure I could have a word, but of course, that would mean you'd have to help me.' He stepped back and leant against the opposite wall again. Pulling a packet of Gauloises out of a top pocket, he slowly lit one before offering them over.

I shook my head 'I gave them up.'

'Sensible, a concern for your health, that could be important to you in the next few days.' He drew heavily on the cigarette and then slowly puffed a smoke ring from his mouth. We both watched it twist and swirl, blue smoke in the blue light, until it finally evaporated in the silence.

It was clear what was coming next. 'The drugs?' I said, flatly.

'Yes, the drugs. Unfortunately your rather enforced involvement in this game means that we will have to change the rules from those I had originally envisaged. It won't be quite the same, but still, I feel that the range of options open to you will make for some excitement.'

I shook my head, I couldn't believe this, but it throbbed painfully at the motion to remind me it was all real.

'You will be transporting a package to Australia for me. The package will contain processed, uncut heroin, and it is worth a great deal of money. It will be your job to bring it safely through customs before posting it to an address I will give you.'

'Posting it!' I looked up at him, surprised.

He drew on the cigarette. 'By hand of course, to an address I will give you. There's no reason why you should meet anyone else, and I'm safe from tedious western law here, I can assure you.'

I raised my eyes to the crumbling ceiling and breathed deeply, before looking directly at him. 'What if I don't?'

Janac smiled with a yellow-toothed grimace. 'I was hoping you would ask that, because I didn't want to miss the opportunity to explain your choices. Choice after all, is the essence of life, and death, as we have discovered in our games so far.' He paused to stub out the cigarette before going on. 'Firstly you could just refuse to take the package, in which case you will remain here and be prosecuted to, how does it go, "the full extent of the law". Of course you can weep and bleat and write letters to the consul, and then the prime minister and the *Telegraph* and have your friends start a campaign but,' there was heavy emphasis on the last word, 'I think you will find that Thai law in this part of the world is remarkably resilient to outside pressure, and that in due course justice will prevail.'

The sneering, sarcastic delivery as much as the words finally tipped me over the edge. 'You're so full of shit!' I spat out.

Janac stepped forward in front of me with a speed that was frightening. I didn't even see his hand move, but I certainly felt it as it lashed across my face. I swore, just once, and gently dabbed at the blood now oozing from my lip.

Janac hissed quietly in my ear. His breath smelt of decay, rotted humanity. 'I'll only take so much backchat my friend, and you just crossed the line. You would be well advised to show me a little more respect.'

There was a long silence as he stepped away and strode once around the room. I watched him, head still, the pulse in my temple pounding out the pace of his steps. Unable to stop a tremor as he disappeared out of my vision behind me. Finally he spoke again. 'Nevertheless, it is a choice you could take. I'm sure the whole thing would take a year or two to work its course, and you never know, a miracle might happen. My people down here could be overthrown, I could be run over by a bus, anything could happen. But really, Martin, I will be disappointed if this occurs. It's not the player's choice.' He paused slightly, shifted, hands back on his hips, the sneer returning after the flash of temper. 'Alternatively, you could just deliver the drugs safely as ordered. Of course if you do that, you will be personally responsible for about two kilos of pure heroin entering the market. I want you to think about that too. The misery that will cause, the families that will be hurt when those drugs enter people's lives. We will be having a special push outside schools with those drugs in fact, get 'em young, like the cigarette companies eh? Not good. So you may feel, in a burst of public spiritedness that has been rather lacking in your behaviour until now, that you do not wish these people to suffer.'

He remained frighteningly still as he continued. 'Which brings me rather neatly to your final choice. You could take the parcel, apparently in good faith, but then run to the authorities in Australia. Now obviously such selfless behaviour must have a personal price – this is the nature of our games. And, much as I would like to make this choice attractive to you, it would be expensive to me. Very, in fact. So I am forced to load it rather heavily to discourage you. You will be followed all the way to the delivery point and for some unknown time beyond it by one of my men. If he feels that you are about to deliver up the drugs to the authorities or in any other way compromise my operation in Australia he will kill you.'

I was breathing fast and hard now, my mind tumbling over his words. I swallowed and wiped the sweat from my forehead. Now he squatted down and I met the soulless grey eyes on a level. I stared into them and saw nothing, not a flicker of life. When he spoke it was slowly. I can't convey the nature of that voice. It was beyond bad, beyond threatening, beyond evil. It was certain and the words were final. He said, 'Now you may feel your miserable little life is a worthy trade for all that unhappiness and rush to the authorities at the first opportunity – at the acknowledged penalty of your life. I must confess I'll be proud of you if you do. Quite a bit poorer and the possessor of a rather dented theory on human nature, but proud.'

'Of course you may be convinced that you are smarter than my man and can elude him, especially in Australia which is a little more like home ground. You could turn the drugs over to the police and escape. This is an appealing proposition. Can you outwit me and my men and get to home base a hero? An attractive choice that avoids all of the unpleasant consequences associated with the others – if you pull it off. Rather unfortunate if you do, since it would spoil the game. A choice with no bad consequences, public or personal? We can't have that. And of course it is possible. My man isn't perfect. So I want you to understand, and this is most important, that it will not finish there. I, personally, will hunt you down and find you. And we will play a final round of our game, Martin. One which you may survive. But at what price?' He ground out the final sentence and I stared into those eyes for another half second. I was numb.

He stepped up and away, his tone was lighter, he'd made his point. 'So, you can opt out and stay here. Or take the drugs and make the ultimate personal sacrifice. But perhaps you'd prefer just to look after number one and deliver the drugs, but at what cost to other people? None of them are good choices are they, Martin? And I know the one you're most attracted to – play to win, outsmart the bad guy. But remember, win that round and we'll play again.' He laughed now, a dry throaty cackle. 'Your choice, you can have a few minutes to think about it.' He started to move towards the door.

'What happens if I just get caught?' I said, stupidly.

He turned and looked at me. 'Well, I guess you die, as my man will have no way of knowing that it wasn't set-up. It's in your interests to do a good job. And his. It has been explained to him that either the drugs arrive safely at the address or your dead body does. Otherwise it's his neck, another concern in your decision perhaps. Maybe not high on the pros or cons of any list, but another life in the balance. I'll be back in say,' he glanced at his watch, 'ten minutes.'

I watched him disappear out of the door and the room fell quiet. I could feel the anger slowly building inside me, until finally I leapt from the chair, turned and kicked it as hard as I could. The chair spun across the room and I hopped around for a while cursing fluidly. None of this provoked any reaction whatsoever from outside and finally I calmed down sufficiently to recover the chair and sit down. I dropped my head into my hands. I had to think.

It didn't take long after that to come to a decision. It was clear that I had to take the drugs. Staying here was just rolling over and playing dead, at best I'd end up rotting in a Thai jail for years and at worst I'd be properly dead. But if I took the drugs the game was on, it could go either way. There was a chance. Whatever I subsequently decided, this was the only option now. I'd like to say that I took the package out of some more noble motives. That in that moment I decided I would get the police involved, hand the stuff over to them at whatever cost. But it's not true, I figured I could just do it exactly as he said and walk away.

He returned a couple of minutes after I had decided, another cigarette dangling languidly from those thin fingers. He looked at me enquiringly.

'I'll do it,' I said, simply.

He smiled. 'Good, excellent, I knew you'd want to play. You're booked on a flight to Sydney later this morning.'

'But . . .' I started and then stopped. Alex, the cop, was from Sydney. And Kate and Scott were flying there today too.

'But . . .?' said Janac, tauntingly.

'But . . .' I thought quickly. I didn't want to mention Kate and Scott. 'But that cop, he was . . .' Had Janac or Alex told me he was from Sydney? 'He was, is Australian, isn't he? He saw me, he might have pictures . . .'

'Did I say it was going to be easy, Martin?' Janac sneered. 'One of my men will pick you up and take you to your plane. They will bring you your things, tickets and passport and of course, the package. You're lucky you already have a visa, which will give you a better chance than going in with one of ours.' He handed over a slip of paper. 'This is the address that you will deliver it to. Just push it through the front door. If you haven't done so within twenty-four hours of arriving in Sydney, my man will assume that you have turned against us. You know what happens next.'

I glanced at the address.

'I suggest you memorise that.'

I looked at him blankly, struggling to keep the inner turmoil from showing. He smiled at me. 'Good luck, Martin, I'm sure news of your progress will keep me entertained for some time.' He laughed, and I could hear him chuckling to himself as his footsteps receded away down the hall.

8

S LAMMING THE TOILET door shut, I collapsed on the seat and tried to get my breathing back under control. God that was close. I'd nearly walked straight into them. I'd spoken to no one since they let me out that morning, right through the flight to Bangkok and the hours of killing time in the airport. I'd done nothing that could be interpreted as trying to get help. Instead, I'd been trying to remember faces, trying to spot the minders Janac had sent to accompany me. I was sure he would send more than one of them to keep tabs on a couple of kilos of uncut heroin. Remembering faces had been the problem, not recognising them.

Until I had decided to check-in for the flight to Sydney, and had just about come face to face with Kate and Scott breezing across the arrivals hall. If I hadn't bolted into the bathroom they'd have seen me. I'd thought it was all right: I was on the first flight out of Ko Samui and I knew they weren't flying till after lunch. But the long stopover in Bangkok left plenty of time for later flights from Ko Samui to get here. I pulled a hand through my hair, and tried to wet dried lips. The bottom one twinged painfully where Janac had busted it open. Christ I was tired, but I had to concentrate. Another slip up like that and it was all over. And now they were on the same plane to Sydney. There was no doubt about it. It was the only Qantas flight down there today, and that was the check-in desk they were headed for. It was the worst possible scenario. If Kate tried to say hello or start a conversation, as she certainly would if she saw me, I was finished.

I could feel the sweat prickling away beneath the strapping that held the two kilos of heroin under my shirt. If the Thai authorities caught me before the plane took off I was dead. Tried, judged and executed. I wiped the sweat off my forehead with the back of my hand. It was still shaking. I needed a drink, or a cigarette, or both. All I wanted to do was get out of here, keep the minders happy, play it cool in Sydney and hope I made it through. And now I had this to deal with. I slammed my hand against the wall as the frustration boiled over. 'Dammit!'

'Steady on, son,' came a very English voice over the dividing wall.

I stood up and took three deep breaths, counting to five on the exhalations. I flushed the toilet, picked up my bag and stepped outside. There was no one in the little bathroom. I caught sight of myself in a mirror. It wasn't too bad. They had let me shower and shave this morning, given me my gear and I'd found some cleanish clothes. Even with just a loose T-shirt on there was no sign of the strapping. But I couldn't look myself in the eye. I swallowed, tried to steel myself. There was no choice. I had to deliver this shit.

I eased out of the bathroom carefully, shivering a little. The air conditioning was on so high it was chilling the sweat off my shirt. At least I had cooled off, the burning panic was gone. The hall was busy, echoing with the click of heels on the stone, the hum of quiet conversations, the occasional public address announcement. Kate and Scott were being processed right now, another couple of minutes and they would be clear. I scanned the rest of the crowd. I had spotted four possible minders so far, all men and all Thais. Now I couldn't see any of them. But someone was out there, someone was watching. The thought propelled me forwards.

I stepped cautiously into the hall, watching Kate and Scott through the crowd, ready to move away, duck and hide if they turned. Kate was gathering up the tickets and passports. Scott picked up his briefcase, moved off. Kate was struggling with the zip pocket on her bag. The blonde hair had fallen forward, hiding her face. Then she glanced over her shoulder. There was a sudden stillness in all those about us. I could see her so clearly. I was looking straight into those blue eyes. And I could see everything. The past. And another future. If I could win. It was a moment frozen in time. For me, a moment of recognition, of decision. She didn't see me. She turned again and was gone. I stood for a second longer. Now I knew what I must do.

Somehow I forced myself forward again. Avoiding the queues for economy I went straight to the first-class check-in. 'I'd like to upgrade this ticket to first class please, whatever it costs.'

The girl looked me over appraisingly. I knew I wasn't that

impressive, crumpled and casual. I snapped my Gold Visa card down beside the ticket.

Now she smiled sweetly, picked it all up and said, 'Let's see what we can do, sir.' There was a half-minute of tapping at the keyboard and then, 'We have one seat left, sir?'

I nodded yes. It was risky because the minders might regard it as an attempt to throw them off. But it was the only way to guarantee not having to face Kate and Scott on the plane. And it worked. I hung back from the gate, drinking watery coffee in a café, until the last boarding call. One of the men I'd identified as a possible minder stayed back with me. Playing safe, he wanted to see me on board. But now I had his number, I knew him. When I arrived at the gate only a handful of people were still queuing. I joined the back, and brandishing my boarding pass like a magic wand, I stepped on to the plane, turned sharp left and disappeared behind the comforting security of the first-class curtain – safe for a while.

I had tried to sleep, but it was hopeless. I gazed around the cabin, dark, the blinds pulled down. The only light was the flicker of the wordless movie on the screen. The only sound the all-encompassing roar of the jet engines. I glanced at my watch, four hours to Sydney. By the time we landed it would be more than a day since Janac's flunkeys had hauled me out of bed. And every second of it had been spent wound up to the max. I tried to concentrate on the decision I had made and the new problems it presented.

The plan had been simple. Do as I was told. Get through customs if I could, drop off the drugs and then get the hell out of there. That was the decision Janac wanted me to make. I'd been all set to play the defector – till I saw Kate. But now . . .? I just couldn't do it. I had to try something, I couldn't let her see me get shot or arrested as a smuggler. Because I knew I didn't stand a bat's chance in hell of making it through customs. Apart from the normal risks, I was known by name and face to an Australian narc. I had no chance. It ended for me in death or jail. But at least I could make Kate believe I was trying to do the right thing when I went down.

And if by some miracle I did make it through customs, the future I wanted was with Kate. If I was to make that happen, I had to do the right thing. And I'd have to be real smart about it or getting through customs would be a very short reprieve. If Janac ever found out I'd gone to the cops, if I made the slightest mistake . . . I pushed the thought to the back of my mind. I'd made the decision, the problem now was how to enact it.

It was clear that talking to anyone was too risky with the minders on me this tight. The guy I had tagged was up here in first class with me. But if I could get a message to Kate, she could call Alex and tell him about the pick-up. It was the only way I had a chance. I could write her a note, and because I'd already told her about Janac she would understand what I needed. And she was a buffer between me and the cops. It was vital that they didn't talk to me at any stage: Janac's minders could still be watching even if I did make it through to and beyond the drop-off. And in Alex I had a cop who knew me, and Janac and his methods, would take Kate seriously and would respond quickly. I fingered the piece of paper he had given me. If you get sucked in and want to join the good guys, that's what he'd said. All the pieces were there. But I still had one problem. How to get the message to Kate without her seeing me.

My options were limited, it was way too risky to walk back down the plane. Unless they were both asleep, I'd get nowhere near them before they saw me. It was also too risky to ask one of the hostesses to give them the note, the minder could see me do it, and his friend or friends back there in economy would see who received it. That left the period between disembarking and customs. It would be easier to approach them from behind, try to sneak up and drop it in a pocket. But first-class passengers would disembark first. I'd have to get off quickly, and perhaps duck into a bathroom and wait there. Or get close to them in the crowd at the baggage claim. I started to sweat a little at the thought of it. This was not going to be easy.

The first problem was to write the note. As casually as possible I reached into my bag on the floor and, rummaging around, found my pen. I slid it into my sock and pulled my hand out of the bag holding a paperback book. Settling back to read it I gently tore one of the plain sheets from the back and slipped that into my pocket. Then I forced myself to wait a full fifteen minutes before I moved. Counting to sixty, turning each unread, unseen page after a minute. Finally I unclipped the seatbelt and eased myself upwards. I walked forward to the toilets. Once inside I quickly started to write.

Kate,

I hope you get this, if you don't I have failed. I am being forced to carry 2ks of heroin into Australia. I have the drugs on me and a gunman watching me. If I make any attempt to get help they will kill me. That is why I cannot talk to you.

I want you to contact the police for me. Tell them you can give them the address where I will drop off the drugs, and the time. In exchange I want immunity and anonymity. They can only watch the drop-off, and must take no action until at least a week has passed. Tell them nothing until they agree to these terms. Janac will come after me if he discovers that I've gone to the cops. All communications must come via you.

While I was on Ko Samui I was contacted by an Australian undercover cop, who was tailing Janac. His name is Alex. He knows all about Janac. His phone number is 02 954 9966. I will contact you a few days after we get to Sydney. When that happens you must pretend that we are only casual acquaintances.

I will drop the drugs off at six p.m., the address is 14 Mount St, Manly. If there is no deal I can drop the drugs and disappear. Do not try to talk to me, whatever happens at customs in Australia, or any other time. You cannot help, only put yourself in danger.

I stopped. But I had to say it, it might be my last chance.

Kate, I love you, I always have and I always will.
Yours always,

I signed it and folded it into a tight square, flushed the toilet and returned to my seat. I thought back over the message. And wondered if Scott would read it. But if I wasn't going to make it, she had to know.

He had me by the arm, another was picking up my bag. 'This way please, sir.' Pressure at my elbow.

I tried to think, but behind me there was a scream, the officer was moving, ducking, yelling, 'Gun!'

I started . . . someone was gently shaking my arm. There was a wonderful moment of relief as I realised that I had finally managed to sleep. I looked around, my head throbbing.

'Put your seat back up please, sir, we're approaching the landing.'

And then I remembered the nightmare was real. I stared at the seatback in front and tried to get my heart under control as we descended into the landing. Occasional roars of extra power from the engines punctuating the drone of their background noise. I couldn't see how low we were until the wheels bumped and the plane shuddered. The engines roared as the brakes went on and I could feel the strap pulling on my waist as we slowed. We had arrived.

I struggled to my feet, grabbing my bag and heading over to the door. As I expected we were let go first. I took only the briefest of glances at the crowd of passengers as I charged through the door. There were no shouts behind me. I was clear so far, slipping, sliding downstream with the flow of people. I felt giddy with the blood that was pumping round my brain. Everything was going slowly, as it does in an accident. In that split second when all the doing is over, and there is only the crash to come.

I followed the few passengers in front through plain corridors. There was nothing I could escape into, only closed doors and private signs. All too quickly we were at the entrance of a large airy hall. I hesitated, panic rising, where was I going to give her the note? Here was the first test already, the immigration officials. I stepped up from the red line to a woman officer and I dropped my bag by her counter, 'Good morning,' I said, handing over my passport. I wanted so badly to check over my shoulder. If I got held up here and Kate arrived round that corner before I was in the baggage claim hall it was all over. But the adrenaline was pumping now and my head was starting to clear. I could feel the supercharged calmness coming on that I had always achieved before big deals.

'You just made it,' she said, flicking the pages apart.

'I'm sorry?' I said, warily, focusing now.

'This visa is only just in date.' She looked at me over the top of a pair of steel-framed spectacles. 'You were aware of that?'

'Yes, yes, of course.' I was ad-libbing furiously. I'd got the visa in London last winter when I was going to take a holiday with an ex-girlfriend, to try and patch the relationship back together. Unfortunately it had needed more patching than we had in us, and we'd never taken the trip. I'd thought that I could use the damn thing anytime. 'Sorry, I'm a little slow this morning, not too much sleep recently.' I smiled.

'Change of plans was there, sir?'

'Yeah. Girlfriend trouble, had to come on my own in the end.'

Stick as close to the truth as you can.

'Well there's plenty girls out here. Have a good holiday, sir.'

There was a thump as she stamped and handed the passport back.

'Thanks,' I said.

I walked down a ramp into the brightly-lit baggage hall. It was painfully open. I finally allowed myself one glance over my shoulder, but there was no sign of Kate or Scott yet. How the hell was I going to do this? There was barely anyone in the hall. It was warm and I could feel the sweat start to build under my waistband. I'd put a light jumper over the T-shirt, which helped break my shape even more, but I was beginning to wonder if that wasn't making me conspicuous. I spotted the minder from first class, just coming through immigration behind me. There was still no sign of the other three probables and I guessed they were held up in the economy crowd with Kate and Scott. This place needed to fill up a lot before I could get near Kate unnoticed.

I found a monitor and worked out which carousel my bags were coming in on. Then strolled over towards the carts and pulled one free. I glanced over towards the customs, red and green lanes just like home. I'd filled in a form on the plane, which I had in my hand.

A buzzer was going by the carousel, the motor ground into action and the rubber belt started to slide. I fought back a rush of panic. What if my bags popped up early? I looked around desperately for somewhere to hide until there were some more people around and saw a camera high up on the wall. I could feel my knees go weak. I moved round, closer to where the bags were coming out, fighting for a grip, feeling the sweat break out on my forehead. It was warm but not that warm. And if I was sweating I should take the jumper off. I dabbed at my forehead as nonchalantly as possible, leaned on the back of the trolley and tried to concentrate on the bags.

Then I realised what I was looking at. The bag popping out of the chute was a battered grey holdall. It was Kate's. God knows I'd carried the damn thing around enough. I didn't have to go near her. I slid my hand into my pocket as the bag came close. Closed my fingers round the paper. I stared at the bag, with its open side pocket. I shifted, put my foot on the stainless support of the belt, fiddled with a shoelace, putting my body between the camera and where the bag would be. The belt was moving so slowly, it seemed to take for ever to get to me. Then in what felt like slow motion I stuck the message in the pocket. Everyone had seen me. I was sure of it. Someone would ask what I had done. I glanced up at the faces opposite and saw the minder. For a frightful second our eyes met. Then his hand moved, gently brushing back his jacket a couple of inches. I caught the dull glow of metal tucked into his waistband. Fuck, that was it. The bag clunked inexorably towards him. He only had to reach out . . .

Then it was gone. The gun, the knife, whatever. And so was he, he'd melted back into the crowd. He hadn't seen the note. That had just been a warning. I was almost staggering from the relief. I could feel my pulse rising, pounding at my temple so loud I was sure the people nearby could hear it. I glanced around, anxious again, still so much that could go wrong. No Kate. No Scott. I needed my bag, I had to get out of here before they arrived. For a second I almost left it, turned and walked away. But no one arrived in Australia with just hand luggage.

There it was, popping up the chute. I grabbed it and threw it on to the trolley, pushing out and moving away. I was sweating like a spit roast. I pushed the trolley ahead of me and started to struggle out of the jumper. Free of the extra clothing I mopped my head with it and threw it on top of the bag. I rounded the corner into the green lane with my heart pounding. It was the last hurdle.

In front of me was a small queue. At the head of it a young customs officer, very young. I pulled the form out of my back pocket and tried to drape myself over the handles of the trolley as nonchalantly as I could. Something made me look over my shoulder and I saw the minder, right behind me. It wouldn't matter if it was a gun or a knife, he'd be close enough to use either if they caught me. I was suddenly frighteningly concious of the strapping and its all too thin covering of T-shirt. It was a struggle not to start pulling the jumper back on, or patting the T-shirt into place.

I gripped the trolley with white knuckles to keep my hands

where they were. The couple at the front were diverted left, where I could see other officers searching bags. The straight ahead option appeared to be clear. The next guy, a smartly dressed man in his forties also went left, so did the next. God they were all going to be searched. There was only one in front of me. Now I was certain they could hear my heart.

Suddenly I was there.

'Bit warm for you, sir?'

I held my form out and he took it. My spine tingled with the presence behind me. I could feel the blade about to plunge in between my shoulders. I breathed a silent scream and then, some words.

'Yeah, after England,' I finally blurted out. You haven't come from England, I thought as soon as I said it.

'That where you've come from, sir?'

I could feel the panic rushing up inside me like a huge overwhelming wave. I had to tell the truth. He was looking down at my form, which listed the place I'd joined the flight.

Finally my mouth moved and the words came out sounding almost normal. 'No, Thailand actually, but I can't get used to the heat. Too much time in the cold and the rain I guess.'

He was looking up now, gazing at me with a pair of placid brown eyes. My stomach and its guilty wrapping burst out into flows of perspiration, but I held his eyes and somehow managed a wan smile. But still he just looked and looked, it was seconds, minutes, hours. I had to hold his gaze. I could feel an irresistible urge to cough or sneeze, to cover my mouth, anything to stop the lies coming out. But I didn't move. I could lie with the best of them.

'Well, doesn't help with the air conditioning broken down. Hope you get used to it before you go home to that lousy pommie weather.' And with a tiny flick of his hand he indicated right and I was gone. I pushed the trolley ahead with a sensation flooding through me that was better than sex. I'd done it. I almost skipped across the hallway and all before me, doors, people, slid apart. I walked outside into the blasting heat and humidity of an Australian summer a free man.

9

W ELL, ALMOST. I still had two kilos of heroin strapped around
my waist. But that was OK, the worst was over. If Alex
agreed to play ball, and did a good job, I was there. I waited
patiently for a cab, and spent the time looking for the minders. In
the flood of emotion leaving the customs I hadn't even thought to
check behind and see if they got through. Whatever, they weren't
close now. I needed to give them a chance to catch up. And I
didn't want to be alone with anyone. I needed a bus not a cab.
Cautiously I went back inside the arrivals hall, checking for Kate
and Scott, and found some signs to the City Shuttle.

It was only now that I realised how totally exhausted I was. I
collapsed on to a seat and stared blankly out of a window. And
there he was, number one minder, arms folded, watching me. As
the bus jerked lumpily into motion he stepped into a waiting cab
and together we slowly pulled away from the airport. This was the
first time I'd been to Australia and I watched the surroundings slide
from light industry through surburban housing and into urban
terracing before we were swallowed up by the towering blocks
of the city centre. All the time the cab was sitting just off our
bumper.

The bus stopped a couple of times outside hotels and I was
tempted to get off. A shower, some sleep, lose my bag. It was
a nice idea. But could I afford to be alone in a hotel room?
They could monitor my calls, check who went in and out. But
they wouldn't have time to set that up. Maybe if I just dropped
my bag off and checked in for now. At least then I wouldn't be
humping it around for hours. The drop-off could be miles away.
The bus stopped again. The Randolph. That would have to do.
I lurched down on to the street and through the doors. I got a
room, picked up the keys and dropped my bag for the porter. I
was in and out of the lobby inside five minutes.

Freed from my bag I walked briskly away from the hotel, and

found a newsagent where I bought a map. Next a café. I found a table and ordered lunch and strong, black coffee. When it came it was strong enough to crawl out of the cup and pour itself down my throat. I ate slowly, forcing every mouthful down a tight throat. Then ordered more coffee before I finally turned my attention to the map. I looked up Mount Street, Manly. It appeared to be miles away. The other side of the harbour. I checked the route map out and discovered that there was a ferry that went over there. It looked a lot less hassle than the bus, which would have to trail all the way round the harbour. It was three thirty. I could be late, but not early. I tried to figure out how far the ferry had to go, how long it would take. But there was no scale on the map. Two and a half hours, there must be plenty of time, I'd better have another cup of coffee.

When I finally left I was buzzing with so much caffeine there was no longer any danger of feeling tired. Giddy and light-headed perhaps, but not tired. I followed the map down to the ferry terminal, and eventually figured out which one to take. The boat, a big catamaran, was full of commuters. The view was enough to take even my troubled mind off its problems for a moment. We powered out of the bay, swinging past the Opera House, with the Harbour Bridge only a few hundred metres away to the left. Hell of a way to go home from work.

I was sitting at the front of the boat, and that now gave me the opportunity to turn and casually scan the faces behind me. I couldn't see either of the guards, but there were several people hidden by newspapers or parts of the boat. Since we'd arrived in Sydney, the surveillance had been much more discreet. The minders were off their home territory and maybe wanted more distance in case I did try to cry for help. Or maybe they figured that the customs was the real danger point and they could relax a little more now. But if Janac's orders were to be obeyed there was a stronger argument for keeping close. How close did they need to be to kill me?

I turned back to the window. Staring out at the harbour, with cascades of beautiful houses tumbling down to every beach and rocky foreshore, I wondered again about Kate. Had she found the note yet?

The trip was a quick one, and it was barely half past five when we pulled up at Manly. I stared out of the window at the motley collection of buildings on the pier. There was a tiny beach off to the left, but that obviously wasn't the ocean beach

I needed. Disembarking I walked past newsagents and fast food outlets and out on to a forecourt, it was a major bus stop. I was looking around to get my bearings on the map when I finally saw the surveillance. The one who had been up in first class with me and behind me at customs was standing none too casually by a newstand. I turned and looked straight at him. He didn't flinch. Stared right through me, as much as you can do with a pair of mirror shades on. Despite the heat he was still wearing his jacket.

On a sudden impulse I started towards him. I half expected him to move away, but he didn't. And I was committed now, getting closer with every step. I was ten yards away and still he hadn't moved. He was obviously not bothered by the fact that I had recognised him, nor that I was making the fact clear. And then it occurred to me that they were going to kill me anyway.

I stopped a couple of yards short. Still he hadn't moved a muscle. The unblinking glass stared at me, a paradigm of dispassion. There was no one else close. 'So,' I said, 'why don't we get it over with here. I give you the package, you blow my brains out.' Not a muscle moved. Seconds passed. Then I heard footsteps behind me. They stopped. Eventually I turned, more mirror shades, another lumpy jacket. One of the four I had marked down as probables. Were there any more?

'I'm sorry,' said the accentless voice, 'but my friend does not speak good English. Perhaps I can help you.'

I stared back, then repeated my question, even more slowly and precisely. This time there was a response.

'I'm sorry, but I have no idea what you are talking about, perhaps you have a little too much sun, eh?' One hand touched his forehead lightly, in a gesture understood world-wide, then returned to clasp the other. I stared again, but the sunglasses betrayed only light and even breathing. Finally, I snorted and turned away. I knew them both and they didn't care. Either they were convinced I hadn't gone to the police and wasn't going to, or that if I did they could get to me first. Or they were going to kill me anyway. I couldn't see what the hell I could do about it either way, so I started walking again, heading across the rows of bus stops. I could feel the guards start out behind me, not far behind. I crossed by a set of lights and almost immediately entered a pedestrian walkway. I walked slowly but steadily, passing chip shops and burger stands, ice cream parlours and trinket sellers, glancing round occasionally to check on Tweedledum and Tweedledee.

Both were about ten yards back, one on either side of the road. Could Janac have ordered them to kill me after delivery? No, there was no point, I was no danger at that stage, once the drugs were out of my hands and safely away what could I do? I had no proof of anything, certainly not against the two goons. The only one I could threaten was Janac and he was safe behind his wall of protection in Ko Samui.

The confrontation was stupid, unnecessary. I started to step out a little bit and could soon see the ocean ahead of me. I checked the map, this was where I turned left. I crossed over, ducking through some children's play apparatus and past a couple of buskers. All around me was the bustle of a busy summer day in a holiday resort, but I felt so far removed from it I might have been on the moon. I turned on to the seafront, surfers were dashing towards the beach, pulling on wet-suits as they went, anxious for a few last waves. Couples strolled along, dodging the occasional skateboarder and more frequent rollerblades. I hurried on, anxious to be finished with it now.

I found Mount Street, turned the corner and glanced over my shoulder. They were a little further back this time, but not much. I slowed again. I wanted number fourteen. I glanced at gates and doors looking for a clue to where I was. Nothing, I strode on. Then took a glance at my watch, quarter to six – damn I was early, what if the cops had got the information from Kate but weren't in place yet? I stopped. There was silence behind me, I turned and looked at Tweedledum and Tweedledee. They too had stopped. Arms crossed, one unmistakably inside the jacket.

We stood there, like nineteenth-century gunfighters. Stand off. I waited, thinking hard. This still didn't make sense, Janac had told me I was to deliver it like this because he didn't want me to have contact with any more of his people. And here were these two breathing down my neck. My mind accelerated. What was the deal? Then I thought about watching cops and nervous fingers on sweaty triggers. How would Alex play it? I swallowed heavily, licked my lips, tried to dry sweaty palms on my trousers. A firefight. I'd be right in the middle. I felt a rush of nausea. Fought it back. There was nothing I could do if the game plan was wrong. The play had been called, all I could do by behaving strangely was provoke definite disaster.

I walked on, head twisting right and left until I finally saw a number. Fifty-three, I was on the wrong side. I crossed over, walking steadily and looking for numbers to check against. The houses were big, plenty of frontage and I allowed the time to tick away, hoping the cops would be in place by now. There wasn't going to be an ambush. They would want the whole gang, not just two of them, who probably knew nothing anyway. Besides, Kate would have made a deal. You could trust the cops. They'd be here, and if they were still unloading cameras and telescopes, or whatever it was they needed, at ten to six it wasn't going to be undercover.

There, a single-storey, off-white house. The fourteen was painted on a peeling board by the front door. It looked a respectable enough place, if a little shabby. I stopped by the gate, but there was nothing to check, the address had been imprinted on my mind for the last day and a half. This was it, whatever it was. My heart started to surge, putting that package through the door was the decisive moment. Whatever orders all these guys had, turned on it. I glanced back at the minders one more time. They were waiting for me. I unclipped the gate and walked unsteadily up the path. The front door had a letter box.

I was by the door now, under the shade of the porch. Out of view of anyone on the street. I pulled up the T-shirt and wrenched the package down and then up, over my head. I stopped, motionless. It was silent, I daren't look behind. Somewhere a dog barked and a child screamed. Then there was silence again, only the buzz of the heat and humidity. I brushed a persistent fly away from my mouth, and roughly pushed the package through the letter box. That was it, it was done. Whatever was to be would be. Slowly, so very, very slowly I spun on my heel. No one. Nothing moved on the heat-baked street. I walked down the path, every nerve firing, expecting the sudden explosion of violence. But there was nothing. It would be later, in a quiet alley somewhere. A sudden crack, a flash of pain. Emptiness. Darkness. I began to realise that it would never be over, I'd be expecting it for the rest of my life. I stepped out of the gate and looked left and right. No one. They'd gone.

I walked down the street back towards the ocean, quickly now. I could feel my grip on reason slipping. Steps coming one after the other, faster and faster, tumbling forwards. I was running, running scared, breath coming in short sharp driven breaths, legs stretching. Arms pumped faster. I exploded on to the main street and ran straight into someone. There was a crash, a shout,

I tripped but somehow stayed on my feet, still running. I looked back wildly. I was still running when I got into the first taxi, and out of it, into the next, through the mall, another cab and finally into a hotel room, any hotel room. Any hotel but the Randolph. In my mind I was still running when the door shut behind me.

10

I LEANED AGAINST the balcony railing and watched the first, blood red streaks of dawn spear through the cityscape. Red sky in the morning, a shepherd's warning. There was a storm brewing somewhere. I turned away and stepped back into the hotel room, closing the door behind me. I didn't want to be on the balcony in daylight. I was sure they'd lost me, but just as sure that they would still be looking. My stomach churned as I moved inside. I forced exhausted eyes to focus on what was around me. Fuck what a mess. I hadn't let the cleaner in for . . . however long it was. I glanced at my watch. The twenty-eighth of January, I think I'd flown in on the twenty-third. Five days.

I sat down on the end of the bed and pulled out another cigarette. Six months of agony to give these up, five days of hell to start again. Mechanically, I tapped the cigarette on the box before reaching for a light. I ripped the cheap cardboard match from the book, last one, damn. The cigarette glowed and I stared at the room. Dozens of cigarette butts scattered around a couple of ashtrays. Glasses and plates sat in unwashed piles on the table. The mini-fridge was open, contents ransacked, along with a couple of full-size bottles of whisky. The bin overflowed with fag packets and take-away boxes. Both the beds were a crumpled mess of twisted, sweat-soaked sheets. I took another drag and pulled the harsh smoke deep into my lungs. I wanted it to fill my mind, cloud my eyes, block it all out.

But nothing seemed to block it out. I pulled the phone towards me by the cord and dialled. 'Room service, is Pauli there?'

The reply was affirmative and I waited briefly.

'Yeah, Pauli, it's Bob in 402, bring me some more coffee would you, and some toast or something, oh and a couple more boxes of matches. Leave it outside, same as usual. Thanks.'

Pauli was the only one I'd talk to, and I wouldn't let him in. I was sure I'd lost them when I ran from the drop-off. Christ why had I panicked like that? It was stupid, suspicious as hell. I knew Janac'd think so. Was he out there looking? Whatever, I wasn't taking any chances. I'd registered under a false name, paid cash for a week in advance, spun them a line about working on a project, not to be disturbed – all that stuff. It seemed to have worked. I was still alive.

The panic-stricken, logic-defeating fear of my flight had slowly fermented into a corrosive, soul-destroying paranoia. It was devouring me. Soon there would be nothing left. I had to stop the rot. I went to the shower and turned it on, full blast, maximum cold. I sat on the edge for a while, my back to the torrent, scared of what I would feel when the cold water washed away the numbness. Then I let myself slide backwards into the jet. I gasped, floundering for air. Breath torn away by the chill. But I hadn't the strength to fight it and soon I was quiet. Sitting gazing at the wall, letting the water drive feeling back into my life. Sucking in oxygen, in huge life-giving heaves. I felt so tired. But my mind started to clear a little, pressure was easing, something had cracked and given way and suddenly I felt the exhaustion of the physically-driven, not the mentally-tortured. I struggled from the shower, pulled off the clothes and left them in the water. I flicked a towel from the rack and tried to find the energy to rub myself down. But it wasn't there. I collapsed on to the bed.

I awoke with a start. Confused, struggling for a time and place. Bright, clean sunlight dazzled through glass windows and doors. A bang on the door, loud. Again. Louder. I tried to speak. I knew I didn't want people in here but I couldn't remember why. The sound of keys, a sudden rush of memory. Flash of fear. I crashed off the bed, scurrying for cover.

'Jesus wept, what a fucking mess!' It was Pauli.

'Get the cleaners up here.' Another voice. 'No, no, use the phone.'

Slowly I stuck my head up from behind the bed.

'Mr Smith?'

The speaker was a tall, well-dressed and equally well-spoken man – had to be the manager. By the phone was Pauli. He was a wiry young man, freckles and a cheery smile: an all right kid.

'I thought I said no one was to come in here,' I complained, groggily.

'Hey, man, that coffee's been outside there for over twenty-four hours, I thought you was dead or something. I had to get the man, I could lose my job.'

Twenty-four hours? I glanced at the clock on the bedside table, early morning. Had I really slept for twenty-four hours?

'And,' the manager was speaking, 'we don't normally allow guests to, er, deteriorate the rooms to this degree. May I suggest that you put some clothes on before the cleaners arrive?'

Pauli fetched a robe from the bathroom and threw it across.

'I'm sorry about the mess,' I said, 'but I had some work to do, it's been a heavy schedule and I must have just crashed out after I delivered it.' I struggled to think. The manager was scanning the room. There was no sign of any work, of any kind. I looked as suspicious as hell.

'Mr Smith, this room will be cleaned immediately. May I suggest that you move your luggage across the hall, to room 404. Pauli will bring the key and give you any help you need.' He snapped his fingers and Pauli trotted from the room. 'You can remain there for the rest of your stay. I would appreciate it if you could allow the cleaners in on a daily basis from now on. Otherwise we may have to ask you to leave.' With that he was gone.

Alone again I shut the door and slumped back against it, gazing at the mess. I was attracting attention, not diverting it. But six days now, I was still alive. No sign of them. What the hell was going on out there? I had to know.

There was a bang on the door. I turned and opened it. It was Pauli, he looked apologetic, held out the new key.

'Hey, I'm sorry, man, I really thought something had happened when I came on this morning and saw that food still there.' His face was creased with a genuine concern.

I smiled to reassure him. 'Don't worry about it. You did OK, I needed to be woken. Look, I lost my bags on the flight over here, and I guess they haven't found them yet. I have a meeting today. Could you get my clothes washed in an hour or so?'

He smiled, relieved, happy to help. 'No worries, man.'

'Ok, hang on.' I went back into the room, found the laundry bag and dumped the sodden mass from the shower into it. 'There you go,' I said, handing it over. 'Twenty bucks in it for you if it's done in an hour.' I glanced at my watch to confirm the time was running.

'OK, man.' He was already moving down the hall.

'Hey, and breakfast, the works, everything, OK?' I shouted after him.

He turned and waved an acknowledgement, nearly tripping in his haste. 'Coming right up for room 404.'

I smiled, good kid. I glanced at the key in my hand, and after picking up my passport and wallet, went across the hall and into room 404.

I stripped off the robe and stepped into the shower. The breakfast arrived just after I had finished drying, and over a steaming plate of bacon, eggs and the rest, I thought it through. Six days after the drop and no sign of Janac or his men. That meant one of two things. Most likely, they had lost me after the drop off. They would be looking for me – even if they hadn't found out about the cops' possible involvement – my running was suspicious enough for them to want to find me. But it was a big city and I would have to be seriously unlucky for them just to come across me. The second possibility was that they had kept on my trail after the drop-off and were still watching me. Waiting to see if I had run for a reason – or just panicked. Which also meant they either didn't know about the cops, or Kate had failed and the cops weren't involved. If they were watching I had to behave as if everything was normal.

The only way to cast any light on this morass of ifs and maybes was to find Kate. I couldn't spend the rest of my life rotting in a hotel room. At least then I could establish whether or not the cops were involved. But I had to be careful I didn't attract any attention to her. If I was going to talk to her I had to do it in such a way that I appeared to be going about my normal business. And it wouldn't hurt to try and be as sure as possible that there was no one watching.

The first step was to get out of this damn hotel, where I was altogether too well known. Pauli was as good as his word. And an hour after he'd got them, he was twenty bucks richer and I had some clean clothes. I left immediately after, without checking out. I had no intention of going back there, but if they were looking for me, I wasn't going to make it easy for them by announcing I had moved on. I left by the back entrance and stepped on to the street nervously. It was already a muggy, cloudy, oppressive kind of day. And it was only ten o'clock. I stood on the steps for a full minute, checking. Only a couple of people walked by, no one in the parked cars, nobody else to pay me any attention. I took a deep breath. It looked safe.

I had got directions from Pauli to the nearest shopping area, and it turned out this was the city centre itself. I headed there ostensibly to buy a few basic things; another map, some more clothes, toiletries and a bag. But it would also give me plenty of opportunity to see if I was being followed. I spent a couple of hours wandering round shops, stopping frequently, checking behind, doubling back, going in front doors and out the side. But trying to do it all in a way that didn't appear as though I was checking. Playing it cool, just out for a little shopping and some air. Nothing. I didn't see or suspect anyone. If I had a tail he was damn good at it. Which certainly hadn't been my experience of the Thai guys before.

Finally I was satisfied. Or at least I couldn't see how any more of it could make me any better satisfied. I found a little pavement café and ordered some lunch. Over the meal I found Rushcutter's Bay on the map. It was only a couple of train stops away and I got there quickly, straight after the meal. I walked down the hill and into the park next to the marina. Then skirted round the waterfront till I was on the opposite side of the bay. The park was quiet except for the chirp of insects and the shouts of some children away in the distance. No one around. My head was a little fuzzy, but I felt better than I had for some time, the sleep and a couple of good meals had done the job. I gazed out across the water.

There she was, *Gold*, unmistakable from the colour. The topsides shimmering in the heat. I found a spot by a tree and settled down to watch. It was a big boat and there were probably twenty people or so on deck. After a while I picked out Kate's mane of hair, the recognition coming with a buzz of pleasure. There had been more than the odd moment when I thought I'd never see her again. The boat was a hive of activity. Stuff being loaded on and off, the deck scrubbed, people working on the winches and gear. Time slipped away. I didn't want to approach in the open unless I had to. I didn't particularly want to talk to her in front of Scott either.

I tried to stay relaxed, lounging against the tree, looking around casually. Smoking the occasional cigarette, just someone enjoying the sunshine. There was no rush, I could afford to wait for the right moment, even if that meant coming back tomorrow. And it didn't look like it was going to be easy to get Kate on her own.

Half an hour later I saw Kate and Scott standing and talking on the aft deck. Hand motions were emphatic, Kate was angry. Some of the others had stopped work and were sitting around drinking out of bottles. Scott stooped towards an icebox and picked up a can. Kate turned away and, without another word, jumped down on to the pontoon and walked off. Alone.

This could be my chance. I watched her progress down the dock, emerging into the park a couple of minutes later, bag on her shoulder, can in her hand. I glanced back. Scott was sitting with about ten others at the back of the boat, showing no signs of going anywhere. I stubbed out my final cigarette, screwed up the packet and walked slowly across the park, arriving at the road about three hundred yards behind her. She was walking quite quickly, heading uphill, back towards the station. But less than half-way there she turned into the second of a pair of hotels. It was perfect cover. I kept moving and went into the first. Got some smokes from the machine, then made a show of asking about the long-term room rates. Picked up a brochure. Checked the availability. Finally I left and headed next door, she'd had plenty of time. I'd go through the same routine, get the brochure with a phone number, get her room, then call her. But as I pushed through the doors she was only yards away, stalled on the staircase, reading a letter.

'Martin!' It was a gasp of total astonishment.

I moved quickly, covering the distance to her in less than a second. I grabbed her hand, pulling her up the stairs and away from prying eyes in the lobby or on the street. 'Your room, which floor?'

'This one.' Voice, face confused. 'Martin, it's . . .'

'Let's go. Now!' I was insistent, electric with the tension.

She hesitated, then turned, we ran down a short corridor and after fumbling with the key and her bag, she opened the door. I hustled her through, slammed it, dropped the dead bolt. I sank my head against the wall. It must be OK, I couldn't be any more careful. But I couldn't stay in here long, I spun round.

Kate was right there, anxious, frightened even, hands to her face. 'What is it, I thought everything was over?'

It was my turn to look confused. 'Over, what do you mean?'

'Alex called a couple of days ago. Said it was all right, you were in the clear, the guys that followed you had lost you, then gone home.' Understanding came slowly, she carried on, 'The cops've infiltrated the gang, they don't know where you are, and they don't seem bothered either. I thought it was over. What's happened?' Her voice was starting to lose its urgency, the fear evaporating, as she saw my face. I was giddy with the relief, unable to believe it was really over, that it could be true. 'You didn't know?' she asked.

I shook my head.

Then she was in my arms. Holding on so tight. Words coming in a torrent. 'God I was so scared for you, I thought I'd never see you again. I didn't realise how much I'd missed you till I thought, I thought . . .' A little sob, tears of relief. I still couldn't find any words. The nightmare was finished. We held each other for a long time.

11

WHEN SHE FINALLY pulled away, it was gently, and not very far. She kept hold of my hands. 'You look awful,' she said, with an affectionate smile, then shook her head. 'I was so scared and worried after that note. It's been impossible to think about anything else. I've just been waiting, hoping you'd get in touch. But terrified every time the phone rang in case it was the police to say . . .' She tailed off, gripped my hands tighter. 'Where have you been? What's been happening?'

I led her over towards the small sofa. She sat down beside me. 'I've been in a hotel in town, hiding up. I thought I'd probably lost them, so I just kept off the streets.'

'You look like hell though,' she laughed. It didn't matter now. I smiled ruefully. 'I've been a little anxious.'

She shook her head again. 'How on earth did it happen, how did he force you to do it?'

I looked at her carefully, blue eyes unwavering, the blonde hair tumbling around a face lit up with concern. I could feel relief being washed away by an incoming tide of new emotions. 'Oldest trick in the book, used his contacts in the police to set me up on a drugs charge. They came and got me after I returned to my room. I should have stayed away, not gone back there. I just never thought he'd try anything so . . .' I shook my head. 'I had no choice, it was stay there and rot in jail for ever or smuggle the drugs. But after they let me out, the minders were on me so tight I couldn't see how to get help.' I hesitated, eyes flicking down, it wasn't quite the truth. She'd been the one that changed my mind.

I carried on, staring at the cheap wallpaper. 'Until I saw you in Bangkok. It was too risky to talk to you, but then I thought of the note. It was my only chance to get a message to the police. I was scared that when I tried to give it to you, I'd have to talk, that the minders would realise I was trying to get you to help.

You could have been dragged into it . . .'

I felt her take my hand again. I looked back at her.

'It's all right, you did the right thing.' Her voice was soft, sympathetic. 'We're both here, safe. It all worked, I found the note when we were unpacking. I phoned Alex and he was great, he had it all set-up when I called back. Told me not to worry, I gave him the number here and he said they'd call as soon as they knew anything.'

So they had been there, watching, with cameras and telescopes. And sweaty trigger fingers. 'And then he phoned again?'

'Yeah, like I said, told me that the two goons went home.' She hesitated. 'He also asked me a couple of times, if you could meet them. They want to ask some questions . . .'

'Kate!' I threw my hands up, anger, but disappointment too.

'I told him what you said, that there was to be no contact. He said they wouldn't force you to do anything. But it would make it a lot easier for them if they could at least take a statement.' I was shaking my head. 'What can the danger be now these guys have gone. I don't see why . . .' softly, persuasive.

'No, Kate, you must understand. First a statement, then it's in court, it's public. If Janac ever finds out I've done this he'll hunt me to the ends of the earth. I can't ever see the cops. That was the deal.'

She nodded slowly, but I could tell she wasn't convinced. 'It's OK, Martin, relax, it's over,' she said quietly.

I swallowed heavily, realising that I'd been shouting. 'It's over.' I said it blankly. I shook my head. 'It's been a hell of a few days. I guess I'm still pretty tense.' I scratched at my eyebrow, rubbed my forehead. Tried another watery smile.

Slowly, she returned it. 'It's OK,' she whispered, 'it's OK.'

I reached out a hand and stroked a stray lock of hair back behind her ear. It promptly fell loose again. 'There were a couple of times when I didn't think I was ever going to see you again,' I said, gently. There was an awkward silence. The only sound was the final sentence of my message to her, creeping quietly closer to the surface. I looked away, staring at nothing. I'd already said it. But I had to say it again, to her face. 'Kate . . .'

But she was gone. 'You need a beer, hey?' she said, already half-way to the fridge.

I took a breath, the moment lost. Or thrown away. I nodded yes.

The top fizzed off, and I took the bottle from her. 'Thanks.'

She sat down again, but this time opposite me, on the edge of the bed. Legs crossed, beer in her lap. 'So what will you do now?'

I was surprised. 'I don't know,' I shrugged helplessly, lost. 'I've paid for a couple more nights at the hotel I was at, I guess I can go back there, after that . . .' I stopped. I had no idea.

'I'm going to be pretty busy the next couple of days. But maybe we can get together sometime,' she said in a neutral voice.

'That'd be nice,' I said encouragingly, 'spend some time together, get to know each other again. I'd really like that, Kate.'

She was picking at the label on the bottle, staring at the floor, then she looked up, suddenly intense. 'We're leaving the day after tomorrow.'

I felt a sudden chill.

I stared at her, and she looked away. 'You're leaving?'

'Yeah,' she hesitated, uncertain tone, 'I have to, I didn't realise it would be quite so soon. But we have to get the boat up to Hong Kong for the next regatta. It's a long trip and Scott wants to get it done . . .' She tailed off. Her ring was tapping against the bottle in the silence. 'He kind of moved it forward . . . he wants to get out of here . . .' She stopped, but tense, something she wasn't saying. Scott had seen the note. He was taking her away.

I felt light-headed, distant. Aware of the silence, its growing awkwardness. But detached, unable to do anything about it. So much I wanted to say. Nowhere to start. I couldn't look at her.

'There's a party,' she was speaking again, I dragged my eyes up. She looked sad. 'Tonight. It's the regatta prize-giving. Why don't you come along? We may not get many other chances to see each other.'

Christ, a party. Just what I needed. 'I don't know, I'm . . .' I shrugged.

She stood, put the bottle down. 'I've got to go send some faxes and organise a couple of things. Why don't you think about it. There's plenty of time. I'll be half an hour or so, there's more beer in the fridge, some food. If you want to come with us, maybe take a shower, shave, whatever. Scott's stuff is all there, shirts, everything.' I nodded, looking away, no idea what to say. I felt her touch my hand. 'Martin, I'm sorry. Let's just try and have a good time tonight, hey?' Then she was gone.

I sat on the chair, dazed, unaware of anything around me, taking occasional, mechanical sips from the rapidly warming beer in my hands. Trying to catch up. I was safe. That was first. That was good. I was with Kate. That was good too. But Scott was getting her the hell out of here as fast as he could. I stared around the room for the first time, noticing the hum of the air conditioning, the sterile air. The hotel chain anonymity of the place was shaded everywhere by reminders of Scott's presence. A pile of clothes in the corner, oilskins on the wallhooks, boots by the door. I finished the beer, got up and went through to the bathroom. She was right about the shave.

By the time Kate came back I was feeling better. Cleaned up and half-way through a packet of beernuts I'd found. She threw a pile of folders and loose papers on to the bed I was lounging on.

'How do I look?' I'd put on the chinos and a polo shirt I'd bought earlier.

'Much better, perfect.' She leant over and kissed me on the cheek. Friends. 'You've decided to come to the party?'

I nodded, mouth full.

'Great.' She smiled, glanced at her watch. 'I'd better get ready.' She was already pulling the T-shirt off as she disappeared into the bathroom.

I listened to the hiss of water, got myself another beer. Found a bar of chocolate. Eventually the shower stopped. 'Where's Scott?' I shouted through.

The bathroom door opened. 'Sorry?' came her voice.

'Scott. Where is he?' I repeated.

'Still at the boat, they had some work to do. I just went to the top of the road to look, they're still there.'

They didn't look like they were working when I left, I thought. She emerged from the bathroom wearing one small towel and rubbing her hair with another. She still took my breath away.

'What time is it?' she asked, towelling furiously.

'Six thirty.'

'Hmm,' she looked annoyed, 'he's going to be late if he doesn't hurry up.'

'What time do we have to leave by?'

'Seven.'

I shrugged with a bad attempt at nonchalance.

'He'll be here by the time I've dressed,' she said confidently, and with a swirl of golden blonde hair she disappeared back into the bathroom.

More sounds of drying, the clink of glass bottles and lids.

'Mind if I smoke,' I said, needing a distraction.

She stuck her head round the door. 'You haven't started again?'

'Just.' I managed a half-smile as I picked up the packet, waved them at her.

'Yeah, go ahead, I'll have one in a minute. Can you pass me that dress on the bed,' she said, disappearing back into the bathroom.

I looked at the black dress. It seemed a rather ambitious description, there wasn't enough cloth there for a skirt, never mind a dress. I picked it up and bashfully handed it into the bathroom with an outstretched arm.

'That's very gentlemanly, not like you at all,' said Kate, taking the garment from me.

'I'm a changed man,' I replied, retiring back to the comparative safety of the sofa. I lit the cigarette.

'You are? Tell me about that. You still haven't said why you left England and don't want to go back.'

That was the last thing I wanted to talk about right now. I sucked on the cigarette nervously. 'Maybe later.'

There was a grunt of dissatisfaction. 'You have at least phoned your family?'

'No. What would I say, "Hey Dad, you may read about me in the papers soon, being shot by some drug smugglers."'

'Martin, it's over.' She peered round the door. I just looked at her. Not feeling so cooperative now. She shook her head. 'We need to get you to the party.' She disappeared, then emerged from the bathroom a few seconds later and turned round to be zipped up.

'I haven't done this for a while,' I said, neutrally, fumbling with the zip with a shaking hand.

'I can tell,' she replied, then, spinning round with a flourish, 'tadaa. How do I look?'

I took in the vision with one long, longing gaze. 'Breathtaking,' I whispered with a sad smile.

She giggled. 'No, you haven't changed.'

'Kate . . .' I started, then stopped. 'Drink?' I asked, quickly. I had to keep it light.

'Oh, yeah, beer please.' She slid past me and reached for a packet of cigarettes on the coffee table. I held out my own, she took it and used it to light hers. She sat down on the bed again. I fetched another bottle from the fridge, passed it over and sat back on the sofa opposite.

'So tell me about you, Kate?' I said, eventually.

'Well,' she took a thoughtful sip of the beer, 'I'm officially the cook on *Gold*, but the responsibilities are pretty limited. They've cut back the budget a lot, but despite that the crew are still put up in hotels and fed in the restaurant. I only have to do the food for racing and the delivery trips. It's pretty dumb, the $40,000 hotel bill would pay for a couple of new spinnakers and three more professional delivery crew. But that's corporate sponsorship for you. No idea where to spend the money in something they know nothing about. And can they be told? No chance. It makes life pretty easy though. The downside is the money. I get paid nothing until they're racing or on delivery. Sitting around in the dock working on the boat just burns up my savings.'

'But you've got Scott,' I said, cautiously.

She gave me one of those looks. 'He's not my keeper.'

I nodded, 'No, of course. So are the budget cuts the problems you were talking about in Ko Samui?'

'Yeah, part of it. You sure you want to hear about that, it's pretty dull for an outsider?' A casual drag on the cigarette.

Whilst I flinched at the implication, 'Yes, of course I do,' I said, encouragingly.

'I guess it starts with Duval. He's the racing skipper of *Gold*, those are the guys in the public eye, the glamour boys who do the interviews. Only the skippers get the serious money in this game because they're the people who can bring in the publicity for the sponsor. And often, to be fair, they put all the time and money into finding the sponsor in the first place. But sometimes they aren't even the best sailors on the boat. So much of the real work is done by the people in the background and they get so little reward for it.'

'People like Scott?' I said, intrigued that she was worried at someone else getting a better deal than Scott. Materialism wasn't exactly her big thing three years ago.

'Yeah. He's more than capable of skippering the boat, but there's all this other stuff involved, mainly finding the sponsor and dealing with them at the top corporate level. And ironically they're exactly the people, like my father, that I ran away from.' She took a big sigh and brushed her hair back away from her eyes. 'I've been trying to help him with that stuff. So he can make the step up and get his own boat for the next race. But the situation has got much worse recently because Scott has got to the point where he's a threat to Duval. He's very popular with the crew and the story goes around a lot that he sails the boat. It's starting to effect Duval's image and we think he wants to get rid of Scott. So now Scott is embroiled in this huge political fight, just to keep any job, never mind get a better one.'

I sipped at my beer as she went on, 'This has all built up over a while and in the last couple of weeks has exploded. Duval's been in England looking for another sponsor, because Gold have just decided that they will pull out in three months time, after the regatta in Hong Kong. We heard from some mates back in Hamble that he was also trying to hire a replacement for Scott, once he has the new sponsor in place.'

'This is for the Whitbread Round the World Race?'

She nodded. 'It starts in September this year. So there isn't much time. Gold have found someone that might buy the boat and run it for the next race. Their people are coming out here to meet everyone and talk through the deal. Using some contacts of my father's I discovered that they want a clean slate. Start afresh, no one is guaranteed a job, not even Duval. So I've managed to set up a meeting with them for Scott, where he can pitch to them as a potential new skipper. We were working on the proposal in Ko Samui. They're all arriving in town tonight. Duval's meeting them at the airport and taking them off to dinner somewhere, presumably to pitch his proposal. Tomorrow's our big day. It's shit or bust now. Duval knows about our meeting. If he gets the money Scott will definitely be out on his arse after Hong Kong.' She took a final drag on the cigarette and exhaled the smoke cloud slowly, staring into space, before she stubbed it out. 'And vice versa,' she added, in a hard voice.

I nodded, silent, but thoughtful. The ambition, the planning, it wasn't like Kate. She had changed.

She glanced at her watch again. 'I don't know where Scott's got to, but we should probably go anyway. He must still be on the boat.' She got up and picked the key off the dresser. 'Come on, let's go party.'

12

T HE PARTY WAS in the yacht club and we walked there in
silence, lost in our own thoughts. It was a low brick building,
sprawlcd across a park, from the road down to the water. The
hubbub of voices grew as we got closer, and I could see that the
party had spilled out on to the terrace. Kate avoided the club
and headed towards the water's edge. We stopped under a tree,
staring out towards the dark and silent shape of *Gold*.

'Damn him, he's gone straight to the party, didn't even bother
to phone me,' she said, quietly.

I let the words dissipate. Then said, 'It's a beautiful evening,'
and it was. The boats sitting quietly at their moorings, with just
the odd slap of a halyard or bang of a fender on the pontoons.
The water glowing in the last of the sunlight, sound from the
party diffused by the warmth and humidity.

'Yes,' she said, looking up at me and smiling, 'yes it is,' and
she took my hand and led me into the club.

We entered through a side gate, standing for a moment to
survey the scene. On our left was the marina, with boats four
deep on the nearest docks. In front was a large, open terrace,
a sea of cheerful expressions and florid movement. At the far
end a band was setting up. Off to the right was the bar, and
set back from that was an open dining room. Kate stepped
forward, I followed, and we were quickly swallowed up by
the crowd. I caught snatches of meaningless conversation in a
babble of English. The men wore variations on a theme; polo
shirts, docksiders, jeans or chinos with lots of bleached hair. The
occasional tie and blazer was the only concession to formality.
The women had tried harder, there were little black dresses and
sparkling, made-up smiles everywhere. Kate drifted through them,
moving easily; turning heads, absorbing greetings, a nod here, a
word there, but never stopping.

Finally, she found what she had been looking for, at the far end of the terrace by the band. There was Scott, with a bunch of other guys, all still dressed in grubby shorts and T-shirts. They must have got there straight from the boat. Kate stopped when she saw them, pulling back into the crowd.

'What's wrong?' I asked.

'Scott's drunk.' Her voice was tight, annoyed.

I smiled, despite trying to be concerned. Everybody was drunk. But Scott did seem to have pushed the boat out a little bit further than anybody else. His face was flushed, swaying unsteadily, traces of most of the evening's consumption down his shirt.

'Come on, I'm not talking to him while he's in that state,' she said, leading the way back towards the main bar.

I put my arm round her. She was tense with anger. 'Hey, relax. You and I were going to have a good time, remember?' I said, lightly.

She nodded, managed a smile. 'You're right,' unwinding a little under my arm.

'I'll get us some drinks,' I said. I left her and fought my way to the bar. It took for ever to get served, and by the time I returned to where I had left Kate, there was no sign of her. If there is one way to feel foolish in a bar, it's standing with a pint in one hand and a glass of wine in the other, looking for a girl who has, self-evidently to anyone watching, found something better to do than wait for your return. This depressing emotion lasted for about ten seconds before I felt a touch at my elbow. With a rush of relief I turned, it was Kate.

'Quick! Come with me.' Real panic in her voice and her face.

'What about these?' I held up the drinks.

'Leave them.' Already she was moving off through the crowd, heading towards the restaurant. I dropped the drinks on the nearest table and struggled to keep up as she explained in staccato bursts over her shoulder. 'It's Duval, with the new sponsors, he's brought them here, the sneaky bastard! We've got to keep them away from Scott. If they see him in that state it's all over.' She indicated a group of noticeably over-dressed men. Suits. About twenty yards away, looking as if they felt as out of place as they were. 'I recognised that guy with the grey jacket, while you were getting the drinks. He's a friend of my father's. I went to check it out and found the whole lot of them.'

We were only a few yards away by now, Kate slowed her pace as one of them caught sight of her. 'Peter, what a surprise, I didn't expect to see you here this evening,' she began. He was silent, looking disconcerted. Kate carried on, 'I'd like to introduce you to an old friend of mine from England, Peter Duval this is Martin Cormac, Martin, Peter.'

I took the proferred hand, but he clearly wasn't interested in me. The pale blue eyes were cold, charmless, and they flickered nervously back towards Kate even as he shook my hand. She was turning that dazzling smile on to the group of men. A mixed bunch of age and build, they were nevertheless all flattered by the attention. Then, with eyebrows slightly raised and a quick but enquiring glance at Duval, she forced him to introduce us.

I took the opportunity provided by the round of introductions to study Duval. He was lightly built, wiry, I guess you'd say, with mousy brown hair that was just short enough to be respectable. Maybe five ten, with a sharp, angular face, battered by the sun. He looked uncomfortable in the shirt and tie. But it was the voice which was the most distracting feature, an unfortunate, grating nasal whine. It wouldn't make him easy to like. I tuned back in on the conversation as Kate was introduced to what, fading business antenna notwithstanding, appeared the most senior member of the group.

'Kate, this is Mr Monterey, CEO of Rollen's Tobacco,' the speaker was the grey jacket Kate had already pointed out, 'Kate is Wallace's daughter, she's out here with that other chap we're seeing tomorrow.'

'Ah yes, of course. Your father is a fine man, I'm delighted to meet you, my dear,' he said, all distinguished silver mane and ample girth, 'perhaps you'd like to join us for dinner. I believe Mr Duval has booked us a table.' He looked enquiringly at Duval, who was squirming, but could hardly refuse. This obviously wasn't part of his plan. So far Kate was ahead on points. She half-turned to me, and the old boy was quick to include me in the invitation. A waiter arrived and we proceeded over to a corner table in the dining room.

As we got to the table the band started up outside. I looked back at the mass of humanity in the main bar. The combination of the music and shouted conversation gave it the atmosphere of a cheap nightclub rather than an expensive yacht club. Duval had taken a chance bringing these people here. I moved in to sit next to Kate. She in turn was beside Monterey. Someone was ordering a couple of bottles of champagne. As we sat down she hissed in my ear, 'Duval has set this up deliberately. He knows Scott'll be pissed. He's brought them here so Scott can make a fool of himself. You have to help me. Go and find Scott and get him out of here.'

'Me? Don't be ridiculous. I'm the last person he'd listen to!'

'Find a guy called Ben, everybody knows him, he's the mate on the boat. Tell him the deal, he'll know what to do.'

'Jesus, Kate.'

She squeezed my arm. 'Please.' Imploring blue eyes.

Duval's nasal whine interrupted us from his position on the other side of Monterey, 'So, Kate, where is Scott tonight?'

She turned away from me, and, talking less to Duval than Monterey, said, 'Still working I'm afraid.'

'But, it's the prize-giving?' said Monterey.

'The boat has to go up to Hong Kong the day after tomorrow, there's a lot to do to get it ready. I'm sure he would have been here if he'd known you were coming.' She looked blackly at Duval. 'Sometimes these events can get a little hectic. After your flight I'd have thought you might have preferred something quieter.'

Monterey glanced at the heaving main bar, smiled at her, 'I think you might be right.' He looked at Duval, an amused glint in his eye. It was pretty clear he knew what the deal was.

Duval bristled, but he wasn't finished. Ignoring the put-down he looked enquiringly at Kate again. 'I'd heard the boys were planning on having a few drinks tonight, maybe Scott's with them?' Then added to Monterey, 'Little celebration, we won the regatta of course.'

Kate turned back to me, face set with urgency. I nodded and said loudly, 'I'll see if I can find him, tear him away from the boat.' I looked at Monterey. 'Perhaps he could also join us?' I said.

'Certainly, I'd like to meet this young man.' The glint in his eye was increasing. He was thoroughly enjoying the prospect of further combat. But as I started to rise there was a big cheer from the main bar. Everybody looked up as the crowd parted like the ocean before Moses, and right in front of us Scott staggered into someone's arms, an empty glass upturned on his head. A faint trickle of beer, or maybe sweat, running down his cheek. The Gold Breweries team had just won a drinking race by a short half. Scott collapsed in the middle of his back-slapping colleagues.

'I guess you won't need to look for him after all,' said Duval, quietly, pulling out a gold cigarette case. 'Though I doubt he'll want dinner, cigarette, Mr Monterey?' He was keeping a remarkably straight face.

Monterey had been staring at the scene in the bar, slowly he turned to Kate. 'Is that the chap we're seeing tomorrow?' he said, mildly.

'I'm afraid so,' she replied, with a tremor.

'Mmmm, what a shame, my dear,' he said slowly, with a sympathetic smile. Then he turned to Duval, accepting the cigarette. 'Good brand,' he said, coldly.

I could see Kate struggling with her anger. I turned to her, tried to think of something to say, to diffuse the situation. She could still recover it, if she could keep her temper. Then I realised I didn't want her to. After a couple of seconds of pregnant silence, as Monterey lit his cigarette and Kate fixed Duval with a glacial stare, she flung back her chair. She strode straight towards Scott as he was hauled back to his feet. I followed at a safe distance. In a voice vibrant with anger, she said, 'Look! See what a fool he is making of you!' pointing back at Duval. He had sensibly stayed with Monterey and the sponsors, and the lot of them had now disappeared behind the surging crowd.

Scott just looked confused. 'Katie, sorry I didn't make it back to the hotel.' The words were slurred and the breath heavy with alcohol. He hiccupped slightly to punctuate the sentence.

I'd seen Kate angry a lot of times and I knew the signs. She was furious now. She slapped him once, hard, on the cheek. 'Don't you see it? What you've done? Over there, the tobacco people. Your future, you moron. You're pissed as a fart, look at you. It's over. No one will ever take you seriously.'

Scott stepped back, obviously a little surprised at the venom, but Kate was still going, 'I'm off, you're disgusting,' she spat. 'Give me the keys.'

Scott slowly fished the keys out of his pocket, but not without some difficulty. Kate grabbed them with little ceremony. Then she turned to me, 'Martin, are you coming?'

The words froze Scott even through the alcoholic haze. He looked at me in a double take, finally realising who I was. Then he spluttered, looking for the words, 'What the fuck's he doing here? He with you? Jesus I'll kill him.' The Western Union couldn't have telegraphed the punch better and I stepped easily out of the way. A couple of the guys grabbed him. I looked wildly between the struggling Scott and the fast disappearing Kate. But there was no choice really, was there?

I hurried after Kate, who was already through the door. 'Kate, are you sure this is a good idea?'

'Too bloody right. I've had enough of that clown.' I dropped into step beside her as she strode across the grass. 'Where are we going?'

'The skiff club.'

'Uhhuh,' I replied, none the wiser. She opened the doors of a pale-blue van and I climbed in. The engine roared into life, horrendously over-revved, crashed into gear and we bumped across the grass towards the road. I sat in silence for a while, trying to catch up, figure out how to play it. I couldn't believe my luck. Scott had crashed and burned and I had Kate to myself. I needed to take it slowly, keep it light.

'What's the skiff club?' I said eventually.

'It's another yacht club, across the harbour.'

'You sure you want to go to another yacht club?' I replied as gently as I could. 'Maybe we could just go somewhere for a quiet dinner or something.'

She was silent.

'Somewhere really nice, you have a favourite place? Just the two of us, like the old days, Kate.' I reached out and brushed away a tear that was sliding down her cheek.

She flinched away. 'I don't think that would be a good idea,' she said tersely, not taking her eyes off the road.

'Why?' I said, taken aback by the physical and verbal rebuff.

'It just wouldn't. The situation is complicated enough as it is, without making it any worse.'

'And asking me to leave with you didn't make it any worse?' I said, my anger building quickly.

She just shrugged, expression grim.

'What the fuck are you trying to do to me?' I retorted, harshly, too quickly. I knew as soon as I said it that it was a big mistake.

She slammed the brakes on, hauled the wheel over and flung the van into the side of the road, narrowly missing a shiny new Toyota. Horns blared as the drivers behind us swerved. 'What makes you think you've got any right to come barging back into my life like this!'

You were the one who came looking for me, I thought.

'Like the old days? Shit! Don't you remember the old days, Martin? Didn't you ever look in the mirror after I left and check for that naked greed I told you about. Didn't you see it, staring you back in the face? I loved you once, Martin, when we met and you'd just started that job, but you turned into some kind of monster, the stuff you did, the money, and for what? Screwing other people's lives up. You say you've changed, but was that before or after you helped destroy the ERM for your own benefit? Before you got yourself hooked up in some drug deal playing your stupid games. Who's next for the treatment, me and Scott?'

She slammed the car back into gear, hit the gas and we roared off, completing the rest of the journey in silence – while I wondered if she had any idea how much that had hurt. I should've got out and taken a cab back to the hotel and got on the next plane to anywhere. But of course I couldn't, I didn't want the evening to end like this, I wanted to stick around till she had calmed down, try again. I had to tell her why I'd left England. What I had learned. But now wasn't the moment.

13

THE CAR ROLLED to a halt on another patch of grass outside
another clubhouse. Kate flicked the lights and as the key
turned the engine died. With one hand the seatbelt was unclasped
while the other reached for the door-handle. She pulled the keys
from the ignition, climbed out of the seat and slammed the door
shut. Not a word was spoken. I trailed inside after her, then
headed for the bar. She was wrestling with the cigarette machine
when I returned with the drinks. I held out the glass of wine, a
peace offering. She ignored it and carried on struggling. I watched
in silence.

'Here, Katie, let me help you with that.' We both turned at the
sound of the new voice.

Kate smiled. 'Thanks, Josh,' she said and held his drink for him.
The newcomer was a big bloke, tanned with a mass of curly blond
hair. He pinned the machine against the wall with one hand, then
slammed it hard, about two feet from the bottom on the left side.
There was a clunk, and he pulled the drawer open easily.

'Isn't that your new employer's product?' he asked, exchanging
the packet for his drink.

Kate looked at him intently, taking the drink from me without
so much as a glance in my direction. 'Not after tonight,' she said,
'how do you know about that, anyway?'

'Small town and news travels fast.' He smiled. 'Are you OK,
Katie?'

She was trying to smile, but it looked like an effort. So she
drank instead, the glass was quickly empty.

'Jeez,' said Josh. 'You're not gonna be all right in a minute if
you keep that up.'

The grin seemed to come much more readily now. 'Get me
another one, Josh,' she said.

I followed the two of them over to a group standing by the
french windows at the end of the room. Behind them, the

lights of the city glistened in the water of the harbour. Kate was welcomed noisily into the group. The boys were shooting the breeze, telling their stories, drinking their beer. If I had felt reasonably comfortable in the other club, I was totally out of it here. The slang was incomprehensible and the dress code was formal at shorts and a T-shirt. And those were only the surface representations. I didn't belong. I knew it and everyone else knew it, but I hung in there. Kate was slowly unwinding – as you would, after drinking steadily for a couple of hours.

It was Josh's loud exclamation and the sudden movement that pulled me up from my analysis of the carpet pattern. Kate was being led away by Marc, a slightly built man with the trace of a French accent. She was laughing. He whirled her out of the bar and down the stairs. Leaving me wondering what was going on. I followed them, along with most of the group, feeling completely lost.

Outside a crowd had already gathered, with people lifting a boat and masts off a trailer. It was the strangest looking craft I had ever seen. It must've been nearly twenty foot long, a wide, open dish shape. But as it grew from the various parts under an army of willing helpers, that wasn't half of it. Two huge aluminium frames were bolted on to either side, with netting joining the edges to the main hull. The rig was enormous, with an unbelievable collection of wires to hold it in place.

The activity grew and soon I saw Kate standing alone, she didn't look quite so happy. I came up beside her. 'Kate, what's going on?' I said.

'We're going sailing,' she replied, more than a trace of defiance in her voice.

'In that! Now?' I replied.

Then Josh came up beside her. 'You'd better get changed into a wettie,' he said, holding out a bright orange rubber wetsuit, 'it may not be too warm out there.'

Kate took it without a word and ducked behind the trailer. Josh turned to me, 'You a mate of Katie's?'

'Sure.'

'Well, maybe you could talk to that bloke over there,' he pointed, 'and see if he'll take the rescue boat out in case we have a problem.' He must have recognised the look of alarm on my face, because he went on, 'Shouldn't be necessary, but it's better to be safe than sorry.'

I nodded and hurried over to the man in question. He was cooperative, though a little drunk as well. He led me out to another jetty where we stepped into a small and rather battered speedboat. Behind us the strange craft, now upright and with its sails towering over the grass, was hoisted on to many shoulders and carried into the water. Our engine fired into life and I threw off the ropes, we backed out into the dark waters of the small inlet.

I watched the boat with interest. I'd done a little sailing, but I'd never seen anything like this. Marc was aboard and starting to fit the rudder, Josh helped Kate on. I could hear his instructions quite clearly, even over the engine.

'Wait up near the centreboard in the middle, Kate, and don't move, OK?'

She nodded. The sails cracked a couple of times as a puff of wind blew through. Josh waded out to the left-hand frame and hung on. There was a third guy already in position on the other side. The helpers, many still in shorts or jeans, were slowly climbing out of the water.

Marc had finished with the rudder. 'All set, guys?' he shouted. The two remaining helpers holding the stern gave a shove and Marc climbed on to the wing and started to pull in the mainsail. The other two flicked themselves out of the water and into the boat as she started to move. Immediately they began to accelerate, heading straight towards us. The engine revved and with a churning of wash we backed out of the way.

'Wow,' I breathed as they flashed by.

'Mate, they ain't even got her cranked up yet,' my driver said.

'I guess that's a skiff, huh?' I asked.

'An eighteen-foot Sydney Harbour skiff, mate, that's what that is. And these blokes are the World Title holders.'

We turned and powered after them, the cheers of the landlocked spectators receding behind us. I watched Kate move out towards the others and soon all four were on the netting of the wing frame. Josh and the other guy standing, Marc sitting at the stern steering with Kate beside him. The boat was nearing the end of the narrow cove that led to the club. In front of us lay the open water of Sydney Harbour. Directly opposite were the bright lights of the opera house, with the bridge under the sails to their right. In front of Kate the two crew clipped something to their waists and then, together, they pulled in the sails and moved outboard.

Finally stepping over the edge of the wing so their weight was supported on the wire at their waist. That in turn seemed to be attached to the top of the mast somewhere. The bubble of water turned into a froth as the boat responded to the new horsepower. The engine churned as we pulled up right behind them. There was a light splash of water as they hit a couple of waves.

I watched Kate pull herself up beside Marc and take the wire from him. She clipped it on. I heard Marc shout, 'OK, out you go,' encouragingly. She scrambled and slipped her backside on to the edge of the wing, tugged her pelvis against the wire to check it would hold, then pushed out with her feet. I smiled, I could see she was starting to enjoy it, and I had to admit, it did look kind of fun, now they were out here. I saw her turn and look back at me, with the biggest smile. I grinned and waved, beer bottle still in hand. 'Yo, go, Katie!' She waved back.

The boat creamed along for about another ten minutes with us churning away alongside. It was a blur of water, moonlight, the chuckle of the bow wave and the throb of the engine. Then suddenly the skiff was spinning and slowing as it turned down, away from the wind. The others were gone from beside her, moving inboard, and Kate started to fall forwards, slamming into the wing about half-way along. She scrabbled frantically at the netting and finally managed to arrest the slide towards the bow. By the time she had sorted herself out Josh had the huge brightly coloured spinnaker hoisted and was headed back up the netting towards her.

He was out on the wire again and the spinnaker cracked twice as he fought to sheet in the sail. Then it filled and the boat shot forward as though it was jet propelled. Kate was thrown backwards into Marc with the acceleration. I saw her desperately trying to get a foothold and just as she planted both feet on to the wing the boat leapt in the air off a wave. I heard her scream as the boat came down with a bang and shot an enormous plume of water out from underneath the hull. It caught Kate full in the face. She was gasping for air, my driver laughing loudly at her antics. But she was still in the same place, the boat was upright and they were charging towards the opera house under a luminous moon at what seemed like a thousand miles an hour. Our speedboat roared as we tried to keep up. The boat kicked and trembled as it skipped off waves and thundered forward under the puffs of wind.

The opera house was only two hundred yards away now, I could see a crowd gathering on the railings, this was not the usual entertainment, but it promised to be special. The boat turned and Kate ducked as the mainsail came whistling over her. The boat wobbled unsteadily as it slowed. But Marc and Josh were already past her and sheeting the sails back on. The skiff stabilised as it began to accelerate. By the mast there was furious action as Josh hauled the spinnaker in. We all watched as the last piece of cloth was tucked away and the bag zipped up. The boat was reaching home now, and we motored quietly beside them.

As we drew slowly back into the dock, there was still a big crowd watching. I noticed one figure in particular, standing alone, knee deep in water, at the foot of the slip. I looked across at Kate, but she had seen him too.

'And where the hell have you been?' Scott's question boomed across the water as the boat drifted in towards him. 'You've been sailing? On this thing? In the middle of the night? Do you realise how long I've been looking for you?' He grabbed the boat as Josh and the third crewman hopped over the side to slow it down. We were already back at our jetty and I hurried round to the slip. Kate was out of the boat, and sploshing through the water towards Scott.

'Look . . .' she started, trying to interrupt his tirade, but got no further.

'It was these idiots, huh? I'll kill 'em.' And with that he plunged into the water, headed straight for Josh. Josh was considerably disadvantaged, having one hand still on the boat and being neck deep in water. Marc was struggling to take the rudder off so that the boat could be pulled in closer to the shore. But Scott got there first, diving at Josh full-length. They disappeared in a huge cloud of spray. I heard Kate scream. And the crowd that had begun to disperse, was regrouping at the possibility of more action. Marc dragged the rudder into the boat and leapt into the water on top of the struggling pair. There was a huge cheer from the crowd. Some were helping pull the boat to safety, as Josh and Marc had long since lost interest in anything but Scott. Others dived in to try and stop them, or just because it was a good excuse for a fight. Either way, they quickly became embroiled. And so it grew.

Soon the entire waterfront was a mass of struggling figures. But I could hear laughter now, and there on the grass foreshore was

Scott. Racked with laughter. The most hopeless case of the giggles you ever saw. He lay there, rolling from side to side in the dust, guffawing. Lungs and chest heaving for air through the howls, tears streaming down his face. Damn him, I thought, where the hell was Kate? Then I spotted her, climbing into the van. I dashed after her.

'Kate!'

The door slammed and the engine started. I banged on the window. 'Kate!' She wouldn't even look at me, I could see the tears on her cheeks. 'Kate!' I screamed frantically as she started to pull off, swerving away and heading for the gate. I ran across the grass and vaulted the fence. If she turned this way I could cut her off. The van spun through the gate, wheels spewing dust and then blue smoke as they found traction on the tarmac. Foot down, she accelerated towards me, seventy yards away and closing. I had to stop her. I jumped into the road, yelling and waving. But with no lights on I would be hard to see. Then she found the switch and flicked it up to high beam. I was caught in the glare of the lights, blinded. I heard the tortured howl of stressed rubber as she braked, but I stood my ground, I didn't trust her to stay braked. This was going to be close. I held my breath.

14

'ARE YOU COMPLETELY insane?!' I opened my eyes. The windscreen of the snub-nose van was three feet away from my face. I looked down, the bumper was inches from my shins. I let go a long, slow breath. My heart was trying to rip its way out of my chest. Kate was still shouting at me, half out of the driver's window.

I found the strength to speak, 'Move over. I'm getting in.'

She stopped raving and glowered at me. But it was an argument I'd already won. She shuffled across to the passenger side and I leapt in the driver's seat before she could change her mind. I slammed the van into gear and hit the gas. We drove off in silence.

I had only the vaguest idea of where we were and no idea of where I was going, but I wanted to put some distance between us and the club – I didn't want Scott pulling another cameo performance like the last one. I drove fast, taking one turning after another, not caring where I went, so long as it was away from Scott. I hauled the protesting van into one quiet, treelined residential street after another, stamping on brake then accelerator, revs high, tyres squealing. It was a couple of minutes before I realised that I needed a longer term strategy. But by then I was hopelessly lost. I pulled the van up in the orange pool of the street's only light and looked across at Kate. She was huddled in the corner, face pale, strained, sickly in the sodium glow. Her whole body shook with silent sobs. Silent tears are the worst. The deepest.

'Let it out, Katie.' I slid closer to her, but she stayed huddled in the corner.

'God, what a shambles,' she choked out, the pent-up sobs released as the tears began to flow, but before I could say anything a violent tremor gripped her. I realised she was still soaking wet, bare arms goose-bumped, lips bloodless.

'You're freezing to death,' I said, turning back to the wheel. I clunked the van heavily into gear. 'I'm taking you back to my hotel, Katie, get you warmed up.' Just as soon as I work out where we are, I thought to myself.

I glanced in the mirror to pull off and saw lights approaching behind me. I hesitated, waiting for them to pass. But instead the car slewed across in front of us, trailing rubber in a black, smoking stain. I stared at the two dark figures that leapt out of the car, struggling to comprehend this sudden shift of pace, of circumstance. A thought half-formed in my head – not Scott again . . . Heels clattered loudly on the tarmac beside me and the door flew open. A blinding light shone in my eyes and something hard and blunt jabbed into my rib cage. A voice said, 'Get out quick or I'll blow your fucking head off.'

No, not Scott. The answer roared through my head before I had even asked the question. Fear rippled through my body in a paralysing wave. Kate was hauled out of the seat beside me, a stammering protest still-born.

'Move!' yelled the voice in my ear, with a more painful jab in the ribs. I started to unwrap my fingers from the wheel. Not quickly enough. A hand grabbed my shirt and pulled me outwards. I crashed to the pavement before I could get my legs out to save myself. The voice was hoarse, urgent in my ear, carried on garlic breath, 'Move when I tell you, arsehole.'

I looked up, Kate was being pushed into the back seat of the car ahead of me. I was hauled to my feet and sent stumbling after her. I cracked my head as I climbed in, slumped heavily into the upholstery.

'Bring the van,' yelled the driver. Something familiar about that voice. My door slammed, someone climbed into the passenger seat. The interior light glinted on the gun, revealed features distorted by a stocking mask. The black snout of the barrel was levelled at us. The engine was already running. More unhappy rubber as we drove off. Kate was beside me. I turned to her, reached out a hand anxiously, 'You OK?' I whispered hoarsely.

'Shut the fuck up!' yelled the man in the passenger seat. I looked at Kate and she nodded, lips a tight line, eyes big, frightened. And she was shaking uncontrollably. Jaw clenched to stop it trembling. And it wouldn't be just the cold now either. I pulled her in towards me, felt the damp of the wetsuit press against my shirt, the cold of her cheek bury into my neck. I glanced forwards. The man in the passenger seat was turned towards us, the gun wedged on the seatback, unwavering. His masked face was in shadow from the flicker of the street lights. But I could see the driver clearly; no mask and a dark swelling still around the left eye. I knew where I had heard the voice before.

'Alex,' I breathed. 'What the hell is going on?' I felt Kate move underneath my arm.

'Shut up!' yelled the other man again, his grip on the gun tightened.

Alex glanced over his shoulder, then back to the road. 'You fucked up, Martin. Should have just done as Janac said, made the delivery and kept your mouth shut.'

I stared at him, my mind refusing to comprehend the obvious, the grotesque extent of the catastrophe. It was all over. Now I would have to pay. And Kate. Oh God, the nausea swept up and choked me. What had he said? 'The fear of the death of a loved one is as strong as the fear of death itself.' That was what he would want now. I pulled her in tighter with a sudden strength and she gasped as I squeezed. The gunman hissed threateningly at the noise, but before he could do anymore, the car bumped hard on a deep pothole. I slid against the door as we swung fast into a turning and through a half-open, wire-link gate. We had entered an old fairground, the headlights lit stalls and booths with blistered paint and faded shutters. We drew up beside a more substantial building with grey concrete walls, mesh covered windows.

The doors opened, hands pulled us apart and out of the car. The van lurched to a halt behind us as we were pushed towards the entrance, the flashlight flickering to show the way. I moved beside Kate and put a protective arm around her shoulder, my mind screaming at me that it was an utterly worthless gesture. I could no more protect her from what was coming than I could feed the world or heal the sick. We stumbled down a dark corridor, crashing into unseen objects every few feet, until we were shoved into one of the rooms. The door slammed shut behind us.

Kate was in my arms, still shivering uncontrollably. My eyes started to adjust to the moonlight that slid tiredly through a small window high up on the far wall. We were in some kind of a storeroom, empty shelves filled the space. Just the one door, the only other way out was the window and it was too small for either of us. No escape.

'What the hell is going on, Martin?' said Kate in a shaky, desperate voice.

I pulled away from her, took off my shirt. 'Here, put this on. It's dry, it might warm you up.'

She took it, turned away and peeled down the wetsuit top and tugged the shirt on over her head. She looked small and vulnerable, shivering in the oversized shirt.

I pulled her back in towards me, trying to warm her body with mine, and whispered quietly in her ear. 'Alex, the cop you went to, works for Janac. It was a set-up, in case I decided to go to the police and succeeded in doing it without the minders knowing. Alex was fed to me as the obvious place to turn for help, but he's one of Janac's men. And I fell for it.' I lifted my eyes to the dark ceiling. 'Janac promised me that the penalty for doing the right thing, giving the drugs up to the police, would be death. The minders should have killed me as soon as they knew that you'd called Alex. He can't have got the message to the flunkeys in time – otherwise I'd be dead already. Then they must have screwed up by losing me when I dropped the drugs off. After that, the only link they had with me was you. And they knew where you were, so they just watched and waited until I showed up.' I shook my head, feeling her wet hair rub against my face. 'And I thought I'd fooled them. I never stood a chance.' My voice was cracked, bitter, broken. I remembered the bruising still visible on Alex's face. At least Janac had hurt that bastard, making the show look real enough in the nightclub. Or maybe it was during the beating afterwards that they turned him. Either way, it made no difference now. There were only consequences left.

'So now he will punish me for trying to turn the drugs over to the cops. I thought I could outsmart the bastard. I thought, God forbid, that I could do some good for once. But I've been a stupid, blind fool and all I did was get you involved and I'll never forgive myself for that. But I swear nothing will happen to you. I'll get you out of this, Kate, somehow, there has to be a way . . .' I couldn't go on, couldn't get my mind round the enormity of what had happened.

After a while, I wasn't counting time, her body warmed up to mine and she stopped shaking. She pulled away and I let her go, moving slowly to the nearest shelves she slumped on to the floor in front of them. I couldn't see her expression in the half light.

Her voice was hoarse, tinged with despair. 'So what's he going to do with us?' she asked.

I stared at her in silence for a moment, leant back against the shelves opposite, still standing. 'It'll be some kind of a game.' I shook my head, I didn't want to think about the game.

'A game?' she sounded surprised.

'You remember I said back on Ko Samui that he had sucked me into this through the games?'

She nodded.

'After I told him about what had happened to me in England, he started these games: the last one was a Prisoner's Dilemma. He wanted to see how I would react. I'm sure he'll do something similar now.'

She shifted, I felt her looking at me. 'What did happen in England? You never told me about that.' There was a tiny spark of life, curiosity, in her voice.

I sighed heavily, hopelessly. I had thought about this conversation so much; my chance to convince her that I had changed, finally, from the man she knew and rejected. But these were not the circumstances I expected to be doing it in. Damn you, Janac. Slowly, painfully, wishing with every word that it was happening differently, I told her all that had passed since that terrible day on the motorway. About the crash and how it had affected my work, getting suspended from the job after the ERM disaster, leaving England and meeting Janac. I told her about the Prisoner's Dilemma machine with its options to cooperate or defect. The parallel moral issue he had made of the drug smuggling choices, and how seeing her had helped me to do the right thing.

I watched her carefully as I finished up, 'Seeing you again made me realise you were right, not me, three years ago. That lifestyle, those values, they're completely shot, there's no future in them. You can't just care about yourself.' I hesitated, she was silent, but tucked her knees up to her chest and started to rock gently to and fro. 'And the conflict that drove us apart – whether to cooperate or defect, to act selflessly or selfishly – that conflict is the point of all his games, including whatever we're now going to face.'

Kate remained silent, head down, rolling her weight off her toes; backwards and forwards, backwards and forwards. I listened to a train rattle across the Harbour Bridge, the sound layered on to the background hum of traffic. Somewhere else in the building there were footsteps, a shout. I heard another car approach, the lights flicked momentarily through the window. A lighthouse beam, a warning flash in the night. It would be Janac, this was what we were waiting for.

Kate was still rocking herself gently, showing no interest in what was going on outside the room, or outside her own tightly wrapped universe. I moved over, sat down beside her and put my arm around her. But she didn't respond, shoulders set, hard and unyielding. She stared ahead, biting her lip. I spoke softly, 'I think he will make us play the Prisoner's Dilemma game, with the machine. Maybe we'll play each other, maybe we'll play him, or one of his men. He may try to hurt you to get at me. But whatever happens you're going to make it, you're all that counts. It's my mess and I'll do whatever it takes to get you out.' I squeezed her to me – but still she was unresponsive. I took my arm away.

Suddenly she looked up, eyes glistening. 'When I first started with Scott we had everything we wanted. A simple, good life; working on the boat, a little money, each other. Compared to living with you, with all that greed, it was wonderful. And now,' she hesitated, 'it's not that I want riches or luxury, just a few basics, some security, somewhere to call home other than . . . other than that damn boat.' She stopped as her voice broke, choked back a sob. 'So I push Scott to get his shit together, to get ahead. But then he just slips back, happy as he is, with what he has. And then I push a bit harder and we end up with a fiasco like tonight.' She stopped, looked around the room as if seeing it for the first time, and shivered. 'And now with this' . . . she swallowed, waved her arm at the room. 'I see so clearly how I've changed, how that's what's screwed it up for me and Scott. And you, of all people, want to tell me that I was right before – here, now? Jesus . . .' She shook the blonde hair, tears starting to roll, dropped her head into her hands.

I saw how she was hurting; that the blame for tonight's row could get confused with this new, infinitely more dangerous situation. I had to make her understand the danger. 'Kate, listen to me. You have to deal with this differently. Forget Scott. Forget your world. Think about getting out alive. When I played Janac before, I knew it was crazy to keep defecting, but there was no choice. No other rational choice. That is the brutal reality of the game. In a world where everyone is selfish, you have no choice but to defect. It would be great if it was different but it isn't – certainly not in Janac's world. He uses the games to force you into his world, into his way of thinking. To force you to defect.

'So you defect and you both get zapped time and time again, much worse than if you were cooperating. It's crazy. I kept thinking this is insane, but could see no way out. We could have gone on taking level three shocks till it killed both of us. At that point you have to wonder what sort of thinking produces solutions like that. But that's what so much of the world is like now. The world of the stock markets, tax dodges, insurance scams, cutting down rainforests for cash. It's all the same thing. The overwhelming acceptance of the defector's attitude is dragging all of us down. But that's the way it is – especially with Janac. You have to understand that. You have to remember, Kate, if you play him, he'll never cooperate. He'll break you if you don't remember that.' I looked at her intently, tightly wrapped up in herself. 'Promise me, Kate, if you play Janac or any of his people, you will defect.'

There was a long silence, Kate sobbing quietly now, her face in her hands, rocking on her heels. But gradually she grew still and the crying stopped. Suddenly she looked up. 'But it has to start somewhere, somebody has to be first if the world is going to change. We won't all start cooperating at the same time, it has to grow from the people that believe.'

'This is not the place for that. No stupid heroics, Kate,' I said harshly.

She was watching me with those ocean-clear blue eyes, the brightly burning intelligence. Finally, she took a deep slow breath and wiped her cheeks, before she said, 'It's OK. I understand.'

I smiled with relief. 'But it doesn't have to be like that for us. It's more likely we'll play each other. If we do, we can both cooperate. If he makes us play against each other, we can make it.'

The eyes stayed on me for a second before they moved away, back to the window. The blonde hair hid her face, but slowly she nodded. The silence and the gloom descended back on us. After the flurry of activity a few minutes earlier everything had gone quiet again. What the hell was he planning? I tried to work tired, stiff muscles, thinking about the pain, thinking about what the game might be. I had to be strong enough. Whatever he had planned, I had to be strong enough.

There were heavy footsteps in the hall, the snap of a bolt, then the door crashed back with a tinny rattle of the shelving. Two flashlights flickered around the room, one found myself and the other settled on Kate. I squinted into the hallway, only shadows, but the voice belonged to Alex. 'You first, Cormac. Outside.'

I stood, this was it. Now was the time. I squeezed Kate's shoulder, but she made no response. I stepped into the hallway with the flashlight still in my face, my teeth clenched, emotions locked down tight. No fear. Show them no fear.

'Search him.'

I was pushed and spreadeagled against the wall. Hands swiftly traced every fold of cloth and flesh. I thought about them touching Kate and felt the first trace of anger emerge.

'Just a wallet and passport,' said another voice, the one that had hauled me out of the car, a pause, then, 'Fuck, there's thousands of US and Aussie dollars in here.'

'Leave it,' said Alex.

A grunt, dissension crackled in the air like static.

'Leave it, boss's orders. If he lives he gets to keep it, part of the game. If he dies the boss wants it found on the body, then we're going to spread some of that shit in the car around to make it look like a drug deal gone bad.'

'Waste of money and good dope if you ask me.'

'You want to take it up with Janac?'

Another guttural grunt, but the wallet was swiftly pushed back into my pocket. My hands were pulled down, I felt my watch stripped away, arms twisted behind my back, a rope bound them.

'So I'm not dead yet then, Alex,' I muttered grimly.

'Not yet. But I wouldn't put a cent on your odds.'

Before I could reply a hand grabbed the ropes and tugged backwards – hard. I yelped at the pain, as bones twisted up in their sockets, into places where they didn't belong. Then the hands pushed forward and down. There was a blow at the back of my knees and I crumpled.

'OK, now the girl.'

'Don't touch her,' I yelled, struggling to hold my balance. But a foot jabbed into the small of my back and pushed me over. My arms tugged at the bindings in a desperate but futile reflex. I crashed to the floor with shoulder and forehead, cursing at the twin shocks of pain. Then a knee pressed hard into my spine, I felt the gun barrel in the back of my neck.

'Shut up,' hissed Alex in my ear, 'I took a hell of a crack on the head to set you up, you fucking arsehole. And I can't tell you how disappointed I am the boss has his own plans for you. But if you don't behave and play the game properly this time, he might just let me sign your girlfriend up for our little stage show on the island. Maybe I'll do the job myself huh? Maybe I'll do it with this.' The gun jabbed harder into the back of my neck. 'How would you like that?'

The seed of anger crystallised and grew exponentially. I twisted hard and lashed out with both feet, but Alex was ready and all that connected was the pistol whip across my head. There was a starburst of perception, vision doubled, tripled, quadrupled. Hands grabbed me on both sides and pulled. My legs wouldn't respond and knees cracked and banged against the ground. A door opened to my left and light poured out. The brightness was dazzling. I shut my eyes and the world started to suck and twist, spinning into a vortex of glittering light. Consciousness slipped a little further out of reach. I struggled against the inviting blackness with eyes open but sightless, stumbled into something solid, a metallic thud. I turned and slid down against it, my hands were pulled in and lashed down hard, while the world slowly formed itself from the surreal kaleidoscope of colour and shape.

A brightly lit room emerged with bare walls, brown paintwork, a dirty grey carpet and a tangle of wires criss-crossing the floor. The room was 'L'-shaped, and I was tied to a radiator on one of the longer, outside walls. A masked figure stood in front of me, cradling an automatic weapon. And Kate was about thirty feet away, with Alex bent over her, securing her to a radiator on the connecting outside wall of the other arm of the 'L'. He glanced up at me and leered. The anger came alive again, 'You son of a bitch, you touch her . . .' I started to shout, pulling hard against the ropes.

'Enough!' The single word stopped me. My heart froze, stumbled on the next beat. I looked round, Janac stood a few feet away, just inside the door. The grey eyes moved away from me and towards Alex. 'Finished?' he said sharply.

Alex nodded, pulling away from Kate.

'Good. Now get out of here.'

The figure with the automatic was already going as Alex nodded again, turned and walked out past me. He glanced down and I watched his lips move silently, 'You're fucked.' The door shut on the three of us and an overpowering silence. I swallowed heavily, tried to wet dry lips, eyes drawn straight to Janac, who was pacing slowly across the room. He was carrying nothing, no gun, dressed respectably in chinos and a collared shirt. He stopped at the junction of the two shorter, inside walls of the arms of the 'L'. Both Kate and I, from our positions in each arm, could see him clearly.

'So, Martin,' he started slowly, 'and Kate, I believe.' He glanced at her momentarily, but she didn't respond. She was frozen, mesmerized. It was a hypnotic presence, emanating control. A power that commanded the silent, instant obedience of thugs like Alex. There was a half smile now, a crack in the thin lips. 'Did you really think I would let you cheat the game?'

Janac let the silence do the work. Failure, brutal ignominious failure crashed in on me. Humiliation overcame all other emotion. I had let him beat me. Now he threatened Kate. And there was nothing I could do. Powerless. I strained at the bindings and a deep roar of frustration built in my chest. It exploded out, a bellow of pain and anguish and hate. I pulled and tugged at the ropes that held me, kicked and lashed senselessly until finally the emotion exhausted itself.

And Janac just watched in an amused silence.

When I was quiet, he said, 'Kick and scream all you like, Martin.' He nodded towards the wall that Kate was tied to, and I followed his gaze, heart still pounding from the energy burned. There was a mattress jammed, by four planks, against the wall fifteen feet from her. 'You will see that we have taken precautions that no sound or light leaves this room. For an hour anyway. Not that there is anybody out there to hear it, this amusement park has been closed down for years.'

I guessed there was a window behind the mattress. I glanced around the room, I couldn't see any other way out. But I couldn't see either the wall opposite Kate, or the end wall of her arm of the 'L' – but the corresponding end wall in my arm contained the door we had entered though.

I shifted my attention to the mess of wires and cables. Now I noticed a grey box with a red button set in the top, right in front of me. There was a similar switch in front of Kate. At Janac's feet was a battery, and two clocks, one facing each of us. A garish yellow and green toy lorry was upside down on the floor, by the wall opposite me. And all the components of this apparatus were connected to each other by the spider's web of wires. But it wasn't the wires running from the lorry that jump-started the sweat on my face.

The lorry lay on its back, wheels in the air, with a cord fixed to the axle. The cord then ran up and over a hook, which was mounted in the wall opposite, and down to where it was fastened to the top of a tin. The tin was precariously wedged half-way on to a grenade. And I could see that the pin was out.

Janac was watching me carefully. 'Yes, that's the game, Martin. It's a good one too.' He lifted an eyebrow. 'You will recall that I told you the penalty for taking the drugs to the cops was death. Well, you tried to do just that and the minders should have carried out the judgement on you instantly. But they screwed it up and so you're still alive. Which is more than I can say for them.' His voice was so cold the chill touched my heart. I might have been better off dead. 'So, as I promised, now you must play another game.' He kicked a heel up and leant back against the corner, folded his arms lightly across his chest. 'And it has worked out rather well, as we have this delightful young lady involved.' He stripped Kate with the grey eyes, she didn't even blink. 'It took me a while to figure out how best to use her. You see I'm not quite sure about your relationship. She's with the guy on the boat. But I think you two go back a way as well. You took too big a chance asking her to contact Alex otherwise.' He waved a thin finger at us both. 'There's something there. Something between you. Old lovers perhaps?'

Despite myself, my arm muscles tensed against the rope and Janac smiled. I cursed myself for allowing the uncharacteristic reaction.

'As I thought. So unfortunately the Prisoner's Dilemma is no good to us. Too easy. You'd both cooperate.' He stroked his lower lip with a finger, before going on. 'At least, I think you'd cooperate, Martin, even you.' A whisper of a smile appeared on the hard face. 'I'll give you the benefit of the doubt, and assume so. And anyway, I have something just as good. It's called the Volunteer's Dilemma. It should really be played with a large group of people, none of whom can talk to each other. But I think with just the two of you, you can talk. And you will have plenty to talk about.'

'You will both see the charming little toy lorry, the grenade and the tin opposite you. Each apparatus is connected to the clocks.' He pointed a finger at them. 'After sixty minutes both clocks will complete a circuit to the battery here,' he tapped it with his left foot, 'and switch on the motors in the two lorries. The lorries will wind the cord on to the axle, pulling the two tins off the grenades, releasing the spoons and – boom. It looks a bit Heath Robinson I know, but I can assure you that it will work.' He smiled at me with a malice that meant it already had. 'The grenades will kill you both, obviously. The L2 grenade is fatal at up to five metres and you're only ten feet away from it. Your death will probably be instantaneous. Messy, but quick. However, there is a way out, for one of you. You both have a button.' I glanced at it, it was just within reach of my feet. A big red button. An apocalypse button.

Janac continued, 'That button will switch on your lorry, popping the tin off the grenade opposite you. Killing whoever hits their button first. But the other individual will have the pleasure of watching the show in relative safety. See,' and he pointed, 'with the grenade up against the wall the blast is directed outwards, sweeping everything in front of the wall with metal. But the shrapnel won't reach round the corner into the other section of the room,' he turned and moved a couple of paces towards Kate, 'to where you sit in safety. If, that is, Martin does the decent thing.'

He backed up, leant against the wall again and turned to me, 'And this is where the volunteer bit comes in. If either of you fires the grenade early, the dual switch in that box in front of you will disconnect the other lorry from the clock circuit. Making the other grenade harmless when the time is up. The survivor will then be released, after a twenty-four hour sojourn, whilst Alex and myself depart for more friendly shores. Of course they will have to explain to the police where they were during a brutal murder in a room full of cash and drugs. Especially since you, Martin, were seen by witnesses climbing into the van with Kate. But I'm sure that's not something you can't take care of with a little quick talking. And so that's the dilemma. Who commits suicide for the sake of the other?'

The empty, emotionless eyes flickered away, then settled on me again. 'You see, I said you might survive the next game, Martin, but at what cost? Well, Kate's the cost. Or have you the balls to take the original punishment that I promised and die like a man?' He crunched a fist into the other palm, and smiled. 'It's good, isn't it? And if neither of you has the guts to do it – you both die anyway.'

It came to me then: a torrent of relief – I could save her. But then came the violent shock of what it would cost. It would be my last act.

And it would also be Janac's. I hadn't lost yet. He was going with me. All the way to hell. I watched him push himself off the wall with his heel. He started moving towards the door, still talking, but I heard nothing. He would take the brunt of the blast if the tin popped off quickly enough. I might make it. I glanced at Kate, maybe the last time. She looked confused, something in my face, Janac would see it too. I had to do it, overcome the resistance. The instinct to survive. Heavy limbs that didn't want to move. A consciousness that didn't want to die. I glanced up, he was right there, opposite me. It had to be now. Now! I lashed out at the button. My foot came down hard with a crack.

But nothing. No winding of the motor. No explosion. No flash of light and death. No tearing of flesh, shards of steel and pain. I was still very much alive. Heart pounding, breath tumbling out in short, sharp jerks. Janac stood grinning down at me. Hands clasped in front of him, a teacher amused at a pupil's foolish error.

'You don't think I'm that stupid, do you, Martin? The circuit comes alive in another minute and thirty seconds. Exactly sixty minutes after that it closes. And you both die. Unless of course someone volunteers to pre-empt it. I'll guarantee the safety of the survivor. You have my word on that. It's the game, and the game is everything.' He strode the remaining feet across to the door. And turned, with one final smile, 'Goodbye, Martin. Don't let yourself down.'

The door swung open, I found some breath, 'You bastard, Janac, you come back in here and I'll take you with me, you son of a bitch!' I screamed at him, but the door clicked shut behind him.

I swallowed heavily, trying to get control. I'd just committed suicide. And now I had to find the strength to do it again. I started to shake uncontrollably. Adrenaline still flooded my body. Fight or flight. And I could do neither. I turned to Kate, she was staring at me wildly, straining at the ropes. Then I heard the click and looked up at the clock. The grenades were live. We had an hour to live.

15

I WATCHED THE second hand of the clock. Felt my pulse loud and heavy in my chest. Every tick of every second matched by two beats of my heart. And it was getting faster. Boom, boom, boom. Tick, tick, tick. Time and heartbeat. Racing towards the vanishing point quicker than I could count them. Slipping away, the moments dissolving . . .

Stop.

I hauled in a huge breath, balled fists, taut muscles. Then let it go, let it all go. Slowly, relax. Think about calmness. Think about being calm. Think about thinking clearly. There was time. Fifty-eight minutes. While there was any time left, there was time for action. There was time to do something. You need to be calm to think of that something. Something to do. Other than hit the big red button and blow yourself to hell.

'I don't believe you did that.' Kate's voice was almost unrecognisable, a strained, terrified whimper.

I turned to her. 'If anyone's going to die it's going to be me.' I said the words, thought about the button. Held on to my idea of calmness. It had to be dealt with. I had wanted her to live, well now I could make it happen. I had to get it under control. I concentrated on my breathing, got it steady. Good. But again Kate's voice snatched me back to the real world. 'I don't believe this. This is insane. You can't die. I don't want you to die.' The pitch was rising, she was close to hysterics. Disbelief. A lot of pain. Staring at the grenade opposite her.

'Kate, Kate. Kate!' I had to shout, break into the gathering momentum of her own panic. Her head snapped round to look at me. 'We have some time. I'm not going to hit the button till we're all out of time. Anything can happen. Take it easy, try and think. How tight are you tied?'

Her eyes were wide open, sweat was pouring off her face, hair matted and stuck to her cheeks. I could see her struggle with it.

Pulling back.

'Come on, Kate, stay with me,' I urged and finally she started to relax, still breathing hard and fast.

She stared into space for a moment. Then turned and said, 'It's too tight.'

'Did they search you? You have anything we can use? Anything sharp.'

She shook her head. 'No, that bastard was really thorough.'

The anger started to build again. But anger was only a whisper away from panic. I fought it back. Stay calm. Think. Maybe they were listening. Would they come in if they thought we could get loose? 'Katie, is there a door that end?'

'No.'

'OK, my door is the only way in here. And Janac knows what will happen if anyone walks through that. They can't touch us for,' I glanced at the clock, it tore at my heart, 'fifty-five minutes. We have that long to think of something.'

Like what? I worked at the ropes, but they were tight as hell, chafing skin off my wrists. Maybe the radiator pipe, but it was solid, no movement. I twisted to look at it. Perhaps there was something sharp on it I could move the rope towards. I was tied to a vertical pipe that entered the radiator at the top. But I couldn't move the bindings up the pipe, too much tension in the rope for it to slide. I felt around what I could reach with my hands. But it was all smooth, with kiddy-safe functionality. I swept the floor with my feet and legs, everywhere I could get to, maybe something metal, discarded, with an edge. Nothing. I told Kate to do the same. Watched her struggle, pull this way and that. Still nothing. And the clock ticked on. Fifty-one minutes.

I felt the panic building again. Dragged it back under control. Panic and you're finished. Only a cool head was going to think of the way out. And there had to be a way out. There just had to be. I stared at the button. The red button. Then I saw it. A hairline crack in the grey case. I must have damaged it when I smashed my foot down. And it was plastic. It would break. There would be pieces, pieces with an edge. Maybe metal inside. But the risk was huge. I wetted my lips. And thought about what could happen when I broke the case. But this was it, what I had to do. What were the options? I glanced at the clock. Fifty minutes. None. Get on with it.

I looked over at Kate, she was struggling hopelessly with the ropes. 'Kate.' She glanced up. I spoke quickly, quietly, 'Listen up. I'm going to do something scary. It's not what it looks like. If it works it might mean a way out. If it doesn't . . .' I hesitated, 'if it doesn't work, you have to know I never stopped loving you.'

She opened her mouth to speak.

'Shhhh. Don't say anything. Look away and keep quiet.' But I was dancing light-headed in the gaze of those blue eyes and I felt the old emotions start to rise. And the thoughts of loss and death made me hesitate; it was an insane idea. But it was the only idea. I stamped on every flickering flame of ordinary emotion. I had to be crazy. There was no time for feelings.

'Close your eyes, look away,' I said coldly.

Slowly, fear etched in her face, she did as she was told. I stared at the box. The edge above the crack was the place to aim for. I raised my foot. Focused on the edge. Miss it by half an inch and it would be the last thing I ever did. I steadied my breathing. And brought my heel down. There was a sharp crack. A stab of sensation in my foot, a millisecond of pure awareness. I was one single nerve, one single feeling – waiting to die.

'No, Martin! No!'

But there was no whir of the motor. No motion of the tin. No burst of fire and flame. I had minutes, not moments left. And the split in the case was opening. I came back down with a rush. Get on with it. I looked up at Kate.

'Jesus Christ, Martin!' She was staring at me, mouth agape.

'It's good. The pieces,' I hissed. I gritted my teeth and swallowed. It wasn't that good. I had to hit it harder, faster. But that meant less accuracy. I glanced up at the clock. Forty-eight minutes. Again the wash of panic. I steadied myself. Raised my foot and brought it down. Harder. And again. Harder still. There was a screech and splintering and my heart pounded at the bars of my rib cage.

But the toy lorry sat motionless. The grenade remained imprisoned. And now the box had split open along the fault line. The lid had sprung away intact. The button was screwed into the lid and it engaged with a switch fixed to the underside. Wires ran from the switch to a circuit board mounted in the top of the box. The confusion of cables that ran away across the floor to the other components were all connected to this board. The chances were that Janac had rigged it to go off if any of those wires were disconnected. I had to be very careful of the circuit board. The box itself was cracked and broken on three sides. And the circuit board had already taken some damage. I took a deep breath and shook away the sweat that was rolling into my eyes. That last hit had been too hard. I'd been lucky.

I kicked my shoes off and gingerly pushed with a toe at the one broken box edge that was not connected to the circuit board. The plastic was hard and brittle. That was good. The harder the better. I levered it away from the base, which was screwed to the floor. It gave suddenly and my foot slipped. 'Shit.' I cursed at the stab of pain. I had slashed my toe open. Hot, red blood oozed onto the floor. I looked up at Kate, grinning like a maniac. 'Something's sharp!'

I flicked the piece of plastic towards me. Dragging it closer with my bloody foot. In the box I could see the circuit board, switch and wiring more clearly now. There were a couple of metal brackets, other pieces that might have edges, if this wouldn't do it. But it would be dangerous trying to get them out. I wasn't going back to the circuit board unless I had to.

I pushed upwards against the bindings and dragged myself off the ground. Slid the plastic into position with my feet. When I lowered myself again I could grab it. It was wet and slippery with the blood. I felt round the edges for the sharpest one. The rope constricted the movement of my hands and fingers so severely it was difficult to manoeuvre the edge into position. Difficult to get a decent grip. To apply any pressure. There was only one section of the rope I could reach. I started to work the plastic across the strands. It was multi-plait, synthetic. I could feel the heat generated.

'Is it working?' whispered Kate.

'I don't know. Just wait. Be quiet.'

I kept rubbing. Sweat mingled with the blood. Poured off my face. Ran in rivers down my bare arms. Every muscle and nerve was focused in my thumb and fingers. Tension and pain building up my forearms and spreading across my chest.

I watched the clock tick down, gave it three minutes. I stopped, felt the rope anxiously with numb, slippery fingers. Something was happening. But not much. I felt the plastic, it was polished smooth, the edge gone completely. The plastic wasn't much harder than the rope. The heat and friction were doing most of the work. Forty minutes left. Difficult judgement. It would be real close. Go back

118

to the box or push on? I had spent minutes on this already. And that circuit board would punish any error. I felt the rope again. Could feel the pressure of time physically, pounding at my skull. No, there wasn't enough time. I had to find something else. I had to go back to the circuit board.

I leant forward as far as I could and peered at the wreckage. Two right-angled mountings on opposite sides of the box bolted the circuit board in place. I could see that the board was cracked around one of the bolt holes. I strained at the ropes for a better look, the crack didn't seem to run through the circuit anywhere. And the cheap, pressed metal mounting would have an edge, it would do the job. If I could separate it from the circuit board without tripping it and blowing myself to a bloody pulp. I steeled myself again. I had to get on with it, I was running out of time. I glanced up. Thirty-eight minutes.

I pushed my right toe into the bottom of the box, and worked it up under the circuit board next to the mounting, where I could support it. Then I pushed down on the top, outside edge with my left heel. It was strong. It didn't want to break. I stopped, what did they make this stuff out of? I had another look at it, there was some whitening of the board around the crack. It would break. It had to, there was no other way, another sharp blow was too dangerous. I started again. The bolt and the solder joints dug into bare flesh. I ignored the pain. Forced everything into it. Still it held. It wouldn't budge. I paused, gathered myself. Ignored the clock. And focused everything. The strength of desperation. The strength of ten men. I needed it now. The pain and fear started in my chest and exploded in a sudden frenzied scream to fill the room. 'Janac you bastard!!' And it gave way with a sharp crack. Instantly my gaze switched to the lorry.

Which sat, with its childish bright colours, in judgement on my every move. And again it decided on life. I let go a mountain of pent-up tension. That had to be the last time. I couldn't mess around with that box anymore. I put my head back, waiting for my lacerated feet to recover, sucking in air, sweat streaming. I blinked furiously, trying to clear my vision. And finally pushed my battered feet back into their shoes. But the clock wasn't waiting. No time-outs in this game. I had to ignore the pain. I sat up. The whole side of the box had come away from the base, with the precious metallic mounting holding a piece of the circuit board to it. I once again shuffled and slid to get it into my hands. Trying to stay calm, trying to work fast. I felt around my prize. I was right, the metal had a jagged, serated edge. The circuit board too, it was hard, the manufactured edge was clean, it might do some of the work. I snapped away the pcb, so easy now, working with fingers not toes, cleared the metal edge and started work. I looked up at the clock. Thirty-one minutes.

The metal had a tiny length of sharp edge. I could only make short movements across the rope, but I could feel the fibres separating under them. I looked over at Kate, who had watched this whole operation in silence.

'It's OK. It's working,' I said.

Her whole body had been on a rack of tension and now she sagged back against the radiator. She must have exercised a superhuman restraint not to talk and distract me during the last few minutes. But we weren't clear yet. I kept working and the clock kept ticking. Twenty-six minutes.

It was brutal work. Slow, painful, demanding of both body and mind. Numb fingers that slipped, wouldn't cooperate, couldn't be seen. Strange thoughts flickering on the edge of consciousness. Concentrate. But what happened if I ran out of time? Would the button work now? I looked at the shattered box. Jesus, that would be the final irony. I glanced over at Kate. Forced myself back, to concentrate on the work. Relax. Keep the fingers moving smoothly. Try not to tense up. Try not to make too long a cut, get the metal snagged – lose time. How much time? I allowed myself a glance at the clock. Fourteen minutes.

I could feel the progress though. Feel the rope thinning, feel the loose strands, feel the fibres gathering around my fingers. But it was hard. It hurt. Kate was watching anxiously. She could see the toll it was taking. Now she started to talk to me, a gentle whisper. Soft-spoken encouragement. You can do it, Martin. We're going to make it. We are going to make it. Both of us. But the muscles were burning. All the way up my arms. The ropes constricting movement, blood flow. Sweat making it almost impossible to grip. Vision distorting. Breath shallow. The short repetitive motion was cramping. I had to stop. I dropped the piece. Flexed my fingers desperately, trying to work them back to life. Slimy fingertips wiped ineffectively against sweat-soaked trousers. Useless. But I had to go on. I fumbled for the metal. Glanced at the clock. Six minutes.

The rope was thinner now, but not thin enough. I wasn't going to make it. And what if my button didn't work? I'd stop at a minute to go. Say goodbye. No. This had to work. But it was getting harder as the rope got thinner. Harder to get the edge up against the right strands. Harder to make the cutting stroke. Frustration building. Desperation bubbling. Panic rising. Pain with every movement. Everything soaked by sweat and blood from chafed wrists. Four minutes.

This was cutting it way too close. It wasn't going to happen. I could feel despair flooding me. Taking over. I was losing it. I couldn't work the metal against the final strands. Couldn't place the tiny edge in the right place. I flexed against it desperately. Every sinew straining for freedom, for life. But it held. Three minutes.

Then I remembered the circuit board. The longer edge. I dropped the metal and scrabbled desperately. There, I had it. I needed that focus now. Had to stay cool. Had to stand above it. Panic would kill me. Because I was all out of time. I pushed the stiff plastic edge up against the final strands. Tensed against it. Pushed with a tool that cut. It was working. Almost too easy. Why hadn't I thought of it before? Two minutes.

But the rope was giving. I could feel it opening strand by strand. And with a final surge of strength my arms exploded out of the bindings.

Freedom gave me the calm that I'd fought so hard for. I could see it clearly. I knew what I had to do. I was at Kate's side. 'Keep still.'

She froze.

'When I get you free, go to the mattress and pull away the planks. We're going out through the window behind it.' There had to be a window. I couldn't be wrong about that. 'Hold the mattress up against the window so no light escapes. Then count down the time for me, quietly.' I heaved on the final half turn that held her and she was loose, 'Go!'

Kate was up without a word, no questions, no panic. Carefully, high-stepping over the scramble of wires, I moved to the grenade that had been opposite Kate. I grabbed the base with my right hand so I had the spoon firmly clamped down. Then I pulled the tin clear, it came away frighteningly easily. The inside was greased. The grenade was slippery as hell. I could feel my pulse start to race. Don't drop it now. I wiped away the sweat from my forehead and glanced over, Kate had the planks clear and leaned her body against the mattress, watching the clock.

'Time?' I hissed.

'Minute fifteen,' she called softly.

I moved as quietly and cautiously as I could over to the other grenade. Tried to wipe my free left hand on my trousers.

'One minute,' came the calm voice.

No time left to be careful. Same routine as before, but one-handed, I grabbed the base of the grenade, held the spoon down and flicked the tin clear in one motion. It was every bit as well greased as the first.

'Fifty seconds.'

I turned and ran back towards the window. Noise wouldn't make any difference now. 'Pull the mattress away, towards the end wall,' I yelled, pointing. She started to move. There was the window with its protective mesh on the outside. We would need a grenade.

'Hey!' The voice was from the outside. It was a guard, attracted by the light from the window – like a moth to a flame. And then he appeared, an apparition in the frosted glass. I was going to kill a man. I jammed a grenade on to the windowsill and jumped back. Kate was ahead of me, almost at the corner. She fell to the floor. I dived and pulled the mattress over us. Swore viciously, almost lost the other grenade from a desperately slippery hand. And time ticked on, seconds. The delay was set long. That bastard Janac. Giving you plenty of time to think about it once you'd pressed the button.

The explosion was flat and short. But loud. My head was ringing as I threw off the mattress. With most of the shrapnel directed away from us by the window recess it had only been hit in a few places. And there the energy of the flying metal had been safely absorbed before it got through. Kate didn't need to be told what to do, she was already at the window, climbing carefully past broken wood and twisted metal. The guard had disappeared and she was half-way through it before it occurred to me that there might be others outside. But there were no shouts as she dropped down. Then I heard the clock tick over. Time's up. The door handle twisted as I pulled myself into the hole. I let the spoon go. There was a yell behind me. I jumped clear, lobbing the grenade back as I went. The shouts turned to panicked warning.

Kate was motionless, staring at her van, which had been outside the window. I had a millisecond snapshot, all the windows had been shattered, blood, flesh and shrapnel slashed and spattered the paintwork. But a deep, basic survival instinct forced me away, before my mind could register the rest. I had to ignore the carnage. We weren't going to be leaving in that, was my only conscious thought.

I grabbed Kate's arm and pulled her down and into the wall just as the second grenade went off. I felt the edge of the blast wave across my back. And then I was moving, dragging Kate with me. Kept us low and against the wall. The lights in the room had gone out with the explosion. We were in deep shadow. I heard shouts behind, but confused with screams of pain. We turned a corner and I stopped Kate. I looked back. There was no one following us. No one moving outside the building at all. Behind me Kate was throwing up. I turned. 'Are you all right?'

She was on her hands and knees, staring at the pool of her own vomit. She nodded slowly, shaking. Spat, blew her nose. 'Did you see him?' she croaked.

'No,' I said quickly, lying. 'Come on, we have to keep moving.' I helped her to her feet, trembling and dry retching. Then took her hand and led her cautiously but quickly across the fairground. Pain stabbing up from my battered feet with every step. We dodged from one boarded-up ride or stall to another. There were no sounds or signs of pursuit. I wondered who had been caught in the blast of the second grenade. I guessed it was a casualty that was preoccupying the pursuers and giving us a headstart. Maybe more than one. I didn't dare to hope that Janac was dead. The gate was in sight. One final, fifty-metre dog-leg and we slipped through the gap in the fence. There was a large brick building in front of us. Behind there was only darkness. No pursuit.

We ran down the side of the building and a park opened out in front of us, with the ramparts of the harbour bridge towering above. I held Kate back in the shadows until I had the chance to take one more look behind. Still quiet. Just the rumble of cars overhead and, somewhere, the distant whine of a siren. We left the cover and ran towards a huge stone pillar, one of the bridge supports. Ducked behind it and ran across the remaining open ground to a road beyond. We slowed to a walk as we made the tarmac, turned left and passed a collection of businesses typical of any surburb; off-licence, take-aways, newsagent and pub. I glanced down at my watch, not there, of course. But I noticed the chafing around my wrists and immediately started to feel the pain from them. I was already limping, trying to keep my weight off the worst of the cuts on my right foot. There was no one around, apart from the cars on the bridge hundreds of feet above us. But it wouldn't be long before the city started to stir. I took us a block back from the shops, then turned left and headed north.

I tried to think through our options, work out what came next, but my mind was a mush of emotional reaction to the close escape. I had seen what that grenade had done to the guard. It could have been me. And it had been me that killed him. My head was spinning with it all. And Kate too, hurrying along beside me, was silent, caught up in her own thoughts. My shirt was soaked with sweat, sticking to her back, the wetsuit top pulled down and flapping around her thighs. I realised she still had bare feet. I pulled up in a patch of shadow. I suddenly felt exhausted, every part of me hurt. 'Kate. We have to find somewhere to hide, figure out what to do, we can't go far without clothes and shoes for you.'

She nodded. 'The skiff club is just down here. Maybe my stuff is still on the grass.'

That would make life a lot simpler. 'OK, let's check it out.'

Kate led through a hilly maze of dark, quiet streets, lit mostly by the moon. I followed, unsure if she knew the way precisely or was just looking for something she recognised. I stopped often, watching and listening. But there were no sounds of pursuit or action. Finally there was a glimmer of light on water, glittering between the chimneys.

'Down here,' she said and turned into the blackness of an alley. We moved even more cautiously down the steep, broken pavement. Silent houses stood over the fences on either side, trees whispering quietly in the breeze. Kate stopped just short of the road, I pulled up beside her and looked across at a theatre.

'The club is just down there,' said Kate, pointing to her left, about to step out towards it.

I grabbed her and pulled her back. 'Wait!' I hissed fiercely in her ear. Something in me had picked it up and then I heard it – the grumble of a car engine in low revs. Its lights appeared, throwing our alley into even darker shadow. It was coming down the street towards us. We both shrank back, pushed under the foliage of an overhanging bush. The lights were close now, and then the car slid past. I caught a glimpse of a shadow inside, the glow of a cigarette.

The car continued, out of sight. Then I heard it pull up. The click of doors, quiet voices. Silence. I moved slightly, and Kate grabbed at me.

'It's OK. You move back up the alley. Wait for me at the top. Stay hidden,' I breathed into her ear. I felt her move off, then I crept down to the corner and edged one eye round it. No more than fifty yards away, Janac's taut skull and cropped hair was framed by the open car window. My instinct had been right. The cigarette flared brightly and glistened off what looked like blood on his hand. I pulled back, pulse and breath surging. He had been hit. But he wasn't dead. And now he'd want revenge. I heard footsteps, they stopped, more talk. I risked another look, a man I didn't recognise was at Janac's door. He exchanged a few words and then moved back into the shadows of the club park. Janac put out the cigarette between his fingers, dropped the butt on the road, and the car drove slowly off. I watched a last swirl of smoke climb neatly into the air for a moment, before the wind caught it and whipped it into shreds. I glanced up the alley, no sign of Kate. I slid back from the corner and worked my way quietly up to the top, body in the shadows, eyes behind me and fear dogging every step.

Kate's whisper made me start. She was hiding behind a wall. I told her what I had seen. 'We have to find somewhere to hide and quickly. Somewhere good that will be safe in daylight, but near some big, busy shops, we'll need food and clothes before we can do anything.'

She thought for a moment as I watched her face. Even in the darkness I could see the strain. And I could hear the fear and exhaustion in her voice when she said, 'North Sydney is just up the road from here. Plenty of shops there, and nearby there's the elevated main road running down to the bridge, underneath it is a park, maybe there's somewhere there.'

I nodded my agreement and Kate led off.

But progress was infinitely slower now. Janac might be round every corner, behind every wall. In each rumble of a car engine, in every imagined footstep. Nerves and senses pitched like tuned piano wire, we moved from one patch of shadow to the next. One at a time, so there was always someone watching and listening.

Instinct had saved us once, now I wanted to trust something more tangible. But it made for agonisingly slow progress. And the more that time ticked on, the more I became distracted by the pain. Physical and mental. I forced it down, concentrated on the movement, on the shadows and the silence, on Kate's signals. But it kept coming back. What the hell were we going to do?

It wasn't long before the sun was warming a glow in the eastern sky and I could feel and hear the city start to stir. Hazy light brought exposure and our visibility chilled me. We had to find cover, hide from the new day. Kate had brought us to the huge network of elevated carriageways that lead to the bridge. We had crossed below these roads earlier, further south, just after escaping the fair. It was here that we needed to go to ground. There were patches of open space, broken up by the pillars and earthworks that supported the highway. I stopped by a wildly overgrown bush of thick foliage that was packed in against a concrete support wall. Already there was a steady roar of traffic above us. This was waste ground, carelessly landscaped, surrounded by roads. There would be no pedestrians.

'This looks good. How far to the shops?'

'Not far.'

'In here.' I took a final, long look around. But could see no one. We weren't even visible from any of the slip roads or nearby buildings. It would be all right. I pushed into the undergrowth, trying to disturb it as little as possible. Kate slid in behind me, dusting our track with her hand. The bush was dense, resistant. Unseen leaves and branches jabbed my face, hands and bare torso in the darkness. But it opened up to a clear patch against the concrete wall which I slid down on to gratefully. The earth was damp and hard-packed. I could feel the traffic on the road through the vibrations in the concrete at my back. Kate slumped beside me, and I realised we were both totally exhausted.

I put an arm round her. I could feel her breathing, still much too fast. 'I think we'll be safe here for a while,' I said. 'We should try and sleep, get some rest. It'll make more sense after we get some rest.' I felt her hair against my chest as she nodded.

'Martin,' she hesitated, and pulled in against me a little tighter, 'thank you. For what you did back there. I'm sorry I was suspicious before. I was wrong about you.'

I squeezed her gently in reply. And wondered if she was right. It had been possible to do it for Kate. What if it had been someone else in that room with me, Scott for instance? What would I have done then?

16

THE HEAT WAS building quickly, even here in our damp, dark little hideaway. Cold wasn't a problem anymore, but water was. My head throbbed with dehydration, lips were dry and cracked, my mouth a desert. Every muscle was stiff and cramped, screaming out for replenishment. The wounds and bruises of the struggle to escape throbbed with a particular frenzy. I shifted my arm under Kate slightly, to try and revive the blood flow. She murmured something and settled into me more comfortably. I thought that she had slept. But I was wide awake and had been the whole time. Thinking about what she had said, thinking about how the hell we were going to deal with this. I felt drained of energy and emotion. The driving fear and tension had gone, only a dull anxiety remained.

'What do we do now?' said Kate quietly. I felt her weight lift off my chest as she sat up, let go a sigh.

'The first thing is, I go and get us some clothes and some food. We'll think a lot clearer after that, and once you're dressed we can move around without so much risk. The shops must be open by now ...'

'What about going to the police?' she interrupted.

I saw the dark lines of fatigue and worry under the red-rimmed eyes. Could she ever forgive me for getting her into this? Could I forgive myself? 'I don't think so. Certainly not if Alex really is a dirty cop. If he's just one of Janac's goons acting the part it might be worth the risk. But if he is a cop, we'd stand no chance. Janac would get straight to us ...' I saw the expression on her face, rubbed a worried hand at my temple. 'It's "us", you're involved now. He'll want you as much as me. I'm sorry,' I said. I turned away, stared up at the rumbling concrete that bore down on us.

'It's not your fault,' she said. 'You were trying to do the right thing, that's important. You made the right choice and I had to help you. This is how it's turned out. Janac's crazy, don't blame yourself.' I looked back at her and she almost managed a smile.

I leant forward and kissed her gently, on the lips, just once. 'Thank you,' I murmured. She didn't shy away. Things had changed. Were changing, slowly. But the danger seemed very distant with the two of us together, safely hidden away. I wondered if she would remain so generous with time, and a continuous background of fear. If I kept her safe, I thought. I have to keep her safe.

'So,' she said, after a moment of silence, 'do we know if Alex is a real cop or not?'

'You only ever talked to him?'

'Yes.'

'So he answered the phone? Did it sound like a police station? Any background noise – that kind of thing?'

Kate looked thoughtful. 'When I phoned him he answered straight away, I don't remember any background noise. The second time he called me, and it sounded like a mobile.'

'So, maybe he isn't, but . . .' I shook my head, it throbbed in my skull. 'It's too risky to go to the cops at the moment.'

'So? So what?' said Kate with a tiny hint of desperation.

'First thing is I'm going to get us some clothes and some food and water. Maybe I can get a paper, see if there is a report about last night. Two explosions, at least one murder – there ought to be.' I paused for a second; 'murder', I'd said it thoughtlessly. But it was me, the murderer. I felt little remorse. It had been him or us, simple as that. I continued, 'It might give us a clue about Alex. You rest up here. We'll talk about it when I get back.'

She nodded, settled against the concrete wall. 'OK.'

I sat up on my haunches. 'I'll need the shirt.'

She smiled. 'Oh yeah, sorry,' and she took my shirt off and slid the wetsuit back on.

I pulled it on with difficulty in the cramped space. I tried to smarten up a little as Kate gave me directions. When I was ready I looked at her – there was a risk involved in this trip, but I couldn't bring myself to acknowledge it. 'I'll whistle when I get back, so you know it's me.'

'Anything in particular?'

'Yeah, "Careless Whisper".'

She smiled, acknowledging a shared past. I remembered trying to persuade Kate to dance to it at the party we'd met at, while she dismissed it as sentimental junk. I turned quickly and slid out under the bush, a catch in my throat.

I watched from cover for a full minute before going out into the open – despite having heard no pedestrian movement in the hours of wakeful, worried vigil. There was still no one around, only empty scrubland and the ever-present roar of traffic. I found my way through the road system and picked up Kate's route. The streets grew busier quickly and before I'd gone half a mile there were shops, and people trying to hurry to work. But with the traffic jammed at endless queues for lights, everyone had the distant gaze of the trapped and preoccupied. I kept my head down, eye contact would only make recognition easier. I struggled not to limp, my right foot in particular hurt like hell. The chafing on my wrists had subsided, but it was still visible through my tan. I would buy a long-sleeved shirt. I glanced up occasionally to check the shops, looking for any sudden motion. Janac wouldn't have the personnel to sweep the whole city. I could get unlucky of course, but my biggest concern was the possibility that Alex could have the cops looking for us as well.

I found a department store, a grinning Garfield in the window. It was so early I had the place to myself. Bored assistants, nursing late nights and grudges against life, weren't interested in me. I gathered two full changes of clothes, jeans and shirts for both of us, plus training shoes for Kate. I added a cheap digital watch, sunglasses and baseball caps, picked up some white zinc sunblock and plasters. On the second floor I found a small backpack to put it all in, then made my way to the check-out. I paid cash.

I put the cap, shirt, watch and sunglasses on and moved to the next project. Food. I found a deli and ordered up six rounds of sandwiches. I glanced at the papers, no mention of the action in the headlines – but it was just as likely that any report had missed the paper's deadline. I picked one up, along with cans of soda and crisps, fruit and chocolate. A local FM station was blaring in the background, playing 'Careless Whisper'. I smiled at the coincidence. The music stopped for a news bulletin. I was only half listening, thinking about Kate, about the past, watching the girl expertly bag the sandwiches – then the words shot into the foreground.

'Suspects are being hunted in connection with a brutal, double cop-killing last night at Luna Park. The officers, who were working on a drug-related investigation, were found dead in the early hours of this morning, minutes after reports of twin explosions in the area. The police wish to talk to anyone who was in the Luna Park vicinity last night or early this morning, who thinks they may have seen or heard something that can help them. They are particularly interested in anyone who saw a light-blue van in the area. We have no more details at this stage, but hope to bring you them soon.'

The report went on, pounding through me. Double cop-killing. Alex was a cop, the others were cops. Janac would have the entire police force after our blood. Pictures. A manhunt. I felt a chill; shooting first, asking questions later. The whole damn country would be looking for us. The world tumbled in on me. I felt hollow, distant, I was drifting away.

'Sir!' the voice was sharp, insistent.

Something snapped and I turned. The sandwiches were ready. I could feel my cheeks burn.

'Fifteen dollars twenty.' The voice was impatient, there was movement behind me, a queue. I fumbled for the money, dumped twenty bucks on the counter, managed to get some control. Desperate to run, I waited for the change, managed a 'thank you'. Piled everything into the backpack. I felt every eye was on me as I left the shop.

I walked fast, straight back towards Kate, fearful of any glance in my direction. I scanned the street from under the baseball cap, behind the shades – looking for the cops, for any sign of recognition. Suspects they had said, no names – yet. But they had found the van, it wouldn't be long. I was into the no-man's land underneath the highways, and almost on the hiding place before I realised the stupidity of what I was doing. I swung away, paralleled the road above for a hundred metres. Slowed down, tried to make it look casual, ducked behind a tree and waited. I listened for a count of sixty before I stuck my head out. There was nobody, nothing. I moved off, looping round to backtrack and rejoin my earlier route. I found a slip road underpass, recognised some graffiti I had passed earlier. I slid into the dark shadow thrown by the bridge and waited again. Endless streams of cars, but no people, no watchers, no tail. Eventually, I made my way cautiously back to the hiding place. I sat outside the bush for a couple of minutes, softly whistling, before I was satisfied and pushed my way into the undergrowth.

I dumped the bag on the ground, suddenly aware of my painful hunger. I sat down beside Kate and handed out a sandwich and soda wordlessly. She tore into it every bit as feverishly as I did, and I waited until both of us had slowed before telling her what I had heard. She listened in silence, chewing until she finished the sandwich. She looked at me with what I found to be a surprising steadiness.

'So we're on our own, no police.'

'No way we can trust them. We've no idea how many men Janac has on the inside. I don't know if one of the dead men was Alex or not.' I picked up the paper. 'I fucking hope so,' I added bitterly, flicking through it. 'Maybe there's something in here, but they probably won't release any details until they've told the families. There were at least three or four of them last night, plus Janac. Maybe they were all cops. All working for him. They must have just left the whole bloody mess there, including the van, and called in the explosion as a disturbance. Who's the van rented to?'

'The boat.'

'So they'll go to Scott. He'll tell them you had the van and when he hears about the drug connection he'll guess that I was with you. And Janac said someone saw us leave the club together. The cops'll have our names as soon as they find Scott. Janac's boys will make sure we're the prime suspects.' I shook my head and swore loudly.

'Shhh,' whispered Kate.

'Sorry.' We were both still for a minute. But there was only the traffic. I saw it as I sat and listened. 'Here.' I flipped the page over to show her. In the late news, a couple of lines, the same story, less detail. I watched her read it. 'If he owns half the police force what the hell did he need me to smuggle this shit in for anyway. The whole fucking thing is just a game!' I hissed suddenly.

Kate looked at me. Neither of us needed to say it. Of course it is, Martin, I could hear the words in Janac's voice. Feel the fear pounding in my gut. I leaned back against the concrete wall. 'We have to disappear, evaporate. No other choices. We have to run and hide somewhere he can't find us. Which isn't going to be easy with every Tom, Dick and Harry in the country looking for a couple of cop-killers. Maybe if we could get out of Australia, we could go to the police in England and get help, but how?'

'The boat,' she said, a note of finality in her voice.

'The boat?' I sat up and looked at her.

'I've been thinking about it while you were gone. No other way.' She shrugged and pointed at the paper. 'This just makes it clearer. We have to get out and quickly. If we stay here they'll catch us eventually. Neither of us knows how to survive on the run, in a totally hostile environment with no one we can trust. We have to get out. Planes are a non-starter, the airports will be watched. Same problem with cruise ships. That leaves a boat, a small one that can cross oceans. It has to be a sailboat. One with people on it who believe in us, who'll take us without argument. There's no choice, it's obvious.'

'That's just the problem – it's obvious. They all know about you and Scott, they'll be watching the boat. And probably Scott as well, in case you go to him for help. So how do we talk to him and get on board unobserved? And even if we make it on without being seen, if the boat leaves shortly after we disappear it's still suspicious. And we sure as hell aren't going to be outrunning anyone with a sailboat.' My voice was heavy, I couldn't see it working, but I didn't have any other ideas.

'The boat's been scheduled to leave tomorrow for a week. Ask anyone on the dock, everybody knows,' Kate pointed out.

That was true. I nodded, 'OK, but Scott might change that plan when he hears about this. And we still have to assume they'll be watching him and the boat. The biggest problem is how do we talk to him and then get on-board unseen?'

She stared at me in silence for a couple of seconds. 'There is a chance. I think I know where we can find him tonight. He'll be up at the Cross with Ben, in the usual bar. Once they're inside, anybody watching him will be taking it easy, they won't be expecting us to know where to find him. So you go in there late on, some time after Scott and Ben arrive. And you could get to Ben, who doesn't know you, maybe give him a message telling Scott to call a number. I'll wait on the other end of the phone.'

I nodded slowly. 'Risky, but it might work. If he's there . . .'

'He'll be there. I know him. He'll go drinking tonight, after all this; me disappearing with you, the cops all over the place, murder suspects . . .' She managed an ironic smile, mixed with grim resignation. 'He'll go drinking tonight, like he always does when there's something he can't face head on.'

I nodded, another thought had occurred to me. 'OK, let's assume he is there, no downside if he isn't, we stand as much chance of getting caught in King's Cross as anywhere else. But there are still problems, the cops might have him down as a suspect, it is his van after all, and stop him leaving with the boat. Or he might have told everyone he's going to stay until it's sorted out, then when he changes his mind . . .'

'We have to take a chance on that, hope someone looked after him last night and can give him an alibi. Either way we have to talk to him to find out. And the boat has to leave sometime. Gold will put pressure on to make it happen on schedule.'

I looked at her dubiously. 'OK. If he's in the bar. If he hasn't been arrested. If he hasn't said the wrong thing . . .'

Kate cut in with a fierce, frightened voice, betraying the tension. 'It's the best chance we've got. I'm not going to be hunted like an animal, until they run us down and put us back in that room.'

I pulled up sharply, looked at her face, lined with a characteristic determination. She had set her mind on this. I put the next question as gently as possible, 'OK. Let's assume it all goes our way, he's in the bar and the boat is still leaving. How do we get on-board unsuspected?'

'A couple of surfboards, we find a quiet beach up north somewhere, paddle a half-mile offshore, Scott leaves the harbour, headed for Hong Kong and picks us up on the way past.'

'How would he find us?'

'Torches, radios.'

I sat back thoughtfully. 'That could work. There'd be no trace. No stolen dinghies, no contact with the boat till it's well offshore.'

'Exactly.'

She had it all figured out. Driven by the desire to get on the boat, back into a safe environment. Back into Scott's safe environment. 'Do you think Scott will help us?'

She nodded. 'Yes. He'll help us.'

'Both of us?'

She nodded again. 'Both of us.'

'He's not going to be happy that I got you involved in all this,' I said sombrely.

'I'll explain you had no choice and neither did I. He'll help us. If he hadn't been such a drunken arsehole I never would have been with you anyway.' She was firm, very sure of herself. But she could see that I wasn't convinced. 'He'll do whatever it takes, once he knows I haven't left him,' she added.

I nodded slowly. Those last words echoing. She hadn't left him.

She was going back to him, back to their boat. To escape the danger I'd got her into. I had to stay with her. I had to help, she obviously couldn't approach Scott or Ben in the bar herself. She still needed me. But I wasn't going to lose her, not that easily.

17

I PULLED THE baseball cap down a little tighter, crossed the street away from a dark and, I now saw, empty police car. Eyes casting about for the owners. Nothing. But over twelve hours had passed since I heard the radio news bulletin, twelve hours for the manhunt to progress. Did they have our names? Were our pictures on television, in the evening papers? It wasn't worth taking the chance of buying one to find out. So I moved through the streets of King's Cross without knowing how great the danger was. And the uncertainty, as much as the risk, played up and down my spine with an icy finger.

After waiting till dark, we had got this far uneventfully, using the train. There were a lot of people here, but these were tourists, party-goers, drunks. Out for a good time, they wouldn't be worrying about cop-killers. No, only the surveillance team assigned to Scott would be worried about that. I'd had all day, sitting and sweating in our hole, to think about this. Now I actually had to do it. I almost hoped that Kate was wrong, that he wasn't there.

But then what? If we stayed in Australia they would catch us. It was as simple as that. Every time we broke cover we were at risk. And the longer it went on, the worse it would get. They would pull out the photos from our visa applications and plaster them all over the media. And the more people that saw a picture of us, the more chance someone would remember our faces. Cop-killers. Drug-dealers. The ultimate threat to surburban security. The police would want us to be caught all right. And they wouldn't rest till they succeeded.

So I had to do this. And he had to be there. And the boat had to be leaving on schedule. The uncertainties had eaten at us all day. Sweating it out in silence. Realising there were no alternatives. Now Kate was waiting by a phone we had found a quarter of a mile north of the station, and I approached the bar. The phone's number was in a message from her to Scott, arranged inside a cigarette packet. I intended to give it to Ben. That was the plan, it was still the best idea we had.

Kate had described the place to me in some detail. I walked up past it once, quite quickly, sweaty palms pressed into my jeans' pockets. There was no obvious police presence. There appeared to be only the one entrance which was manned by a couple of bouncers. I crossed the road a hundred yards further up, then strolled back down towards it, studying it carefully. It was a biggish place, bracketed on either side by smaller shops. There was no one hanging around, watching the entrance. Maybe he wasn't here. I paced myself to tag on to the back of a large mixed group about fifty yards short of the door. I was almost in amongst them, happy, smiling faces. And no shouts, no yells. No one came after me. This was it. I was up to the door, ahead of the stragglers. Part of the crowd.

'Five dollars, mate,' said the bouncer, I nodded. 'Pay the girl.' And he waved me inside. I parted with the five bucks, the precious baseball cap still well down over my eyes, and moved in. It was dark and it was loud and crowded and it was perfect for the job. If they were here.

I moved towards the bar and queued patiently in the three-deep huddle. I glanced around, as naturally as I could, checking people, checking the space. The room was long and rectangular with one central oval bar, and a band at the far end away from the door. I couldn't see Scott. But nor could I see most of the room. I found myself at the front, with a jolt of panic at the sudden eye contact with the barman. Before I realised he was waiting for me to order. I got a beer and bailed out without incident. I started to work my way round the room.

I moved with infinite care, stopping every couple of feet to peer out from under the peak of the cap, take another sip, plot the way forward. The place was jammed solid; music, lights and voices pounding the brain in successive, relentless waves. I side-stepped a lurching drunk, still scanning the restless, shifting sea of faces. Each one registered, assessed for recognition or threat, discarded. I couldn't see Scott. My heart and head fought over the correct emotional response. Elation at the short-term escape, or despair at the long-term prospects – or lack of them. Elation was winning when I stalled mid-stride, felt beer slop on my hands.

Scott sat locked in deep discussion with a second man that fitted

Ben's description; leather skin, thinning bleached hair pulled back into a pony tail, paunchy, medium height. They were at a table near the band. Just like she said they would be. I watched them for a second, tingling with the knowledge the surveillance could be only yards away. I took a big pull at the beer. They were in full view of eighty per cent of the room. I doubled back slowly and went round the other side of the bar, away from the door. I worked my way along the side wall until I found a free seat at a table, about half-way down. From here I could see them and most of the rest of the room. I needed some time to spot anybody watching them.

I sat back and waited. The hunted, hunting the hunters for once. But the tension in my neck was making me only too aware that a single tiny error would reverse the roles again. The beer was helping. I shifted the cap to clear a bead of sweat, struggled to drink slowly. I didn't want to face the barman again. A couple of songs went by, pretty average covers of blues numbers, but plenty of people were dancing. I couldn't see anyone else on their own, most were at least couples, or groups of three or four. Those few individuals that were around kept moving, cruising, in and out of the shadows, looking for prey. No one was paying Scott any particular attention. Kate had been right. It was safe, as safe as it would ever be.

It wasn't long before I got my chance. Ben finished his drink with a flourish and headed towards the bar. I watched him go, swallowed mine back heavily. This was it. Get it over with. One way or the other. I stood up and started out towards him. Trying to move smoothly round tables, past people, and not to focus too much on him. I pulled the carefully prepared packet of cigarettes out of my pocket. Tapped one out and paused to light it. Watching him, letting him get ahead. He stopped to wait for a girl carrying drinks to cross his path. Then he shouldered his way into the crowd.

I took a couple of breaths and stepped closer, empty glass in one hand, cigarettes in the other. Head down. I took a soothing drag. Time ticked away. I jostled for position, studied the mock brasses. Checked the faces, no one interested in anything other than the next drink. He was second row, I pushed up beside him. We were deep in the middle of the crowd, I'd never get a better chance.

'Cigarette?' I said, as casually as my trembling body would allow, holding the pack low, at waist height.

He looked at me, curiously, as you would. The balding pate and forehead wrinkled slightly. He shook his head. 'Don't smoke,' he said in a soft accent – South African, definitely Ben.

I pushed the packet further up, under his nose, the rolled message sticking out invitingly, my hand shaking. 'Please,' I said, in a voice that was a lot more desperate that I intended. I saw him tense, thought he was about to tell me to piss off, or hit me, when he glanced momentarily at the pack. Kate had written on the inside of the lid, 'Take it! Kate.'

I saw his eyes widen.

'Don't say a word, read it where no one can see you, take a smoke as well,' I hissed, through a fixed expression of nonchalance.

He stared at me, bewildered, but he was cooperating mechanically. He pulled out the note and a cigarette, palmed the note neatly into his pocket. I lit the cigarette with mine, a steadier hand now, and for a second our eyes met. And I saw the light of comprehension start to burn. He nodded his head a fraction, then turned away. I let the jostling bar queue work me backwards, shoving forward in front of me readily enough. The critical moment passed. No crash of tables and chairs as the trap snapped shut. It was done. Now I had to get the hell out of there. I pulled the peak down and shuffled through the crowd. Trying to sway a little and look drunk. I stepped outside, the fresh air hit me. I sucked it back, still tensed, ready to run.

I checked up and down the street and started off in the opposite direction to the station and the phone. I needed to see if I was being followed. There was half an hour before I had to meet Kate. I made my way through the back alleys and bars of the Cross. The tension slowly unwinding in my muscles. I couldn't believe I'd got away with it. Maybe I hadn't. I forced myself back to the job, checking for a tail. There were all sorts on the streets. Punks, preppies, skinheads, bikers, drop-outs, tourists of every national flavour, and all ceaselessly moving around. It seemed hardly possible that there was anyone in the bars there were so many people on the street. I stopped occasionally at a shop or restaurant window, spinning round quickly to see if I could spot a tail. Like before, if there was anyone behind me, they were a lot better at this than I was. Which was possible, but finally I convinced myself I was clean. It was time to get back to Kate and find out if it had been worth the risk.

She was where I'd left her, sitting in the shadow of a wall by the phone. 'Did he call?'

'Yes.' She looked up, smiled, but there was a trace of concern in her eyes.

'Well?' I said urgently.

'It's going to work.' She didn't seem particularly elated though.

'Thank God for that. Let's go, Kate.' I reached out my hand. 'It was all right after he got the message? They didn't draw any attention to themselves?'

She pulled herself to her feet with my help. 'I don't think so. Ben figured out the deal.'

I nodded, indicated down towards the station. 'Let's keep moving, get out of here.' She started to walk. 'So what did he say?'

She stared down at her feet as she spoke, 'We got lucky. He went back to Josh's place with Ben last night. They were drinking till five in the morning, slept there, woke up at lunchtime and didn't get back to the hotel till mid-afternoon. He missed the eleven o'clock meeting with the sponsors.' She shook her head, still staring down. I glanced away to check the street. The station was on the other side, we needed to cross the road.

'When he finally got back,' she continued, 'everyone was waiting. You can imagine, the police wanted to grill him then and there, Rollen's still wanted to talk to him – though God knows why after everything that's happened. And on top of it all he was hungover. He told the police we had the van before he realised what it was all about. Janac was right – someone saw you leave the club in the van with me. When Scott found out he went and got completely trashed.' She hesitated again, glanced up at me, the concern was back.

'So they have our names,' I said, neutrally. I could hardly blame Scott.

'And a description. From Scott. But no pictures,' she added.

'They can get those from our visa applications. It's just a matter of time.' I looked at Kate, the long blonde hair hidden under the cap. Pulled my own down tighter in a reflex, as a well-dressed, middle-aged man strode past us close by.

When he was gone Kate continued, 'He told the cops where he was last night, and that he knew nothing about what happened with the van. And he couldn't answer any more questions because he had to go to a meeting. Ben was there to back him up and so there wasn't much the police could do. They went off to check his story with Josh, told him they'd be back, but it should put him in the clear.' She sighed. 'Then he went and saw the Rollen's people, but they just wanted to tell him that Duval had got the deal. After that he came straight down here with Ben. He told me he wanted to avoid the police till they figured out what was going on.' She snorted with disgust. 'More like he wanted to avoid sobering up, in case he figured out what was going on.'

'But that's perfect. You told him the right story to give them tomorrow?' I cut in.

She nodded. 'Far as the police and everyone else is concerned we're through and I can go to hell. He's out of here. Bound for Hong Kong, leaving on schedule.'

I wish, I thought, but I said, 'Then we're clear, it'll work.'

'Yes,' said Kate. 'But . . .'

'But what? What's wrong? He will do it?'

'Of course he'll do it.' She paused as we stopped at the kerb, waiting for a break in the traffic. 'But he's suspicious of you. Like you said, angry with you for getting me involved.' I grunted. 'And he wanted to know why I left the club with you both times.'

'What did you tell him?'

'To shut up and listen, he was drunk and deserved it and anyway this was more important than his petty jealousies. But, Martin, if, when, we get on the boat, you must remember – I'm still his girlfriend. OK?'

I felt the hairs on the back of my neck prickle as I stepped out to cross the road.

'Martin?'

I could feel her eyes on me, as she followed. I stared resolutely ahead. But I had no choice. 'OK,' I said tightly, glancing at her, then quickly, 'what else did he say?'

She was as keen to shift the topic as I was. 'He liked the plan, but he had a better spot, North Narrabeen beach, right at the top end. There's a lake there and a little river provides a good rip current that will sweep us out through the break. They'll be there at midnight. He'll wait about half a mile offshore, closer if he can get in, he didn't know the depth around there.'

'Not too close, we don't want to attract any attention.'

'It'll be OK, it's a quiet beach, especially at night. We need a torch and a radio. A handheld VHF, they'll be listening on channel 71. We'll be Danny Boy. If we see the boat to the north of us, and the coast is pretty much north/south there, we must call on the radio for Northern Lights, if the boat is to the south we call for Southern Cross. If they're offshore we say "Come in Southern Cross, Come in Southern Cross." If the boat is inshore of us, we just call "Southern Cross, Southern Cross, this is Danny Boy." They won't talk to us unless they're having real trouble finding us.'

'He's got it all worked out.'

'Yes, he's pretty good at organising. The other thing he said was that once we get out beyond the headland there's anything up to two knots of current going south down the coast. We've had a couple of days of the seabreeze weather so the current'll be running tomorrow night for sure. We must stay on the beach until we see the boat lights. They'll be motoring up the coast slowly. The forecast is for this weather pattern to last another day or two before there's a southerly change. So it should be calm wind-wise tomorrow night. But there's quite a swell running from a big storm out in the Pacific.'

'Oh great,' I said, unenthusiastically.

'You'll be OK, Martin. He said we should have a practice in daylight and remember not to panic.'

'Thanks. So where is this North Narrabeen?'

'That's the bad news. It's miles up the coast.'

'Well, how do we get there?'

'Get the ferry to Manly and start walking.'

'Jeez. How far?'

She checked her watch. 'We've got twenty-eight hours.'

I sighed heavily. 'So we need Circular Quay again then, right?'

We were walking into the station now.

'Yeah, that's right.'

We were silent until we got on the ferry and managed to find a spot by ourselves. It was quite cold out on the water, and I wondered what it would be like tomorrow night, in the damn ocean. 'We haven't really got twenty-eight hours though, have we?' I started. 'We've got to get the boards, torches and radios, for instance.'

Kate shuffled in closer to me, perhaps to keep warm. 'Uhuh, we pass through a few shopping places on the way, we should be able to buy everything we need.'

Instinctively I checked for my wallet, it was still there. The irony of using Janac's ten thousand dollars to fund our escape from him had not escaped me. Nor, I'm sure, had it escaped him. Especially after he had let me keep it. Then it occurred to me that those things wouldn't be that easy to buy, you needed specialist shops for VHF radios and surfboards. I said so.

'Well, we could steal them,' she said.

I was surprised, but what difference did a couple of stolen radios make? People were dying in this thing. But stolen radios and surfboards might be reported to the police, and someone might put two and two together. Better to buy them. Even then there was the chance of being recognised. But we should take the short-term risk, rather than leave clues behind as to our escape. If we were recognised at least we could run, discard the plan. Whereas once we were on the boat we were committed. If Janac figured it out after we were on-board, we were history. I said as much to Kate and she nodded. We settled back in silence.

Despite it all, it was good to have her with me. It made a difference. We had slipped back into the comfortable, easy-going relationship of four, five years ago. The best days. Perhaps that was what had provoked Kate's warning – guilt.

18

I GLANCED AT my watch, 12.15 a.m. and no sign of them. Still, boats weren't like buses, and those weren't usually on time either. It was cold tonight, out here by the ocean. Even without any wind, and we weren't in the water yet. Kate had got a full wetsuit, but the shop had only had a shortie that would fit me, no arms and no legs. It was all I was wearing. I had buried the rest of our clothes and gear as soon as it got dark enough to do it safely. It was an isolated stretch of beach, and I was happy that it wouldn't be found. I shivered involuntarily.

'You OK?' Kate lay beside me on the sand, and had felt the shudder.

'Yeah, just a little nippy, but I'll be OK.'

The moon appeared briefly from behind a cloud, lighting up the surfline crashing on to the beach a few hundred yards from our hiding place. It had been a difficult twenty-four hours.

The walk had been a nightmare. Even with the protection of the plasters and socks I had bought, my cut feet had deteriorated badly. We had stumbled on till daylight, totally exhausted. When the sun peered gloomily over a horizon as cloudy as the situation, we were still a couple of miles short of the goal. And we had neither radio, torch nor surfboards for tonight. Then we got lucky. We walked past a marina just after dawn. Leaving Kate on lookout on the road, I'd broken into four boats before finding everything I was looking for. I guess handheld VHFs in waterproof bags are the kind of thing most sensible boat owners take home with them. The fourth had been too stupid or too lazy – everyone had a torch. I'd had to take a pile of other junk from all of them as well – to make it look like your normal, everyday, marine ransacking. All the other stuff had then been dumped in Narrabeen Lakes. I didn't feel good about it.

We'd got to the beach just after nine and there had been a lot of surfers out already, it was a good day then. There was no wind, and the glassy waves were providing long rides. We trudged on until we reached the rocky headland at the northern end that Scott had described. We'd found a spot up in the grass at the back of the beach and slept till lunchtime. It had been the wind that had woken me, and when I rolled over to check out the water I could see nearly everybody had gone. The onshore breeze was blowing the tops off the waves. Even I could tell the surf was nowhere near as good.

Kate had still been asleep, blonde hair strewn over the sand. I left her in peace, and sat and watched the waves and those few surfers who were left. It didn't take long to see what Scott had been talking about. Everyone new into the water or riding all the way to the beach walked out at the river mouth, in an area of flat water, and scarcely needed to paddle before they were shot past the break by the outflow. I looked again at the point in the moonlight. I had been over it in my mind so many times I was sure I could do it in my sleep. Which was good, because I was probably going to have to.

I stifled a yawn and checked my watch again, twelve thirty-five. They were late now, no question. Something must have happened. There was no wind out there. Maybe engine trouble. Maybe cop trouble. I gripped the radio and stared at it. I had no idea how much battery power was left. I hated to use it before we needed it.

'They're late,' I whispered hoarsely to Kate.

'I know,' she muttered.

'Have they got enough people to handle the boat?' I said.

She looked at me. 'I hadn't thought about that.'

'What?'

'There's only three of them, Scott, Duval and the first mate Ben. They'll be relying on us for the rest of the manpower.'

'So you think they're having a problem handling the boat?'

'No, no, three's plenty just to get it off the dock and motor up here, but it isn't many to go all the way to Hong Kong with.'

'I see what you mean, it looks suspicious.'

Kate nodded. 'A little.'

I stared out into the darkness of the ocean. 'There's nothing we can do about it now,' I said. Then after a silence, 'Why is Duval coming? I wouldn't have thought he and Scott would want to be stuck on a boat together.'

'He's the only other person on the payroll, apart from Scott,

Ben and myself. The brewery won't part with any money they don't have to, so extra delivery crew were out of the question. We didn't have any choice.'

'They're going to be fun together after all this sponsorship hassle.'

'Yeah, we might have got someone to do it for free, but there was no time to get it sorted with Scott moving the departure forward.'

I grunted an acknowledgement. It was lucky for us he had.

I wasn't going to worry about it, there were too many other things to worry about. The boards had been a problem. We'd finally had to bite the bullet on that and go and buy them. There was a surf shop a mile or so from here, back in Narrabeen itself. It was one of those places run by an enthusiast, it just reeked of the sport. Old posters and broken boards competed for space with the glistening new models and the dayglo displays of accessories. It had been no fun being out in the open in daylight, with no idea of how well publicised and widespread the search had become. But the sunglasses and caps had done the job and we'd had no trouble.

We had gone in one at a time, an hour apart. Kate had been first since I considered that less risky for her, and came back with a lurid short board and wetsuit. Then it was my turn. The salesman had been helpful. Although he had baffled me for a while with arcane talk of soft rails, moderate rocker and lots of volume in the nose, once I'd explained I only wanted something I could just have a go on, he had dug out a huge second-hand board from the back room. It was ten foot if it was an inch. It was a semi-trailer to the Ferraris that decorated the shop. I must have looked dubious, but he explained that this thing would keep me afloat, whereas the short boards would sink under my weight. That sounded good to me. It had belonged to some old timer who just wanted to see it go to a good home. That seemed like a good omen too, and I had paid out the hundred bucks he had asked.

When I got back to the beach Kate had ribbed me mercilessly about my learner's truck. It was all very well for her to gloat, she'd done this before. She might scoff but it was certainly a fine piece of work, the grain of the wood gloriously brought out by the varnish. It was so different from the gaudy short-boards. I had already fallen for it. This was my passport out of here.

I stared back out to sea. With no moon all I could see of the ocean was the phosphorescence of breaking surf. And I could hear it. There was a big swell. I remembered Scott's words about practising and wished I'd taken the advice. But after the surf shop we had just wanted to hide up. Too much exposure in the harsh light of day. Especially as it meant losing the cap and the shades to get in the water. No, the idea of getting picked up while grabbing a few practice waves had been too scary. The downside was that I now had no idea what I was in for. Kate was a pretty good surfer and we'd gone through the basics of paddling through the break. But I had a feeling that talking about it and watching wasn't going to be the same as doing.

If the boat turned up. I glanced at my watch again, quarter to one, where the hell were they? I scanned the non-existent horizon, there was nothing out there but blackness. Forty-five minutes, what could hold them up for forty-five minutes? I looked at the radio. They were not supposed to talk to us unless something went wrong. Had something gone wrong? I clicked the switch, and dialled into channel 71. There was nothing but hissing. I tried a couple of the buttons and found that the one called squelch seemed to suppress the noise. Now there was just silence.

'What are you doing?' whispered Kate.

'I thought we'd better listen on 71 in case they've got problems and they're trying to talk to us.'

She nodded in agreement, 'Good idea.'

I listened to the silence as the minutes ticked away. Maybe they were out there and their lights had failed. No, they would at least have torches. Maybe the cops had forced them to stay. Or spent hours searching the boat. But if that was the case they were still under serious suspicion. Or someone had pulled strings inside the police. I tapped at the radio restlessly. And finally gave in, I clicked the transmit button down, 'Southern Cross, Southern Cross. Do you read me, over.'

'They're not supposed to talk to us!' hissed Kate.

'Shhh.' I turned the volume up as loud as I dared and the squelch down as low. I listened intently to the crackle of static for another couple of minutes. Nothing. I switched the radio off.

'Nothing has gone wrong, Martin. Just be patient,' muttered Kate, staring out to sea. I felt her go tense before I heard the words, 'There, a light, I see them!'

I stared out into the blackness, following her arm.

There it was. A light. I was sure I saw a light. There, again, it topped a wave. The tiniest glimmer. It was still a way off, or maybe it wasn't. I had no idea of distance out there, it was impossible to tell. 'How far do you think?' I asked Kate urgently.

'Maybe a mile out. We should go.'

I eased up to a crouch. 'Here, you take the radio,' I said. 'Tuck it in the wetsuit, it'll be safe there till we need it.' I watched Kate slide her torch in with it, and then helped her with the zip. She already had my wallet and passport in a plastic bag. I stuck my torch in the shoulder strap of the wetsuit. I had a good look around, this was the high-risk part, getting in the water. Suspicious as hell, a couple surfing at night. Nothing stirred, not even the grass. No moonlight romancers. I strapped the leg rope on and picked up the board. It wasn't light that was for sure.

'Let's go,' I said, voice cracking a little with nerves.

Kate led out from the dunes and headed down towards the ocean. Hefting the weight under my arm, and with a final look around to see if she had attracted any attention, I started to trot down the incline after her. Almost immediately the leg-rope got tangled round my feet and I tumbled forward, stifling a curse. I bounced to a stop with a mouthful of sand and the board on my head. I struggled to a sitting position.

Kate was beside me 'You OK?'

'Yeah.'

'You're supposed to put the leg rope on after you get to the water,' she muttered.

'Shhh.' I pulled her down flat onto the sand, 'Don't move.' We lay still for a couple of minutes, but it seemed that no one had noticed. There was no one to notice.

'Happy now?' asked Kate, finally.

'Yeah, OK, let's get it over with.'

I pulled the Velcro strap off my leg, coiled it in my left hand, picked up the board with my right and tried again. This time I did at least reach the sea safely. I reattached the leg-rope and waded out until I was waist deep. Kate was about ten yards away to my left. I watched her push the board forward, jump on and start paddling, looked easy enough. Maybe I should be a bit more over that way though. But it was hard to tell in the darkness.

I didn't see the wave, not until it broke into white water. Then, a hiss, a wall of foam, over my head! There was no time to do anything. I stayed on my feet, for a moment, then they were sucked from underneath me as firm sand became slurry. I crashed into the water and was immediately dumped on by another wave. The board had gone from my arm and I thrashed around looking for it. There was a jerk on my leg as the board surfed inshore without me and was brought up by the leg-rope.

I was spluttering, choking. I couldn't find the beach under my feet. Everytime I came up another wave crashed on my head. Everything was salt water and sand. The board tugging at my leg like an anxious puppy on a lead. Finally I managed a breathing space and looked over my shoulder – only to see the mother of all waves creaming towards me. I started stroking frantically, I could feel myself rise on the face of the wave, but I just paddled like hell regardless. Suddenly I was surging forward, seemingly weightless in a mound of frothing water. The beach rushed towards me and I just held my breath and hoped, a surge of adrenaline coming with the speed and motion. The wave expended itself with a crash and threw me nose-first into the sand. I grabbed at the beach desperately as it slipped through my fingers. The leg-rope was slack then came up taut again as this time the board was washed back offshore. I could already feel the backwash trying to suck me back out. But somehow I managed to find my feet and I threw myself up the beach, clear of the water. I dragged the board towards me on the leg-rope and finally it was all quiet.

I collapsed back on the sand. What a disaster. Surely someone must have seen me. I couldn't get caught now, not like this. I had to get back out there. No more screw-ups. I must have drifted too far to the right, in the main break. I needed to go further into the river. Breathing heavily and still blowing water from nose and mouth I sat up and looked around. Where the hell was Kate? There was no sign of her. And she had the radio. The thought made me reach for the torch. Gone. A cold chill blew over me, this wasn't good, I had to get out there. I got back on my feet and picked up the board. No sound from the beach, I heard a car move past on the road, but it was hidden by the dunes. This time I walked into the middle of the river before trying to move offshore. The bottom was much rockier here and I slipped painfully on my damaged feet as I tried to pick my way forward in the dark. There was a much more gentle rise and fall of the swell, I could hear the break out to my right. I was waist-deep now, pushing the board with my hand. It all seemed calm and gentle compared to the previous occasion. I stood still and looked and listened carefully.

Ahead of me the point poked out. Still no sign of Kate. I could feel the water washing seawards around my waist. This was the place. I pushed the board forward, leapt on and started to paddle. The first few strokes were placid enough, then I could feel the board start to rise underneath me. It wobbled and I stopped paddling to hang on. Immediately it started to spin and I could feel the next wave lifting the board at an angle. I stroked strongly on the right side to straighten up. And dropped down the back of the wave in reasonable shape. This wasn't too bad. I took another couple of waves before snatching a quick look around. It was so damn dark.

I was already a long way out from the beach and I seemed to have been swept south too, as I was a lot further out from the point now. I must be beyond the break, I could see the white tops curling away inshore off to my right, but here there only appeared to be the gentler rise and fall of the swell. I looked forward again as the nose started to rise. This was a bigger one, much bigger. The board seemed to be climbing for ever before it finally pushed through the crest and dropped heavily into the trough behind it. I clung desperately as the board fell and slammed into the back of the wave. There had been white water there, it was close to breaking. I started to paddle quickly, trying to move offshore, past the break. The next one was bigger still. But I almost had the technique, paddle fast into them then just at the top, as the board goes light under you, grab hold and hang on for the ride down the back. But as we topped this one the moon once again popped out the back of a cloud and I saw the wave from hell.

Twenty yards away and it was much, much bigger. Already a jagged comb of white water was snapping at the top. If that broke before I got to it, it would carry me all the way back inshore. I paddled harder, tearing at unfamiliar muscles, the memory of being caught in the impact zone all too recent. The board flew as I sliced towards the break. I struggled to keep my position, willing the heavy board towards the wave. The nose started to rise. I daren't look up but it already seemed darker, the bloody thing must be curling right over me.

Still I was going up, the board was almost vertical. I was going over backwards! I started to slide off the board and I grabbed frantically at the nose. I had to push that over the top. The darkness turned to white and for an instant I thought I was gone. My heart missed a beat. I'd be ripped and shredded as I was launched back towards the beach. Then I was through it. Flying down the other side in the enormous trough. I looked up, did it have a bigger brother? But there was nothing, almost flat water. I could hear the crash and roar as the monster thundered inshore, taking all the energy of ten waves with it.

This flat spot was my chance, and I paddled as hard as I could to get offshore. If I was outside the impact zone of that thing, I would be completely safe in another couple of hundred yards. I counted to sixty and paddled like hell. Breathing fast by forty, it was a struggle just to keep going for the full count. The waves now were big, but they were a long, unbroken swell. I could enjoy the rise and fall as I dipped over them. At the count of sixty I thankfully sat upright to take my bearings. The board was stable and I had plenty of time to look around. I was a long way out. All I could see of the beach were the streetlights on the road behind it. Even the headland, which had been so close, was lost in the night. But much more importantly where were Kate and the boat? I scanned the darkness. An eighty-foot boat with lights wouldn't be easy to spot from the board in these waves. I stood no chance of finding Kate. Was she all right? She could look after herself, I reasoned, she was the one with the surfing experience. Kate would be all right, she had the radio and the torch. They would find her. Maybe they had already found her.

I watched anxiously for what seemed like an eternity. A profound sense of loneliness overcame me. I started to shake like a leaf from cold and emotional reaction. It was a big ocean and I was out here on my own. I couldn't go back in and I couldn't call for help. I tried not to think about sharks. Waves of panic tumbled over me – maybe Scott had found Kate and gone without me. She had said he was suspicious. He wouldn't have believed his luck when he found Kate alone – he'd have picked her up and left me.

No.

It wasn't like that, Kate wouldn't let him. She loved me, I was sure she did. She wouldn't leave without me. She would make Scott search this ocean to eternity to find me. Please, let it be so. I was on the edge, exhaustion, emotional stress and just plain fear – all were slowly levering me over into the abyss.

I slid up the face of another wave. A red light. It was them. Lost again in the swell now but I was sure it was them.

'HEY!!!'

I screamed at the top of my lungs. A frighteningly high pitched, fear-laced sound came out. I leant forward into the prone position and started to paddle. Stroke, stroke, forcing tired arms, stiff and cramped with cold, to work. Paddle like hell, Martin. I counted to thirty. Slid upright even as the board glided over another wave. There they were, but a white light, a stern light, they were going the wrong way, they were leaving.

'HERE, OVER HERE!!'

It was a better sound, deeper, controlled, it would carry further. I pushed back down on to the board and started to paddle again. Muscles searing, I forced myself to count to sixty this time, I had to get closer so they could hear me. They were looking for a torch not listening for a voice. The engine would be on, Christ they'd never hear me. I forced myself harder. It doesn't matter if it hurts. If not now, then when? If not now, then when? I repeated my college training litany over and over. Losing count. Ten more strokes. Choking with the pain. I took a faceful of water and swallowed some.

I let myself slide upright, wheezing and coughing, spitting out the water, trying to get the breath together to shout. I managed a blurry look, tried to wipe the salt from my eyes. It was another couple of seconds before I could see anything. A wave moved under me and I stared at the suddenly revealed horizon. A red and white light this time. It didn't make sense. The white disappeared and the red switched to green even while I watched. I slid back down into the trough. They were manoeuvring, that's all I needed to know. They were still looking and they were closer. I bellowed off another 'over here' and started to paddle.

My arms felt as though they had lead weights attached to them as I dragged them through the water. I seemed to be going so slowly, making so little progress. The board was so heavy. I counted to thirty strokes. It was a desperate last effort. If they couldn't hear me this time, I was finished. Twenty-eight, twenty-nine, at thirty I slid upright, sucked in everything I had and yelled.

'AAAHHHH!!'

I rose up a wave and they were right there.

'Martin?' came a voice across the water. It was Kate.

'Yes!' The shape became clearer and bigger with every second. I could make out the mast and rigging now, even in the troughs, and hear the engine. I watched them turn slowly to come beam on. And suddenly it was there, the gold hull looming above me, rolling wildly as it sat across the swell.

'We'll throw you a rope.' That was Scott's voice. The line came flying across the water towards me. I grabbed for it and then Scott was shouting again. 'There's a sling in the rope end, put it round your chest, then jump off the board, we'll pull you in.'

I did as I was told and was dragged the twenty yards towards the stern of the boat. Leg-rope tugging the board behind me, struggling to breathe as the line pulled me forward and under. I floundered on to the transom and eager arms grabbed and pulled me as I struggled to get a grip on the wet paint. My arms and legs were stiff and unwieldly struggling through the lifelines. And I was blind, eyes closed and stinging with salt water. I was suddenly desperate to be inside, to be safe.

Then I was there, collapsed on the hard deck. Unable to move, but happier than I had ever been. I could still feel the leg-rope tugging.

'We'll get rid of this,' a voice said, I felt hands on the Velcro strap.

'No! The board, we've got to keep it.'

'One day in the water and he's already a surf freak,' growled another voice.

'No. I don't want it found,' I spluttered, still trying to clear the water out of my eyes so I could see properly. There was some crashing and banging and I felt the board beside me. I patted it. Good board, did well. A hot cup of coffee was pressed into my hands and a blanket thrown over my shoulders.

'Are you all right?' It was Kate's voice, full of concern.

'You were real lucky, man, we only heard you because we had the engine throttled back to pick Kate up,' said another voice.

'What happened to you, where did the torch go?' It was Kate again. I couldn't speak. I just shook my head. I blinked fiercely and my eyes cleared. 'Martin, talk to me, are you all right?' She was beside me, arm round my shoulders.

I nodded, tried to smile, tried to speak. 'I got caught in the break, ended up on the beach, lost the torch, lost you. I thought you'd left me.'

I glanced up. Scott was glaring at us. I started to pull away from Kate.

'I can't believe we're doing this, Scott.'

The voice came from behind me. But Scott's attention was diverted, he looked up. 'Shut up Duval, I'm the skipper.'

'If I'd known this was what you were planning I'd never have allowed it. I can't believe I fell for that crappy line about picking up crew in Newcastle. These people are being hunted by the police in connection with a double murder. Killing cops, for Christ's sake! We're helping them escape. Do you realise what that means?' It was the nasal whine again, urgent, tight, angry. I shifted round so I could see him.

Scott stood up straight and glared at Duval. 'I told you they didn't do it, some bent cops set them up – they can't go to the police.'

'That's their story,' retorted Duval quickly.

I could see Scott was getting angrier, I could imagine he wasn't happy at having to defend me. But I didn't have the strength to intervene. I sat there numbly, sipping at the coffee. Scott managed to ignore Duval, 'Ben, help me get these two below and warmed up. Duval take the goddamn wheel and steer north. We'll talk about this later.'

Then he was beside Kate, and leading her away, an arm round her shoulders. A hand was proferred. I looked up and recognised Ben. I accepted the help, and he pulled me heavily to my feet. I kept hold of his hand as I said, 'Thanks. Nice job in the bar. I guess we never really got introduced. I'm Martin.'

'Sure. I'm Ben.' He shook with a firm grip from a gnarly hand. But there was a pleasant enough expression on the easy-going face. It didn't look like I was going to get any hassle from him.

The boat was rolling awkwardly under the swell, dead in the water. We staggered down the deck like a couple of drunks. I leant on him heavily as I struggled down the companionway into the warmth and light below. Duval was left with no one to argue with. Moments after we got below, the engine revved and the boat started to turn. Scott brushed past us and peered out the hatch. He came back inside. 'Just checking,' he said. 'I wouldn't put it past that bastard to try and take us back into the harbour.'

Kate was already out of the wetsuit and tucked up in a sleeping bag. Ben led me to the next bunk and some towels. I slowly peeled off the wetsuit. He returned a few moments later with some dry clothes. 'Here you go. There's a bag of spare stuff we pulled out for you, oilskins, clothes, on your bunk, back there,' he said.

I looked up in time to see him indicate the bunk beside me, where Kate was sitting. 'Thanks,' I said, again.

'No worries.' Then he moved to the galley and poured two bowls of an excellent chicken soup. I sat up to eat mine, propped uncomfortably on the edge of the bunk. But there was nowhere else to sit. I looked around. In fact there wasn't much else at all. A spartan galley, lines of bunks down each side of the boat, and in the middle the companionway ladder. Scott leant against it and watched us eat.

'You better go on deck, Ben, and keep an eye on Duval. Make sure we're headed well offshore. I think oh three oh is about the bearing. I marked it on the chart back there,' he said. Ben nodded and moved past him up on to the deck. I could feel Scott watching me. I kept my head down and kept eating.

'You're quite a star, Martin, you've been all over the media,' he said, finally.

I looked up at that, spoon half-way to my lips. I wanted to ask him if they had got pictures of us, what was in the reports, the details. But something in his face told me this wasn't the time. And that maybe I didn't really want to know.

But Scott wanted to tell me. 'Yeah, like Duval says, tough guy, cop-killer. The story is you lost a lot of money in the City, did a runner, drifted, fell in with a bad crowd, all that shit. Failed wheeler-dealer turned drug-smuggler. The perfect mix – dope and high-finance. They're really doing a number on you. They want your blood.'

Slowly I finished the spoonful. I leant forward and put the bowl down on the galley. 'Good soup,' I said quietly. I didn't want to know any more.

'There was only one thing missing – sex. But they got that covered now too. They got Kate down as Bonnie to your Clyde. There've been reporters all over the yacht club, all day. I heard that some fuckwit off another boat sold a picture of Kate in a bikini to a paper.'

I felt Kate shift beside me, the clink of the soup spoon dropping. Neither of us said anything. I could see Scott's jaw grinding.

'And when the cops turned up this morning, they wanted to

know all about you – maybe even trying to find a little fact in all this fiction.' His voice was a chain saw grinding on metal. 'It is fiction, isn't it?'

I met his eyes. 'Yes,' I said, simply. I heard Kate put the bowl down behind me, felt her curl into the bunk.

Scott watched us, unblinking, before he went on, 'So when they turned up, I had to tell them I only met you once. All I knew was that you were an old boyfriend of Kate's. Turned up out of nowhere and whisked her away.' His eyes shifted to Kate. He went on, 'And then I had to tell them I didn't care where you were, Kate. You were nothing to do with me any more. I did a great job too. They all believed me.' He sounded so hurt.

'The cops searched the boat before we left, but half-heartedly. They believed me. So did the media circus, cameramen everywhere, some arsehole in a boat even followed us a couple of miles out of the harbour taking pictures, that's why we were late. And they all believed me when I said you could go to hell, Kate. They all believed me, everyone, even my mates. Fits in with their little story, doesn't it?' His voice was rising. 'Broken-hearted lover flees scene of his humiliation. Jesus, you'll be on the front page of tomorrow's tabloids half-naked, with a story telling how you've run off with this clown on a sex, drugs and killing spree, while I, the spurned lover, sail off to Hong Kong alone.'

There was a terrible, anguished silence. I couldn't imagine what it had cost him to stick to his story with this storm raging round his head. But it came home to me hard that this was the perfect cover for his departure, our escape.

But now he turned to me, jabbed a short, stubby finger into my chest, pushed his face up close to mine and hissed, 'And this is all your fucking fault. You've been nothing but bad news since we met, you've really fucked it all up. You got Kate involved in this. I don't mind for myself, I can take the shit, but you put her in danger and I can't allow that. I'd love to take you back to Sydney and give you to the cops and whoever else it is who wants you, but I can't do that now without making things worse for Kate and probably the rest of us as well. So I guess I'm going to have to take you with us. But if you lay one finger, you so much as look at her on this trip, you'll be swimming home. Get it?'

I nodded, slowly, neutrally. He stared into my eyes for another second and then he was gone. They were both gone. Kate offering no protest as she was bundled off to the other side of the boat. I was left to crawl painfully into my bunk and, for the few brief minutes allowed me before I caved in to sleep, think about the fact that now she was Scott's. And there was nothing I could do about it.

19

I BRACED MYSELF hard against the boat's motion, waiting for the pause at the top of the roll, before I continued lurching towards the companionway ladder. I could feel the storm-driven chill of the night seeping through the closed hatch. The crash and howl of the southerly gale had been with us since the pick-up twenty-four hours earlier. I glanced at the time, nearly two in the morning and a four-hour night watch to do. It didn't get any darker or colder. I hunched deeper into the borrowed oilskins and struggled to zip them up, juggling two hands for a job that needed three or four, what with holding on to the boat and my coffee. Too hard. I gave up on the zip, I'd wait till I could put the coffee down on deck. And now the hatch cover was stuck. Cursing quietly I jammed my hand against the red glow of the night light to get some purchase against the handle and heaved. The hatch gave way with a bang, and the trickle of cold air became a flood. I shook the spilt coffee off my hand and stuck my head out.

I didn't even hear the wave. The bow must have gone in just as I pulled on the hatch and the green water came rolling back down the deck while I was worrying about my coffee. Whatever, I missed the signs and the first I knew was water cascading through the hatch, straight down the neck of my unzipped oilskins. I was soaked. A four-hour watch to do and my only set of dry clothes was wringing wet. I stood there on the ladder for a second or two, cursing under my breath, then struggled through the hatch, nursing the remaining coffee.

There were no friendly greetings as I emerged on deck. Although Ben nodded, Scott merely glanced at me from his position behind the wheel. His attention switched straight back to the boat, spinning the wheel a couple of turns and forcing her down the next wave. The sudden lurch of acceleration as she started to surf nearly had me on my backside. I grabbed at the top of the mainsail winch just in time. It spun under my grip with

Ben tailing the sheet to keep some pressure in the sail. Over the stern, a creaming tail of spray and phosphorescent wake was carved through the heaped-up seas behind us. I moved aft more carefully, and jammed myself safely into the corner of the cockpit opposite Scott and Ben. I sipped at the mug and the odours of coffee, sodden oilskins, sweat-laced thermals and adrenaline all wafted upwards.

It had been, at best, a tense twenty-four hours. It was probably only the advent of the gale, and the demands of sailing the boat in difficult conditions, that had stopped us tearing each other's throats out. I had been woken a couple of hours into that first night by the noise of Duval and Scott, 'discussing' the situation. From what I could tell, Ben had had to intervene to stop it coming to blows. As for myself and Scott, we had simply ignored each other. What was harder was the fact that Duval was no longer talking to any of us. Which only affected me since I shared a watch with him. Four hours of stony silence on deck wasn't so much a problem when it was blowing forty knots, but it wasn't going to be much fun when the sun came out and the wind went down. But, since this was a rescue mission, not a holiday cruise, I was hardly in a position to complain. The only person on board who was talking to everybody was Ben. And it was Ben who was beside me now.

He peeled away the layers of clothing from his face and, shouting to make himself heard, said, 'This looks like it's in for a while. It's good, we'll get some miles done before it blows out.'

'How far have we come?' I yelled back.

'About two hundred and fifty miles.'

I glanced at the rig, three reefs in the main and the storm jib up, and we'd averaged just over ten knots for the last twenty-four hours. 'Not bad,' I shouted into his ear – small talk, there had been precious little of that recently.

'Yeah, the faster we do the run up to the corner of Papua New Guinea the better, then we can back off as we go through the reefs and islands up there, do a bit of fishing, some snorkelling maybe.' The boat slowed as it came off another wave and the sudden increase in apparent wind whipped the last few words from his mouth and carried them away down the boat. I settled for a smile and a nod by way of reply. I nestled the coffee cup in my hands and let the steam warm my face. That was the problem with Southerlies, they might be blowing us the right way, but by God they were cold.

I felt a tap on my shoulder, it was Ben again.

'Where's Duval? We're off watch here in five. Skipper wants him up on time.' He jerked his head at the bulky figure. 'Four hours at the wheel and ready to hit the sack. Better deal with it pronto.'

I flicked the remaining coffee into the ocean and climbed back down the hatch without a word, turning on to the port side where I knew I would find Duval. Second bunk along, there he was, only a thatch of hair appearing from the sleeping bag. I shook his shoulder through the damp cloth. No movement.

'Duval! You're on deck. Scott wants to get off watch.'

Then I turned and shouted forward, 'Hey, Kate, you got any more of that coffee.' She stuck her head round the corner. Backlit by the red night lights I couldn't see her face, only the mane of tousled hair, silhouetted and glowing.

'Sure,' she disappeared, to emerge a moment later with another steaming mug. She moved towards me, one hand on the bunks to keep her balance and the other holding the coffee. The headroom was so tight, because of the flush decks, that even she had to crouch and duck her way past the hardware bolted on to the deckhead. It was a new experience for me, this boat. The ones I'd sailed on previously had all this junk hidden behind panelling. But not a race boat, too much extra weight apparently. The result was I went everywhere doubled up and still cracked my skull all the time.

'Here you go,' she said, offering the cup.

'Thanks,' I replied, reaching out to take the mug. The boat rolled and pitched her towards me, she grabbed for the passage wall to brace herself as I took the coffee, but she was very close to me now. My heart thumped a little, we'd hardly spoken since we came on board.

'You OK?' she asked, in a concerned tone.

'Fine, I don't get sick. Well, I never have done so far anyway.'

'No, I didn't mean . . .' her voice tailed off, she glanced at the hatch. 'You know what I mean, how's Scott treating you?'

'Ignoring me.'

'This isn't going to be a fun trip, we just have to deal with it the best we can.' She forced a weak smile, that didn't reach the blue eyes.

I nodded. 'It's OK.'

'Scott's really wound up about all that newspaper stuff. I keep telling him it's rubbish, that it covers our escape, helps keep me safe.' She paused. 'He knows that's true, but it made him look a fool in front of everybody and coming so soon after losing that sponsorship deal ... it's really got him down. I don't think he realised how much he wanted that till he'd lost it.' She glanced down at the recumbent figure of Duval. 'He said anything?' she asked.

I shrugged, with an ironic half-smile. 'He's not spoken to me either.'

She leaned closer, whispered in my ear, watching Duval, 'He's a shit, keep your eye on him, I wouldn't put anything past him.'

'What do you mean?'

'Just watch out for him.'

I nodded, and she squeezed my arm gently, then slid past me through to the navigation station. Duval still hadn't moved. I was about to shake him when a voice came down the companionway. 'Duval, get your arse out of bed. You're on watch.' I looked up, it was Scott, peering down the hatch and more than a little miffed. 'Wake him up,' he said, brusquely. Duval still hadn't moved. I shook his shoulder, and kept shaking, finally there was a response.

'OK, OK, I'm there,' he muttered as he rolled over and slowly struggled into a sitting position. He glared at me with those empty, pale-blue eyes. I pushed the coffee in his face. The steaming cup drifted a smoke screen between us. He took the coffee, but didn't back down from my stare. I thought we were going to be transfixed like that for ever when the boat shot forward under me, I lurched and snatched at Duval for support. This was a big wave and I could hear the roar of water past the hull. The carbon construction seemed to amplify everything, but even so this was a hell of a surf. The bone-jarring crunch came next as she pitched into the wave in front. The boat slowed as though it had been driven into a brick wall, then came a crack like a pistol shot and the roar on deck of a thousand buffalo. 'Jees! The bloody coffee's all over me.'

Duval was wiping frantically at his lap when Ben hollered down the hatch. 'All hands, everyone up, the vang's blown.'

I dropped the empty coffee cup and stumbled towards the hatch. The boat had slowed considerably with the power that was lost from the mainsail now the vang, which held it down to the deck and stopped it blowing open, was broken. The waves twisted and turned the disabled boat viciously. It was a struggle just to get out of the hatch. I staggered on to the deck.

'Martin, you take the halyard, it's that one.' Scott was yelling with the full force of his lungs to make himself heard above the flogging sail. 'Ben's on the mainsheet, Duval'll do the genoa.'

I looked behind me, Duval was already out of the hatch, dressed only in his thermals. Prima donna he might be, poor seaman he wasn't. We all moved to our positions, down below I could hear the engine rumble into life. Kate hadn't even needed to be told about that one. I watched Scott bend down and flick her into gear, the revs built and the boat churned forward. Now he would have enough steerage way to get *Gold* into the wind so we could drop the mainsail, still flapping like a broken wing above us, on to the deck. With everyone in position and eight knots on the dial Scott picked his wave and swung her round.

'Now, smoke her, Martin!' he bellowed. I had only been shown this by Ben a few hours previously, on my cook's tour. I clicked off the spinlock and let the mainsail halyard, which was holding the sail up, run round the winch as fast as I dared. It seared through my hands. But the yards of Dacron were tumbling down on top of me and before I knew it the rope went slack. It seemed incredibly quiet when the flogging stopped. The bow was pulling away from the wind and the genoa filling. I could hear Duval ease the sheet as the sail filled, and once more the boat began to accelerate. There was one more lurch as a final wave caught her broadside before Scott had her back under control and headed north with the wind behind us. Figuring it was safe to move I scrambled out from under the sailcloth that had buried me. Emerging I saw Ben, still holding the now useless mainsheet, turn to Scott, 'What d'you reckon, boss?' he said.

Scott looked thoughtful. 'Rehoisting in this stuff is going to be impossible with five of us. Have a look at the vang and see what's wrong.'

But Ben was already on his way to the hardware dangling limply off the boom. 'The hydraulics are blown,' he shouted back to us.

Scott looked annoyed. 'Again? There'll be fluid everywhere down below. Someone just shout down and tell Kate what's happened.'

Figuring I was someone, I bent down to fight my way past

the sail to the hatch, but before I could get there Kate's voice emerged, 'It's OK, I already found the problem. It's up by the mast. Fortunately we've got plenty of coke on board.'

'Coke?' I looked at her enquiringly.

'It breaks down the hydraulic oil.'

'Listen up, guys,' Scott, who had been conferring with Ben, brought our attention back to the matter in hand, 'it's a quick repair, but it could be a while before this weather drops off enough to get the main back up. Duval, you take the wheel, Martin can help me and Ben with the sails, then go down and give Kate a hand with the mopping up.'

Duval and I nodded, silently. I was surprised at his easy compliance with Scott, maybe he was settling for the quiet life.

It was a full ten minutes before we had the mainsail folded, and another ten before the jib was poled out and the trisail hoisted. Everything is hard on a boat rolling downwind in a big sea. Ben started on the repair, while Scott went below to sleep. I did as I was told, and joined Kate. The hydraulic connector that had blown apart was situated by the mast, below decks. Kate had got to it just in time and contained the leaking fluid to a small area of deck. Paper towels were soaking it up and then dropped into a plastic bag. I sat on the floor beside her and began wiping up the rest.

'Most of the worst of it is done, we'll wash it over with the coke to get the final bit off,' she said, looking up only briefly, but I caught a glimpse of that dazzling smile.

I nodded.

Above us Ben was dismantling the broken connector. 'The damn seal's gone again. It happens all the time this does,' he muttered.

'I thought as much from the efficient damage control operations down here,' I replied.

'Some of the new boats have got rid of all the hydraulics, they just use a block and tackle to whatever purchase is necessary. Often it's a lot simpler, at least as reliable, and when it does break you don't get all this crap.'

'How many systems are on the hydraulics?'

'There we go!' he said, as whatever it was came undone. 'The outhaul, backstay, cunningham and the vang. It wouldn't be hard to change them. But with the boat's future up in the air, there's been no point and no money.'

I nodded, I knew all about that from Kate. I looked at her, the blonde hair was soaked now, and stuck to her face. She looked pale in the dull glow from the overhead light. I had a suspicion she might not be feeling so good, despite her thousands of miles. The combination of the motion and the enclosed space, with the smell of the hydraulic fluid, could turn the strongest stomach. I was lucky, I seemed to be immune to motion sickness. I caught her eyes and she smiled wanly. There was something of our time together in that look. Then a feeling made me glance aft, and there was Scott, lying on his side in his bunk, staring at us. He held my gaze for a full couple of seconds, then rolled over without a word.

20

SOMETHING HAD CHANGED, my eyes were just as gummed up as normal, I could smell and feel the damp and the sweat. But there was no noise. The accompaniment of nearly four and a half days of sailing, the constant foaming of water, the clatter of sails and winches, the shouts carried on the wind from on-deck. It was gone. I levered myself upright. So was the motion. I sat there without bracing myself, I could hardly believe it. Every muscle throbbed and every joint was stiff. I felt as though I had been on the booze for about three months and was waking up sober for the first time. I swung my legs over the edge of the bunk and gingerly tested my feet out with some weight. Not bad. They, at least, had healed and improved.

I rubbed my eyes and peered around me. The spotless boat I'd joined in Sydney had disappeared under an avalanche of wet oilskins, clothes, scraps of food, discarded tools and sails. What a mess. In the middle of it, on the little island of order that the galley represented in this ocean of chaos, was Kate. She looked over at me from the pan she was stirring,

'How are you feeling?' Apart from the occasional smile, that was almost the first communication we'd had since that incident when the vang failed. I was sure Scott had been on to her again, after that. Every time I'd tried to get near her, physically or metaphorically, she'd kept a distance between us.

But then, the conditions hadn't exactly helped. The storm had finally abated, at least the clouds had gone and the winds had swung a little to the east and warmed. But it had continued to blow like hell out of a clear blue sky. Ben had muttered darkly to me on a couple of occasions, that it wasn't supposed to be like this. But it was. The weather had turned life into an exercise in survival. You were on watch, sleeping or eating. Anything else was a waste of energy. Even conversation. I was exhausted. I had started the trip exhausted and it had just got worse. Scott, Ben and Duval, even Kate, seemed to take it in their stride, but I'd suffered.

I summoned up my last reserves of energy in an effort to appear cheerful. 'Good, I feel good. Where did the breeze go?' I asked.

'Blew out a couple of hours ago. Just upped and disappeared, along with the sea. Nice, isn't it?' she said.

'It's so peaceful, it's wonderful.'

'Unfortunately we're only making about four knots, we should turn the engine on.' I grimaced. 'But Scott reckons we'll struggle on under sail for a watch each so everyone can get some rest.'

'There's no big hurry, is there?'

'Nope, we're miles ahead of schedule so far. We've got to start on this mess though. Get the oilskins hung up on deck, wash or dry the clothes, collect the trash.'

I wasn't so keen on that, the last thing I needed was work, and said so.

She smiled. 'You'll feel better for it when it's done. Or at least that's what Scott says. Personally, I'm on your side.'

I laughed. 'Good!'

She glanced up from the bowl, and I held her gaze for just a second. But it was long enough. She knew what I meant.

There was a loud crackle and buzz of static from the back of the boat.

'Shit.' It was Scott's voice. The volume of static eased.

'Bloody hell, Scott, I'm trying to sleep.' That was Duval.

There was a creak of floorboards and the snap of a switch, the static disappeared.

'You're on watch in ten minutes anyway Duval, better get up.' Scott again. I heard him climb on deck through the aft hatch.

I turned back to Kate. 'Who was Scott talking to on the radio?'

She looked up from the pan, shrugged. 'No idea, probably a weather forecast.' She went back to the stirring for a moment, then said, 'But it reminds me.' She glanced up. 'Scott left most of my stuff at the hotel for me. He thought it would look good for the police. He was thinking about phoning the hotel, to see if there was any news, or if my bags were still there. He thought it would add to the cover story. And we would maybe get to hear what was going on back there. But I thought it might indicate that he was still interested in what happened to me – maybe attract more suspicion than it would deflect. What do you think?' The blue eyes settled on me.

'He can phone the hotel from out here?'

'Yes, of course. You can make a ship-to-shore link to the coast station on the SSB radio, and then connect to any land phone number through the radio operator.'

I nodded automatically, 'I think you're right, there should be no communication, he's forgotten about you, doesn't care.' Kate nodded her agreement and said, 'I'll tell Scott to forget the idea.'

'It would have been good to know what was happening in Sydney though,' I said, but my mind was going back to an incident in the storm. It had seemed insignificant at the time, but now I wasn't so sure. I moved across the boat and checked aft, Duval was in the far bunk, apparently asleep again. I moved forward of the mast, as far away from him as I could get, indicating to Kate to join me. I kept my voice down, 'A couple of days ago I came below in a major rush, there was a crisis, that genoa halyard that was chafing through, remember?'

She nodded.

'I came down the back hatch and Duval was on the radio. I didn't think much of it at the time, I didn't realise we had a phone facility. And a second after I got down here the halyard blew and all hell broke loose. But there was something about his reaction.'

'What do you mean?' said Kate.

'Well, he jumped, I thought I'd just surprised him. But the more I think about it now, it was like I'd caught him doing something he shouldn't, a guilty reaction.'

'What are you trying to say?'

I looked at her anxiously. 'Well, what if Janac got to him before we left? One of his bent cops could have told Duval to call them if Scott gave anything away about our whereabouts. He's been real quiet after that first row when we came on-board. We know he doesn't want us here, if he believes all that stuff in the papers, maybe he'd book himself some insurance by informing. Maybe he even approached them before we left . . .'

Incredulity and concern were chasing each other across Kate's face – incredulity won. She said, 'Don't you think that might be getting just a little paranoid?'

'You were the one who said we shouldn't trust him.'

'I said he was a shit. I had it in mind that he'll have you doing all the work on your watch, while he festers in his bunk – not that he might turn us in. I mean, deep down, he's one of us, he's a yachtie.'

I looked away, perhaps she was right, but something inside me didn't want to give the idea up.

There was a thump behind us, I looked round. Ben was cursing, having just slipped on the layer of trash that covered the deck.

'Goddamn, we really have to clear this mess up, you know,' he said.

'You want some soup, either of you?' Kate was already half-way back to the galley.

I nodded and launched myself off the sloping hull to take the bowl.

Ben shook his head. 'Nah, it's pretty hot on deck. It's going to be a scorcher down here before long – you'll be after cold drinks in half an hour. We're less than a thousand miles off the equator.'

'Where are we?' I hadn't taken much interest in such issues up till now.

'The Coral Sea. About two hundred miles south of the south eastern tip of Papua New Guinea. From here it's all glamour. And we're so far ahead of schedule that we can afford to take our time.' He paused and looked around him a little less enthusiastically. 'But we got to get this bun-fight cleared up first. There's an island we can maybe stop at, Rossel or something, about two hundred miles up the track, we can do a better job there. But we'll do the best we can for now. Soon as you've finished that soup Martin, we'll get started. I'll give you a hand for half a watch, then Scott will help.'

Two hours later Ben and I had made a big impact on the cleaning, everything that was wet was hung in the lifelines or draped on deck. The sails were all packed and most of the garbage was either picked up or small and degradeable enough to be washed into the bilge. I was pumping them out when Ben emerged from on-deck.

'We're nearly there, Martin, there's only the bilge to do. You want me to wake Scott to give you a hand?'

I glanced at Ben, raised an eyebrow. 'Wake him up? To pump a bilge? With me?'

He smiled. 'I guess not,' he said.

It was exactly what I didn't want and the reason I'd been busting my butt for the last two hours. 'No, I'll manage it easily on my own.'

'Good, I'm about to take a shower, then crash.' He disappeared back up the companionway.

Pumping bilges is one of those tasks best undertaken with the brain disengaged. In such a fashion it is over quickly enough. You get a rhythm going that you can maintain, then just keep at it until you hear the satisfying sound of sucking air rather than water. It didn't even take half an hour before I was finished, and I headed back up the boat to see how Kate was getting on. Ben had showered and then, like Scott, hit his bunk. Their snores now echoed in unison through the quiet of the boat. With Duval at the wheel, and a good excuse to be down here, I had a chance to talk to Kate again with no one else around. But she too was out cold in her bunk, with a pile of sandwiches left on the galley. Nothing for it but to see how Duval was getting on, maybe I could get something out of him, some clue about what he was up to.

I climbed up through the main hatch. The glare was unbearable after the gloom of below-decks. I stood there for a full minute, with my eyes all but closed, gradually easing them open as they adjusted to more light. Now I understood why sunglasses were such a prized possession to these people. Ben was right about the heat too. It was warm below, but up here it dropped on you like a heavy cloak. Eventually I could peer around me. The boat was sailing gently along on a broad starboard reach. I'd learned a bit of sailing in the last few days and had a better grip on the game now. Although there was barely a ripple on the water Duval was coaxing about four knots out of her. The motion was almost soundless. He seemed to have engaged the autopilot and was lounging with his back against a stanchion, reading a book.

'How's it going?' I said, stumbling my way across the deck towards him. There was clothing and oilskins strewn everywhere. All of it steaming in the heat. He looked up from his book, barely nodded, then went back to reading. That's a good start I thought. It's going to be hard conducting a discreet interrogation if he won't even talk to me. I tried again, 'I've finished up down below, she's a new boat. Kate's made some sandwiches, you want one and maybe a Coke?'

'Thanks,' he said, without taking his eyes off the book.

I went back down the companionway and dug a couple of Cokes out of the icebox. I had no idea where all these came from, but there seemed to be an inexhaustible supply replenishing the cooler at regular intervals. I grabbed two sandwiches to go with them and returned on deck.

'There you go,' I said as I handed Duval his. He carefully marked the page in his book and took the sandwich and drink. I sat down opposite. The Coke cans hissed as we pulled back the rings together.

'To light winds,' I offered the informal toast.

He ignored me, concentrating on the sandwich.

I stared at him. 'You don't like me, do you?'

He looked up that time. 'As far as I'm concerned you're not even here,' was the acerbic reply.

'You want me off the boat that bad, huh?'

He lowered the sandwich, wrinkling his nose in sudden distaste, and stared at me with unblinking blue eyes. 'I didn't want you on it in the first place. You could cost me my career, all the years of effort could go up in smoke, "pooff".' He made a magician's motion with his hands. 'Vanish.' And with that he put the sandwich aside and went back to his book.

I chewed heavily on mine, it had gone dry in my mouth. I took a drink to try and wash it down. Well, my friend, I thought, if you've told Janac where we are there is every possibility that I'll vanish, just like your precious career. And you'll be going with me.

21

I CHECKED THE time, just before one, I'd only got another hour to go. I wiped the gathering beads of perspiration from my forehead again, and shifted a little to try and get comfortable. It was just about the hottest part of the day and it made the freezing Southerlies seem like a pleasant dream. There was nowhere to escape the heat. The awning we had rigged over the cockpit yesterday morning, when the wind completely ran out, had helped a lot. But with this Easterly filling in and building, it had had to come down when the sails went back up. So Duval and I took it in turns to steer, whilst the other struggled to stay in the patches of shade provided by the sails.

It was just as bad below decks. Despite our efforts to dry everything it was like a sauna down there, as all the ingrained damp of the heavy-weather sailing steamed quietly back into the atmosphere. At least the air moved up here. Not much, as we eased along on a starboard beam reach, but it did move. Down below, with only the two hatches and no windows, another feature of these damn racing boats, there was precious little throughput of air. I felt I'd breathed some of that stuff four or five times already. But Ben assured me that with the Easterly slowly filling in, things would get better. For a while at least. Thirty miles or so ahead was Rossel Island, the eastern tip of the Louisiade Archipelago, which spread out from the south east toe of Papua New Guinea. After a stopover there we had to head north west, and unless the wind changed this would turn us downwind once more. The apparent wind would shift aft and the cooling breeze would disappear. This much I had learnt in a couple of minutes at the chart with Ben that morning.

That, at least, had temporarily relieved the other principal occupational hazard – boredom. Especially when Duval was steering. Then I knew where he was, so watching him wasn't a problem either and there was little else to do. In the lightish airs he could click the autopilot on when he needed to adjust something and do it himself. I didn't even need to be on deck. When I was steering it was a little harder. Having to look after the boat and keep an eye on him. But in the last thirty-one hours he had made no effort to go near the radio. He had just sprawled on the foredeck, reading what seemed to be an inexhaustible supply of books.

Nothing else had happened either. We hadn't seen a boat, never mind search planes or helicopters. Nothing, just mile after mile of empty ocean. I had started to think that Kate might be right, maybe I was paranoid. The deep concern had slipped away, leaving me with just a faintly ill-at-ease feeling. And, nearly two hundred miles on, I had only had one conversation with Kate. It's almost impossible to talk to someone alone on an eighty foot boat with three other people around. Particularly when they seem to be ducking you. I didn't want to admit it but I was fast being forced back to the conclusion I had reached during the storm. She was avoiding me. What that meant, gave me something new to worry about.

'How's it going Martin?'

I looked over to the aft hatch, where Ben was emerging. He at least, and he alone, was still talking to me.

'You're not on for an hour yet Ben, what's the problem?'

'Too hot to sleep down there, thought I'd come up and sling some lines over the back, see if I can't catch us something to alleviate the tinned diet.' He sat down on the cockpit floor and started to untangle the line and lure. 'Don't know why I didn't think about it before, while I was up here myself. Too tired, I guess. Pretty hard work that weather.'

I looked at him with interest. He hadn't shown much sign of tiredness, and I said as much.

'I guess you get used to operating in that stuff, so it doesn't show too much. But I still feel it all right. I'm not getting any younger either,' he answered, head down over the fishing tackle.

I'd been curious about that as well 'So how old are you then, Ben?'

He looked up. 'Me? I'm thirty-eight. Too old for this shit, that's for sure.'

'You're older than both Scott and Duval,' I said, it was half a question and half a statement. I'd lowered my voice too, and glanced forward. But Duval was fifty feet away, in the shade of the genoa.

'Uhhuh,' he replied non-committally, head back down over the fishing lines. He seemed to be making a bigger tangle, rather than a smaller one.

'I'm also confused over who is the skipper,' I said. 'Scott's in charge, but back in Sydney Kate said it was Duval?' I half knew the answer to that question, but I wanted to get him to talk about it. Partly because I was interested and partly because if I didn't talk to somebody about something soon, I'd go crazy.

Ben looked up again, and this time he leaned back against the cockpit side, and studied me a little more closely. 'They both are. The responsibility shifts depending on what the boat is doing. It's Scott's job to prepare the boat for each regatta, or race. During that time, like now when it's on delivery, he's the skipper. When the preparation is complete and the boat is practising or racing Duval takes over. There's a few borderline areas but that's roughly how it works.' He stopped, but didn't go back to the tangle in his lap. It seemed like someone was going to talk to me for a while.

'Back in Sydney Kate said being the racing skipper was better?' I asked quickly, before the moment disappeared.

Ben smiled. 'Did she now? Well that depends on your outlook. Far as I'm concerned Scott's the man. But he gets none of the public recognition, and little of the money. The two jobs are totally different. Duval is the front man, he nobs it with the guys who pay for all this,' he waved his arm dismissively at the couple of million dollars worth of hardware we were sitting on, 'he does the interviews, has his photo taken, and he carries the can if the boat doesn't get results. I guess he's responsible to the sponsor for value for money. The problem is that a lot of that stuff can lose you respect with the guys. The ones that sail the boat. Some of the things you have to say and do, whether you mean it or not, it's hard not to look ridiculous.'

'Like what?'

'The self-promotion, press releases about yourself, pumping up your profile in the magazines and papers. The kind of stuff you have to say to make the sponsors pay attention, makes you look foolish to the people on the inside. The problem is that you need those same people to sail and run the boat. Duval comes from multi-hulls, single-handers, so it wasn't a problem for him before.

He didn't need anyone else. But when he got into the Whitbread, well, he found it was different.

'He needs the boys, the crew, to respect him. And they don't have so much respect for someone who spends all his time writing his own press releases. With Duval it's even worse.' Ben shifted slightly, and paused a little to think. I'd underestimated this guy, he certainly knew what was going on, and his different perspective to Kate's was interesting.

'We're in the Southern Ocean, OK?' he continued. 'It's blowing like hell, forty, fifty knots and building, forty-foot waves. The chicken chute is up and the boat is smoking. It's absolutely freezing, so cold you can't touch metal without gloves on or you stick to it. The boat's on a knife-edge of control, adrenaline's going so hard you can smell it. You know you should get the kite down, but who the hell is going forward to do it? No one. And anyway it's a race. He who pushes hardest and stays in one piece, wins. So on you go, faster than you ever been, till something gives.

'Finally the driver gets it wrong and wham, she spins out to windward. The pole's in the water, and the kite's in shreds. The main's pinning the boat down, a couple of guys are floating out the back on lifelines – all kinds of hell. Anyway, it sorts itself out eventually after you shit yourself for ten minutes, gets back upright and off you go. Trouble is, half the kite's still up there. So now someone has to get it down. But it's worse, much worse. You got to go up the rig to retrieve the halyard, cause there's only one left, since we've done this once already.

'You're all standing there waiting for someone else, usually the bowman, to be dumb enough to get going on it, when Duval comes on deck and starts blowing off about how much time we're losing with no sails up, and why isn't it sorted? It isn't his job, he's the skipper right? One of the boys has to go, so who you going to do it for? You look at Duval, and you see this guy making more money in a month than you get for the whole damn race. He gets himself on telly, in the papers, it's like he sails the boat on his own. I mean, I don't care too much for all that, but even so, you can't help but be a little bit jealous, can you?' He paused, pulled his sunglasses off and wiped them on the tail of his T-shirt a little self-conciously, perhaps at the nature of this last revelation. I was silent, waiting for him to go on.

The sunglasses were carefully replaced, and he continued, 'So, am I going to risk my neck to make him look good? We could just leave the damn thing up there till the breeze backs off a bit after all, but we're racing. So who you going to put it on the line for? Not Duval, he can go up there and fetch it himself far as I'm concerned. No, you do that stuff for Scott, because the first time it happens he's already got the harness on and he's looking to you to get him up that mast. He leads by example, you know? And he's only got to do it once because the next time the boys'll sort it for him. He's out there with you, taking the risks, for no money, just like you. And when you finish he's in the bar, getting trashed and doing crazy things with you. The boys'll follow him anywhere, do anything for him.

'But Duval? He must've done it once on those big multi-hulls. No one else to do it for him. I'm not saying he doesn't have the balls. But, now, I guess he just figures there's only so many risks you can take. He isn't up for it any more, and the boys don't respect him so much. Especially with all that bullshit self-promotion he has to do for the sponsor. And Duval loves that stuff, he goes over the top on it. So that's why he needs Scott. On his first Whitbread he didn't have him and he did all right, but me and Scott were on *Eagle* and we beat 'em good. So next time around Scott's first on the payroll, and we take five out of six legs. I'm not saying that it's like that on all the boats, but it is on this one. Some of the skippers, they manage to do both jobs. Scott and Duval into one. But it's a hell of a fine line. You see them doing something dumb to keep the crews on-side, and you know if they get caught the press'll chew their arse and the sponsor walks. They risk their neck on the boat and get hurt, the result goes down the tube and the same thing. It isn't easy.' He paused again and sighed heavily.

'But Katie, she doesn't see any of that. All she sees is Duval with his big fat pay cheque, and the fast cars, getting invited to all the smart parties. You know as well as I do that she was brought up with that stuff, her old man is high-up in some big company back in England or something. So she sees it all and figures why can't Scott do that job? Everybody says he's good enough, and he is, on the boat. But he can't ever do all the other stuff that Duval does. He's the wrong kind of guy, he's a sailor's sailor, not a media man's sailor. That's the difference. He isn't ever going to give her those things, however much she pushes him. I think he'd like to, but it isn't going to happen. It's worse because she never sees the stuff Scott is good at, so she doesn't appreciate it. Hearing about it isn't quite the same. So, sure, the racing skipper is the glamour boy, but Scott's my man.'

He stopped, and looked at me with an uncertain smile, I could guess what was on his mind. But I didn't think he'd have the nerve to say it. And I was right, he just looked away. There was an uncomfortable silence.

'I never realised. You see these things from the outside, and you never know,' I said quickly, for something to say.

He shook his head ruefully. 'I could tell you some stories, there was a boat back in the '77 race . . .' but he stopped again. I had heard it too. The sound of Duval's footsteps coming back down the deck, I looked up.

'You want me to take her for a while?' he said.

I glanced back at Ben, but he was gone, aft with his lines. 'OK.' I moved aside, as he stepped in behind the wheel.

I was just about to move forward to chase the shade, when Scott stuck his head out of the hatch.

'We want to come off five degrees if we're going to make that island.'

'What island?' said Duval.

'Twenty-eight miles ahead, we're going to stop there, get cleaned up, see if we can get ashore and have a look around.'

Duval was shaking his head. 'No way, Scott.'

'What do you mean no way? We're days ahead of schedule.'

'You know I have business to do in London. You pressured me into this trip, now you want to rub it in by cruising up there?' Duval's voice was tight, serious.

Scott climbed out of the hatch, his jaw set. Ben was looking back from the stern, with a mixed expression. I just kept very still, this wasn't my beef.

'I pressured you into it?' Scott started, his voice mocking Duval's anger. 'You know there's no money, who else was going to do it?'

'You could have found someone,' said Duval in his resentful nasal whine.

'I could have found someone?' Scott was incredulous. 'It's my responsibility to find a replacement so you can go back to London and tidy up a sponsorship deal that I have no interest in? This is my last trip, I fly back from Hong Kong to a British winter and no job, and you want me to hurry it?'

'That's bullshit, Scott.' Duval was angry now. 'You go home at the end of your contract, after the brewery sell the boat. That's when the regatta's over in Hong Kong. It makes no difference when you get there, you can holiday there or here.'

'What makes you think I'm going to do the regatta?' said Scott icily.

Duval was quiet, when he replied his voice was flat, without the menace the meaning delivered. 'You will, Scott. The new guys don't start work till Rollen's get the boat. You break that contract, you'll never work on a race boat again.'

Scott looked, and sounded, stunned. 'You really think you're that powerful, don't you?'

Duval stared at him, expressionless, the sunglasses a mask. Scott shook his head. 'Where do you get off, Duval? OK, let's just get there. Forget the island. The sooner I'm out of sight of you the less likely I am to throw up on you.' He turned to go down the hatch, but started when he saw me. I could see the thought cross his face, like a summer cloud on a field. But he said nothing.

22

I LEANED BACK and closed my eyes. I felt the boat push my feet out of the shade and into the sun at the top of its roll. But the shadow cast across my face by the genoa strengthened. I opened my eyes and the silhoutte above me was unmistakably Kate's. I sat up quickly and shaded my eyes so I could see her face, she was smiling nervously.

'I just had a long talk to Scott. We have to talk also, I have some things to say.'

I nodded, and she sat down beside me. She gazed at the water for a while. 'You have to understand, Martin, that he thinks everything is being taken away from him. The only two things he cares about. Duval's destroying his sailing and you're threatening his relationship with me. There's nothing else in his life.' I looked at her, but she was still staring at the ocean. 'Maybe he should've tried harder to replace Duval on this trip. But you, he didn't ask for, and he's got. And while you're here, you just remind him constantly that someday, maybe soon, I might leave him. He hates you for that.' She paused, glanced up. 'This situation with you and Scott is impossible. Every time you look at me it winds him up, it's getting worse and worse. I can't stand all the tension and hate. If at least you two can get along, we only have to worry about Duval. Do you understand?'

I was the one who looked away. It crossed my mind how artificial this conversation would seem under more normal circumstances. It would never be necessary with the luxury of distance and the separation that afforded. When I looked back she was staring at the ocean. I spoke softly, 'I can get a good job back in London, a good one, Kate. It won't be like it was three years ago. That's all over, I've changed. Come back with me. You know,' I hesitated, striving to see her reaction, but she was quiet and still, as though hypnotised by the static motion of the bow wave. I plunged on, 'You know you're too good for this, for him. You know that, and you know that he'll never make you completely happy. You've changed too and there are so many things he can't give you that I can. The break will only get harder the longer it goes on. Be honest now, Kate, and everyone will be hurt less in the end.'

There was only the chuckle of the forefoot ploughing up the Pacific. The faint rise and fall of the boat's loping passage. But her shoulders were starting to tremble and before she looked up I knew she was crying.

'Don't, Martin, please don't.' She put her hands to her face, and when she spoke again it was through them. 'I have to think, I don't know . . . I'm not sure about anything anymore. Please just stay away for a while. It's too difficult . . .' She buried her face in her hands, and stifled the sobs.

My hand fell on to her shoulder and squeezed it gently, just once. 'It's all right, Kate. That's best for everyone. Please just think about what I said?'

She nodded, a tiny movement, but it was there. There was nothing more to say or do.

I looked past her towards the stern. It was empty. A memory churned my stomach and then a cold fear gripped me.

'Where's Duval?' I said quickly, everything else forgotten. I was already on my feet, heart racing. I flew down the deck and was half-way through the navigator's hatch before he had even managed to rise from the seat, the microphone still in his hand. His look of guilty surprise was enough to tell me who he'd been radioing.

'You stupid bastard, Duval!' I screamed.

He was too taken aback to offer any resistance, verbal or otherwise. I grabbed the microphone from his hand, ripped the plug from the set and hurled it across the boat. In the same motion I hauled him out of the seat and threw him into the bulkhead. The impact knocked all the air from his wiry frame. I was back on him in a second, both hands round his throat, he was no match for my size and weight. But then I felt Ben's arm, trying to pull me away.

'Hold it, Martin.'

'I'll kill him,' I shouted, tightening my grip. Duval was starting to struggle desperately, his face turning red. Then Scott was there as well, pushing between us. The fear and frustration of the past weeks boiled over and then condensed into the energy of pure rage.

I tucked my legs up and found a purchase against the side of the chart table. Then jabbed backwards, hard. We couldn't move far and Ben hit the companionway ladder at speed. His grip slackened at the impact and I ripped free. Scott was off-balance after the sudden movement and I caught him guard down, just below the rib cage. He staggered back, then tripped over Duval who was on his knees, gasping for air. They went down together. I caught my breath but the half-second hesitation gave Ben a chance to grab hold again. He had my arms and propelled us both forwards before shoving me face down on to the chart table.

'Let me go, Ben, this isn't your fight!' I yelled.

'No way,' he muttered grimly.

'He was on the goddamn radio for christsakes,' I spluttered. I pushed up again in a last effort to break free and we staggered back across the narrow deck. But Ben held on and now Scott was on his feet, still breathing heavily, face twisted in pain. 'Hold him, Ben,' he muttered, 'I'm going to fucking kill him . . .'

The sudden crash of the explosion was incredibly loud in the confined space. I looked around wildly for where the shot had come from, and there stood Kate, a rifle at her shoulder, aimed up through the hatch. A wisp of smoke drifted away from the muzzle. Nobody was moving now, although I could feel Ben slowly easing his grip. Nothing but the sound of distressed breathing. Kate spoke quietly. But there was an emotional force behind the words that held everyone's attention.

'This ridiculous, macho crap will stop immediately. Let him go, Ben.'

Ben relaxed and I sank on to my knees. Scott was only feet away, clutching his ribs, staring at the floor. But it was finished, we were all spent. I watched Kate step over to the radio. It crackled and hissed with static, faintly we could all hear a monotone voice reciting a weather forecast. She clicked it off. 'This is tuned to the emergency channel. Who were you talking to, Duval?' Kate swung to face him as she spoke, the rifle barrel following her movement.

He was still crouched on the floor, wheezing, and when his head came up his face was bright red. 'Weather forecast, it's in the almanac, transmitted out of Darwin.'

There was silence.

'That's bullshit,' I muttered.

'Shut up, Martin,' said Kate curtly. 'What Martin is concerned about, Duval, is that you are trying to report our presence on the boat to the police. Are you?'

Duval slumped into a sitting position on the deck, back against the bunk. His face was a mask. 'No.'

'Bullshit, the cops got to him before we left . . .' I started to protest.

'Quiet, Martin.' Kate looked at Duval, 'The two cops that died worked for Janac, the man who's after us. That's how he found Martin last time. I went to the police, to this guy called Alex, to get help and he told Janac where I was. When Martin contacted me Janac caught us.' Heavy emphasis and a pause, 'You call the cops and tell him where we are, and Janac will find us, and there's a good chance you will get us all killed. Do you understand?'

Duval was silent.

'Do you?' The rifle waved again.

'Yes,' he said tightly. 'I didn't make the damn call. I was listening to the weather forecast.'

Kate stared at him for a couple of seconds before finally saying, 'Stay away from the radio from now on. Secondly, stop this petty crap with Scott. And you too, Scott. It's only a bloody sponsorship deal, for goodness sake, it's not the end of anybody's world. Now shake hands. Do it,' she insisted. They weren't happy, but they did it.

'And you two,' the rifle waved at Scott and myself, 'listen good. This ridiculous jealousy trip will stop, Scott, there's nothing between me and Martin. Right?'

'He's the . . .' Scott began.

The rifle slammed down on to the deck.

'Whoo, honey,' it was Ben now, 'that could go off.'

I glanced at Scott, and got a look of such blackness I should have dropped dead on the spot. The look slowly passed, finally he nodded. Kate turned her attention to me. I went more easily, I held up my hands compliantly.

'We have a long way to go on this trip, and we have to do it together,' she continued. 'From now on we will behave like normal human beings.'

There was an uncomfortable silence. It was Ben who broke it. 'Kate, may I have the rifle now?'

'Certainly, Ben,' and she handed it over. 'That will be all,' she said, turning on her heel and walking forward. Scott followed after her. Duval headed up through the hatch, back to the wheel without another word. I sullenly watched them both go.

Ben was looking at me. 'It's OK,' he said eventually, 'if he'd been making a link call they would have shifted him to a working channel, not left him on the emergency channel. And there was a forecast.'

'It was cover. And he had plenty of time to switch it back, he was still in the seat when I got here, but he must have been able to hear me coming all the way down the deck,' I said quietly.

Ben nodded thoughtfully. 'I guess, it's possible,' he said. His hands were automatically checking the rifle. He was handling it comfortably, professionally even. 'I'm surprised she knew how to take the safety off,' he added, tersely.

I watched him for a while. 'Where the hell did that come from?' I asked.

'There's a special rack built in the engine box,' he replied, head down over the weapon.

'I mean, why is it on board?'

'Standard in these parts.'

'Why?' I said, surprised.

Ben looked up, 'Pirates.'

'Pirates? You're kidding me? This is the twentieth century, they went out with Blackbeard, didn't they?' I wasn't sure whether I sounded worried or amused.

'Not out here, they didn't. Mostly they're from Indonesia, Thailand, but some Malays and maybe even the Chinese as well. It's a real problem, especially once you get further north. Two hundred attacks in the South China Sea year before last, and that was just the ones reported to the International Maritime Bureau. Mostly merchant ships they go after, especially around Singapore, but still, they're out there. That's why we have this baby, three shotguns and a revolver.'

'Shit, it's an armoury,' I said, no longer surprised – more astonished.

Ben hefted the rifle up, replaced the magazine and smiled.

'You've done that before, haven't you?' I said.

He nodded. 'A little, I did some time in the army at home. Before I got on to the boats. Don't get the chance to shoot much these days, just a few rounds when we're out here maybe.' He looked at the weapon. 'This use to be the standard issue rifle for the Brits, the L1A1. But they replaced it and the Sterling sub-machine gun with the SA80 assault rifle. I heard some of the blokes, especially after the Gulf, think that's a worthless piece of shit anywhere but the range, but this one,' he cradled the rifle, 'is all right. I'd better put it back.'

'Let's just hope we don't need it,' I said, pointedly.

'Yeah, right,' said Ben, with a grim expression. He turned and moved up forward. I shook my head, but I felt a little better. I had a feeling that if there was any shooting to be done, Ben'd be doing it.

23

THE ISLAND LOOKED beautiful as it slipped by to leeward, turquoise reefs and verdant scenery. I imagined endless white, sandy beaches. But it was probably better that Scott had decided not to stop. This trip would only be tolerable when it was over. The wind was helping, it had freshened to a good sailing breeze as we headed past Rossel Island and out into the open water of the Solomon Sea. It had also backed a little, following our turn to the west as we cleared the island, and helping us maintain speed by providing a better sailing angle. Combined, the effect was enough to keep the motor off, but not so much that it was an uncomfortable motion.

I had stayed on deck as the afternoon had slipped away through Scott and Ben's watch, and now Duval and I had taken our night positions. It was cooler already, and with the sun accelerating towards the horizon shade was no longer a priority. He was steering, and I sat in the middle of the cockpit, near the two sheets if anything needed adjustment. It was also just far enough away that neither of us felt any compulsion to talk. Not that there was much chance of small talk from Duval. Down below I could hear the voices of Scott, Ben and Katie, the fight forgotten, laughing over a beer as she prepared dinner. As I watched the sun disappear and the night close in the glow of light from the main hatch and the buzz of voices became more and more painful. I had never felt lonelier.

I stared mournfully out to sea, watching a light off to port. It was a single white, dipping and ducking, I presumed with the waves, and then it disappeared. Over the horizon I guessed. But with nothing else to do and far too much to think about I kept watching. Twenty minutes later it reappeared, in the same place. I couldn't figure that out. It certainly looked like the same light, but if it was travelling parallel to us I should be seeing a green starboard light as well as the white stern light. And all there was was the one, erratic white. I watched carefully and it stayed exactly on station for the next twenty minutes.

The existence of any other ship on the ocean was cause enough for concern in my paranoid state, and this sort of behaviour made it worse. I thought about telling Duval, but it could wreck the truce, mentioning more of my suspicions. So it came as a surprise when his voice butted in on my thoughts. 'You been watching that light?' I turned and looked at him, he was staring out at it. 'It's been there for a good twenty minutes now,' he went on.

'More than that,' I said, 'I was already watching it before. It disappeared for a while and then came back about twenty minutes ago.'

Duval turned and looked at me, then nodded slowly. 'He's only showing that one light too, no green.' Was there something in his voice, a little edginess? 'Reach down and fetch the binoculars will you?' he asked.

I hopped down the aft hatch and picked them up off the hook by the chart table. When I reemerged Duval spoke as I sat down beside him.

'What do you see?'

I put the binoculars up to my eyes. The image danced around as the boat moved, but slowly I pieced together the picture. I could see that the light was from a lamp inside a cabin. It was moving separately to the cabin structure so it must have been hanging. Occasionally it hid itself behind the wood work. That explained its erratic nature. Apart from that I could see little more of the boat. Nothing to indicate its size or type. The only clue was the superstructure around the lamp, which looked old – it probably wasn't a modern cruising boat or a sailboat. Not the police and not the kind of fast launch I thought Janac would use.

I reported all this to Duval as I watched. He listened in silence until I took the binoculars down.

'I'm gonna alter course towards him, see what he does,' he said. I looked over at him. His face was lit by the glow of the compass. He was a little twitched about something. I didn't think he believed our story about the cops working for Janac. If he had reported us the only thing he'd be expecting would be the Australian Navy. And they wouldn't be messing around following us with only a lamp showing. Maybe he was worried about the pirates Ben had mentioned. Minutes more passed by in silence. Finally, he glanced at the compass and said, 'I've altered course twenty degrees towards him so far, and he's still paralleling us.' He looked at me. 'I'll come back on course and we'll track him on the radar. You know how to use one?'

I shook my head.

'No, OK, take the wheel and I'll go set it up. We're steering three twenty, which is a little high of the rhumb line to keep the speed up.' He looked back at the compass. 'And we're on three twenty, just about now.'

I took the wheel from him and he stepped over to the main and genoa sheets to give them a small trim before going down below. I wedged myself in beside the wheel and checked the course, three twenty it was. As Duval disappeared down one hatch Ben emerged from the other carrying a couple of plates. He picked his way carefully aft, no mean feat with both hands full, even though the motion was an easy one.

'Supper's ready,' he said. 'Special tonight, the last tin of that chicken.' He smiled broadly.

I pointed out towards the light still bobbing along to leeward and said, 'Duval's just setting the radar up to track that guy.'

'What is it, cruising boat or something?' said Ben, staring at the light, just as it disappeared for a second time.

'Except that it's paralleling us, and not showing a green light.'

'Or any lights now,' said Ben. 'I'll go and tell the boss. Hang on to these.'

I clicked the autopilot on and took the two dishes from him. I bent down the aft hatch. Duval was sitting at the chart table, tweaking the radar. He accepted the plate with a grunt of thanks and turned back to the screen. As I sat up again, Scott appeared at the main hatch. I could see Ben pointing out where the light had been and repeating my description of the happenings.

Scott nodded, then disappeared again with Ben following him. I slurped at the chicken, it was damn good. Scott's voice drifted up from the aft hatch. I glanced down, he was bent over the radar with Duval, who was explaining, 'They're keeping station about six hundred metres off, I've set the bearing and range indicator up on them, so it will be easy enough to track them.'

'Set the alarm for closing within two hundred metres or moving out to a thousand,' responded Scott, gruffly, not polite, but not exactly rude either. There was a silence, Scott stared fixedly as the dot glowed and then dimmed with each sweep of the radar.

'Probably just another cruising boat looking for company,' said Duval.

'Damn funny way to behave, running without lights, and tracking your course change.'

Duval shrugged. 'Just wanted to stay with us I guess. Maybe his lights are broken.' His voice was devoid of inflection, as expressionless as you could make it.

It didn't sound like Scott was convinced. 'I still don't like it,' he said finally, 'we'll set up a zig-zag pattern. Twenty degrees one side of our course for fifteen minutes, then twenty degrees the other side for another fifteen minutes. Keep doing it, see how badly they want to stay with us.'

'Hell, Scott, that'll slow us up nearly as much as if we were going upwind.' Anger was creeping into Duval's voice.

Scott stared straight ahead. He was visibly struggling with his temper. In the end he brought it under control. 'Just do as I say please, Peter. Steer the pattern.' He looked up at me and said, 'Martin, come down here and watch this thing on the radar. Duval will show you how it works. Report to me in half an hour.' He backed out of the navigation station, without looking at Duval, and went forward. Ben glanced at me and then followed his skipper.

I stepped down the hatch, carefully keeping what was left of my supper upright, and slid onto the chart table bench beside Duval.

'This is kind of strange,' he said, flatly.

I nodded my agreement. If it was Janac, why would he wait? Why not move straight in? I stared at Duval, but the face, bathed in the red glow of the night light, was giving nothing away this time. 'You think it could be pirates?' I said, finally.

Duval was still staring at the radar. 'Maybe,' he said.

So that was what he had been worried about.

'But it's unlikely,' Duval shook his head, 'they don't usually operate this far south. It's probably just another cruising boat.' He started fiddling with the radar again, I watched him for a couple of seconds, then he turned and said, 'It's simple enough, we're in the centre, this dot,' he pointed, 'is them. If they move from position let me know. Just in case you fall asleep, I've set these rings up as alarms. So it will buzz when they close to less than two hundred metres, or move out beyond a thousand. You turn off the alarm here, OK?' I nodded. 'Right, let me through then.' I shuffled sideways so he could get out.

'Hey,' I shouted as he disappeared up the companionway, 'what about your supper?'

'Forget it,' came the reply, 'I'm not hungry.'

The cubby hole that formed the chart table and navigation station was probably the most comfortable place on the boat. I'd seen Kate working in here a few times, she seemed to do most of the navigating. The motion was bad because it was so far aft, but that was no problem for me. I settled back against the cushions and watched the green blip. Thirty minutes later there was no change. Despite Duval's two course alterations they remained fixed on our beam. I was about to go and find Scott when he and Ben appeared beside me.

'Well?' he asked curtly.

'No change,' I replied, equally abruptly.

'Might as well, Skip,' said Ben.

I looked round to see what they were talking about as Scott reached over my shoulder and picked up the radiotelephone.

'All ships, all ships, this is the yacht *Gold*, over.'

The transmit button clicked off, and we all listened intently, nothing.

Scott tried again.

And again.

Still silence.

He replaced the receiver and shrugged. 'If they were a cruising boat they should be listening on 16. It doesn't prove much, a lot of people are pretty slack about radio watches.'

'What's the range of that thing?' I asked.

'About twenty miles.'

'Is that all!'

'We have the SSB, the one with the radio microphone you hurled across the fucking boat this afternoon!' Scott retorted angrily.

I stared straight ahead at the radar.

I heard Scott take a deep breath, then he resumed in a more reasonable tone, 'That will go a few hundred, or even thousand miles when the conditions are right. But, assuming that the microphone still works and we can talk to anyone at all, I can't call for help just because this guy is tracking us – whatever we suspect.' There was a heavy pause for emphasis. 'He has to do something before we can justify calling another boat, especially commercial shipping, off course to help us. What do you say to them now? Would you steam a couple of hundred miles to check out these guys following us? It's like walking down a street and thinking the guy behind you might be going to mug you. When do you scream help?'

'But surely by the time they have . . .?' I started to say.

'Yeah, that's the problem,' Scott shrugged, unwillingly granting me the point. 'So, all right, if it's this Janac bloke we do have a case for calling ships off course since we know he's trouble. But if it's not him we might be giving ourselves up by broadcasting. The Australian authorities or your buddy Janac could just as easily pick up our transmissions and our relayed position, which we would have to give to get help. And they may be out there looking for us if Duval called them. Which we can't discount,' he glanced upwards to where Duval was on deck, 'whatever he says. The second problem is, that if we have an ordinary pirate out there and we start calling for help, he may figure we're weak and come right on in. At the moment the only thing stopping him might be that he doesn't know who we are or how much of a fight we could put up.' Scott paused. 'There's a hell of a lot of ifs and buts. But the biggest one comes down to, is it Janac? Well, he's your problem, what do you reckon?' finished Scott harshly, staring at me.

I hesitated, wiped my hand across my mouth nervously, then said, 'Give it more time, see what he does. There's too big a downside to screaming for help at the moment.' I paused. 'But we should maybe try and check out that microphone, or swop it with the other one,' I added, pointing at the working VHF microphone.

Scott nodded, 'Yeah, that's right, can you get on to that, Ben?'

'They're not compatible, we've had the problem before. But I can try and fix it, although electronics isn't exactly my field.'

'Do your best. We'll keep a listening watch on the SSB and the VHF on the emergency channels, if we hear any chat let me know. It would be worth making contact. It would be good to find someone close we can hook up with for company. The problem is, there aren't too many cruising boats in this part of the world, especially at this time of year.'

'Why?' I asked the obvious question.

'Well, it's the hurricane season for one thing, and the pirates have something of a reputation.'

'This may sound dumb, but what are we doing here?'

Scott smiled. 'We don't have any choice for one thing. The boat has to go to Hong Kong and it isn't going to fly there. But hurricanes aren't too much of a problem, we have the best weather forecasting equipment you can buy on board.' He gestured at the bank of screens, printers and radios. 'As for the pirates, I guess it's like riding the subway in New York. You think it'll never happen to you, and you can't stop going out because of the possibility.'

'You can take a cab,' I said.

Scott grimaced. 'Not if you can't afford one,' he replied.

The time ticked on, and Duval, despite his reservations, kept making the course changes right on cue. The second thirty minutes was about due when Scott reappeared once more.

'Same deal?' he said.

I just nodded, he could see for himself, the green blip was right there.

'You ever fired one of these?' he asked.

I looked round. He was holding a pump-action shotgun.

'No,' I said, swallowing heavily, 'but I've done some clay pigeon shooting with the ordinary sort.'

'Good, it's the same principle. Put the cartridges in here,' he spilt a handful on the nav table, then loaded a couple, 'and this,' there was the ominous schung-schung sound as he worked the action two-handed, 'puts one in the breech. OK?'

I nodded again and he handed me the gun. I took it wordlessly and dropped it in beside me. My mouth was completely dry and I was sweating enough to soak my shirt. But I shuddered.

On the dot of ten Ben poked his head round the corner and said, 'Any change?'

I shook my head as I turned to look at him. He was every bit as grim and serious as Scott. The rifle was held loosely at his side. I wondered what Duval was thinking now.

'Nothing. Is that radio working?' I said.

'I've pulled it apart, there were some broken connections which I've tried to solder back on. I've no idea if it works, though.'

'Maybe we should try it?'

'You heard what Scott said, we could just give ourselves away to the cops or Janac. We don't figure they'll do anything till they've sized us up in the daylight. We don't want to provoke an early attack by using the radio.'

Ben hefted up the rifle. 'It may not come to using this, but we should make it clear to them that we aren't to be messed with lightly. But as I say, I think they'll wait till it's light to have a look at us.'

'Unless they already have,' I replied.

'How do you mean?'

'At the island, they started tracking us almost as soon as we were past it. Maybe they were watching us from the shore. We would never have seen them in the vegetation. Simple enough to jump on a boat hidden in one of the bays and then chase us up here.'

'Maybe . . . I'll take over, I'm on for the next four hours.'

I heaved myself out from behind the chart table and scrambled up the companionway. Emerging on deck the wind had freshened a little. I glanced at the speedo, we were charging along at a healthy ten, eleven knots. Scott and Duval stood by the wheel, deep in conversation. And Duval looked anything but sceptical. I clambered up the pitched deck, grabbing the runner winch for support, and planted myself beside Scott. He turned to me and said, 'Is Ben by the radar?'

I nodded an affirmative, then said, 'I don't understand why they're waiting. They could have been watching us from the island. They might have already checked us out.'

Scott looked at me sombrely.

Duval murmured his agreement from the wheel, steering with a concentration and intensity I had not seen in him before.

'You think we can out-run them?' I asked.

'That's what we were just talking about. We've come off the zig-zag pattern and headed up a bit. This is about as fast as we can go without setting a kite.' He eased himself over to the hatch. 'Any change?' he shouted down. I couldn't hear the reply, but it was clear enough from his expression that there wasn't. I stared out into the dark to where the unknown boat must be.

There was silence for a while, Duval steering, Scott standing and staring out to leeward, hands in his pockets, deep in thought. He balanced himself easily against the motion. I wedged myself between the runner winch and the guard rail. The only light came from the phosphorescent wash rushing past to leeward. All our own navigation lights were now out. It was clear what he was thinking: Janac, pirates or just some innocent fishing or cruising boat?

'Why is he playing this game, why doesn't he just get on with it?' Scott finally asked, of no one in particular.

It was that moment that it hit me with a certainty that was as solid as it was frightening. It was part of the game. Janac's game. That's why he was holding off. He was telling me it was him out there. I stared dumbly into the blackness. Trying to deal with the realisation.

Scott may have sensed something. He turned towards me and glared. I glanced across at Duval. And Scott followed my gaze. Then he said, slowly, 'It's Janac, isn't it, Duval?'

'How many times do I have to say it, goddamnit, I didn't call anyone!' Duval snapped back.

There was a heavy silence as Scott considered us both. 'Well, the bastard's locked on to us good and proper. And he's not going away,' he said with a grim finality. Then he relapsed back into his meditation, staring out to leeward.

Eventually I said, 'What about setting a spinnaker?'

'A kite? Five up on a Maxi boat?' Scott sucked his teeth. 'It would be difficult, not impossible in this breeze, but difficult and risky. We could band it up like a cruising chute. But if it went wrong we would be real slow for a while. The other problem is that we'd have to come off another thirty degrees to set it. We'd be sailing right at them, making it easy for them to close the distance. For all we know they could be flat out trying to keep up. Heading towards them might encourage them to have a go now. No, I'd rather wait on the spinnaker till we know for sure that we need more pace and definite evasive action, and the kite will take us away from them. We'd look pretty stupid pulling the rig out trying to get a spinnaker up.'

He paused for a moment, then looked at Duval and did something I had never seen him do before – check with him, 'You OK with that Pete?'

'Yeah,' came the reply, 'but it would be worth banding the chute ready.'

'Right, come on, Martin, you can give me a hand.' He moved off forward, with me trailing behind.

By the time I got down below, Scott already had the spinnaker out of the bag. He had his head down, and was sorting through it. He held up a corner to the weak red glow from the bulkhead light, then started working his way along the edge of the sail. I braced myself against the companionway to watch. 'This is the only one we've got on board. We have a rule about no spinnakers on deliveries.' He smiled briefly to himself. 'Some friends of mine once dropped a mast with a kite up on a delivery. Got caught in thirty-five knots, hadn't got enough power on the grinders to trim it fast enough, couldn't get it down, and eventually they rolled the pole in and that was that. Bit unlucky, I've done a lot worse in the Southern Ocean and kept the stick up. But there you go, shit happens.'

I nearly said, I know, but settled for nodding.

'OK,' he went on, 'if we're going to get this up, we need to band it tightly from all three corners. It's already done a bit, but the only time we were going to use it was when it's light, in which case if you band it too hard you'll never get it open.' He handed me the corner he had arrived at. 'You pull this forward and I'll work down it with the wool.'

I took the big heavy stainless ring from him and pulled it and the spinnaker with me as I walked towards the bow of the boat. I was careful with my feet and kept one hand on the hull as the motion up here was even worse than back aft. Scott followed me up with the ball of wool in his hand. Slowly we worked our way down the sail, with me holding the cloth in a bunch and him tying it in place with lengths of the wool. I began to understand what we were doing. The wool would hold the spinnaker closed till it could be fully hoisted. Then we would pull on the sheets, and pop the wools, opening the kite as though we were unzipping it. I grunted as the light dawned.

'You get it now, Martin?' said Scott. 'The distance apart of the wool is the crucial thing. Too far apart and she'll pop before you get it up, too close and you have trouble breaking it open. We have fancy methods of doing it when we're racing, big socks that you just zip it up in, but they're all in the container on the way to Hong Kong.'

I nodded with a certain amount of admiration, he sure as hell knew what he was doing.

We spent another ten minutes on the spinnaker, tying the wools in from the three corners, until it was completely banded up. Scott then packed it back in the big, square bag, with each of the corners carefully pulled out and tied off, so that it would be hoisted the right way up and untwisted. Finally Scott was happy, and as he straightened up from the bag he said, 'OK, Martin, you get some kip, I'll wake you for the next watch.'

I watched him turn to go aft, before I said, 'Scott.'

He stopped, glanced over his shoulder.

I hesitated, I was committing myself, but it had to be done. 'I think we should start trying to contact people with the SSB now. Ben thinks he might have fixed the microphone.'

He turned to look at me more carefully, before replying, 'You think it's Janac?'

I took a deep breath. 'I think that we should assume so.'

'Is that the same thing?' He was scouring my face with his eyes.

'To all intents and purposes.' I looked away. 'After catching Duval on the radio this boat turns up – and the way he's hung back, like he's toying with us,' I shook my head, 'I have a bad feeling about it.' That was putting it mildly, I thought.

He nodded slowly, grinding his jaw grimly. 'I'll get Ben on to it,' he muttered. He opened his mouth to say more, but stopped, turned and stalked away.

24

Four hours later, I was back at the radar watching the unwavering green blip tracking us, when Scott slid in at the chart table beside me. He reached up and clicked on several switches and the screens flickered into life. I had never seen this stuff powered up before. He turned a few dials, then pulled a keyboard and mouse out from behind a board and I realised that the monitor in front of us was a computer. He started up some software, the mouse and keyboard clicking in unison. The colour screen slowly began to draw what I recognised as a weather satellite picture.

'Where's that from?' I said.

'The aerial's on the back of the boat, the satellite passes overhead every couple of hours at most. This one we just picked up now.' A couple more key-presses and a grid flashed up on the screen. Scott reached over and pressed another button. I recognised our position, in latitude and longitude, on that one. He looked back at the computer monitor. The picture was now complete.

'We need to know what the options are.' He seemed to be thinking aloud as much as talking to me. He carried on, 'Bit premature possibly, since we have no idea how fast they are or what their plan might be, but it's good to have the scenario in your head before any action starts. Just like a race, and since we got all this kit, we might as well use it.'

'We're about here,' he said, pointing to a position on the grid. 'The cloud pattern you can see is from the weather system that's providing us with this east north easterly breeze. What we need to know is what's going to happen next.' He gazed at the screen for a while. 'You can see new systems developing on this thing before they appear on the weather fax. But there's little doing here.'

'The what?'

Scott turned to his left, and reached up to a printer above his head. More buttons and lights, then he glanced at his watch. 'That thing is a weather fax. We should get a forecast through any minute. All the big weather stations world-wide send out forecasts and information on radio signals. The machine is built to receive and print them out.'

As he spoke it clunked into life, the paper spat out the front and the print head whirred.

'Like that,' said Scott. 'It'll take about ten minutes for that to finish. How's he doing?' He nodded over towards the radar, which I had completely forgotten about. 'Looks about the same, huh? Maybe moved in a little bit.' He paused. 'About three and a half hours before we get any light. I wonder if he'll make a move before then?'

The question hung in the air while we sat and watched the fax churn out the picture in silence. After a couple of minutes, Scott opened the table lid and pulled out a chart. He refolded it and then smoothed it down in front of us. Once again the position was brought up on the screen, and this time plotted on the chart. I looked over his shoulder. I could see Rossel Island behind, the Louisiade Archipelago spreading out to the west of us and ahead, a small, distinct chain of outcrops called Duffen Reef. Scott tapped the pencil thoughtfully on the chart. Then said, 'We need an edge. Something we can do that they can't. But until it's light we don't have much idea of what their capabilities are.' The watch was checked again. Now the ruler came out and the distance to Duffen Reef was measured. 'Forty miles,' he said softly. 'We get there about sun up. It might just be dark enough . . .'

'Dark enough for what?' I asked suspiciously, as he drew a line on the chart – between the two biggest islets. It was the only part that wasn't marked as solid reef. I peered at the chart, there was a neatly drawn three in the tiny white gap signifying clear water, 'Through there? Three what? Metres?'

'No, fathoms, eighteen feet, plenty of water there. The biggest problem is hitting that channel accurately, with pace on. That's the idea. If it's an old shitter of a boat, which we think it is, they probably won't have this kit.' He tapped the position indicator. 'I doubt they would try to follow us through there in the dark. They may do it in daylight, but slowly, and even if they do, the best they can do is follow. It allows us the freedom out the other side to chose an angle, get the kite up and see how fast this baby really is when she needs to be.'

I let out a low, breathless whistle. 'What's the kit?' I said finally, nodding at our position flashed up on the lcd.

'Satellite position indicator, works out where we are from a ring of satellites above the earth. At best it's accurate to maybe one to ten metres.'

'And at worst?'

'About a hundred. They're American satellites, they transmit a civilian and a military signal. The military one is a lot more precise, but unfortunately these sets just receive the downgraded civilian version. During the Gulf War they didn't have enough military kit for all the boys out there. So they had to give them civilian equipment, and then make the civilian signal full military accuracy to allow their own people to use it normally – we could do with that facility now, but I think this will be good enough.'

'How wide is that channel?'

Scott smiled. 'About a hundred metres. That's the fun bit. The only other little problem with this plan, is that the satellite chain isn't quite complete yet, and it has an unfortunate tendency to go off when you most need it.'

I didn't say anything to that one, just watched as Scott hit more buttons. A graph appeared on the display, which said 'Satellite Availability'. I looked across the horizontal row, at 0600 there were three marked to appear.

'Three?' I said, in case I had read it wrong.

'Should be enough to give us a good fix. Best chance we've got.'

I was silent.

'If it is Janac,' he added, as though I should have said it and had missed my cue. 'There'll be enough light to see that by the time we get there. If it looks like a cruising boat we'll just turn round and come back out the way we went in. But if it is a cruising boat, I doubt they would follow us all the way in there anyway. It's a dead end to anyone sailing under normal circumstances.'

He turned round abruptly and reached for the weather fax print out. It tore off easily enough and was smoothed out in front of us. Again Scott studied it in silence.

'Well?' I could hold my patience no longer.

Scott shook his head slowly. 'It isn't good. This system is moving away, the breeze is going to disappear. If we head downwind, we'll track it for a while.' He paused to look at the computer picture again. The ruler flashed quickly with some measurements.

'It's moving a lot faster than us, though. Whatever we do it'll over-run us by this evening. With no wind we're dead meat to those guys.' He looked sombrely at the radar picture and the ever-present green blip. 'This boat isn't made for motoring. That channel is the best, perhaps the only chance we've got. It's ten miles around, the only way through. We make it and they don't, then we've got a ten-mile head-start, or at least till it gets light enough for them to try and follow us.'

I sat silently, nodding was as much as I could do. Once again Scott pulled forward the keyboard. The weather picture disappeared and after a few more keystrokes up came a chart, much like the one we had in front of us. The cursor danced at the mouse's bidding for a minute or two, and then Scott sat back.

'We're sailing three twenty-five at the moment. We can come off to three ten and head for Hong Kong, come up five degrees and go for the gap. Or stay as we are and just hit the south west end of the reef.' He grunted. 'We'll slow up about a knot if we bear away to Hong Kong, plus it takes us towards him. Whereas we hold this speed and go away from him if we head up.' He stared at the blip in silence for a while. 'I don't think we have any choice. My call is we go for it.' He hoisted himself out of the chair and climbed up on-deck.

It was just before five when Duval dropped through the hatch behind me.

'What's happening?' he said.

I looked up from the screen that I was studying so intently. I felt like the green blip was burned on the back of my retina. 'No change, he's still there, but just maybe he's pulled back a little bit. That's because the breeze has picked up?'

Duval nodded, serious, unsmiling, 'Yeah, it's hitting twenty knots in the gusts now and we're doing just under thirteen ourselves.' His eyes were red and puffed, I realised he'd been on deck for about eleven hours.

I looked back at the screen. 'Maybe he has gone back a touch.'

'Could be thirteen knots is too much for him. It's a fair pace for anything but a modern motor yacht. Still nothing on the radios?' he asked.

'No.' I shifted uncomfortably and changed the subject before he could mention the SSB and its damaged microphone. 'But you can just about see the islands on the radar now. He has to have realised what we're up to.' I pointed to the screen as I spoke.

'Or he thinks we're running blind into a dead end. One of the two. He can't have any idea what we can do with this boat. I'll wake Scott up, he'll be talking me in.'

I sat and watched for another twenty minutes, slowly becoming more and more convinced that he was altering position. By the time Kate arrived for a look I was sure.

'He's going back, I'm certain of it now, coming into line, but also losing distance.'

Kate nodded and climbed up past me. I heard Scott's voice, 'Hey, Katie, this is your last time on deck, the light is starting to come up and we don't want them to know we've got any women on board.'

'Scott, be serious . . .' but he didn't let her finish. I don't think he even said anything, the look must have been obvious enough. She came back down and passed the nav station without so much as a word.

A couple of minutes later Scott appeared below. 'I'll take over now, Martin, you stand up here by the hatch and relay my instructions to Pete. Once we get in there it's going to be noisy, with this swell breaking on the reef. I don't want to have to leave the nav station to talk to him. Ben's going on the bow to watch the water.'

I was quite relieved to be moving after three and a half hours jammed behind that chart table. I stepped out of the hatch and tripped on the liferaft, which had been moved on deck.

'What's that for?' I said, warily.

'Just in case we screw it up,' Duval replied grimly, staring fixedly ahead.

I looked around. There was the faintest orange glow away to the east, slowly spreading its way into the sky, the first sign of day. In front the deep, blue water of the ocean gave way faintly to the moonlit, azure shimmer of the shallowing reef, and then on the far horizon the flecked white of breaking waves stood out in the gloom. Somewhere in there, was a channel. I peered intently behind us, but could see nothing of our pursuer.

'He's there,' Duval muttered.

I hunched down by the hatch, alternately watching Scott, ahead and behind. Occasionally I passed up messages – down a couple, up one. I guessed he meant degrees, but couldn't believe that

Duval could steer a boat under sail that precisely. We thundered on, thirteen and a half on the dial, water foaming at the forefoot, headed straight for a reef in the half-light. I switched my gaze from the bow to the stern and finally I thought I could see something. The sun was coming up on our starboard quarter and there was the faintest sign of a silhouette against the lightening sky behind us. Slowly it picked itself out of the blackness and the boat's superstructure emerged. I got Scott to pass up the binoculars. I could just make out the high deck house I had seen before, surrounded with davits and tackle. The boys were right, it was no cruising boat.

Ben dropped down beside me and took the glasses. 'It's a local boat for sure, with that profile. And she wouldn't be chasing us in here if fishing were on her mind,' he said, matter of factly. But the words caught me with a sudden chill. 'Hang on to this, Martin,' he handed me the rifle, I took it uncomfortably. 'I'm going forward, it's going to get a little wet up there.' And he moved silently forward. I looked back again, I could see the white of the bow wave now, and the dark of the hull against the lighter black of the ocean. They were not that far away.

'We're no more than five minutes from the reef, guys, get organised up there.' Scott's voice, belying no tension, emerged from the hatch.

'Everyone's in position, Scott,' I replied. Ben was perched on the plunging bow, already soaked.

'Ease the genoa just a tad for us will you please, Martin.' It was Duval this time, voice as cool as ice. I was choking with nerves, I wasn't even sure my voice was going to work. I moved forward and the winch groaned as I eased the heavily loaded sheet off an inch.

'That's fine,' came the call from astern. I hurried back to my station. Scott called another tiny course change. Behind, the hull of the boat was finally visible against the horizon. Rolling quite heavily, she looked like a big, squat, round bilge fishing boat.

'I can hear the surf.' Ben's voice crackled through the radio by Scott's head. I started, I had expected him to shout. But he was seventy feet away, we'd never hear him. I looked forward into the half-light, there was little of the deep blue left to go, and a hell of a lot of reef and white water. Where the fuck was this channel? And now I could hear the thunder of rollers. It seemed there was nothing quite so frightening as hearing the crash of surf from a sailboat in poor visibility.

Crack!

Except that. The unmistakable report of a firearm.

'They've opened fire,' I called below to Scott, my voice a squeaky croak.

Scott looked up at me grimly. 'At least we're doing this shit for a reason. Come up just a fraction now,' he said. I passed the message on to Duval. We plunged on, into the open, gaping mouth of the reef, jagged, white teeth appearing either side of us. Another shot from astern, but again not so much as a splash to show where it had gone. A flat, dull report muffled by the thunder around us. Nothing like the movies, no whining richochet to add to the effect.

'Surf either side, clear ahead, but it looks shallow,' came Ben's voice again, distorted, metallic and far away from here.

'Keep her steady,' said Scott. I passed the message on, then glanced down, he was working furiously. First on the chart, then on the computer. Checking and checking again. By now the sound of the surf was everywhere, I daren't look up. Stick to your job I thought, don't want to screw up now. I braced myself hard, just in case.

'Come up five now,' came the call from below. I looked up to pass it on, there was thundering water all around us. No turning back. I glanced at Duval. His face was calm, but his knuckles were white.

'Surf everywhere, I can see no clear water,' hissed through the radio.

'Did you hear that!' I shouted at Scott, the fear lacing through.

'Keep it steady,' he said urgently, 'it's shallower than I thought, it may break in the channel. But there should be enough water.'

'Hang on everyone!' Duval screamed over the noise. 'We're going to get a ride on this one!'

And then the bow dipped as the boat surged forward in the foaming water around us. I was just plain terrified now, hanging on for dear, sweet life.

'Yeehaaaa,' I heard Ben scream from the bow. He had almost disappeared under the froth of creaming sea. Beside me Duval fought the wheel as though we were back in the gale. The sails clattered and banged as the acceleration blew them into the middle of the boat. Empty of wind, all the power was from the ocean.

Power we could barely control. One mistake on the wheel, if we went broadside to this baby all the liferafts in the world wouldn't save us.

Then suddenly we were clear. Racing ahead of the breaking water. Ben was running back from the bow, fists clenched, 'Yes!' he shouted.

I looked up at Duval. His normally expressionless face was illuminated by the widest grin I've ever seen.

'What a blast.' He shook his head disbelievingly. 'Who needs drugs when you can do this shit?'

Ben was back beside us, dripping wet and breathing heavily. 'That was better than the Southern Ocean!'

We stared at each other, smiling, laughing. We did it. They did it. I looked behind, there was a solid, white wall of breaking seas, their phosphorescent glow a row of white fangs in the gloom. From here you wouldn't dream of going in there.

Scott emerged through the hatch to reinforce what was becoming apparent, 'They haven't followed us. They're a mile back on the other side of the reef. We cracked it. Now let's get the kite up and put some distance between us.' His business-like voice cut through the adrenaline-drenched high on-deck. 'Ben, set the spinnaker up, hoist this side, pole on the headstay.' He leant down the hatch and yelled, 'Katie, we're far enough clear of them now, come up and take the wheel so Peter can help with the hoist. Stow that rifle below, Martin, we won't be needing it, for a while at least.' He followed Ben forward. I dropped down the hatch and jammed the rifle into a bunk.

I struggled along the passage, the deck leaping and jumping under me. When I emerged from the main hatch Ben already had the spinnaker on the foredeck and was clipping the gear on. The boat was pounding forward now, heeled over, spray coming back in chunks. I caught one of these full in the face but barely noticed. Scott dragged me up to the mast and handed me a rope. 'This is the spinnaker halyard,' he shouted, head shaking to flick away the water running down his face, 'you're going to hoist it here, while I tail the rope on the winch, right behind you there.' He pointed. I looked back and could see Duval moving round the cockpit, setting up the sheets on to winches. But Scott was still talking, 'As soon as it gets too hard to pull, you leave it to me to finish with the winch, then go back and get on the handles to help with the sheet, OK?'

I nodded.

'Ready forward,' shouted Ben. He was crouched by the leeward lifelines, balanced against the waves crashing over him, shirt and hair flapping. He seemed barely aware that the ocean and the boat were making a concerted effort to pluck him off and take him away.

Scott was already in the pit behind the mast, he yelled back, 'OK. Once she's clear you're on the sheet, Ben. Ready, Peter?'

Duval was standing by a windward winch with a rope loaded and in his hand, he nodded.

'Bear away for the hoist, Kate,' Scott shouted aft. She spun the wheel as Scott looked back to me, 'Let's go, Martin.'

I started to pull, there was eighty or ninety feet of this, and I figured none of them were going to be any easier than the one before.

'Com'mon, Martin, put your back into it,' screamed Scott. I could feel him pull on the rope from his position behind me, it was whistling through my hands so fast I was hardly contributing anything. I went at it harder, breath starting to rise, snatching at the rope from the mast as fast as I could. 'Good work, guys, over half way.' I could hear Duval's encouragement, but it was getting tougher now with every pull. I couldn't use just my arms any more, but had to lean my weight on it. I could hear Scott's laboured breathing. Then I felt Ben run down the deck past me and I knew we were close.

'Five feet, she's starting to pop, Scott, we need a grinder,' shouted Duval.

I could hear the kite begin to open. I didn't need any more telling, the halyard was already impossible to move. I leapt past Scott, who was loading the rope into the self tailer on the winch, and landed by the coffee grinder handles.

'Go, Martin!' urged Ben, who was struggling to control the spinnaker sheet. I wound like hell, but with arms already weak from the halyard I might have been climbing a mountain towing the boat.

'Guy's set, Katie, steer it to help him,' I heard Duval shout through the blood pounding in my ears. Then he was there beside me, the extra power on the handles made the difference. The spinnaker gave a final crack and set full. The boat lurched, staggered once under the new sail area, recovered, then lifted up her skirts and pounded forward.

'Well done, Martin, bloody good effort, take a break, I'll wind for a while.' Duval patted me on the back, I looked up through my heaving breath and the sweat running into my eyes and smiled. 'We'll make a grinder of you yet,' he added.

I was still recovering five minutes later, by which time the others had all settled down. Duval was back on the helm, Kate had taken over trimming with Ben winding the handles for her, and Scott had disappeared down below. Behind us I could just see the other boat as we both bobbed up on waves. But under Duval's deft touch she was getting further away pretty quickly. The boat was surging forward, spray licking back all the way to the wheels as she heeled to the breeze.

'What now?' I said to no one in particular.

'Scott's gone down to have a think about it,' said Ben, in between bouts of winding. 'You might as well get some rest while you can.'

That was what I wanted to hear, I picked my way aft through the hardware and loaded ropes and slid into the hatch. Scott was once more bent over the chart table.

'You're still worried, Scott,' I said. It was a statement.

He looked up and shrugged. 'They could pick their way through there in full daylight.' He looked back at the radar. 'They haven't tried it yet, but there must be nearly enough light now. It's given us a headstart, but not much. I'd like to see them turn around and go chase someone else. But they're not going to, are they?' He looked at me directly.

The elation of only moments before disappeared. I was silent.

'You've really dropped us all in the shit, haven't you?' Scott said with a sudden flash of temper.

I tensed, hackles rising. 'Now wait a minute, he might be after me, but Duval was the one that got them on to us,' I retorted.

Scott didn't respond immediately, the anger seemed to drain as fast as it had arisen. 'We don't know that.' He was looking right through me, his voice tired. 'We don't know anything.' He looked back down at the charts. I waited, but he didn't push the point any further. Instead, rubbing his forehead he slowly went on, 'The only plan is to put as much distance between us and them as we can. Which means sailing at whatever angle takes us away from them the quickest.'

I nodded, having no idea how he could work that out. He picked up the computer mouse, and more images flashed up on the screen. This time it was a section of a complex spider's web pattern, radiating from a central point. The mouse clicked a couple more times and up came a number.

'Which,' said Scott, 'if this latest forecast is correct, is three hundred.'

'How the hell does it work that out?' I said.

Scott looked up and managed a weak half-smile. 'Some other time, Martin, some other time.'

25

I CRAWLED INTO the nearest bunk, guilty at the realisation that I had already had more than my share of rest. Duval had steered for almost three straight watches. But he's the best in the world, an internal voice replied, what can you do? Nothing but wait.

I shifted constantly in my efforts to sleep. And finally managed a semi-concious daze that made it impossible to distinguish between dream and reality. Scott's calls from the chart table and occasional excursions to confer with Duval. The wash and bubble flowing inches past my ears on the hull outside and the occasional hiss and crackle of static on the empty radio as Scott mayday'd for help. Kate's shouted commands from on-deck, the clank and whirr of the winch gearing inches away on the inside of the hull, the crack of the sails and all the time half aware that I might be called on at any moment. Was this what it was like to race these boats? The continual tension of something happening all around you. The only buffer was the bunk and permission to go down and rest. I was almost grateful when Duval came to fetch me.

'Your turn on deck, Martin, we can only afford to rest one at a time now.'

I rolled over to face him, he looked exhausted. I heaved myself out of the bunk. 'What's happening?'

He nodded sombrely. 'Came through the gap about half an hour behind us. While the wind stayed up we were pulling out, but it's been dropping for the last hour or so. At the moment they're tracking us, same speed, about ten miles back. Scott's sure they must have radar because they're right on our line.'

'They gonna catch us?' I couldn't hide the urgency in my voice.

'By mid-afternoon, unless we get some more breeze from somewhere.'

I just stared at him. Thought about that room. The clock and the decision. Another game. I forced the thoughts away. 'Maybe we'll get someone on the radio,' I said, stepping up to the ladder. I looked back, Duval was asleep before he hit the bunk.

I could sense the change as soon as I went on deck. The early morning triumph had evaporated. No one greeted me as I emerged into the heat of the day. The atmosphere was grim, occasional commands the only communication. The boat too was muted, she still hustled along well enough, but not with the crash and thunder of the dawn. I realised that all this had been apparent from the bunk. I just hadn't wanted to think about it.

'Take over the handles from Ben please, Martin,' said Scott, tight lipped and curt. The lines on his face were etched ten years deeper than when I had left him this morning. I nodded and went forward. Ben straightened away from the coffee grinder winch handles and rubbed his hands together, I could almost hear the muscles creak. I stepped into his place and listened for the commands from Kate, but she spoke to Ben first, 'Ben, you want to go and fix us up something to eat and drink?'

Ben nodded.

'Give the radio another try when you go past,' I murmured as he left.

Kate and Scott may have been grim and silent, but they sure as hell weren't driving the boat any less hard. Ten minutes later and my shirt was soaked in sweat. I stripped down to my shorts and started to feel better – at least I was doing something. As we got into a rhythm the atmosphere cleared a little, the commands were less tense. The irony of the three of us working together so closely went unacknowledged. But none of it stopped the inexorable speed drop as the wind slowly deserted us. Every ten or fifteen minutes the pole would ease forward another couple of inches as Scott brought the boat higher to try and squeeze a bit more speed out of the lighter breeze.

Ben kept us fuelled with water and chocolate for a couple of hours and then took over the trimming from Kate, and we worked on. I was sweating it out as fast as I could drink it. I could feel my skin tightening with the sun, even through my tan, but sunburn seemed of no concern. I ground on, listening only for the two words that meant anything, trim and stop. Even through the leather gloves my hands were blistering on the smooth handles. My back was cramped and aching from the bent position and my arms – they just plain hurt. By midday the speed was down to ten knots. When Kate checked the radar they were only seven miles back. Even I could work that one out – they could do thirteen knots, so at best we had a couple of hours. I pounded those handles fit to break the chains, watching Ben's face intently. He barely spoke now, I knew when to wind from his expression. His eyes, hidden by the shades, can never have left the spinnaker. Not once had it collapsed in the hours since I came on deck. The front edge was always just curling, working at a hundred per cent, just like they'd told me it should be.

Finally Scott called Kate to take the sheet back, Ben patted me on the shoulders and I fell back to let him take my place. I slugged back a pint of water and held my head in my hands. It throbbed, all of me hurt.

'Get your shirt on, Martin, and out of the sun for a while. We don't need a case of heat stroke. And get Pete up so Ben can take a spell,' said Scott, I needed no second bidding. But when I got below Duval was already at the chart table, bent over the SSB radio. I started, the sight of Duval at the radio providing a jolt of memory of our earlier antagonism. But I said nothing this time. The radio crackled and hissed, much as it had before. I started to speak, but then Duval's hand shot up for silence, and out of the static I could hear another human voice. Not much, but enough.

The button on the transmitter clicked and Duval spoke into the microphone, 'I repeat, this is the yacht *Gold*, we have been fired upon and are under pursuit from an unknown vessel. We require urgent assistance, they will be alongside us in one hour. Please give me your position. Over.'

We both waited, the air not even disturbed by the sound of breathing. The radio crackled again, I could barely distinguish it as words, but Duval seemed tuned in to the sound. He leaned forward intently, then there was silence. Once again he clicked down the transmit button on the microphone and spoke, painfully slowly and clearly, stopping to spell out the yacht's name, 'This is the yacht *Gold*, under attack from an unknown vessel, please acknowledge.'

The radio was silent.

We waited for another minute but there was only the noise of static, nothing that even Duval could distinguish as words. He tried again, simplifying the message still further this time. Still no reponse.

'They can't hear us, for christ sakes,' he turned on me angrily, fist shaking the patched up microphone, 'this thing's fucked.'

I stared at him. 'You don't know that, we could be out of range.'

'I can hear them!' he retorted angrily.

'That crackling sound? It's not exactly a crystal clear signal is it? It could be a more powerful radio, even I know that.' I was starting to get angry now, my emotion feeding on his, winding each other up. The truce that had kept relations smooth between us finally crumbling in the face of one shortened temper.

'This is all your fault, pal, you've been screwing my life up from the second you got in it. This guy's chasing you, I say we just put you in the liferaft and let him have you.' He threw down the microphone.

'How the hell do you know it's him? If you didn't phone up the cops and bring him down on us in the first place! Huh? Come on, tell me, how do you know Duval?' My accusation hung in the air for a second.

Then he responded, 'Fuck you!'

I saw the right coming with the words, and caught his arm in motion. I threw my weight at him, and off-balance from the misjudged blow he went down hard against the companionway ladder. I was on top of him instantly, kneeling on his chest, slapping open handers to his face. 'Come on, Duval, tell me you did it, I know you did,' I taunted him. Several stones lighter he was powerless with my weight on him, but he writhed and wriggled like a trapped snake. All the time screaming back at me.

I didn't see the blow coming that caught me from behind, but I heard the words that went with it as I crashed sideways off Duval under the impulse of Ben's foot.

'Pack it in, you morons, there's no one sailing this boat now.'

I groaned slightly at the pain from my shoulder, Duval was silent. Everything was silent. The rush of ocean along the hull had almost disappeared. Then there was a huge slap and a crack as the boat rolled upright on a wave and blew all the wind out of the sails. Ben was already on his way even as Scott's voice came down the hatch. 'The wind's gone, let's have the engine down there.' Differences forgotten Duval struggled to his feet and turned to the radar. I watched grimly as he fiddled with a dial, the scaling ring slid in to the green blip.

'Three miles, we should see them soon,' he said.

The engine choked and belched and finally kicked into life. There was a clunk as Scott dropped it into gear on deck, and I felt the propeller start to bite. But I wasn't exactly thrown backwards by the acceleration. Ben reappeared. 'Let's go talk to Scott,' he said. On deck the boat speed dial was reading between eight and nine knots. The spinnaker was already down and Scott was on the foredeck bagging it. Kate was winding the mainsheet into the centreline to stop it flapping, the boat steering on the autopilot. The wind had gone completely.

I helped Kate with the mainsail, as Ben went forward to help Scott. Within seconds they were both trotting back down the deck. Scott taking the wheel and clicking off the autopilot.

The five of us gathered together again. But the tension in the air now had nothing to do with love or money. Only death and its urgent possibility. And it was getting nearer with every passing minute.

'We got a radio contact, but they can't hear us,' Duval told the assembled group.

'We kind of figured that,' said Scott. 'I don't want to remind you two, in particular,' he stressed the last words heavily, 'of your responsibilities to the rest of us. You will cut the fighting and do your jobs, OK?'

Duval and I nodded silently.

'They are what? Two, three miles back?' He looked at Duval.

'Just under three miles back and five knots faster,' he replied.

'So they'll be up with us in about half an hour. As I see it we have two choices. We can surrender or we can fight. I'll accept the wishes of the majority.'

'We should put Cormac in the liferaft and let them have him,' said Duval with a chilling simplicity.

'That isn't an option,' said Scott with a fierceness that was more surprising than Duval's coldness. 'Even if it's just him they want, it isn't going to happen over my breathing body. Any other suggestions?'

Duval stared at Scott. 'OK, how about we play it cool, talk to them and we see what they want, money, whatever, and we give it to them.'

There was a silence. My stomach churned, I wiped away guilty perspiration from my forehead – and glanced at Kate. She was watching me. 'Don't even think about it,' she said quietly.

Scott glanced at us both. 'We stick together,' he said. 'That's final. No more discussion on it.' Then he turned to Ben, who was next to him, 'Ben?'

'We fight for sure.'

Kate was next, she had looked away, and was staring at her feet. 'Kate,' Scott said, trying to bring her out of her reverie.

She looked up suddenly, and spoke softly again, 'We fight.'

Everyone was looking at me, but I had no choice. I wetted my lips, and then nodded, 'We fight.'

'OK,' said Scott, glancing over his shoulder, 'I make it four to one. That liferaft's all yours, Duval, if you want it. You stick with us, you do as you're told.'

Duval shook his head with a bitter expression. 'You crazy bastards.'

'Make your choice, Duval, we don't have time for this.'

He took a deep breath. 'OK, I'll stay and I'll fight.'

'All right, we haven't got long, we'd better get with it,' said Scott. 'First, we'll all get the main down, then Ben and Martin get half the sails up on deck, we'll pack them round the inside of the cockpit. The Kevlar should stop most things, they make bullet-proof jackets out of it. I'll wrap the other half around the nav station. Kate, get all the ammunition into there, you'll be with it, reloading. You can also use the radio from there, keep trying that boat, see if they can hear us. You can steer for now. Duval, get the weapons into the cockpit, and some food and water. We'll leave the liferafts up here, protected by the sails. Also the first aid kit. Anything else you think we might need, grab it, I want everyone in the cockpit together, except me.'

'Where the hell are you going?' said Duval.

'Up the rig with the rifle, might be able to keep them out of range with the extra height.'

There was silence, then Ben's quiet voice, 'No Scott, that's my job. You know you can't hit a barn door with that thing.' More silence, I could hear the pulse thumping in my temples.

'He's right, Scott. Ben's the best shot by a hell of a long way.' It was Duval speaking.

Scott ground his jaw, then he said, 'I don't like it but I don't have time to argue, let's get it done.'

Action helped, the mainsail tumbled down on to the deck and was hurriedly flaked on to the boom ready to be rehoisted. Then Ben and I tore into the sails, we worked feverishly, heaving them aft and packing them round the inside edge of the cockpit. Down below I could hear Scott cursing and swearing as he struggled to move sixty-kilo sail bags into position round the nav station. Time ticked away. And the chasing boat got bigger and more threatening with every backward glance. As we shoved the last sail into place, Scott emerged from the hatch. He was soaked in sweat, took one look aft then shouted below as he climbed out, 'We haven't got long, Duval, where the hell is that rifle?'

Duval emerged behind him, passing up the weapon, spare magazines and several boxes of ammunition. Ben was already pulling the climbing harness on. He took the hardware from Duval, accepted a bottle of water from Kate and packed it all into the bag clipped to his waist, he slung the rifle on his shoulder, then nodded.

'I'm ready,' he said.

Scott was hurrying forward to clear the halyard. I moved to the handles, Duval to a winch for the tail. Ben clipped on to the halyard and was almost immediately flying upwards.

'Third spreader should do it,' said Scott through gritted teeth as he swung into the handles with me.

'OK,' replied Duval, 'five feet, slowly now, two feet, hold. That's good.'

Scott stood up from the winch. 'Tie yourself off, Ben, in case the winch or halyard goes.'

'Have done. I'm OK, you sort yourselves out. I can see the whole boat from here, they're nearly in range.' The reply drifted down to us from sixty feet up.

The three of us ran back to the cockpit. Duval had done a good job; food, water and first aid equipment all stood in separate piles. Enough for a couple of days. Kate sat carefully loading a shotgun, her feet on the wheel, steering. Beside her lay two more, a pistol and a flare gun. I grabbed the pump action I had had earlier and checked it.

'They're all loaded,' said Kate tersely.

Scott took the second shotgun from Kate and Duval picked up the third. Then he settled into position with his back to the forward bulkhead, staring aft. On one side was the autopilot control, on the other the wheel.

'I'll take it from here Kate,' he said. She slid away from the wheel, and took the pistol Scott proffered her.

'Get down below, Kate, try those guys on the radio again, and keep trying,' said Scott.

She nodded and was ducking down the hatch. Then Scott caught her arm and said, 'Maybe you got a spare cigarette, huh?'

She turned back, with a wry expression, and handed him a packet. 'No one so fanatical as the converted, Scott, hey?'

Scott shrugged, took the cigarettes and offered the packet as Kate disappeared below. Duval and I both accepted. The match flared, Scott lit his own, held it out for Duval, then me.

'Now we wait,' said Scott, flatly, waving the match to kill it.

26

T HE TROUBLE WITH waiting is you get time to think. My first
thought was Kate. The second was a fear of dying. And the
third was doing something about the first two. Scott had obviously
gone down the same path. He stubbed out the cigarette and, with
a glance at me, slipped quietly below to see Kate. He must have
been saying all the things that I wanted to say. Goddamnit, this
was a new game, all bets were off. I finished the smoke, flicked
the butt over the side and waited. Finally, he came back out of
the hatch and sat down. He lit another cigarette carefully, his
hands were shaking, and took a deep toke. He looked at me, no
expression.

'You bastard,' he said, in a whisper.

I couldn't look at him.

'You've both been shitting me all along.'

What the hell had she said?

I struggled to find a reply, but then he was on me and we
were all through with talking. And restraint. I fell backwards,
a charge of adrenaline at this new, closer threat. His hands were
round my throat. I began to choke and gag, struggling harder,
getting more desperate. Suddenly Scott froze, locked on me, but
letting me breathe. I stopped struggling, twitched my head to see,
there was a shotgun barrel at his temple. It was Duval.

'Now, Scott,' Duval's voice was under control, almost urbane,
'he's our ticket out of this, we can negotiate with them, use him,
that's who they want.'

'Duval.' Kate had appeared at the hatch.

'Shut up, Kate!' Duval never took his eyes off Scott. 'Well,
Scott? What do you say now?'

I looked at Scott's face, and every emotion was crossing it.
I held my breath. With Ben up the rig there was little I could
do about it against the two of them, except . . . I felt the deck
quietly for the shotgun. But, almost imperceptibly, Scott's grip

around my throat was loosening. He looked from me to Duval. 'Take the gun off me, Duval,' he said, his voice emotionless.

'Sure, just trying to get your attention.' The gun moved quickly away. 'There's no reason for us all to die, Scott.'

'Just why are you so sure that it's him they want, Duval?' Scott was staring at him intently now, but his hands were still around my throat.

'They wouldn't chase us this hard for money, would they?' he answered, still in that calm, persuasive voice.

The next move was never made. Ben's voice crashed in on the scene, 'What the hell is going on down there, they're almost on us!' The rifle cracked out from above, emphasising the point.

Scott rolled away from me for cover against the opposite cockpit coaming, grabbing for the gun. 'He stays here, Duval,' he jabbed a finger at him, 'and you just remember who you're supposed to be pointing that dammed gun at. And you –' the staccato finger swivelled, punching the air at me, 'this is a long way from finished.' He rolled and peered over the coaming out the back of the boat. I followed his gaze, shotgun retrieved and held a good bit tighter than before.

The boat topped a wave behind us, close enough to see detail – rust streaks, flaking paint – she rolled and swayed with the swell. No one was visible on deck. She was overhauling us fast when there was another crack from above. I saw the splash, Ben had put a shot ten feet off her bow. The engine note changed as they slowed down. But they hadn't chased us for twenty hours to be put off by a few shots. Almost at once they started to move out to our starboard side. Duval flicked the wheel to keep them astern. I heard their engine gun and saw the bow wave pick up as they accelerated. With the greater speed it quickly became obvious they could get alongside even round the outside of a much bigger circle. Duval turned tighter, but they maintained the angle to draw level slowly.

There was a grim silence on board as the rifle cracked again above our heads. This time I was sure I saw it kick up some woodwork. Duval kept tightening the circle, but slowly they gained on to our beam, getting closer. A figure appeared from the wheelhouse and immediately Ben loosed off two shots. They were only four, maybe five hundred metres away and I could clearly see the wood splinter on the topsides. But the figure stood its ground long enough to get off a burst of rapid fire. We all ducked instinctively, and I squirmed up against the sail-packed coaming.

'Machine pistol,' said Duval, his voice hollow. 'He'll never hit us from there.'

But my mouth was completely dry, my tongue felt round cracked lips. We were totally dependent on Ben to keep them out of range. Duval lay on his back to steer, occasionally ducking his head up to check their position. Every so often Ben would loose off a round. More often than not he would hit them. Scott rolled on to his back and shouted up to Ben. 'How you doing up there?'

I looked up at Ben, who seemed reasonably comfortable under the circumstances. He was seated on the third spreader, with his legs wrapped round the mast. He had the rifle propped upright on the horizontal. He looked down at us. I saw him tighten his grip on the rig as the boat crashed into a wave. We had turned through a three quarter circle and were now headed into the wave pattern, rather than running parallel to it.

'OK, but I could do with another heading, I can't shoot and hold on at the same time.' Ben's voice carried down to us easily on the apparent wind of our motion. He grabbed at the mast again as we lurched into another wave. They weren't too uncomfortable down here, but sixty feet up the motion was magnified ten-fold.

I had a quick look over the cockpit edge. 'They've dropped on to our tail and started to creep forwards,' I said, glancing at Scott.

He grunted an acknowledgement, turned to look at Duval. 'They're trying to keep us on this heading so he can't shoot. We have to keep them at a distance, if they get close enough to use that automatic properly, we're history. Spin it round and let him fire.' Immediately the wheel went down and the boat swung round side-on to the pursuer. Ben didn't need to be told, the rifle burst into action. He fired steadily and accurately. Nothing panicky about it. I gripped the butt of the shotgun tighter and wondered whether I would be as cool when my turn came. I saw the wheel house windows go, but couldn't see if anyone inside was hit. The boat kept coming regardless, altering course to close with us side on.

The automatics would almost be in range. At that instant two figures appeared on the deck, both opening up with a long raking burst. I squeezed even tighter down behind the sails, as I heard some of the rounds thump into the side of the hull. Duval spun the wheel hard to starboard to take us back away from them. Ben fired again, three times, then I heard him whoop.

'Yes, got you, motherfucker,' came the scream from above.

I took a chance and stuck my head up just in time to see one of the figures drag the other back into the wheelhouse. Jeez, I breathed, he really did hit one of them. But something was wrong. Duval was staring across at the other boat, the wheel forgotten as our turn tightened and tightened.

'Scott!' I yelled.

He was already reaching for the wheel, pushing Duval to one side. I felt the boat respond to the rudder as he regained control. I got to Duval, he was shaking, breath coming hard and fast, sweat pouring off him, eyes closed.

'He's killed somebody,' he moaned. 'It's all over.'

Then Scott was there, leaning forward, one hand on the wheel, the other grabbing Duval's shirt, hauling him up to eye level like a rag-doll. 'Yeah,' he breathed into his face, 'and when he's killed enough, they'll fuck off and leave us alone. Now snap out of it.' His voice was hard and his face set in stone.

Scott held him there for a long second, then pushed him away, moving back to the wheel. Duval didn't look like he was going to be much use to anybody for a while. He slumped back, wild-eyed, staring at Scott.

'They're still closing fast,' I said, urgently. Ben's rifle cracked again, and again. They were so close now I could hear the shots breaking glass and splintering wood.

'I think he's gonna spin round one side or the other and try and get men aboard,' said Scott, 'or maybe just soften us up a bit with that automatic. I'm gonna take us through one eighty away from him as soon as he makes a move to a side. When I spin the wheel you get your shots in, OK?'

I just stared at him blankly, but I understood. I glanced at Duval, huddled in the corner, looking from one to the other of us. I picked up his discarded shotgun, crawled over and shoved it into his hands. 'You understand?!' I yelled in his face.

He looked at me, then the gun, licked his lips once, and then nodded. I glared at him, but there was no time for more. I crawled back to my position.

Ben was firing almost continuously. He had them all pinned inside but they were so close, even from my lying position I could see the bow, looming over our stern. Then he stopped, I looked up, Ben was changing clips. Scott swore, low and fast and fluent, a torrent of abuse damning everything that moved. This was the moment they had been waiting for, the bow twitched to the right and they surged up alongside. Scott whipped us away to port, the boat rocking wildly under the rudder load. But the transom swung in towards them even as the bow moved away. They were close and broadside on. I heard the sound but it didn't register, until Scott screamed, 'Grappling hooks!'

He started to rise but then the automatics opened up. They picked the targets carefully. A steady salvo slammed into the bulkhead behind me, and thudded into the sails in front. I squeezed deeper in behind them, all thoughts of sticking my head up and shooting washed away in a torrent of fear. Ricochets rang off the transom metalwork as the aerials disappeared in a four-second burst. But it was when I heard the muted, choking scream from the mast that I knew we were finished.

I looked up in time to see Ben fall away backwards, held only by the rope at his waist. The rifle slid from his grip and crashed down to the deck. He didn't move.

Anger washed away the fear. I kicked my legs against the cockpit and half-rolled, half-slid into a firing position. I felt the shotgun recoil in my hands, but can't remember aiming or pulling the trigger. There were two more deafening reports in my ear, and a scream as a body fell across me. I kicked frantically at it, struggling with the warm, twitching figure. There was a thud as feet landed on the deck next to me. Battered training shoes. I pushed and fought to get free, turning towards them. And saw Scott lying on his back, pumping the next round into the chamber when the shotgun was beaten from his hand. The next blow caught him across the head. Duval staggered to his feet, but turned and fell back clutching his arm as one more shot was fired.

Then it was quiet, except for the whimpering of the body still lying nearby. I could hear Duval breathing heavily on the other side of the cockpit. There was a gun barrel under my nose. My hands were still gripped round my own weapon. There were other hands trying to take it away. The flash of gold jewellery. I could see my own knuckles, white and tense, locked to it. Then shouting and I felt something whip across my face. I put my arms up to protect myself and the shotgun was gone. I could taste the salt of the blood on my lip. This wasn't happening – it really wasn't happening.

Strong arms lifted me and I was dragged forward. Stumbling to get my legs to work I tripped down the deck. Crashing into the hardware. They pushed me through the main hatch, and I bounced off the steps and thudded into the floorboards. Pain flooded through every cell of my body. I didn't move, I had no wish to get up. But they were on top of me again, shoving me forward, into the forepeak. I slid through and landed on my face. The hatch clicked shut behind me.

It was completely dark. I could see nothing at all. I waited for my eyes to adjust, but even then there was nothing. I was right in the bow, beyond the waterproof collision bulkhead. The only way out was the way I'd come in and that hatch was locked by four clips on the other side. If there was no light, there was no air. How was I going to breathe? I panicked and threw myself at the door, screaming, banging, sobbing. The answer came quickly, with a burst of automatic fire. I slammed myself down. But silence followed fast, and when I looked up there was a ragged line of holes through both the internal bulkhead and the deck. Sunlight and precious air streamed in.

I slid back against the hull and squatted in the uncomfortable V'ed bottom of the boat. There were no floorboards up here. The carbon black sides of the hull were bare and shiny. The whole forepeak was completely stripped. Nothing. There would be no escape this time. I shivered slightly, despite the humidity and heat. One glance down at the clammy T-shirt told me why. I was covered in blood. I gazed at it in horror before ripping the shirt off. No wound. But of course, it was someone else's blood. I threw it forward.

I sat there, in shock I suppose. I had no rational thoughts. No thoughts. Everything was over. It was all numb. I heard a woman scream. They had found Kate, but I had nothing left for anger. I had no energy for any kind of emotion. It was all spent. I could only listen to her yells. But they were getting closer, coming down the boat towards me. The hatch flew open, and Kate half crawled, half fell through the hole. It slammed shut behind her and I heard the clips go back on. I don't think she even realised I was there as she turned and kicked at the bulkhead furiously.

'Kate!' I shouted it, as I reached out for her.

She stopped and turned. 'Martin, you're hurt!' She moved towards me as I looked down.

My chest was covered in dried, caked blood. I shook my head, 'No, somebody else's.'

'Whose?'

'One of them, Scott got clipped on the head with a rifle butt, but I think he's OK. Duval was shot in the arm, and Ben . . .'

She looked at me wildly. 'Ben?'

I shook my head. 'I'm sorry. He's dead.' My tone was flat, as spent as I was.

She stared at me blankly. 'Dead?'

I nodded.

'Dead?' she repeated, shaking her head slowly from side to side, as if trying to deny what I'd said. I moved forward to comfort her, but she shrugged me off, her fists balling. Then she started to hit me, more and more, on and on. The choking sobs coming fast and shallow.

After a while she calmed down and her head sunk into my chest. We were just left there hanging on to each other in that despairing embrace.

27

THERE WAS NO past and no future. Time had lost all meaning. It could have been seconds, minutes, even hours later when the hatch flew open again. I eased my grip on Kate a little, and looked at the light streaming in. The gun barrels waving, combined with the shouts, made the message obvious.

'They want us out,' I said.

She let go a little, and stared at me.

'Be brave,' I said, without feeling the slightest bit like it myself. Her hand slid down my arm until it found mine. She gripped it tightly, and then turned and led the way out through the hatch.

We stood there, blinking, even in the below-deck half-light, swaying slightly with the motion of the boat. Someone had switched the engine off, and only the occasional creak from on-deck broke the silence. It sounded as though the fishing boat was tied up alongside. We were the centre of a semi-circle of grinning men, all Asiatic. There was no Janac. Fuck. There was no Janac. My head went light with relief. It seemed impossible, but it was just a pirate boat. It wasn't me.

Just pirates? Murderous thieves. The relief condensed back into fear. They all carried automatics. Spare magazines, knives, scarves and shirt tails dangled flamboyantly. Except for one, who stood in the centre – neater, apparently unarmed. He was slightly-built and probably a good six inches shorter than me. But he seemed to be in charge. He moved forward and leered at Kate. I had barely twitched in response when arms grabbed me from both sides. It was obvious what was on his mind long before he got to her. I struggled but as soon as I started to get loose there were more hands on me. Someone kicked my legs out and I fell noisily to the deck, to be pinned there by four or five of them.

'You bastards, leave her alone!' I screamed, still writhing as I watched the drama unfold. A couple of them had moved to grab her arms, but as they were about to discover, it was her legs they should have been worried about. She let him get close enough to touch her without offering any resistance. Obviously encouraged by this passivity he reached forward and slid his hand under her shirt. I saw the cloud fleck her eyes and knew what was going to happen. But he missed it, too busy exploring her breast. I heard myself bellow, 'No, No!' without knowing to whom or for what. No one heeded the warning anyway, and Kate brought her knee up into his groin with a violence and speed that surprised even me. He doubled up and fell away with an exhalation of extreme pain, and almost immediately began to retch. There was a frozen moment while we listened to his agony. And then all hell let loose. Kate disappeared under a wave of bodies and I found a surge of strength in the certain knowledge that we were both about to die.

It wasn't the gunshot that stopped time again, but the gasp of bubbling, bloody agony that followed it. Everyone was still, none more so than our assailants. Except for Kate's would-be rapist, who noisily choked and bled his life on to the deck in front of us. It took several seconds for me to realise that this transformation was because of another arrival. And it was only when I heard his voice that I began to realise what had happened. It was white hot with a fury that chilled me even through the strange foreign sounds. But there was none of the lilting sing-song of the native speakers. No, it was a hard-edged American accent. The men pinning me down pulled themselves away. Then I saw him.

Janac.

Numbly, I watched him lower the hammer on the same revolver I'd seen on Ko Samui. He stood by the companionway, face set in a cynical, yellow-toothed smile. A couple of days' beard stubbled the freckled tan. He wore a set of heavy fatigues, coolly untroubled by the heat. But a bandage covered the left hand. I was empty, light-headed, nauseous. I struggled through the gathering wave of emotion, got myself to sit up, look around. Kate lay on the deck close-by, curled up protectively, her shirt tattered and almost ripped off her. There was a livid scratch across her back. I moved towards her. No one tried to stop me. I touched her. She flinched, silently, glanced at me through the hair matted with sweat and pain across her face. What was it in her eyes? Sadness? An accusation? Hatred?

'These people, they got no goddamn discipline.' Janac's voice.

Behind him the mob of pirates stood with their heads lowered, fiddling with their weapons. It was clear who was in charge. Kate struggled to sit up, covering herself with what was left of the shirt. 'Here,' Janac turned and barked out a command. Immediately one of his men peeled off a T-shirt and threw it to Kate. 'You certainly are a beautiful woman though,' the grey eyes flickered over her, as she pulled the shirt on, 'but rules are rules.' He holstered the revolver.

Then he looked at me, hands on hips, nodding slowly. 'Quite a performance, Martin – you've led me on an impressive dance.' He pulled a pack of cigarettes out of the breast pocket of the fatigues. He offered them but I shook my head. Kate wasn't even looking at him. 'Especially that stunt in Sydney. Do you know how much it cost me in bribes to turn those two cops? Then you go and blow them away.' He paused, with a dangerous stillness. 'And you cheated the game – again.'

The game, always the game.

I waited in silence. He lit the cigarette, with the same Zippo, before continuing. 'Although I suppose we did establish a certain willingness to die for the girl – which is progress of a sort. And then before I know it, you're out here. Somewhere in the wide open Pacific Ocean.' He shook his head. 'You haven't made it easy for me, Martin.'

'How the hell did you find us? Duval?' I said, words tumbling out unbidden.

The thin lips cracked into a smile, 'Well, you know how hard it is to trust the police to do a good job. Even when you're paying a few of them for some overtime.' He paused. 'But credit where it's due, you did all right, you disappeared completely for a while. And even I believed Scott was so mad at you, he was going without you. You nearly got away with it. But at the end of the day, that's what winning's about.' He tapped his forehead gently, with a thin finger. 'Thinking it through and covering all the options. And I had my little insurance policy in place.' He gently blew a smoke ring.

'To be fair to him, he thought he was doing the right thing, reporting a couple of fugitives to the forces of law and order. Covering his own ass in case the story came out, of course, but public spirited none the less. Trouble was, they were my forces of law and order.' He took a long, deep drag. Then considered me carefully through the exhaled smoke. 'You knew it was me, right from Rossel Island, didn't you?' I said nothing, but he nodded slowly. 'I could have taken you out, all the way back there, but that would have been too easy. You needed time to warm up for the next game, start falling out with your buddies.

'I must confess to an element of luck in predicting that Rossel Island was the place to catch you, when he first called. I was relieved when we got the position and heading update on the second call and it was clear that that was where you were going. It could have taken a week to catch you if you'd gone through the Archipelago any other way, especially at the speed that tub goes. And it cost me enough trouble and money getting that thing here. And now you've killed three more of my boys, aside from this asshole.' He nodded at the inert body swimming in its own blood. 'Two of them shot by that guy with the rifle,' he waved a hand upwards, 'and one when we boarded.' He squatted down to my level, and sucked a piece of tobacco from his teeth. He spat it out on the floor between us. 'And then there is this.' He held up the bandaged hand. 'So I think you would have to agree, Martin, that it's pay-back time.'

The words hung in the air between us. I stared back at him. I was almost beyond caring, almost beyond fear. I knew we would all die. We would die in the game. And it was the unknown element of the game that did instil the fear in me.

'I always promised you a final game, Martin. And this is it. No way out this time. Nowhere to run.' He stood up and stepped back, crushing the cigarette with a booted foot. 'I must say I've had a lot of fun figuring out exactly what it will be. But not as much as I'm going to have watching you play it. To start with I thought my little computer game would be ideal. But it's kind of difficult to run it on the boat, and there wasn't time to get it down here. It was hard enough finding a boat that would do the job. So we'll have to use an old-fashioned alternative. I think you'll like it.' He paused. 'Sure about the smokes, might be your last chance?' he went on, pulling the pack out and waving it at us again.

I shook my head.

He stepped back a pace then squatted down to our level again. I gazed into the grey eyes for a fraction of a second, but there was nothing. Only dilated pupils and blood-shot crazy paving. 'So can you guess what we're going to play?' he said in a quieter voice, gently exhaling smoke as he spoke.

He didn't have to tell me – the Prisoner's Dilemma. I was back where I started.

'As you can see,' he went on, 'the four of you have been split up. The others are on my boat. Each of you two will play against one of the other pair. I'll come back to who is playing who later.' He flashed a smile. 'Now each member of each pair will be asked the same question. But you don't have to answer till dawn tomorrow. So you have all night to think about it. The question is simple, I wanted to keep it simple. Strip the game down to its bare essentials. So the choice you are making is clear. Tomorrow morning I will ask you, are you a cooperator, or a defector? Your answer is just as simple; I cooperate, or I defect.'

He stared at us for a second or two and in the silence I managed to ask, 'The others, they're all right?'

'Well it wouldn't be much fun playing against a dead man, would it, Martin?' he snorted derisively, stood up, backed away. 'One of them has a flesh wound which we sort of treated and the other a headache, they're fine. So, to resume, you and your opponent will be asked to cooperate or defect. If you both decide to cooperate, then you both get to play a little game of Russian Roulette with me.' The revolver replaced the cigarette in his hand. 'At odds of six to one.' He opened the cylinder and dropped out all but one shell. It clicked shut and spun in a single movement. The gun was pointing directly at my forehead. It was so close, I could read Smith and Wesson on the barrel. I looked past it, at his eyes again, they were on fire. But then he was smiling and the gun was down.

'But not yet, Martin, not yet,' he said. 'If you both decide to defect, then the odds on the roulette get a lot worse.' The cylinder was open again, and two more shells were loaded. It flicked shut and span. 'Two to one,' he rasped. This time the gun was pointing at Kate. He shook his head. The gun was lowered. 'Not good, not good odds at all. All right for Bobby in the movies maybe, but I wouldn't want to be facing that one for real in,' he glanced at his watch, 'fourteen hours. So I guess right now cooperate looks like the answer? But of course there's a catch. A Prisoner's Dilemma catch.'

'You bastard,' I breathed.

'I know you know all about it, Martin, but forgive me the indulgence. I want to finish my speech for your pretty little girlfriend.' He took a couple of steps forward, leant right into our faces and said, 'If one of you answers defect and one of you answers cooperate, then the cooperator dies and the defector goes free.' The grey eyes danced over us, I could feel his breath on my face, see the pulse in his temple. I licked my lips, swallowed. He still hadn't told us who we were playing.

'But,' there was a slow smile, 'we still have to pair you up.' The smile spread into a grin. 'This is what makes it all so special.' He paused, but I knew what was coming. 'Martin, you will be playing Scott. Because he's this young lady's boyfriend. Or should I say was? Did you already blow him out, Martin?' he laughed, a loud sound in the silence. And then stopped, suddenly, spun away, then turned again. The cigarette jabbed at me for emphasis. 'Which means, Martin, that you have to watch her play Duval first.'

I felt, nothing. Everything . . . and nothing. I stared at him, at the glitter of amusement in the grey eyes. I forced myself to speak, it was still barely more than a croak. 'If we survive that, what happens?'

'You go free, with your boat and a bit of food and water. All over. Penance paid. I told you before, you may survive, but you have to play.'

'Why the hell should I believe you? Why don't you just kill me, that's what you want?'

'You know that's not true. And save me the hero speech, this is the way it's going to be. You get a chance to live. What chance depends on how you answer the question. The fun bit for me, is you thinking about that answer, all night. What will you decide Martin? Against Scott? Are you a cooperator or a defector? It's beautiful, Martin, it's all turned out so well. Sweet dreams people, I'll see you at dawn.'

It was in a dream that I watched him turn and go. The rest of the crew came to life at his departure, and bundled us brutally back into the forepeak. I crashed to the hull, cheek against the cold, black carbon, listening to the fishing boat untie and motor off. Some time passed. I don't know how long. After a while I moved cautiously to a sitting position. 'So it was Duval all the time,' I croaked, but the words had no venom. I looked at Kate, sitting in the tiny streams of light coming through the bullet holes. The blonde hair was frayed with sweat and dirt. The face lined and worn, a century older. But her body was still tense and defiant.

She looked back at me. 'Forget it, Martin. It makes no difference now. No more than any of the other reasons we're here.' She was right, of course. We sat in silence.

Eventually I said, in a voice I now recognised as mine, 'I'm so sorry, Kate . . .'

'I wouldn't blame yourself for the behaviour of this psychopath,' she said distantly.

'No, but if I hadn't got you involved, if . . .'

'We've talked about that already, Martin.' It was an exhausted voice.

We lapsed back into our own thoughts, defect or cooperate? Self-preservation or sacrifice? It just went round and round and came out the wrong place everytime. I'm better off if I defect. I . . . am . . . better . . . off. Me.

'I studied the Prisoner's Dilemma at Oxford,' Kate said suddenly. I looked at her, unsure how to respond. She sat with an unnatural stillness, leaning against the hull, staring at the ribbons of light filtering into the dark space. 'I had a theory about it,' she went on. 'I thought if people could understand, maybe things would be different. It was like a changing theory in science, like what happened in the sixteenth century with Copernicus.'

I shook my head blankly.

'Everyone believed that the earth was at the centre of the universe. Then Copernicus came along and said it was different, that the sun was at the centre, and the earth and the other planets revolved around it. It was a theory that shook everything people believed in, the whole of our understanding was turned on its head. We were no longer the centre of the universe. A paradigm shift, that's what they call it.'

'So, what's that got to do with the Prisoner's Dilemma?' I said.

She wearily pushed the hair out of her eyes and looked across at me. 'That was my solution. The problem with the statement "I am better off, whatever he does, by defecting." was the assumption that the individual comes first rather than society as a whole. A lot of people think that there is no alternative, that they have to look after themselves rather than the group. That's what happened in the eighties, in the way people like you behaved. But I wanted to change the paradigm, to say that we, the group, are better off whatever the other guy does, if I, the individual, cooperate.' Our eyes met for a second before she turned away.

'So in the electric shock game,' I said carefully, 'if I had cooperated and Janac had defected all the time, I'd have got a level five blast till it killed me. But at least one of us would have survived – him. Rather than taking a level three each, until it kills or maims us both?'

'Precisely. The group is better off. Cooperating, acting for the common good has to be the right answer.'

'A nice theory,' I said. 'But we're not in the lecture hall now – we're talking about real life and real death.'

'We should be able to trust others to do the decent thing,' she said. 'Even when it may reduce our own chances of survival.' She hesitated, staring at the deck. 'But you're right, now I keep getting the wrong answer.' There was a crack in her voice that hadn't been there before. 'It's such a good theory . . .' she went on, 'the group is better off if I cooperate, but now . . . with Duval? And for you and Scott!'

'That's why he's doing this, Kate. He knows all about us. It's been the game, all along, to test me. To see if I'm a defector or a cooperator. And now, with Scott to play against? And I have to watch you play Duval first? Christ, I bet Janac can't believe his luck. I'm just so sorry you all had to get involved.' Silence again. Then I said, 'What about the radio?' with sudden, ridiculous hope.

She looked up. 'I never got them to hear me. I heard them a couple of times but then it went dead.'

'They took the aerials out with the first burst.'

'They were too far away anyway,' she replied.

The silence grew out of the gathering gloom and enveloped us once again. The right thing to do was clear. The answer should be to cooperate. That was what my life had taught me. Right back to Kate and I breaking up, the currency dealing, the motorway accident, all Janac's games. If all the trauma, loss and sacrifice had any point at all, that was what it was about. That society couldn't survive on self-interest. We, some of us, had to act for the good of us all. I could do that. I could see myself, a good job, paying my taxes, letting people into traffic queues . . . But, against Scott? Would he see it? I could remember his hands around my throat all too clearly. The anger. The hate, that was what Kate had said. All directed at me. Would he put that aside? If he didn't and I cooperated, I was dead.

'Kate,' I said, hesitating, 'what do you think Scott is going to do?'

She looked up and shook her head slowly. 'It's no good, Martin. It's got to come from you. It comes from inside. Are you a defector or a cooperator? I know that what is between the three of us seems important, but ultimately you make a simple choice – can you trust him to do the right thing for you both?' She sounded so old, tired, weighed down with an understanding beyond her years. 'And for me,' she carried on, 'god only knows how hard it is. I know what sort of a person Scott is, I know him too well. And I still love him,' her voice was breaking again, the self-control slipping away. 'However confused my feelings are, and with what I now feel for you. We have shared so much over the past three years. If I tell you and affect your decision, if I was wrong, if anything happens to either of you . . .' Her voice had gone. I realised I could barely see her in the gloom, it was nearly nightfall. I crept over to her, and pulled her gently into what was left of the light.

'I can't do it, I can't defect.' She tensed again. 'My whole life I've been fighting against that attitude, that crap, it's destroying the world.'

'It'll destroy you now, Kate, if you let it. You must defect and take your chances, because you know he will.'

She pulled away slightly. 'Scott won't let him.'

'Scott won't be able to stop him, Kate. He'll try, all night probably, but . . .'

She shook her head slowly. 'I can't. I really can't. If he cooperates and dies because of me.'

She didn't have to go on. I knew how hard that was to live with. 'Kate, he won't. Everything about him screams out that he'll defect. The choice is a chance of life with maybe his blood on your conscience, or certain death.'

'To me? You think he'd do that to me?' she said, very still.

'What do you think?' I asked and then I thought I saw her nod. Just the merest hint.

'And you?' she asked. 'Can you trust Scott enough to put your life in his hands, can you cooperate?' It was dark now. I could feel her breath on my neck, her lips were inches from mine. We both waited for my answer, and when I breathed it into her mouth, our lips just caressing, I was sure I meant it.

'I have to,' I said. 'For you, for me. I have to cooperate.'

It would mean redemption, the penance paid. And Kate would understand I'd finally changed. If we both lived, it was the difference, the promise of a new world.

28

I DRIFTED BACK into conciousness, slowly, too slowly. I could feel Kate's weight across my arm. I caught my breath. She shifted slightly and pulled me in a little tighter. I didn't want to disturb her, so I lay still, listening to the gentle rhythms of her heart, the rise and fall of her breath. And stared through the holes in the deck at the changing patterns of stars. The boat rolled slowly to the motion of the waves and the thrust of the engine.

Cooperate or defect? I was still thinking about it when the first glow of light filtered through, and I heard the clips go on the hatch. No more time to think. It was time to decide. I rocked Kate gently to wake her. But she still came to with a start, her eyes fearful, the nightmare real. I nodded silently at the hatch, grey musky daylight struggled through it. She sat up and rubbed her eyes, then sighed deeply into clasped hands. I watched her hold that position for a few seconds. But the voices outside were getting impatient. She looked up finally, and kissed me softly, whispering a barely audible 'good luck' through a dry throat.

'You too,' I said and held her tight for a couple of seconds, before taking her hand and leading the way.

As I emerged through the hatch I was pushed to one side and gagged. Janac was standing at the base of the mast. 'Sorry about the gag, boys and girls, but we don't want to spoil the surprise for anyone, do we?' he said.

One of the others handed me a paper and pencil, and then hung a small box round my neck.

'So you just have to write the answer down on the paper, and stick it in the box there. Not quite as high-tech as my computer game, but it'll have to do.'

I was pushed even further away from Kate as I started to write.

'Cooperate or defect remember, no maybes, no conferring, a spoiled paper gets everyone a bullet in the brain,' he added with his cackling laugh.

The pencil disappeared as soon as I had finished. My hands were shaking and the writing looked like a five-year-old's. I'd done it. I folded the paper and placed it in the box. As the lid snapped shut my arms were grabbed and pulled behind me. I tried to tense my muscles against the cord, but they kept pulling tighter until it had bitten deep into the flesh. Just moving hurt like hell. No escape this time. I was spun round to face Kate. I glanced at her. They had done the same, hands tied behind her back, a cloth forced into her mouth. I daren't look in her eyes.

Janac spoke again. 'Good,' he said, with a delighted grin, 'we're ready. The die is cast, the hand dealt, the wheel spun. Let's do it, and may the losers be damned.'

We were pushed up the steps on to the deck. I glanced quickly upwards and choked my anger into the gag. The bastards had left Ben up there. I started to struggle against the pushing hands and was promptly slugged over the head. My knees folded and I tipped forward, unable to save myself, crashing into the winch pedestal. I lay there, dazed, struggling to focus. But hands grabbed me and forced me to my feet. I saw the trail of blood down the mast. The dark, dry stain on the deck. I looked away quickly.

'Squeamish, huh?' taunted Janac. 'Holy shit, you are going to have a lousy day.'

I glanced at Kate. She had seen it too. The tears streamed clear streaks down her grey face. I lunged desperately at Janac, but again a blow dropped me to my knees.

'Careful now, Martin,' said the voice, in a measured tone from above me, 'it's my game after all, and I might just change the rules and blow your girlfriend's brains out. Much as that would disappoint me.'

I forced my breathing to slow, and squeezed my eyes shut against the pain from my head. And didn't twitch a muscle. I must have lain there for several minutes. The boat was quiet and still. There were few waves and no wind. The engine was off again. Precious time I thought, there could be so little left. And I'm spending it gagged and trussed, too scared to move. Then I heard the other boat bang alongside. We had been waiting for Scott and Duval to be delivered to us. There were some heavy thuds. I wondered how bad Duval's arm injury had been. Bad enough to be a lot worse after a night without hospital treatment. God, what kind of a time had they had. Duval injured, and Scott trapped with a man he despised who held the life of his girlfriend in his hands.

Knowing that Kate was with me. He didn't deserve that, he didn't deserve any of it. None of us did.

I was jerked to my feet. The other three were already lined up by the guardrails on the port side, all on their knees, about six feet apart. It flashed through my mind that I could just slide into the water, that drowning might be better. But that was no chance at all. I wanted a chance. I was pushed into line beside Scott. He didn't even look at me. Just stared straight ahead.

The rest of the scum were gathering around Janac to watch. Lounged over the pedestals and guard rails. A blur of chatter and laughter. The sickness I felt in my stomach started to spread. I closed my eyes quickly, but the feeling was infecting every part of my body. Think about Kate, my mind said, think about Kate. I looked around, Janac already had her box open. He stepped back and unfolded the paper carefully. His voice rang out. One word. But not in English. The mob was hushed. I twisted my neck to watch Kate as he reached for the box round Duval's neck. Her head was down, her shoulders slumped forward.

Once again he turned to his men, unfolding the piece of paper. Again, one word. But the same word. The onlookers cheered, waving automatics in the air, bandoliers and headscarfs flapping. A couple loosed off rounds before a disapproving glance from Janac silenced them. What were they cheering? Two cooperates or two defects? The revolver appeared, Janac looked pleased with himself. It must be two defects. I stole a glance at Scott, he still stared straight ahead. There was a little dried blood on his forehead, but no expression, no emotion. I heard the chamber click open and my eyes went back to the gun. He held it upside down to show it was empty, then pulled a shell from the clip at his waist and carefully loaded it. Time seemed suspended as he hesitated over the next move. Then he loaded another. And another.

They had both defected. I didn't know whether to laugh or cry. And I couldn't do either. I was choking on emotion I couldn't describe. She had done it. Thank God, she could be dead now. That bastard Duval. But then I heard the chamber shut. Two to one odds. My eyes dragged back to her. The chamber span. He levelled the weapon at her forehead. She didn't flinch. I couldn't believe she was going to die. I couldn't believe how much I loved her. I wanted to scream, to pound, batter, bloody the bastard who tortured us. He was looking straight into her eyes, finger slowly increasing the pressure on the trigger. I flinched away.

Click. The relief left me dazed, giddy. She was alive. She was going to make it. Now we had a chance. My mind raced ahead, out of control, unaccountable. Till a tiny voice said, maybe she was going to watch me die.

Then the pistol report exploded. Duval. I looked back. Janac was staring at the smoking gun with a faintly amused expression, as though he hadn't expected it to go off. As Duval slumped forward I saw the gaping hole where the back of his head had been. The body hit the deck, twitched, blood spreading quickly around it. And I knew I was going to throw up. The warm, acid vomit surged up against the gag. I choked hard as I tried to swallow, my lungs started to fill. But hands ripped the gag off and beat my back. I spat and heaved and choked, and finally sucked in air, beautiful air. I blew my nose clear and immediately found the gag back in my mouth. I writhed against the acrid taste of my own puke. Janac was talking to me, 'Whoo, Martin, that could have been a real bummer. We wouldn't want you suffocating on us and cheating me of all the fun, would we?'

I looked up at him, hands on hips, still that cynical smile on his face. I flexed against the bindings one more time. And the scream came from deep inside – and pounded soundlessly against the cloth of the gag. And then I was looking at Kate. She was sitting on the edge of the cockpit. Near the rest of them. The reprieved sitting with the torturers. She was twenty feet and a lifetime away. I ached now. Ached with fear and hate and longing. And a tiny bit of hope. It could be all right. One of them was pulling her gag off. The beautiful mouth I had kissed such a short time ago. But her expression was blank. You've got to be happy I tried to tell her, staring it into her eyes. He took the same chances as you. You had no choice. He acted for himself and you had to respond in kind. Dog eat dog, Kate, I shouted at her in silence. And men eat men.

Still she stared ahead. Unwillingly I followed her gaze to where Duval had been. There was no sign of him. It was as though he had never been. They must have pushed him overboard. She sat there, transfixed. I cast my eyes up at Scott. He was set in stone. I hadn't seen him move since the start of this. What did you answer, Scott? Cooperate or defect? But there was no reply from the passionless, unblinking eyes. He didn't even look at Kate. Does he love her,

I wondered? If he lives and I die, how will they talk about me? What will they say? Will she tell him about last night? Will they even stay together? I could feel the tears forming. So sad. It was all so desperately sad.

But then the hands were at Scott's neck, and my heart jumped into my brain and pumped it into overload. The little ivory inlaid lid clicked back and the thin fingers delicately pulled the paper out. I watched him carry it away to the others. They were restless now, on the blood scent. I heard the word, but couldn't register it. Was it the same as last time? Or different? He was walking back towards me. My heart was pounding so hard all I could hear was the blood flowing. His hands were on the box round my neck and I noticed how beautifully manicured the nails were. I shuddered uncontrollably. A sick mind and perfect hands. His voice came through the haze, a radio tuned to the wrong wavelength, 'So what was it, Martin? What did you decide? What is the future for mankind?'

He turned away again and the word was lost to the thunder in my head and the cheers from the crowd. I glanced around wildly for some clue to my fate, Kate had looked up, she was staring at us both, she looked confused. But Scott, he was looking right at me. His eyes, what was that expression in his eyes? I heard the revolver hammer click back. But it wasn't pointed at me. And the chamber wasn't spun. It was clicked slowly into place on a live round. No, Scott, it can't be, how could it? He turned away from me now, to look at Kate. She was on her feet, she looked so frightened. I glanced back to Janac, he too was staring at me. A thin smile twitched on his lips, as his finger closed around the trigger. Something was wrong, terribly, terribly wrong.

The realisation came at me with a rush – the son of a bitch was going to betray the game. The thunder in my head turned to a roar and the roar said – do something. A reflex rooted deep in the ages of man twitched the right muscles and my legs straightened in a spasm. One foot found a stanchion behind me and the sudden purchase propelled me forward with a gagged roar of incoherent anger. I flew at Janac and struck hard bone with the top of my head. The world exploded in a cascade of light. But I heard the gun go off in the same instant and the blind, hot rage drove me on. All this, to play his fucking game, and then he just kills Scott anyway.

We both went down hard, I twisted to take the impact on my

right shoulder, Janac under me. I heard him gasp as I hit him in the midriff this time. I felt rather than saw the muscle spasm the double blow had effected. The speed and violence of the move had achieved the impossible and given me the advantage. I had the bastard cold. I rolled on to my feet as his hands twitched protectively, instinctively across his stomach. His eyes were glazed, unseeing. He was down and I was going for the kill – foot raised to stamp on his unprotected throat. But even as I lunged at him my supporting leg went from under me. In the fury of the onslaught I had forgotten the others. I hit the deck again, but this time I was unprepared. I took it badly, landing on my back across something hard and unyielding. Pain flashed up my spine and seared through the cortex, deep into my brain. But sensation lasted only an instant longer. As the next blow struck home, everything went black.

I was going down for the last time, kicking hard but hopelessly, arms tied. Waves crashing over me, unable to get back up for another breath. I sucked in water, blowing, snorting, gasping – but conciousness kicked in to save me and I came to with a sharp stab of pain. I stared wild-eyed at the blurred, red-filmed scene around me. Janac was leaning on a winch pedestal nearby, hands across his belly, eyes focused on some other reality. One of the Thais stood over me, water dripping from the bucket in his hand. Kate was held by another. She was struggling hard, twisting, turning, all the time yelling at Janac – a stream of frenzied invective. Suddenly she was free and beside me. Her hand touched my temple.

'Kate, I didn't defect,' I gasped out.

Then she was gone, pulled away by strong arms, now struggling again, spitting, screaming. I twisted round, blinking quickly to clear the blood and water from my eyes. Scott was crumpled, beaten, slumped against the guard rails, eyes closed. But still alive.

I turned back as Janac eased himself upright. He walked a couple of paces, bent down gingerly, and picked up the revolver from where it had landed. Spoke some words. I was grabbed on both sides by unseen hands and dragged back towards the guardrail, dumped beside Scott, who still hadn't moved. This time they stayed with me, hands firmly on my shoulders. Janac watched this, then turned towards where Kate was still struggling. He raised the gun and shouted, 'Silence!'

Kate stared back, her gaze steadier than either his voice or the weapon. But everyone responded. Emotion and violence ebbed away into a surreal quiet. Janac slowly lowered the gun, and turned, once again, to face me. The silence lasted for ever. My battered body screaming at me for a pain relief I couldn't provide. But Janac could. With the revolver that hung in a white-knuckled grip by his side.

When he finally spoke, his voice was so quiet that I struggled to hear him. 'So help me, I should kill you all,' he whispered, staring at me. His tongue flickered out to wet the thin lips. His hands, working blind, slid the six-chambered cylinder open. Two empty shells clattered on to the deck. One live round was left. This was it. I swallowed heavily. Fuck him. I wouldn't give him the satisfaction of thinking I was afraid. I held his gaze, my hatred reflecting every watt of the anger I saw in his face. He would surely kill us now. I expected him to reach for another round. But he didn't.

Instead, his free hand came up to the tunic's breast pocket and pulled out a crumpled cigarette packet. He flicked the top and eased out a smoke with his mouth. It drooped sadly, its back broken. Janac looked down at it, snapped off the damaged end, then pulled out the Zippo and lit what was left. The tiniest spark of hope flared in me along with that cigarette. He took two long drags, inhaling deeply, exhaling slowly. The action seemed to soothe him, the anger dispersing with the smoke that drifted slowly away on the somnolent air.

Finally, he spoke again, 'Gutsy move, Martin,' he said. The tone was different, still quiet, without the anger, but tinged with something else that I couldn't pin down. Certainly, all the earlier sadistic exuberance was gone. 'Stupid, but gutsy. What the hell do you think these people would have done to you if you'd taken me out . . .' He shrugged a shoulder at them. 'I'm the only thing between you and them. Me and the game, we're the best chance you and the girl have got. You should know that.' He paused, pulled on the cigarette till it burned fiercely down to his fingers. Then he flicked it into the silent, watching ocean, which responded with a quiet hiss.

But for all the nonchalance he was tracking my thoughts with the precision of a hunter. 'You thought I was going to kill him anyway.' His words disturbed the exhaled smoke, a cartoon bubble over his head. 'You were about to see your cooperation, your brave stand for conscience, rendered totally worthless.' A trace of a smile flickered across his lips. 'I understand the desperation, but I didn't anticipate the reaction. I underestimated you again, Martin, didn't think you'd have the balls for something like that.' There was a heavy silence. We gazed at each other through the soft, early-morning light. I was completely still, my face a mask. Revealing nothing, unsure which way this was going to go. 'So,' he went on, finally, 'I'll forgive your reaction to my little joke.'

Joke? Christ, some fucking joke.

'And you turned out to be a cooperator,' he continued, quickly this time. 'I was wrong about that too. When I saw Scott'd cooperated I thought it was perfect. I was sure you'd defect, Martin. I'd get to kill Scott, and you'd have to live with it for the rest of your life. You and the girl. Perfect unhappiness. Divine lack of bliss.' Now there was definitely a wry smile, the yellow teeth flashed. 'Perhaps I should have just killed Scott. Who would ever have known?' Then the smile disappeared and I suddenly saw what it was in his voice – a sadness. 'I couldn't do it though. We have to play the game. I said that all along, you must play the game. The game is everything. I'll respect your decision.' He shook his head, a disappointed father. 'You were one of us, Martin. You could have been one of us. You could have been free now. You and Kate together.' But somewhere in his voice, his face, there was a recognition that with Scott's blood between us, Kate and I could never be reconciled. 'That was your destiny, Martin. And you have denied it. So now you and Scott must take your chances, at six to one.'

Six to one, two cooperators.

The chamber spun with a rattle and clicked shut. And the gun was raised and levelled at Scott's forehead. I don't think he even knew. His head was still down. I can't imagine what he went through the time before. Knowing he was about to die. Knowing that it was my fault. Knowing that I would be left alive. I had seen it all in his eyes. That moment had finished him. His head was still down. He didn't know it when the gun went off.

The report ripped through the still air. Jarring, brutalising the quiet. It happened so quickly, Janac had moved so fast. Death crashing back into the party so suddenly even the watchers were surprised. But slowly, the stunned silence was replaced by an animal murmur of satisfaction rippling out through the crowd. It grew, fanning the flickering flames of emotion that threatened to engulf me. Burning, searing hate and anger; glowing, throbbing pain and fear. Ben, Duval, now Scott. I fought to extinguish everything but the hate. I'd hate that bastard till I saw him in hell. My head went down, eyes closed. Focus on the hate. Forget Kate. Forget everything.

'Goddamn it, Martin. That should have been you. Six to one.' It was Janac. More life in his voice. I felt one of the men beside me move, heard the splash as Scott's body went over the side. Just like Duval before him. I heard the chamber click open, the tinny rattle as the empty shell bounced on the deck. The solid clunk as the fresh round clicked home.

'So here we are, Martin. The final act. Live or die? The odds must be on your side now. You should make it. But of course, each spin is a separate event. No causal connection to help you. Just the odds, they're with you.'

Slowly I raised my head, took in Kate, crying silent tears, wet streaks down her face, frightened eyes. But I had no fear now. Only the hate. I looked Janac in the eye. Still bloodshot. Still crazy. Come on you, bastard. Do it. Do it now. We've come all this way. Let's finish it. The chamber spun once again with its death rattle, snapped shut in the smooth, practised movement. Pointed at my brains. Six to one. Fuck you, Janac, I murmured into the gag, with no more strength for screaming. You haven't beaten me. And you know it. His finger tightened and the hammer fell. Fell on to an empty chamber. Fell with a hollow click. A click. The sweet sound of life.

Epilogue

J ANAC DID LET us go. With some food and water, even some diesel. We motored and sailed for four or five days I think, I don't remember too well. They found us as we neared the Australian coast. First a fishing boat, then soon, the Navy. There was a trial. A media circus. But Alex's disappearance supported our story. The jury believed us and we got through it – together.

We're still together, Kate and I. It hasn't been easy. I'm sure it never will be. Time heals they say. But he'll always be with us, in the quiet moments. In the dark. Alone and together, Scott will be there. But we can be there for each other too. We can share it.

It would have been so different if that first shot had killed Scott. Just a joke? Maybe. Or did my crazy charge stop him? That and the cooperation. Perhaps as I had thought back on Ko Samui, the selfless answer had the power to set me free.

But I'll never really know, never understand. How can you understand? Grasping at the motives of a madman could send you crazy. Whatever happened, he didn't kill him then. And so everything is the same, but different. I did the right thing. I can be there for Kate. It's going to be all right. Sometimes you just know these things.